Praise for Johnnie Clark's previous book, GUNS UP!

"Some of the toughest combat ever described on paper."
—*Los Angeles Daily News*

"This book is hard to put down, the sort that can cost you a night's sleep."
—*Eagle* magazine

"Eloquently capture[s] the flavor of combat in Vietnam from the perspective of a young Marine—the man on the point of the spear . . . Clark tells it like it was. . . . He writes about his personal experiences in sharp and explicit detail."
—*Marine Corps Gazette*

By Johnnie M. Clark
Published by Ballantine Books:

GUNS UP!
SEMPER FIDELIS
THE OLD CORPS
NO BETTER WAY TO DIE

NO BETTER WAY TO DIE

Johnnie M. Clark

BALLANTINE BOOKS • NEW YORK

Copyright © 1995 by Johnnie Clark

All rights reserved under International and Pan-American Copyright Conventions. Published in the United States by Ballantine Books, a division of Random House, Inc., New York, and simultaneously in Canada by Random House of Canada Limited, Toronto.

Library of Congress Catalog Card Number: 95-94450

ISBN 0-345-38981-6

Manufactured in the United States of America

First Edition: October 1995

10 9 8 7 6 5 4 3 2 1

DEDICATION

To Jesus Christ for loving me in spite of me, for forgiving us when we can't forgive ourselves.

To Nancy, Shawn, Bonnie Kay, and Mom. To Tony H., Chris, Audi, Elsa, Brett, Tony P., Greg, R. Bob, Phil, Paul, Sean, Regina, and the Do Jang. To Pam, Ernie, and Betsy.

To the heroes of the Chosin Reservoir and the Pusan Perimeter. To all the men who fought in Korea.

Special thanks to the men of the Chosin Few. Without your help I could not have written this book. My thanks and eternal friendship to Win Scott, Executive Director of the Chosin Few C/1/5/ 1st Marine Division.

To Gunnery Sergeant Francis Hugh Killeen, one of the real legendary characters that make the United States Marine Corps unlike any other military outfit. A lot of this book came straight from his life. Thanks for trusting me, Gunny. I'd be honored to carry your ammo anytime, any place.

To my gunny. Alpha Company, 1st Battalion, 5th Marine Regiment, 1st Marine Division . . . August 3, 1968. To Sergeant Corey Coughlin, thanks for the tough memories. To the Nam Corps. Though always outnumbered, we never lost a battle and killed the enemy at about twenty to one. The last American combat troops left Vietnam in 1972. The war ended in 1975. If there was a military defeat, it sure wasn't the U.S. military and it sure wasn't my Marine Corps.

Semper Fi

KOREA 1950

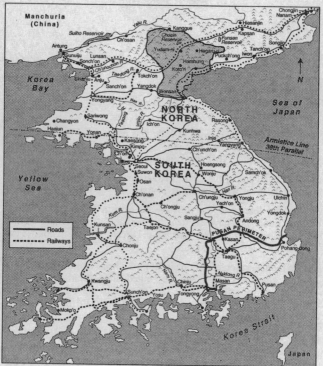

MSR TO CHOSIN RESERVOIR

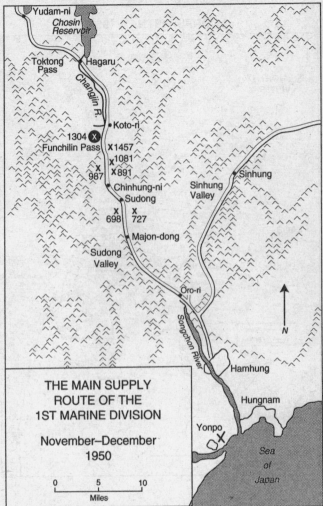

Yudam-ni

Chosin Reservoir

Toktong Pass

Hagaru

Changjin R.

Koto-ri

1304 X
Funchilin Pass
X 1457
X 1081
X 987
X 891

Chinhung-ni

Sudong

Sinhung

Sinhung Valley

X 698
X 727

Majon-dong

Sudong Valley

Oro-ri

Songchon River

N

Hamhung

Hungnam

Yonpo

Sea of Japan

THE MAIN SUPPLY
ROUTE OF THE
1ST MARINE DIVISION

November–December
1950

0   5   10
Miles

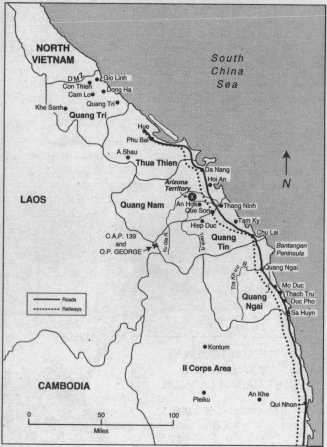

I CORPS VIETNAM 1968

NORTH VIETNAM

South China Sea

DMZ
Gio Linh
Con Thien
Cam Lo • Dong Ha
Khe Sanh • Quang Tri
Quang Tri

Hue
Phu Bai

A Shau
Thua Thien

LAOS

Da Nang
Hoi An

Arizona Territory

Quang Nam
An Hoa
Que Son

Thang Ninh

Hiep Duc
Tam Ky

Quang Tin
Chu Lai

C.A.P. 139
and
O.P. GEORGE

Vu Gia R.
Thanh R.

Bantangan Peninsula

Tra Khuc R.
Quang Ngai

Quang Ngai
Mo Duc
Thach Tru
Duc Pho
Sa Huyn

• Kontum

II Corps Area

CAMBODIA

• Pleiku
• An Khe
Qui Nhon

Roads
Railways

0   50   100
Miles

N

PROLOGUE

Wounded Marines got stiff like cardboard, their faces turned ash gray. They were frozen and already dead but they didn't know it yet. Their dying eyes would gaze up at you pleading or shift back and forth trying to let someone know that they were still alive inside the hardened corpse. Sometimes they would still be able to cry; the tears would freeze the eyes shut. It was easier that way on the boys who had to stand by helplessly.

He watched as they marched past, through the crusted snow, tattered boots, and shoe packs crunching with each weary step, heads bowed against the Manchurian wind that drove sleet down like needles against any exposed flesh. He wanted to call out a warning—or was it just good-bye—to part of himself that he saw down that treacherous ice-and-gravel road weaving through jagged, frozen canyons at the top of the world. Odd, how warm he felt while their breaths came in labored gasps of steam, coughing foul air out of their burning lungs. He shivered violently.

CHAPTER ONE
Yokosuka Naval Base, Japan
August 1945

PFC Jessie Slate stretched his six-foot muscular frame and rechecked his military alignment. He turned and gave the rack beside him a good solid kick. An obscene gesture in the form of a middle finger rose slowly from under the Marine-issue green wool blanket until it was fully extended beside the white stenciled letters PFC BROKEN WING USMC.

"Three days and a wake up, Wing!"

"Chay-ta-gahi-be-woldoni."

"Same to you, pal."

Broken Wing sat up yawning and looking like a twin brother to the Indian on the nickel.

"Stupid and not loyal. Should have never let you in Code Talker School."

"I should have left you on Bougainville."

"Have you told Kate you are leaving the Corps?"

Jessie Slate's strong, handsome face tightened and the humor in his gray eyes vanished.

"Why?"

"She is your wife."

"We're divorced. She's got her own life."

"Your son?"

"They're better off without me! She's fine with her father Jeremiah. Drop it, Wing."

The broad acne-scarred face rarely showed any change in

2

expression and Wing's monotone voice was just as deadpan as his granite face. He put out his right arm, showing the tarnished silver-colored bracelet he had carved from the downed P-51 Mustang on Bougainville. He pointed at Jessie's matching bracelet with the Navajo wind-god symbol engraved on it.

"Blood brother does not abandon warrior going into combat."

"Stick it in your skivvy shorts, Wing! There ain't no combat in China. You'll be coaching the Nationalists. Support troops and guard duty and that's it."

Slate checked his watch.

"My God! Paddy's waiting on me right now! Hurry up, I might need you for moral support."

Jessie snatched up his Irish pipes and ran for the barracks door. He shivered in the cool morning air, then hustled nervously across the asphalt parade ground. Gunnery Sergeant Paddy Francis Killeen stood with arms folded under a glaring light that hung over the chow-hall door. He flicked his broad, flat nose like an old fighter and bit down on his pipe. His large, furrowed brow and wild, bushy eyebrows were as easy to read as a compass for anyone that knew him. Jessie loved the thick-necked old Irish bear and Killeen thought of Jessie as his own illegitimate son.

"And I thought you'd be needin' a special invitation from the commandant himself."

"Sorry, Gunny. That stupid Navajo got me arguing about China again."

"China you say, lad?" The old salt's eyes opened wide.

"Yes, sir. He wants me to go to China with him and—"

"No, don't be doin' it, lad." Paddy scratched at the back of his thick neck with the stem of his well-chewed briarwood pipe.

"Well, I'm not, Gunny. I'm surveying out. But I thought you loved your China duty?"

"That I did, lad, and your father, God rest his gallant soul, he loved it too, Slate. The mysteries of the world are all there to be solved." The gunny's big round face softened at the happy memories.

"Well . . ."

" 'Twas a different time, lad. Before the Japs invaded China and long before any of this Communist garbage. Not much shooting then."

"Shooting? Is there a shooting war or not?"

"To be sure, Marine. And you with only a few days left in God's Marine Corps. You'll have no business shippin' out for China."

"But I never heard about any—"

"Don't you be troubling yourself, lad. You take that discharge, catch the first hop to Nouméa. Patch things up with the lovely Kate. Make a home for your wee lad." Paddy winked and slapped Jessie's shoulder.

"I'm not doing that," Jessie grumbled.

Paddy's big rugged face contorted with compassion. "And you'll not be seeing Kate or your boy?"

"I send them money. But I'll not interfere in Kate's life again and it's nobody's business but mine."

"And what a thoughtful lad 'tis that you're being."

Gunnery Sergeant Paddy Francis Killeen's Irish tone said more than his words. Jessie's scowl deepened, and even the old salt knew that he had reached the limit of Jessie's endurance.

Jessie shrugged angrily, "Nobody said anything to me about a shooting war in China."

The gunnery sergeant's bushy eyebrows lifted.

"Civilians won't be needin' to know about China, PFC Slate! Will you be playing the pipes this lovely morn or not?"

"Yes, sir, I will."

"You'll not be wantin' a dry mouth on the pipes, lad. Now, me, speaking for meself, I'll be in poor form on the pipes if a terrible thirst should come upon meself in the middle of the Garryowen."

"Yes, Paddy, I can see why that would be a concern."

Paddy gave a nonchalant glance to his left, then his right. The parade ground was dark and vacant. He nodded to follow as he headed around the chow hall. Just around the corner of the building he produced a small bottle of Irish whiskey from his hip pocket. He took a long swig, smacked his lips, and handed the bottle to Jessie. Jessie imitated the gunny in every way, until the fiery liquid hit his chest like a shot of battery acid. His right eye closed without a request from his brain. He handed the bottle back to the gunny, turned to walk back to the front of the chow hall, and ran square into Broken Wing, who was standing behind him. Jessie jumped back, startled, and stomped on the gunny's spit-shined dress shoes.

"Wing!"

"By God, PFC Slate!" Gunny Killeen shouted.

"Oh! Sorry, Gunny," Jessie apologized. "But this blasted Navajo should have to wear a cowbell. He's like a ghost, for God's sake!"

"You'll have to reshine my shoes, Slate. I'll not be givin' the colonel reason to purge me out of the Corps."

"Yes, sir."

"Smelled whiskey," Broken Wind mumbled.

Gunnery Sergeant Paddy Francis Killeen grunted and looked at the Navajo with a curious expression that was evident even in the dim light.

"How's he do it, Slate? Could the Navajo be half foxhound, would you think?" He handed the stoic Indian the bottle of whiskey and studied Broken Wing like a detective.

"He's like a ghost, Gunny. I tell you he's uncanny and he can smell booze anywhere within a two-hundred-yard radius."

"Don't I wonder what the Chinese will be thinkin' when they see a real American Indian and I'll be glad to see that collision for meself."

"You!" Jessie said. "You're going to China, Paddy?"

The burly old gunnery sergeant's brown eyes opened wide, and in the dim yellow light coming through a chow-hall window, there seemed to be an indignant frown on his leathery face.

"And do I look like a man who'd run from a fight, lad?"

"Is the whole Corps going over, Gunny?"

"That would be less than a platoon's worth if the Army has their way!"

Jessie nodded that he understood. Rumors of a great purge were everywhere; it was coming down on the Corps like a guillotine. Congress wanted cutbacks and the Army wanted the Corps dissolved completely, if possible.

"Look, Gunny." Jessie glanced over his shoulder at Broken Wing. "Do you mind, Wing? I'd like to talk to the gunny alone."

"A-chi yeh-hes."

"Intestines don't itch!" Slate bellowed.

"Yes," Wing said stubbornly.

"Well, go scratch 'em then, but let me speak with the gunny."

Broken Wing grunted and walked around the building.

"Paddy, I want the straight scoop," Jessie stated.

"Speak your mind, lad."

"I feel sort of responsible for that stupid Indian."

"Yes."

"Well, he was gonna get out of the Corps when his hitch was up after the war and I sort of hoodwinked him into staying in. Don't get me wrong—it was all innocent enough and I did it for his own good. But if that sap is really heading into a shooting war . . . well, for God sakes, I named his son!"

"I know what you're tryin' to say, lad, but—"

"No. No one knows, Paddy. If that stupid Indian is going to China, so am I!"

Paddy Killeen scratched at his broad chin.

"I don't see how you can, lad. Situation being like it is."

Jessie Slate's square jaw clenched tight. "I won't walk out. I did that once and it cost my best friend his life."

The old salt studied the sudden rage in Jessie's face like

a father looking at his son for the answer to an unspoken question.

Fifteen minutes past reveille the garrison stood at attention on the parade ground. The morning sun was up and a cool breeze greeted the formation.

Jessie stood at attention beside the gunny, the Irish pipes at the ready. His heart, already pounding in anticipation, picked up speed as the colonel and the ten-plus lower-ranking officers appeared at the edge of the parade ground. Soon a few Japanese visitors began to appear behind the line of officers, filling up a small bleacher section.

The regimental review began with the first chord of "Bonnie Charley Now Away." The review ended with the "Marines' Hymn," and by the time the last note sounded, Jessie felt as though he had just finished a marathon.

With the command to dismiss, Gunnery Sergeant Paddy Francis Killeen flashed his big contagious grin and hugged Jessie hard enough to crush the Irish pipes.

" 'Twas just fine, lad! Couldn't be prouder if you were me own boy." He leaned closer. "I'll see what I can do about China duty, lad, but don't be gettin' your hopes up. Be in my office at 0800 tomorrow." With that he winked and walked away.

Jessie followed Broken Wing into the gunny's tiny, windowless office. A single bright lightbulb hung overhead. Gunny Killeen sat behind a small olive-green desk. Three wooden chairs that looked to be stolen from an elementary school were the only other furniture. A photo of a two-star general pinning the Bronze Star on the gunny's chest hung on the starboard wall. It was signed, *Semper Fi, Paddy ... Your friend, General Rockey*. The room reeked of cheap pipe tobacco. Jessie's heart felt heavy as he sat before the gunny.

Gunnery Sergeant Paddy Francis Killeen clamped down on his briarwood pipe, his bushy eyebrows pinched together and large forehead wrinkled in serious thought.

" 'Tis a shame about the last fight, lads."

"Those swabjockeys insulted the Corps, Paddy!" Jessie pleaded.

"We was framed," Broken Wing said, his Indian-nickel face showing absolutely no expression.

"It'll do you no good now, lads. Here you stand, temporary PFCs and still reserve status, and there's this satanic purge upon us."

The old salt tapped his pipe against the new notice on the wall behind his chair. "China, lads. In the old Corps, gentlemen, China was the crowning achievement of a Marine on active duty. I had to have two hash marks, be a corporal with an excellent record to even be considered. And sorry liar I'd be if I said things weren't tough back in the old Corps. With Haiti and Nicaragua on a man's record . . ." He paused and closed one eye and pointed with his pipe. "And your father! Jack Slate. A Marine's Marine and one more of the old Shanghai Marines. A fine man. And the great O'Cleary, who could match any liar in the Marine Corps if he set his mind to it." He raised one eyebrow. "He could tell a tale better than the shamuses in the old country. . . ."

Jessie paused to consider his words carefully before interrupting Paddy in the middle of what would surely be a wonderful tale. At almost any other time Jessie would have sat believing every word with the faith of an altar boy, but today, time was short. Men were being released from active service based on a point system. Five points for each Battle Star, five points for each personal decoration, two points for every month overseas, one point every month in the service. It hadn't mattered before. He wanted out of the Corps anyway, but he could not let Broken Wing go into combat alone. He had left Charlie Rose alone and it would haunt him until he died.

"Gunny."

"Yes, PFC Slate."

"I want China duty."

Paddy tapped the notice with his pipe and winked. "Crowning achievement to any Marine's career, lads. The mysteries of the world are all there to be solved."

"Yes, sir."

"How many points would you be havin' as we speak?"

Jessie glanced at Wing for help in the figuring. Wing's stone face was as blank as usual. Jessie did a quick figure.

"Well it's five points for each Battle Star?"

"It 'tis," Paddy Killeen concurred.

"And five for each personal decoration?"

"True enough, lad. And the two of you with Silver Stars."

"Two for every month overseas."

"Yes. And one for each month in service. So where's that leave us, PFC?"

"Near as I can figure quickly, ninety-five points, Paddy."

"And Wing's the same, I'm guessin'?"

Broken Wing nodded silently.

Paddy scratched his head with the pipe and closed one eye. "Well, lads, that leaves us a wee bit short now, doesn't it? The first notification of releases said 180 to 200 and that represented July through September of 'forty-five. And you say you have ninety-five during that time? Broken Wing is fine, being as he already volunteered in time."

Jessie nodded silently.

Paddy grunted. "Now, I'll be promisin' nothing. But I think that if I was to plead your case to the colonel and tell him that you'll be signing up for four years, two years in China . . ."

"What!" Jessie stood up in shock.

"There'd be no other way, lad." Gunny raised his hands like a preacher looking for divine intervention.

"Four years!"

"That would get you regular Marine Corps. No more temporary PFC. No more reserve status, and the Chinese women are clean, lad." Paddy's voice softened.

Jessie sat back down, chewing on the inside of his

mouth, his slate-gray eyes darting back and forth. He rubbed his jaw and sagged in his chair.

"I don't know."

Paddy tapped his pipe on the desk and nodded. "You're right, lad. If something was to happen to ya, I'd feel responsible. Why, you're like me own son. You take that discharge and run with it. 'Tis no shame in it, Slate."

"Where do I sign, Gunny?" Slate snapped angrily.

Paddy slapped down two papers as if he had pulled them out of the air. "Right there at the bottom of both these, lad. The first one's to volunteer for China duty and this one's to reenlist."

Paddy's grin was infectious. It had nearly reached both ears when he pulled out a bottle of Irish whiskey. Jessie had not yet crossed the *t* in *Slate* when he noticed a most unusual and unattractive occurrence. Broken Wing was smiling, not his usual crack-in-the-granite smile, but slightly yellowed teeth were showing. It was enough to give a man a chill.

"A fine decision, lad," Paddy bellowed as he snatched the papers from under Slate's pen and quickly shoved a glass of brownish-red whiskey toward Broken Wing. Paddy filled another small shot glass and Jessie reached for it but was left holding air. Paddy held the glass out for a toast with Broken Wing. They touched glasses.

"To reenlistment," Broken Wing said.

"To China," Paddy answered. They drank.

Jessie stood up, glaring at Broken Wing. "You planned all of this?"

Gunny Killeen reached into a drawer and slapped down some official papers. "Here's your orders, Slate."

"My orders? How could you . . ."

Paddy smiled. "You'll land at Taku Bar, a seaport north of Tientsin."

"I already had orders for China! Without reenlisting?"

Broken Wing hummed the "Marines' Hymn" but showed no emotion.

"Now look on the bright side, lad," Gunny Killeen said. "At least we lied about the shooting! And with a handsome mug like yours, Slate, your only combat will be with the lovely Chinese women."

CHAPTER TWO

PFC Jessie Slate peeked out of his bedroll. It was dark and chilly, and the command for helmets, packs, and weapons made waking up and getting into formation even more miserable than usual. Sergeants and corporals rushed about with lanterns, breaking the company up into squads and handing out C-rations for breakfast. Everyone was griping about the Corps.

Gunnery Sergeant Paddy Francis Killeen approached the second squad of the first platoon with a pipe in his mouth, a lantern in his left hand, and an M-1 over his right shoulder.

"Listen up, lads!" He pulled the pipe from his mouth and pushed his helmet back, revealing his broad, furrowed forehead. "Today you'll be ridin' the rails, escortin' a Standard Oil crew the 120 miles from Tientsin to Chinwangtao. We'll have a flight of Corsairs on station above, and we'll need to guard potential trouble spots along the way. One platoon will get a tunnel and the other a rail bridge."

"Say, Gunny, who is it we're fighting anyway?" a young Marine with a Southern drawl asked. "Japs still here in China?"

"Matter of fact, the Japs are still here, lads. But it won't be the Japs shootin' at you."

"Wait a minute, Paddy!" Jessie blurted.

"You have a question, PFC Slate?" Paddy said in a voice that reminded Jessie of his rank in no uncertain way.

Jessie paused for a moment, then softened his tone. "Yes, sir. I thought there was no shooting war going on over here."

The old Irish bear grinned mischievously and pointed his pipe at Jessie. "Now a man of experience would certainly be pressing the matter to call this a war, laddie."

"But somebody will be shooting at us."

"Aye. Communists, I think."

"You think? You don't know?" Jessie narrowed his steel-gray eyes.

"It's a bit of a tricky question. You see, the Nationalists and the Communists stopped fighting each other long enough to fight the Japs during the war, but now they don't see eye to eye. We supply the Nationalists, who are Chiang Kai-shek's boys, and we'll not be going about the country without their permission. The people would see us as an invading army." Paddy pointed his pipe at the squad of wide-eyed Marines. "So the Nationalists are allies. But you won't be wanting to trust them with your back, lads."

Somebody gave an "oh brother" whistle.

Paddy turned to head toward another squad, then stopped and looked over his shoulder. "The Marines have never had any trouble determining who it is that needs killin', and I'm not thinking we will this time either. Eat your chow and get saddled up!"

The ancient train struggled every inch of the journey through the thick, wet, gray mist of early morning, like an old horse pulling a plow that was cutting too deep into hard ground. Jessie shifted in a useless effort to get comfortable on the hard wooden bench of the swaying open-air passenger car. He looked over at PFC Broken Wing, who was trying to sleep on the bench beside him with his head on his pack and his helmet over his eyes. He and this crazy Navajo had been through a lot together. No point in making

the present moment an exception, Jessie thought, and
pushed Wing's helmet back.

"How can you sleep? Don't you want to see the great
mystery of China?"

Wing opened his right eye. "Trees and hills. Seen before."

"Remember the old Pineapple Express, Wing?"

"Huh?"

"You know, that funny little train on Hilo. When we
were getting ready to hit Iwo Jima."

"Oh, yes."

"This reminds me of that train. Minus the stink of rotten
pineapples."

"This one has the smell of old wet dogs. Worse."

"Not much worse." Jessie pulled his collar up and shivered slightly in the cool mountain breeze. He made a quick
check of the Marines nearest him in the dirty, crowded passenger car. Most of the platoon was sleeping, except for the
squad riding on the roofs of the cars.

"Ever think about O'Cleary?" Broken Wing asked quietly.

"Yes. I think of him all the time."

"Great man."

"Great Marine."

"Remember what he used to always say when things got
bad?"

Jessie smiled. " 'No better way to die than to die a Marine.' Why do you ask?"

"Iwo was proper."

"Yes. Perfect place for a man like that to die."

Jessie stared through the gray mist at the rolling foothills
and the patches of deep woods that seemed in need of rain.
Ambushing this train would be easy. He glanced at his
.30 caliber Browning automatic rifle, sitting on bipod legs
on the sandy wood floor. He could not look at that twenty
pounds of steel without remembering Bougainville. The
BAR's firepower and Broken Wing's reloading skill had

probably saved the entire platoon on that miserable little island. Got them Silver Stars too, thanks to Gunny O'Cleary making such a big deal out of it. Funny, he never thought he would be packing the BAR again. Great weapon, accurate and powerful, but there were times when carrying the M-1 seemed like a better idea, and certainly a lighter one. Jessie shook off a chill and pulled out his wallet. He stared at the photo he kept of his son and ached inside.

"Got a letter from Jeremiah back in Japan," Broken Wing said from under his helmet.

Jessie blinked. "Jeremiah? You mean Jeremiah Polk?" He put the wallet back in his pocket.

"Your father-in-law."

"You mean ex-father-in-law!"

"He said Kate and your boy were fine."

"How come he wrote you?" Jessie asked suspiciously.

"Been writing. He tells me about Bible."

"Yeah? Is that all he tells you?"

"He took Gunnery Sergeant O'Cleary's death pretty hard."

"Figured he would. They were best friends in the old Corps."

"Killeen too."

"What?"

"Gunny Killeen and O'Cleary and Jeremiah. They were all at Belleau Wood together."

Jessie clenched his square jaw and glared down at Broken Wing.

"You mean Killeen and Mr. Polk know each other?"

"Yes."

"Why didn't Paddy tell me that?"

The aging locomotive suddenly lurched from a heavy brake. Metal shrieking against metal echoed through the surrounding hills. Broken Wing lifted his head from the wooden bench of the old passenger car. Jessie snatched up his BAR and leaned from the open window to see ahead. A tepid breeze wafted the smell of coal and fog and steam at him. A burst of small arms fire came from the front of the train.

"Slate! Get that BAR up here!"

Another burst of gunfire shot from the jungle brush and sang off the ancient passenger car.

"Sounds like .03s," Broken Wing muttered.

The thump of mortars echoed from a small hillside two hundred yards to the right of the train.

"That ain't!"

The first round hit well off target, but the size of the explosion looked like it had been a 60mm mortar round. The old train rattled as it shifted into reverse, and the big cargo cars jarred with sudden movement. Jessie jumped off the passenger car, with Broken Wing close behind, and ran toward the wheezing engine. Bullets whined off the steel wheels.

The cracking of small arms fire increased as they neared the front of the train, which was slowly picking up speed in reverse. Up ahead, trees had been felled across the tracks and stacked into a barricade. Captain Fitch, lying behind a jagged stump, pointed toward muzzle flashes seventy-five yards up the track on the small hill bordering the trestles. Fitch was a thin, no-nonsense, scholarly-looking man of about forty. He was a veteran of Tarawa and Okinawa, a well-respected, spit-and-polish Marine with no sense of humor.

Jessie hit the ground nearby and opened fire on the muzzle flashes. A Chinese soldier rolled down the hill with the first burst of BAR fire.

"Great shot, Slate!" Captain Fitch shouted. Another explosion resounded from the rear of the train. A huge tree cracked like a gunshot as it fell across the tracks, blocking any potential retreat. "Who's covering the rear, Gunny?"

"The construction crew! They're armed."

A mortar blast hit the tracks just beyond the barricade of trees, and a second quickly followed, only closer. A third and fourth hit almost simultaneously as mortar rounds walked up the track toward Jessie, and a squad's worth of Marines fired at the enemy-held hill.

"Incoming!"

Jessie shoved his face into the red dirt, covering his head with both hands, and waited for the mortar round to fall through his spine. He clawed at the ground, trying to dig himself under the earth's surface with his fingernails. In the distance, another series of hollow thumps echoed from the enemy hill. The rattle of a Nambu machine gun opened fire from the left flank and bullets ricocheted off the retreating train. Marines scampered over the tracks to take cover on the other side as the new threat opened up again. Jessie pulled his face out of the dirt, spat, and searched for the enemy machine gun. A mortar round hit the tracks to his right, showering Broken Wing and Jessie with rocks and wood splinters from the railroad ties. The Nambu opened fire again, and Jessie saw the flash.

"There he is, Wing! In that brush right beside the big yellow-colored tree! See him?"

"No."

"Just feed me!" Jessie barked, then swung the Browning automatic rifle around, dropped the bipod legs, and took aim.

The Nambu shot another burst, and Jessie sighted in on the flash. He flipped the weapon's small lever to fast-fire, allowing the BAR to fire 550 rounds per minute. The target was a good three hundred yards away, but the BAR was the most accurate automatic weapon in the world, and Jessie had slept with it longer than most men sleep with their wives. A burst of automatic fire would hold its pattern for about six hundred yards. He squeezed off a full magazine. The enemy machine gun went silent. A small cheer went up from the Marines on the other side of the tracks, but it was quickly muffled by another mortar blast.

"And Gunny said there wasn't any war here!"

Another mortar round hit close by and something slammed into Jessie's left shoulder like the business end of a sledgehammer. He rolled, grabbed his shoulder and groaned.

"Come on!" Wing shouted as he pulled Jessie to his knees by the back of his jacket.

"Slate! Over here!" Gunnery Sergeant Paddy Francis Killeen shouted from the opposite side of the tracks.

"Yeah, Paddy! You're just the man I wanna talk to!"

Jessie clutched at his left shoulder with his right hand as Wing picked up the BAR and the two took off in a full-out, hunched-over run. Another mortar round sent up a geyser of rocks and dirt into the air. They dove in beside the gunny.

"You hit?" Paddy asked, his eyes remaining fixed on the terrain ahead through binoculars.

"Yeah. This is your fault, Killeen!"

The gunny squinted, straining to see something ahead more clearly.

"Wing."

"Yes, Gunny."

"Can you see where that mortar might be placed?"

"No, sir."

"Must have preplotted the position from behind that hill, I'm guessin'."

Jessie spat angrily. "I don't want to upset anyone here, but I'm still bleeding."

Paddy glanced at Jessie's right hand clutching at his wounded left shoulder. Blood was beginning to ooze between his fingers. Paddy gave a scoffing grunt.

"Now, you would hardly call it a mortal wound, would you, laddie?"

"Well it still hurts!"

"How'd you manage to get yourself hit, Slate? Didn't you learn anything in the last war?"

Jessie shook his head and groaned.

Sometimes he wanted to kill Paddy, though most times the man was like a father to him. And Paddy had taught him to play the Irish pipes, the traditional instrument of the Seventh Marines, making him the regimental piper. For all that, right now Jessie wished he were heading for Florida and had never met Paddy Killeen.

Suddenly, a flight of three dark blue, gull-winged Corsairs ripped by low overhead. The Marines cheered loudly. They flew over the enemy hill where the mortar positions were suspected, then climbed high into the hot blue sky. One by one each plane tipped its wing and dove down at the hill, firing their .5 inch guns. Two one-thousand-pound bombs tumbled lazily from each plane. Muffled explosions followed, and a moment later black smoke curled into the clear blue sky. The mortar rounds ceased. A blast of small arms fire erupted from the rear of the stalled train.

"Gunny!" Captain Fitch yelled from farther up the track.

"Yes, sir."

"Get Slate and Wing back there to help out those Standard Oil men!"

"Aye aye!" Gunny shouted and turned to Broken Wing. "Wing, take the BAR and give 'em some firepower back there!"

Jessie grabbed the BAR and got to his feet. "This BAR goes nowhere without me!"

Broken Wing muttered something in Navajo that no one understood and took off after Jessie. They sprinted past the hissing steam engine just as another fusillade of small arms fire erupted from the rear of the train. Some of the gunshots sounded like the old Springfield .03s, but some of the weapons being fired from the surrounding hills and brush were modern M-1s. The tracks veered to the left slightly and the caboose was in sight. The Standard Oil men were spread out properly. They were showing incredible fire control for a bunch of civilians, Jessie thought as he and Wing neared the end of the train. Then Jessie saw something that nearly stopped him in full stride. A gray-haired old man with one arm of his black-and-red flannel shirt pinned up was walking calmly behind his line of skirmishers, pointing out enemy muzzle flashes with a single shot from his .45 caliber military Colt. A hard shove from behind pushed Jessie out of his momentary trance.

"Lobe-ca!" Broken Wing bellowed.

"Fish shell? Torpedo?" Jessie muttered his question as he ran for the bearded, one-armed man. The same word in Navajo spoken with four different inflections will carry four different meanings.

The one-armed man turned around at the sound of Jessie's oncoming steps.

"Jeremiah?" Jessie said. "Jeremiah Polk!"

A bullet thudded into the wooden caboose. A series of incoming shots sang off metal and rocks. Broken Wing plowed into Jessie, knocking him onto his stomach beside the BAR and at the feet of Jeremiah Polk. Wing hit the dirt beside him. Jessie rolled onto his left side and looked up into the leathery face of the one-armed old man. He couldn't believe his eyes. Maybe he'd been wounded worse than he thought. Did he miss Kate and his son so much that he was hallucinating?

"Better get that BAR working, PFC Slate, or our reunion might turn into a wake."

"It is you! What are you doing here, Jeremiah?"

A sharp elbow from Wing brought Jessie's attention to the front.

"Treetops at 1400," Wing said as he shoved a magazine into the BAR and took aim with his M-1 in that direction.

Jessie sited in on a group of tall trees about one hundred yards away. Jeremiah casually strolled toward the other side of the tracks, where the right flank of his half-moon perimeter of construction workers ended. The trees lit up with muzzle flashes as the enemy opened fire at Jeremiah, revealing their position. Jessie squeezed off a five-round burst at each enemy flash he spotted. The limp body of a man dropped out of one tree and the Standard Oil men yelled. Jessie took aim at another muzzle flash and the first burst blew another enemy soldier out of a second treetop. Again a cheer went up.

"That's my son-in-law on that BAR, boys!" Jeremiah shouted to his men.

A wave of pride swept through Jessie as he searched out another flash and opened fire at a third treetop. Something fell. It looked to be a rifle. Then, as suddenly as it had all started, it ended. The enemy ceased fire, and silence surrounded the hissing train for a full five minutes before anyone spoke.

"Guess they had enough, boys!" Jeremiah yelled.

Jessie turned an angry scowl toward Broken Wing.

"Hurt bad?" Wing asked.

"What? Oh, the shoulder? Yeah, it feels just swell," Jessie snapped sarcastically.

"Good."

"What is Jeremiah Polk doing in China, Broken Wing? This is no accident. You and Gunny are in on this somehow, aren't you?"

Broken Wing said nothing.

"Slate!" Jeremiah shouted.

Jessie got to his feet as Jeremiah and a tan-faced Standard Oil man carrying an M-1 walked up smiling.

"Mr. Polk, what are you doing here?"

"Jessie, this is my foreman, Byron Sims. Byron, this is PFC Jessie Slate, my son-in-law."

Byron stuck out his hand and Jessie shook it. He looked to be about fifty years old, but he had the strength of a young man. His hand was callused and as rough as he looked.

"Pleasure to meet you, Slate."

"Nice to meet you, sir."

Byron Sims turned and slapped Jeremiah on his good right shoulder. "You teach him to shoot like that in a church, Preacher?" Byron said with a chuckle. "When's your next sermon?"

"Preacher?" Jessie said.

"Yes, of sorts, I guess," Jeremiah replied. "I run a little church for the men in the company at Chinwangtao. We didn't have a real pastor, so I sort of got elected. By default, you might say." He smiled.

Byron Sims held out his hand again. Jessie shook it.

"Slate, it was an honor to meet you. I better get these men to work on that blockade or we'll be here all night. Another forty miles to Chinwangtao!" He turned and shouted, "Let's get that track cleared, men! Hurry up!"

Jeremiah faced Broken Wing and laughed out loud. Wing gave a blank stare in response.

"Good old Broken Wing. It must be divine providence. As God is my witness, I'm happy to see that ugly face of yours!" Jeremiah slapped Wing on the shoulder and laughed.

"We talk again," Broken Wing said with a nod, and headed toward the front of the train.

"What are you doing here, Jeremiah?" Jessie asked.

"I thought I was here for Standard Oil, but God may have another purpose."

"What are you really doing here? Is Broken Wing in on this?"

The old man's soft blue eyes turned hard. "I'm supervisor for Standard Oil. Came here from New Caledonia when the war ended. You're still a little slow on the important matters, aren't you, Slate?"

Jessie looked at the ground. "How is Kate, sir?"

"She's fine. Your boy is too." Jeremiah's words knifed through Jessie like a bayonet.

"PFC Slate!"

Jessie turned to see the Navy Corpsman, jogging toward him.

"Yeah," Jessie answered.

"Gunny Killeen says you're wounded."

Jessie touched his shoulder. His jacket was soaked with blood. For the first time since he saw Jeremiah Polk, he realized he was in a lot of pain. Jeremiah looked at his shoulder and grimaced.

"Get taken care of, Slate. We'll talk when we get this train back to Chinwangtao. How about tomorrow after church?"

"Where is it?"

"It's the only church in town. You'll find it."

CHAPTER THREE

The Seventh Marines were garrisoned at Chinwangtao along with an outfit of Chinese Nationalists who were bandits on weekends. The town had a lovely church, a few houses, forty gin mills, and two hundred houses of ill repute. Older women still had their feet bound up so tightly from childhood that their feet never grew bigger than a five-year-old child's. Gunny Killeen said it was to keep them from running away and to make them unattractive to the slave dealers who ran the whorehouses in Shanghai. Beggars were everywhere. One approached with his hand out as Gunny Killeen and Jessie made their way through the town, toward the church.

"You'll be givin' no greenbacks to the beggars, lad," Gunny cautioned.

He grabbed the man's face with one large hand, shoved him into a nearby wall and kept walking as if nothing had happened.

"The beggars are not as they would seem, lad. They beg to raise money for the Communists."

Jessie believed it. He had already seen enough in China to change his vision of the world. Everything the old Shanghai Marines had told him over the years was true. The women were everywhere and were of every type. White Russians who had escaped Russia during the revolu-

24

tion. Half-Italian and half-Chinese women from Italian soldiers who were once here as allies for the Japanese. Germans left here from the thirties. Chinese women as clean and delicate as flowers.

They stopped in front of a small, gray stone church, nestled amidst white cherry trees, flowers like the colors of the rainbow clustered in stone gardens that were linked by a narrow cobblestone pathway.

In front of the church, to the right of the steps that led into the double front doors, was a line of eight pinewood coffins, their lids lying beside them.

"Who died, Gunny?"

" 'Tis the church charity, laddie."

"Charity?"

"Indeed. Might appear a small thing, but not so. You see, lad, in China whoever has the misfortune of comin' upon the recently deceased is responsible for the burial and all costs thereof."

"You're joking."

"Oh, no. The law. Economics, you see. Eventually the smell would get so bad that some poor soul would fork over the loot just to breathe again. So the church leaves empty coffins out, plain, to be sure, but functional. They'll be filled by early morn."

A group of men were just entering the church. Among them Jessie recognized Mr. Byron Sims, the Standard Oil man he'd met after the train ambush. Three Chinese women and one Chinese man hurried past Jessie and the gunny, bowing as they went.

"A prettier Lord's house you'll not be finding anywhere in China, I'll be wagering."

"It really is beautiful."

"Come, lad, we'll not be missin' the singin' of 'Amazing Grace' just to hear your jabbering." Paddy gave Jessie a push toward the double mahogany doors.

In the cool air of the church, Jeremiah stood at the pulpit wearing a white shirt and dark blue tie. Jessie couldn't fight a slight grin, having never seen the man in anything other than work clothes and suspenders or bib overalls. Jeremiah's blue eyes caught sight of Jessie, and his face lit up with a smile as he said, "Would you turn to page 241 in your hymnal, please."

By the time the service was over, Jessie didn't know whether to be mad or glad he had come. He wondered if the sermon had been prepared with him in mind. Jeremiah shook hands with everyone as they were leaving. Gunny, Wing, and Jessie were the last out. Gunnery Sergeant Killeen grabbed Jeremiah's hand and shook it hard.

"Wonderful sermon, Gunny Polk."

"Thank you, Paddy, and thank you for coming." The two old salts paused with hands clasped and looked into each other's aging eyes.

"Semper Fidelis, old friend," the gunny said.

"Where to, Paddy?"

"It'll be truck-guard duty on the road from Taku Bar to Tientsin."

"Tientsin Barracks?" Jeremiah asked with a hint of concern in his tone.

Gunnery Sergeant Killeen gave a nod. "We leave tomorrow."

"I'll look you up if we get down that way, Paddy."

"And I'm expectin' no less, Gunny Polk."

They shook hands again and Gunnery Sergeant Killeen walked away, pointedly leaving Jessie and Broken Wing alone with Jeremiah. Jeremiah immediately took Broken Wing's hand and shook it.

"I'm so glad you came, my Navajo friend."

"Me too," Wing said quietly, as if embarrassed.

"I'll continue to write you regularly. I should enjoy any reply you feel led to sit down and pen to me."

Wing gave a nod and walked away. Jessie had an urge to grab the Indian by the back of the neck. He was now sure that Broken Wing had conspired with Jeremiah to get him to China.

"Let's walk through the garden and talk, Slate."

"Okay, Mr. Polk."

No one spoke at first. Jessie felt horribly awkward. Jeremiah finally paused by the small bench beside one of the flower gardens and motioned Jessie to sit beside him.

"How in the world did you end up in China, Mr. Polk?" Jessie asked. "I thought you were moving to Hawaii when you left the nickel mining company in New Caledonia."

"Money. I had old contacts here from my cruises in China back in the 'twenties and 'thirties. Had a friend in the shipping business in New Caledonia who knew that I spoke Chinese and had done some logging way back. They told Standard Oil I was the man for the job, and here I am."

"Logging?"

"Yes. See, China has a tree that grows this special kind of nut. When oil from the nut is mixed with crude oil, it brings the crude up to a very high quality."

Jessie nodded and tried to pretend to be interested, but there was no sense going on with meaningless chitchat. He swallowed hard and blurted out the inevitable question.

"Are Kate and Charlie here, Mr. Polk?" He felt a cold chill and immediately wished that he hadn't asked.

Jeremiah looked him in the eyes as if searching for something. "Jessie, I served with your dad, and no finer Marine ever wore the uniform. I served with Gunnery Sergeant O'Cleary, and he loved you like his own son. O'Cleary was closer than any brother to me. Now, as if it were God's plan, here you are serving with another old friend that I respect above most men, and he thinks of you, in his own words, as his 'very own illegitimate son.' "

Jessie chuckled. "It is strange, isn't it?" he said quietly.

"The Lord works in mysterious ways. Not until I spoke to Broken Wing this morning did I even partially understand why you ran out on my daughter and your son."

"It's none of Wing's business."

"You named your son Charlie Rose."

"No! Kate named him Charlie Rose."

"Your best friend, who died on Vella Lavella. You blame yourself."

"I ran out on him to marry Kate! He died so I could chase a skirt!" Jessie jumped to his feet and began pacing.

"Men die in war, Jessie, and other men feel responsible sometimes. You can't blame yourself. It's time to forgive yourself."

Jessie spun around to face Jeremiah. He could feel his face flush with anger and pain that had been bottled up, slicing at his insides for over two years.

"Forgive." Jessie said the hated word through clenched teeth. "There's no forgiveness for what I've done. Is Charlie Rose coming back to his family? Is he going to give me a big hug and tell me he didn't mind dying?"

"You can't take all of the blame."

"I don't!" Jessie yanked his wallet out of his trouser pocket and fumbled madly through it until he found what he was looking for. He pulled out a folded piece of paper, yellowed with age, and threw it at Jeremiah. "I blame you! I blame Kate! I blame God! And I blame me!"

Jeremiah looked stunned. He blinked as if not believing his ears, then slowly picked up the paper and opened it.

"It's a letter from Kate to you. What's this got to do with me?"

"Read it. Read it out loud, Jeremiah."

Jeremiah cleared his throat.

"Dearest Jessie,

　This is the most difficult letter I have ever had to write. I'm scared and confused and have no one to turn to but you. I love you, and no matter what your decision might be after reading this, always remember that I blame myself, not you."

"Hah! Famous last words, huh, Mr. Polk?" Jessie said scornfully.

Jeremiah paused, then continued.

"There is one other person in my life whom I love and would rather die than hurt. I think that you saw the very special relationship that exists between my father and me.

I've been feeling sort of sick lately, so I went to the doctor. He says that I'm pregnant. I'm not sad about having our baby, darling. I love you, and part of me is thrilled, but Jessie, this will hurt my father so deeply that I honestly fear for his life. He had a mild heart attack last June, just a few weeks before you came to the island. Our doctor, Doc Guiet, thinks that this sort of shock might be too much—"

The old salt's voice broke and a tear trickled down his cheek. He cleared his throat and went on.

". . . might be too much for Dad to bear so soon after the heart attack.

Do not misunderstand the purpose of this letter, Jessie. Dad will forgive my sin because he will know that the Lord has already forgiven me. We will find a way to live with my disgrace. But if you really meant what you said about wanting to marry me, and if there is any way you could get back to Nouméa soon enough, then there would be no reason to risk hurting my father. If you are not ready to make such a commitment, then I need to know that soon.

I know that this letter must be a shock for you. I'm in a bit of a shock myself. Whatever your answer is, Jessie, I'll understand.

All my love,
Kate."

Jeremiah Polk sagged visibly. His shoulders slumped forward and his left hand dropped until it nearly touched the ground, as if the letter had become suddenly very heavy.

"Then what?" Jeremiah asked with eyes staring at the ground.

Jessie plunged his hands into his pockets and looked skyward with eyes closed. "The letter came the same day the Northern Landing Force left Guadalcanal. We didn't know the destination. I tried to get O'Cleary to help me get back to Nouméa, but Lieutenant Pomper got wind of it. He had a thing for Kate, remember?"

"He was the one that came into the café all of the time?"

"Yeah. That's him. Class A scumbag. I had jungle rot on my foot. We hit Vella Lavella. Pretty rough at first, then the Japs took off. We were on patrol, trying to outflank a group of nips that were hitting some New Zealanders farther down the beach. . . ." A lump that felt like a softball swelled up in Jessie's throat, and he turned away to breathe and fight back crying.

"Go on, Jessie. Tell me."

"Lieutenant Pierce, he bought it on Iwo Jima. Pierce and O'Cleary needed two runners to get word to the New Zealand troops on the beach that we had a blocking action set up. Me and Charlie Rose volunteered. Gunny O'Cleary didn't want me to go, he didn't think my foot was up to it. . . . God, I wish I'd listened to him."

"How did Charlie Rose die?"

"We made it back to the New Zealanders. Their C.O., a colonel, was hit bad. The medic told us a PBY was coming for him. We gave the message to the medic who was working on the wounded colonel. I asked him if he'd look at my foot before we left. While he took the message to the second in command, Charlie Rose told me that he heard the PBY was taking the wounded colonel back to New Caledonia. Charlie knew about Kate. I made some stupid comment about wishing I could be on that PBY. He said, 'You're *gonna* be on that PBY, boy.' "

Jessie paused and swiped angrily at a tear.

"Finish, Slate."

Jessie took a few steps and stopped. He turned around to face Jeremiah. His gray eyes swelling up with tears, he forced the words out: "Charlie Rose came up with this plan, see, and I did it. We doctored up the jungle rot on my foot to make it look worse." Jessie laughed the kind of laugh that had no more feeling than a cough. "He mixed powdered mustard with some water in the half shell of a rotten coconut. We smeared it around the jungle rot on my foot. It looked bad. I told him I didn't think it was right! I told him I'd be like a deserter! But Charlie kept saying, 'There's plenty of fightin', boy, all the way to Tokyo. You can't let your own baby come into this world a bastard, it ain't right, Jess. . . .' " Jessie could hold back no longer. A flood of tears poured from his eyes and he sobbed openly as he turned away.

Jeremiah stood up and put his arm over Jessie's slumping shoulders. "There now, son." He gave Jessie's shoulder consoling pats, and neither one of them spoke for a while.

Finally, Jeremiah stepped back. "So you were evacuated back to Nouméa, and Charlie Rose was killed going back to your old position."

Jessie nodded.

"Why didn't you tell Kate any of this?"

"I couldn't at first. I couldn't stand it! Then I tried. I tried! I tried to tell her! I tried to tell her in Hilo, but everything fell apart and I couldn't get to her before we shipped out for Iwo Jima."

"Now wait. I was with O'Cleary in Hilo the night he got you that liberty pass. He told me that he watched you get on that Pineapple Express."

"I did. I met Kate and the baby in Hilo. She blew up when she realized I hadn't read any of her letters. I didn't know she named the baby after Charlie Rose. She told me to go away for an hour. I told her that I would explain every miserable detail when I came back, because she wouldn't listen right then."

"What happened?"

"I got in a big brawl with a Marine named Duffy Johnson. Got thrown in the brig by shore patrol. I tried to call Kate to explain the next morning. She was gone."

"Tell her now."

"No! I've ruined her life enough. I'm married to the Corps, and if I'm lucky and if there really is a God, maybe I can get killed so I don't ruin anybody else's life!" Jessie turned and walked away.

"Wait! Jessie!"

"Leave me alone," Jessie mumbled as he kept walking. He walked until he found a slop chute, and drank until the sun disappeared.

CHAPTER FOUR

During the next couple of months, Jessie's thoughts of Kate and Charlie were dissipated by constant movement and changing orders, as the First Marine Division settled into the poorly defined job of helping the Nationalists organize, train, and defend themselves against the Communists. Few if any of the enlisted men knew what was going on, and, as is Marine Corps custom, anyone who asked was given a standard answer: "You a diplomat or a Marine?"

There was no regimental designation for machine-gun companies. The old machine-gun companies were called D Company. In 1943 the Corps changed D Company to Weapons Company. Jessie and Broken Wing were attached to Weapons Company and could be ordered into any outfit in need of a machine gun or an extra BAR team. They were considered weapons experts, having qualified with nearly every weapon the Corps used while serving with the Paramarines in the war. Weapons Company would be permanently stationed at the Tientsin Barracks, where they could be used to teach weapons training to the local Nationalist division.

Tientsin was a city of two to three million people. It was attainable by the Hai Ho River from the sea, a one-lane road coming from Taku Bar, or by rail from Chinwangtao. It appeared to be good duty, since slop chutes and women were said to be gleefully abundant in Tientsin if a Marine ever got liberty to see it.

The First Marine Division camp and headquarters was a huge area on the outskirts of town. It was big enough for tank maneuvers, infantry training, a rifle range, prison camp, and base hospital, with plenty of room left over for barracks. Big tents were spread into a tent city, but most of the barracks were old warehouses, about a block long, half a block wide, and stretching up five stories. Each floor was set up for a storehouse, with an office at the end. The ceilings were about twenty feet high. The freight elevators did not work. The only heat was from oil stoves, about ten to a floor, the size of fifty-five-gallon drums, ancient drip-and-burn oil heat, each encased in a box of sand with a wood frame. You had to go all the way down and out into the courtyard to the head. It would be a sobering winter.

After the first couple of weeks, they brought in double bunks, and these were placed in stateside barracks formation, two companies per deck—engineers, motor pool, and some tankers. There were various offices and old store-rooms throughout the warehouses that NCOs could lay claim to, but only NCOs—corporals and above. The whole setup was unlike any Marine Corps base that any of the men had ever seen. It was total confusion. Old Marines going home, new recruits coming in. Constant changes in regulations. No one knew up from down, and odd-looking, non-Marine characters seemed to be all over the place.

Gunnery Sergeant Paddy Francis Killeen's quarters and office were at the south end of the third floor. He poked his big Irish face out of his door a moment after Jessie and Wing had fallen onto their bunks.

"Slate! Wing! My office on the double!" His voice echoed through the cavernous barracks.

Jessie punched the springs above him.

"What did you do now?"

Broken Wing grunted and slowly climbed down. Jessie

pulled on his shoes and followed the Navajo to the gunny's office. Wing slapped the bulkhead three times, hard.

"Advance!"

They opened the door, and Paddy motioned them in with his pipe as if he had something confidential to say.

"Shoulder healed up, Slate?"

Jessie shut the door behind him. "Good as new, Gunny."

"What is it, Paddy?" Wing asked.

"Well, lads, it's like this. General Rockey is coming in."

Broken Wing looked at his shoes and shook his head, "General inspection?" he grumbled.

"How can we stand in formation for a General Inspection when half the outfit are wearing combat jackets and dungarees?" Jessie asked.

"There it be, and the colonel got wind of it. Now you know the purge is gaining momentum."

Wing nodded.

"What are we down to, Gunny?" Jessie asked.

"Don't know, but they're handing out BCDs for breakfast."

"I know, Gunny. Remember Andy Jones down in Motor Pool?" Jessie asked.

"Good Marine. Had him in my outfit on the Canal."

"Saw two MPs hauling him away. He said he was getting a BCD for giving some lieutenant the finger."

"Andy? Bad Conduct Discharge?"

"Yes, sir, Gunny."

The old salt looked down at his cane-wood desk and shook his big head in disgust. "When a fine Marine like that is sent packing for nothing, I'm guessing that I don't have to tell you men how important this mission is."

Gunnery Sergeant Killeen stood up, tapped his pipe, and moved quietly over to his door. He put an ear to the door, then opened it quickly. No one was there. He shut it, went back to his desk chair and motioned the two Marines closer.

"The situation is this, lads. Some of these men haven't

been issued dress green uniforms in two years. Some don't even have greens! We will fail that inspection and heads will roll. Now, the colonel procured a moonlight issue of greens, and we'll have 'em in Taku Bar tomorrow."

"How'd he swing that, Paddy?" Jessie asked.

"Never you mind, let's just say a certain stateside outfit won't be issued greens this winter."

Jessie rubbed his square jaw and shook his head as if disturbed by something.

"And what would you be thinking, PFC Slate?" Paddy snapped impatiently.

"I'm thinking there's more to this than we're being told."

"It's true enough, lad. The captain is seeing a promotion in this. But some of our boys will flunk inspection for sure without new uniforms. Some were forced to wear their greens in the field when we first got here, and they could be looking at a BCD. But never you mind any of that! Able Company will not be marching onto that parade ground looking like a bunch of GIs!"

The United States Marine Corps takes more pride in their uniform than other services. Buckles and brass must shine like the sun. All leather oiled, soft and shining. A man must be able to shave using his shoes as a mirror. Everything must be in perfect alignment. The buttons on your fly must be perfectly aligned with your belt buckle. Each sleeve and trouser leg must be tailored perfectly in length. The cover on your head must sit exact, according to the type of cover you are wearing, the barracks cover judged precisely by the finger widths from the bridge of the nose to the bill of the hat. Even a loose thread is not just a loose thread in the Marine Corps, it is an Irish pennant.

"What is the plan, Paddy?" Broken Wing asked suspiciously.

"When the uniforms come in, we'll size every man in the outfit. Then we'll load the uniforms onto trucks, which you two will drive into Tientsin. I've discovered a tailor in town with a big sign in the window that says, 'Worked for the British Army for twenty years.'"

"Guess that's one way to get to Tientsin," Jessie grumbled.

"As you were! Who's in command of this mission, Marine?" Paddy said firmly.

"Sorry, Gunny."

The gunny's massive round shoulders relaxed and he gave a grunt. He stuck his pipe back into his mouth and began again.

"You two are scheduled for the truck-guard detail into Taku Bar. I want you to just wander on down to the dock on your way back."

Jessie and Wing exchanged unhappy expressions. The guard detail into Taku Bar was considered a real "garbage detail." Almost punishment.

Paddy checked his watch. "Pick up the truck at 0800 down in the motor pool."

"Who is the guard detail?" Broken Wing asked.

"The new boots."

"What?" Jessie exclaimed.

"Somebody thought they should have some experience on a detail."

"Gunny, I heard scuttlebutt that those guys only had three weeks of boot camp and are actually finishing boot camp at the French Arsenal." Jessie hoped he was wrong.

"True enough, lads."

"That is nuts," Broken Wing said.

Nothing made sense in the Marine Corps. The Corps was busy handing out Bad Conduct Discharges to real Marines, combat veterans, to bring down the number of Marines in the Corps, and at the same time enlisting boys who didn't know an A-2 machine gun from an M-1 rifle. It was all too insane to understand. But one thing Jessie and Wing did understand: do not question or doubt Gunnery Sergeant Paddy Francis Killeen.

A loud knock on the door brought the meeting to an end.

The door opened and Captain Fitch strode in with an official pinch to his narrow brow. Everyone came to attention and saluted.

"As you were," he said hurriedly. "Gunny, we got more trouble."

"Sir."

"One of our Marines on guard duty just shot and killed another 'stealy boy.' "

"Bandit Nationalist, sir?"

"Probably."

"Why are we supporting these Nationalists, Captain? You know that they're common bandits, and it's as plain as the red rain."

"We are not politicians, Paddy. If I made policy, we'd support the Communists. That is not the issue right now. We now support the Nationalists, and unfortunately just killed another one."

"What do you want me to do, sir?"

"I want every man on guard duty issued twelve-gauge riot guns with number-nine bird shot. Take the M-1s away immediately."

"Aye aye, sir."

"And belay the regulation that one man be armed with his service-issue M-1 in every party of four Marines."

"Sir?"

"Have to, Gunny. Too many M-1s being lost in the whorehouses!"

"Aye aye, sir."

Captain Fitch turned to Jessie and Broken Wing, standing at parade rest.

"What have these two done now?" he asked like an angry high school principal, which was exactly what he was in 1941, or so said scuttlebutt.

"Not a thing, Captain. Just sending them out on the Taku Bar run."

The captain nodded, turned and left. An instant later he poked his head back into the room. "Paddy, will you or

Slate be playing the Irish pipes at the Leopold Building next week?"

"The lad will play, sir. Good experience."

"Slate, I'd like to hear the gunny's song."

" 'Pi Brocht of O'Donnell Dau,' sir?"

Captain Fitch looked at the gunny. "That's the name, isn't it, Paddy?"

"Aye, 'tis, sir."

"Outstanding. Then you'll be at the Leopold Building, dress blues, 1900 hours. General Rockey should be in attendance, and, naturally, if he has a specific tune that he wants to hear, you'll go with that."

"Aye aye, sir," Jessie said stoutly, trying to subdue his sudden urge to request a transfer to the Sixth Division in Tsingtao.

Only the very rich or those with contacts in high places could hope to see the inside of the most famous hotel and nightclub in all of China. His lips were turning to ice just thinking about playing the pipes there. He wondered why Paddy would not play.

By 0900 the next morning, Jessie was already getting sleepy at the wheel. The one-lane road leading from Tientsin to Taku Bar looked somewhat out of place in China. For starters, it was concrete, and the stretch from Taku Bar to Tientsin was raised up above the paddy fields. It felt as if you were driving on a very narrow and very long bridge at times. The road was never intended to service the big Marine 6-BYs. When two 6-BY trucks met, it was trouble. Every so often there was a side road or a platform, and a truck would have to back up until the driver found one of these side roads to pull off. Loaded had the right of way, ammo next, then rank.

There was a village every few miles, and each village had a wall around it like some miniature kingdom. The population of these villages varied from as little as fifty people to as many as thousands. Some of them were dangerous, depending on what warlord was operating in the area. It was scary. Marines had been ambushed on the Taku Run, three wounded. If the warlord was getting his pay from the Communists, he was the enemy, and if he was a Nationalist he might still be the enemy, and if he was a bandit he was definitely the enemy. It all made life quite interesting for Marines, especially since none of the men had ever been initiated into the political complexities of China. To most Marines, diplomacy meant deciding between a left hook, straight right, or locking and loading the M-1.

Jessie and Broken Wing put the squad of six boot Marines in the back of the truck where they belonged. There was a machine gun mounted on the top of the truck, which none of the boot Marines knew how to operate. The new recruits did not question Jessie or Broken Wing when they pulled out of the Marine depot at Taku Bar and headed toward the dock. The boot Marines loaded the crates of uniforms into the truck without question. That was the beauty of Gunny's plan. Recruits never questioned anything. The mission could not have gone smoother.

Once back at Tientsin Barracks, the gunny and Captain Fitch took the moonlight issue and set the whole thing up like an assembly line: crates of greens trousers, blouses, overcoats, and piss cutters. No leather belts, although you could have them made in Tientsin. Each man in the company would stop at one crate, try on trousers until he found a fit, then take an additional pair and on to the next crate. Last came the quarter-length dress shoes. Many of the men that came into the Corps during the war had the three-quarter shoes. This had been the source of many a court-martial for improper dress. Shoes were like gold. China had not produced shoes in fifteen years. In fact, the famous "Flying Tigers," who got a few hundred dollars for each Jap plane they shot down, actually made more money smuggling shoes, or so said the old salts. A pair of dress shoes would go for a hundred dollars.

At the end of the assembly line stood Paddy, who carefully placed each man's chevrons in his blouse pocket. Then Jessie and Broken Wing pinned each man's name, rank, and organization to the uniform. A detail had been sent out by the gunny to steal fourteen twelve-foot lengths of three-quarter-inch pipe from the engineers. These were rigged up as clothes racks, uniforms hung on them and loaded onto the truck.

Jessie and Broken Wing took the truck in search of the former British tailor, with orders to press each uniform and sew on the chevrons. It could not help but mean a promotion for all concerned. Captain Fitch's company would be the only Marines in the regiment not caught off guard when the general inspection hit.

At 1700 hours Friday afternoon Jessie slowed the truck to a stop near the International Bridge, which spanned the Hai Ho River leading into Tientsin.

"What's all of the commotion?" Jessie asked as he slowed for Marine MPs blocking one end of the bridge.

Broken Wing sat up straight and pointed. "Look!"

Stretching over the main beams of the big steel bridge was the partially naked body of what appeared to be a young Marine, hanging, tied by hands and feet. His pale upper torso was smeared with blood from cuts and gunshot wounds. A sign with something written in Chinese was pinned to the dead man's Marine Corps trousers. Rage swept through Jessie as he scanned the hundreds of curious Chinese civilians crowding the riverbanks to see the dead Marine. A long line of civilian cars and rickshaws had been ordered by Marine MPs to the side of the road to wait.

"What's up, Corporal?" Jessie asked as a Marine MP with an M-1 jogged up to the truck.

"They murdered one of our men!"

"Who?"

"Who knows? But it's about to get bad here."

"Can we cross?"

"Yeah, go on across." He pointed at a black '37 Ford. "Not you, Mac! Pull over!"

"Hey, Corporal. One more thing. We're looking for a tailor shop. The guy's got a big sign in the window that says, 'Worked for the British for twenty years'?"

"Give it up, buddy! Every Marine in China's already tried."

"What?"

"The redhead, right?" the Corporal said with a wink.

"I don't know what you're talking about. We want to find a tailor."

"Yeah, yeah. I hear ya. Follow this road down about six blocks and turn right. Think it's the fifth or sixth street. There's a mining office next door to it."

Jessie gave the corporal a thumbs-up as he pulled onto the bridge. Two Marines perched perilously on the main beams edged toward the body to cut it down as the truck passed under. Marine Corsairs crisscrossed the sky above. Jessie glanced at Broken Wing's angry eyes. He thought of the beach landing on Vella Lavella and remembered standing with Charlie Rose staring numbly at the first dead Marine he had ever seen. The man had been decapitated. He shook himself to clear away the memory.

The city was crowded with foot traffic. A few cars plowed through waves of bicycles, honking their horns constantly. At the sixth street, Jessie wheeled the big truck cautiously around the corner, plowing through the sea of people with a steady rapping on the horn. He moved slowly down the street, honking the people out of the way, with Wing checking one side while he checked the other.

"There it is," Wing said, pointing.

Midway down the crowded, noisy street a dark green stone building was wedged between a long row of wooden buildings, each littered with hanging laundry and signs of all sizes advertising everything from turtle eggs to chicken heads. Two Marines, one tall and the other short, stood on the sidewalk in front of the tailor shop smoking cigarettes. Jessie pulled up in front of the green stone building and parked. The two Marines on the sidewalk sneered as Jessie and Broken Wing got out.

"What's this, Mac? Somebody running bus tours now?" the short Marine on the sidewalk said.

Jessie gave the man a curious frown. "You talking to me, Marine?"

The short Marine flipped his cigarette into the street and shook his head in disgust but didn't speak. Jessie looked at Broken Wing. He shrugged, and they entered the tailor shop. A small bell rang when the solid oak door shut behind them. An old Chinaman with a gray beard stood smiling and staring almost trancelike at Broken Wing from behind a small counter stacked high with blue silk curtains. At the back of the room was a stairway leading to an upstairs apartment. At the top of the stairs, locked in by a short bamboo gate, sat a small blond-haired Caucasian boy holding an old tennis ball and looking downstairs like a prisoner longing for freedom. Something in the boy's eyes drew Slate like a magnet. He walked hypnotically to the bottom of the stairs to study the child's face, but the kid disappeared in the upstairs hallway.

"See a ghost?" Broken Wing asked quietly.

Jessie scratched his head and shrugged. "Just a cute kid," he mumbled, and came back to the tailor's counter. The Chinaman was still staring at Broken Wing.

"Maybe he sees ghost," Broken Wing said in a dry monotone.

The Chinaman blinked from his trance. He held up an American nickel. "Is you?" He pointed at the Indian on the coin, then pointed at Broken Wing.

"No," Wing said.

"You here for meet singer? Go away! You here for Tailor Chung? Is okay."

"Singer? What singer?" Jessie asked.

"Go away!"

"No, we are here to get uniforms tailored."

The Chinaman smiled awkwardly, nodded, and began looking around the counter. He pulled out a tape measure.

"No, sir. Not just us. We have a whole company of uniforms that need to be pressed and have the stripes sewn on."

"Yes. Very good." The old man turned and shouted something in Chinese. Two young Chinese men came out of a back room. They rushed out to the truck and began unloading the uniforms.

CHAPTER FIVE

Jessie pounded hard on the bulkhead of Paddy's office three times.

"Advance and be recognized!"

Jessie opened the door and stepped in. Paddy pointed his pipe at him from behind his desk. "Lad, tonight is important."

"I know, Gunny."

"It has been confirmed. General Rockey himself will be in attendance, along with many lower-ranking officers. He has requested 'Amazing Grace' on the Irish pipes."

"I'll do my best to make you proud of me, Paddy."

"Good, lad. There'll be dignitaries and diplomats and the like. Europeans all stay at the Leopold—you know the type."

"Yes, sir."

Paddy scratched at the back of his broad neck with his pipe. "Yes, well of course, you'll be doin' a fine job. Taught you meself, didn't I?"

"That you did, Paddy."

"Well then, off with you." He waved Jessie away with his pipe and pretended to be busy with paperwork.

Jessie turned to leave, opening the door.

"And Slate . . ."

Jessie looked back. "Yes, Gunny?"

45

"You'll be lettin' no surprises upset the playin' of the 'Pi Brocht of O'Donnell Dau.' " Paddy's order sounded a hint of concern that Jessie could not understand. It was almost as if he were not speaking about the music at all.

"I thought I was playing 'Amazing Grace.' "

"So you are, lad, so you are, and you'll play well."

"I'll do my best, Paddy," Jessie said as he searched the old salt's face for an answer to this sudden concern.

"All a man can ask."

"Will you be there, Paddy?"

"The likes of meself couldn't get through the door, laddie. No enlisted allowed in the Leopold. You'll be going as a member of Colonel Riggs's staff, along with Captain Fitch and Captain Ross."

"But I was bringing Broken Wing with me to help with setting up and all."

"Sorry, Slate. He won't be allowed in. Now off with you and good luck."

The Leopold Building was an impressive structure. It would have been just another building in most American cities, but in Tientsin, it dominated by its size and architectural strength. Chinese doormen rushed out to open the doors of the colonel's Packard sedan. Jessie retrieved the pipes from the trunk and followed Colonel Riggs through the revolving glass doors and into the lobby. Jessie stared, wide-eyed. He felt like a country boy visiting the big city. The deck was pink marble, with large Oriental rugs spread generously around luxurious couches and large wing-back chairs. The desk clerk was Caucasian and wore a tuxedo.

"Colonel Riggs and staff for the Leopold Room."

The desk clerk checked a list of names on a clipboard. "General Rockey's party?" He sounded European.

"Yes."

The clerk rang a bell. "The bell captain will lead you to the elevator."

By the time they reached the elevator at the far end of

the lobby, Captain Ross and Captain Fitch caught up. The elevator was made of teak and had ornate cast-iron doors. A Chinese bell captain pushed number 20. Not a word was spoken all the way to the top. Jessie looked down at his spit-shined low quarters and wished that he'd buffed them one more time. The scent of jasmine filled the elevator from a tall vase of long purple flowers.

When the elevator door opened, the group stepped into a large foyer and was greeted immediately by a man in a tuxedo. He bowed politely and motioned the Marines toward a lovely Chinese hat-check girl standing behind a counter. Behind her was the clothing room. The men handed over their covers, each receiving a small slip of paper with a number on it. Two large, leafy green banana plants sat on either side of the club's entrance. Just beyond that, a waiter stood at a station with clipboard in hand.

An orchestra was playing a rendition of "Shoo Shoo Baby" as Jessie followed the officers into the club. The head waiter checked his list, then bowed and snapped his fingers for another waiter to lead the group to a table.

"May I take your instrument, monsieur?" The head waiter sounded French. He was speaking to Jessie.

"I guess so."

"I will place it on stage behind the piano, yes?"

"That would be fine, thank you."

The grandiose room covered half of the twentieth floor. Plush, rose-colored carpet surrounded a slick teak dance floor on three sides. The fourth side abutted the stage. Each member of the orchestra sat behind a large wooden shield embossed with the glittering letters LR and what appeared to be some sort of Russian family crest. The waiter led the group through the packed nightclub, finally stopping at a table near the right corner of the stage, close to the piano.

Not exactly prime seats, Jessie thought as he scanned the room for pretty women. The waiter bowed and held out his hand toward the table. Everyone waited for the colonel to be seated first. Jessie, following Marine etiquette, then waited for the two captains to be seated before sitting down himself. His rear end had only touched the black cane seat of the chair when the officers suddenly stood up.

"Attention!" Captain Fitch said smartly.

Jessie sprang to his feet.

"At ease, gentlemen," a guttural-sounding voice replied from behind Jessie.

"General Rockey, a pleasure to see you, sir," Colonel Riggs said.

"Thank you, Colonel."

"General, this is Captain Fitch, Captain Ross, and PFC Slate."

"Sir."

"Nice to meet you, sir."

"Sir."

"And this is my aide." The short, stocky, broad-faced general turned to present a smiling, pleasant-looking major standing behind him. Both men wore Purple Hearts on their dress blues, so at least they weren't permanent "office pogues," and therefore worthy of respect. "Major Franks."

General Rockey frowned, as if searching for something as the men acknowledged Major Franks. Jessie stared in amazement at the three stars on the general's shoulder.

"Where's that old warhorse, Colonel?" the general asked, scratching at the short gray stubble on top of his nearly bald head. He looked like he played center for a good college football team.

"Sir?"

"Gunnery Sergeant Paddy Francis Killeen. Where's my Irishman?"

"Well, sir, he sent PFC Slate in his place."

"Yes, I am aware of that, and I can't wait to hear him play. But that old warhorse should be here to see his prodigy."

Jessie suddenly felt like a nervous kid on his first day of school. He thought of his mom sending him off each morning. If she were alive, she would be so proud of him for finally learning an instrument. He'd been training for a moment like this since the last war ended.

"I suppose it's my fault, sir," the colonel said. "Enlisted men are not allowed in the Leopold Room, and there was only an invitation for four."

The general frowned and chewed at the inside of his mouth as if in thought, then smacked his lips. "Yes, I see your thinking, Colonel. Now, if you will allow one of your captains to accompany my aide, Major Franks will take my staff car to pick up Gunny Killeen. I'm sitting with the ambassadors from Spain, France, and the United States of America." General Rockey winked and nodded at Jessie. "If they can't manage an invite, I guess we'll have to over-run and secure this slop chute, huh, son?" He grinned, then paused, studying the medals on Jessie's chest.

"Yes, sir," Jessie said, standing as stiff as he had ever stood in his life. He liked this guy. Matter of fact, this guy was already his favorite general. He was also the only general he had ever met.

Captain Fitch escorted Major Franks toward the door as a waiter brought four glasses and a bottle of Irish whiskey.

"Compliments of the general," he said as he poured each man's glass to the brim and left the bottle in the center of the table.

"Wow! Real whiskey!" Jessie blurted, then straightened his gaze and clamped his mouth shut.

"You bet," General Rockey said.

"They serve only the real stuff in the Leopold Room," Colonel Riggs added. "A toast." The colonel held up his glass and the other two men quickly held theirs out.

"I'd like to make this toast, gentlemen," General Rockey said. "To the Irish pipes and to the Corps."

"Aye aye," Jessie said as they touched glasses. He slugged his full glass of whiskey down in one gulp and slapped his empty glass down at the same moment that General Rockey did. Jessie and the general stared at each other, each with his hand still on the empty glass. General

Rockey looked at Colonel Riggs and Captain Ross. Each had barely sipped his drink and both glasses looked full. The general burst out laughing, a deep, guttural laugh that was wonderfully contagious. Jessie laughed out loud too, until he caught sight of the colonel's glare. Laughing in the face of your commanding officer was not good, and laughing at your commanding officer was tantamount to asking for a career change. Jessie swallowed back the rest of his laughter. The colonel and the captain threw back the rest of their drinks.

"Colonel Riggs."

"Yes, sir."

"Would you allow me to borrow the company of your young pipes player? I want to introduce him to a couple of people at my table."

"My pleasure, sir."

The general turned and walked toward a large table that faced the stage from the front edge of the dance floor.

The room was filled to capacity. Nearly every man not in uniform wore a tuxedo. Women were dressed in long gowns that sure hadn't come from the average Ben Franklin store. The general's table sat directly beneath a large, mirrored ball that hung from the ceiling, reflecting thousands of pinpoints of light around the room. Seven men and four women sat at the general's table: three Marine officers in dress blues, one British officer, and three tuxedoes. A fast scan of the women at the table showed nothing worth risking brig time for.

"Ladies and gentlemen, I'd like you to meet our Irish pipes player, Private First Class Jessie Slate. I served with his father, Sergeant Jack Slate, in the Great War, and was with him when he died on the Yangtze aboard the USS *Panay* in 1937. He was a real hero, and judging from the decorations on this young man, I'd say he's walking in his father's footsteps."

Jessie's mouth fell open. With a stunned expression he turned to the general to speak, but General Rockey had already begun introductions, and most of them had been made by the time Jessie recovered from his shock.

"The French Ambassador and last, our host, the owner of the Leopold Building, Mr. Sergei Leopold the Fourth."

"Yes. It was my grandfather who took the unfortunate step," Mr. Leopold said with a Russian accent, as if avoiding the inevitable question. Leopold's eyes were small and cold black, and his eyebrows swept up at the temples, giving him a rather sinister appearance.

"Pleasure to meet you, sir," Jessie said.

"The pleasure is mine. I have always wanted to hear the bagpipes."

"Thank you for asking me to play."

"The general must take credit for that."

"Well," General Rockey said, pointing at the stage, "when I heard you found this singer, I guess I got a little selfish. Something I wanted to hear all my life."

"All of Tientsin is abuzz about our beautiful American with the voice of an angel," Mr. Leopold explained.

The French ambassador cleared his throat like a woman. "And the mademoiselle, she sings in the language of love also." He smacked his lips and motioned as if blowing a kiss. Jessie faked a grin and fought an urge to smack the *sis* out of the feminine little Frenchman.

Mr. Leopold smiled and nodded. "Yes, this is true. She speaks French, also."

"Where did you find her?" Jessie asked.

"That good fortune belongs to Sir Jerald Huxley, the British consul," Mr. Leopold said as he held out his hand to reintroduce one of the monkey suits to his left.

A thin, handsome man with a pencil-thin moustache dabbed his mouth with a napkin and gave a nod of acknowledgment.

"Good fortune and distinct pleasure, Mr. Leopold, to be sure," Sir Jerald Huxley said with a very correct British accent. He looked a lot like Douglas Fairbanks, but there was something arrogant about him that made Jessie cringe.

"She was singing in the large Protestant church here in Tientsin, but I first made her acquaintance when she rented one of my boarding rooms on the second story of a tailor shop owned by my family," Huxley continued. "I believe, Mr. Leopold, that fortune smiles on those who seek her."

The table chuckled politely, and Mr. Leopold held up a glass in a toasting gesture.

"Yes. So, Sir Jerald came to me. 'Mr. Leopold, you must hear this angel,' he told me. So I go, I hear, and she is magnificent! I beg her to sing at the Leopold Room, but she says no. I persist. I send her flowers every day. I offer money. She tells me she has never sung professionally, only in church. I tell her, sing one song, just one song. I offer more money. She has a child and is in need of money. She says yes! We are so happy."

General Rockey cleared his throat. "When I heard how Mr. Leopold found her, I remembered Gunnery Sergeant Paddy Francis Killeen. He played 'Amazing Grace' on the pipes while we were at a chapel service on Guadalcanal. Things were mighty bad. The boys began to sing the words along with him, and I never quite forgot it." The general's voice softened. "Anyway, I put two and two together and decided to pull some rank, with Mr. Leopold's help. So you'll be playing the pipes to 'Amazing Grace,' PFC Slate."

"I'd be honored to, sir. Although, I have to warn you, sir, the Irish pipes are not normally used as accompaniment for singers. They're kind of loud."

"Yes," Mr. Leopold interjected. "I have this planned. You will be at this end of the stage, no microphone. She, at the opposite, with microphone."

A nervous quiver rolled through Jessie, and for the first time he knew that he was experiencing stage fright.

"When am I on, sir?"

"She will sing three songs, then you play."

The band did a light drum roll as a thin, long-nosed emcee approached the microphone.

"Welcome to the Leopold Room, ladies and gentlemen. It is with great pleasure that we present the lovely and talented Katherine Monea." He held his hand toward the far left curtain as the lights dimmed and a spotlight appeared high up on the glittering rose-colored curtain. The band broke into a lighthearted, familiar tune. The long muscular leg of what had to be one spectacular dame peeked out from behind the curtain a solid fifteen feet above the stage.

Jessie whistled quietly. "Man, that gal has some gams!"

General Rockey leaned close to Jessie. "She's about the prettiest thing these old eyes ever saw, but mind your manners, Marine. I've discovered that she's the daughter of an old friend."

"Aye aye, sir." Jessie spoke with eyes glued to the sparkling red high heel dancing in the air above the stage as she began to sing a song about stars and moonbeams.

The stage curtains separated.

A stunningly beautiful woman in a skintight red gown appeared, sitting on a sparkling silver star suspended from the ceiling by barely visible wires. Her long auburn hair flowed well past her bare white shoulders.

General Rockey nudged Jessie with an elbow. "She looks better than Rita Hayworth, wouldn't you say, young Slate? Look at those eyes, big and blue as God's ocean."

Just then the girl's flawlessly beautiful face became clear to Jessie's eyes, and his stomach caved in as if someone had kicked it. It was Kate.

CHAPTER SIX

A flood of emotions washed over him. Surprise turned to fear, followed by regret, and then lonely aching. He pinched his eyes closed and tried to clear his thoughts.

This was a setup. Had to be. And Paddy was in on it. Jeramiah too, probably. And Broken Wing. Jessie looked at the general. The general's eyes were on Kate. Was he in on it? Did the general know that Kate was his ex-wife? He'd said that he was an old friend of her father, so he must know.

"Well, what do you think, young Slate?" General Rockey asked without taking his eyes off Kate. "Makes me wish I was twenty years younger!"

Jessie leaned back in his chair, took a few deep breaths and tried to clear his mind. He had to be rational. No way out now.

"She's the most beautiful woman I've ever seen, sir," Jessie said sadly.

His tone must have struck the French ambassador, who leaned forward to see around the general. "A man should never be made sad by beauty."

"Only if he's lost it, Mr. Ambassador."

The ambassador gave him a curious smile. General Rockey glanced at Jessie for a moment, then turned to applaud as the song ended and Kate sauntered sassily from the stage. The band began playing a Latin beat, and a few moments later Kate rumbaed onto the stage in a bright yellow ruffled skirt, bare midriff, and delicate yellow halter top that looked overworked. Jessie recognized the familiar beat of "Rum and Coca-Cola" before she started singing it. Every man in the Leopold Room who was not with a lady stood up cheering, more for the lady and the dress than for the song.

He wiped sweat from his forehead with his sleeve. He had almost managed to forget how beautiful Kate was. He took a deep breath. "Think clearly," he mumbled quietly to himself. Just don't act like a fool, he thought. Don't get emotional, and don't stammer when you speak to her. Ask about Charlie, just talk about the boy and get your mind off her body. She wanted the divorce, right? It's old news. Gotta go on with life. She's probably got a dozen saps after her right now, and I ain't gonna be one of 'em. "That's it!"

"What was that, Marine?" General Rockey asked.

"Nothing, sir. Just talking to myself."

The general laughed. "She has that effect on me too."

Kate sang two more songs, then stepped off the stage. Even in the dim light her silhouette as she approached the general's table stood out like every man's dream. There's no avoiding it, Jessie thought as he stood with the others. Sir Jerald Huxley immediately stepped toward Kate, embracing her. She graciously accepted the seat he offered her directly across the table from Jessie.

A rush of adrenaline sent a nervous quiver through Jessie's stomach and into his throat.

General Rockey held out his hand toward the beautiful woman. "PFC Slate, I'd like you to meet Katherine Monea." Kate's shimmering auburn hair curled gently to the middle of her bare back. She flipped it over one shoulder as she turned to meet the PFC. Kate's smile evaporated into a stunned expression, which brought on an awkward moment of silence.

Jessie felt as though his soul had just sunk into the

quicksand of those big blue eyes, and for a moment it seemed he was struggling for his life.

"Yes, General. Miss Monea and I have met before," he finally said.

Kate gave a nervous smile. "It seems so long ago."

"It seems like yesterday to me, Miss Monea. But you're right, it was a war ago, wasn't it?"

Kate smiled as she twisted a napkin. "Very nice to see you again, Mr. Slate."

"Well, Marine," General Rockey said with an obvious smirk. "You are a multitalented young man." He turned to Kate. "PFC Slate will be your Irish pipes accompaniment for my request, Miss Monea."

"Oh, I did not know that," she said haltingly. "Have you played the bagpipes for long, PFC Slate?"

"Not long. Little over a year. I hope that I can do your voice justice."

"What do you think, Gunnery Sergeant?" General Rockey asked. "Can he play?"

A strong hand came down on Jessie's shoulder. Gunnery Sergeant Paddy Francis Killeen, in dress blues with a chest full of medals, stood smiling beside him.

"Yes, sir, General. The lad's soul is emerald-green."

"Good to see you, Paddy."

"Thank you for inviting me, sir. I know Miss Monea. Used to bounce her on my knee when she was just a wee lass."

Jerald Huxley raised an eyebrow in Kate's direction. "I say."

Kate was on her feet and heading for Gunnery Sergeant Killeen. "Paddy!"

"And how's my darlin' lass? Maybe she's too big to give old Paddy a proper hello?"

They hugged and she kissed him on the cheek. "It's so good to see you again."

"I say. A bit of a reunion, it would appear?" Huxley's tone was tense and smug. Jessie disliked him intensely.

Kate gave the gunny another hug and went back to her seat. She kept her eyes away from Jessie. It hurt.

"May I have this dance, Katherine?" Sir Jerald asked. He pulled Kate's chair out as she came to her feet. The men at the table stood politely. Huxley followed Kate onto the dance floor.

Jessie felt a tug on his sleeve from the gunny. He pulled his eyes off of Kate and Huxley dancing and realized that he was the only one at the table still standing.

"As you Americans say," the Frenchman said, smiling, "she leaves them standing."

Jessie tried so hard to distract himself with small talk during the dance that he didn't notice the music had ended until someone touched his shoulder.

"May I have this dance, PFC Slate?"

He turned to find Kate standing over him. The men at the table stood again, with more than polite interest. Sir Jerald did not look pleased. Jessie would have gloated if he hadn't been so nervous about dancing with Kate. He stood and took her by the arm.

"I'd be delighted, Miss Monea," he said, and led Kate onto the dance floor.

They looked into each other's eyes as they began to dance.

"I want to see Charlie," Jessie said.

Kate blinked, as if surprised by the sudden statement.

"Of course, Jessie. You can see him anytime."

"Where is he? Did you bring him here?" he asked with slight disapproval.

"Of course not. I have a housekeeper with him, Mrs. Young, and she's wonderful."

"Do you read my letters to him?"

"Yes. They're sweet."

"Does he understand 'em?"

"I think he does. I show him your picture and tell him that the letter is from his daddy." Kate smiled, and Jessie melted inside.

"You look beautiful, Kate."

"You're looking well too, Jessie."

An awkward moment passed.

"That guy, the Englishman—he looks serious about you."

"Jerald is a wonderful man. He loves to hear me sing." Jessie glanced at Kate's figure. "Me too."

Kate blushed just enough for him to see pink in her silky white cheeks. She was just as irresistible and sincere as he remembered. Maybe more sophisticated, more sure of herself, but there was nothing phony about Kate. He wanted to kiss her so badly that it hurt.

"Kate."

"Yes."

"Kate. I, ah, I'd like to have a minute alone with you." She took a moment to make up her mind.

"Okay, Jessie. Let's go backstage," she said at last, then led him through the crowded dance floor to a stage door that said KEEP OUT in four languages. A Chinese doorman in a tuxedo bowed and opened the door as Kate approached.

"Kate."

Jessie and Kate paused to see who was calling. Sir Jerald moved around a couple dancing and walked briskly up to Kate without looking at Jessie.

"Kate, where are you going?" he said, too pleasantly.

"I've agreed to give Private Slate a tour of the place," she replied.

"Would you like me to go with you?"

"That's not necessary, Jerald," she said gently.

"If you need me, I'll be right here."

"Why would she need you, Jerald?" Jessie showed his teeth in a mock smile.

"That's Sir Jerald to you, boy," the Englishman said testily.

Before Jessie could snap back, Kate took his arm and ushered him through the door. "Don't worry, Jerald," she called back over her shoulder, "I won't be long."

"I should hope not," Sir Jerald grumbled.

Jessie, burning with rage, turned, intending to go back and give the Englishman the biggest haymaker he'd ever thrown, but Kate's face emerged so quickly in front of him that before Jessie could take a step, her lips were on his and her arms were around his neck. He was so stiff with rage that he barely felt her full weight as she clung to his neck, her feet not touching the floor. But he could feel her tongue pressing gently to get through his clenched teeth, and slowly but surely his anger subsided. He finally put his arms around her. The kiss was long and hot enough to turn his rage into desire. Jessie put his hands on Kate's hips, glanced around to see that they were alone and the door closed, then pushed Kate back against the wall and pressed his body against hers. He could feel her tears against his face, and pulled back slowly to look at this beautiful woman, the mother of his child. He brought his hands up to Kate's shoulders. And then, inevitably, the face of Charlie Rose appeared in his mind.

"Have you talked to your father about our meeting?" he asked.

She nodded. "He told me the whole story."

"So then you know why I couldn't come back to you."

"What happened to your friend wasn't your fault, Jessie."

"I left him to die alone so that I could get on the PBY evacuation plane. So that I could get to Nouméa and marry you, to keep our son from being born a bastard."

"But mostly because of my letter. Jessie, you didn't know Charlie Rose was in danger. You have to stop torturing yourself!"

"I've tried, Kate. It's no use. I can't forgive myself for what I did."

"And you can't forgive me. You couldn't even tell me what it was I couldn't be forgiven for! Even at the cost of your own son's happiness."

Jessie released Kate's shoulders and stepped back. He

looked at the floor and searched for words. "There's no hope, is there, Kate? I've made a mess of everything I touch."

"There's hope, Jessie. But not where you're looking. Of course you can't forgive yourself! You don't have that power. You aren't God. But you can ask *Him* for forgiveness. Give yourself and me a break. Get on your knees and pray."

"You sound like your dad."

"Good!"

Jessie fought back a lump in his throat. Kate's eyes were misty. He touched a tear on her cheek. "I love you, Kate."

"You've caused me so much pain."

Kate turned her head and shoulders to the right and suddenly unleashed a roundhouse right to Jessie's jaw that snapped his head sideways. He blinked, shook his head, and tried to work his jaw to see if it was broken, then faced Kate with what had to undoubtedly be the most dumbfounded expression he'd ever worn.

"That's for not confiding in me! For hurting me and baby Charlie." She began to cry. Her chin dropped and she fell against Jessie's chest.

He put his arms around her and gave up trying to hold back the tears. They flooded from his heart until he heard himself sobbing and asking God to forgive him. After a while he straightened up and tried to control the emotions pouring from him. The massive weight of his guilt felt bearable for the first time. Maybe it was just the nearness of Kate, he thought as he lifted her chin and kissed her lips. Somewhere the music stopped. A microphone buzzed.

"And now a special presentation by the Leopold Room in honor of and at the request of Lieutenant General Rockey . . ."

Jessie didn't hear the rest of the introduction. Kate gasped and pulled away, wiping tears from her face. She covered her mouth and looked horrified. "Jessie! We're on! They're introducing us!"

"I love you, Kate."

"I love you too. Now get your bagpipes! You play a prelude, then I'll come in."

A rush of adrenaline shot through Jessie, and for a moment he thought that he might leave the ground. He pulled Kate closer and kissed her hard, then left the room, rushed to the other side of the dance floor, leapt onto the stage in one bound, and retrieved the Irish pipes from behind the piano. He touched the sore spot on his jaw and chuckled, then quickly tuned the pipes to the chanter.

". . . accompanied by Private First Class Jessie Slate of the United States Marine Corps."

Jessie bowed from the corner of the stage in front of the piano as the lights in the room dimmed, leaving a light on Jessie and another light on Kate at the far end of the stage. The emcee held out his hand toward him. Jessie took the first deep breath and began playing. Kate came in after a short introduction, and to his surprise, he could actually hear her over the pipes, though barely.

> "Amazing grace, how sweet the sound.
> That saved a wretch like me!
> I once was lost but now am found,
> Was blind but now I see."

The applause was genuine and continued even as Kate and Jessie made their way from the stage. Jessie took Kate's hand, stopping her before reaching the general's table. "I'd like to introduce you as my wife."

"No, Jessie. A lot has changed since Nouméa. I've been seeing other men, and I'm sure you've been dating other women, and I'm not jumping into something until we're sure."

"I'm sure, Kate."

"I won't take that chance with baby Charlie." She hesitated, pondering her next words carefully. "And there's one man I've been dating here in China whom I care for very much."

Jessie felt his heart sink into the pit of his stomach. "Huxley?"

"Yes."

"Are you engaged?"

"No," she said, looking down as if embarrassed. "But he has asked me. And he will ask me again."

"Are you in love with him?"

"I don't know," she said, and then, "I don't think so."

"Neither do I," he replied.

Someone grabbed Jessie by the arm. "Be moving, lad. General Rockey is waiting to see you two."

"Coming, Gunny." Jessie mumbled his words the way a man might speak after being kicked in the groin. He turned back to Kate. "Guess the general and Huxley are waiting on us," he said, trying to hide his devastation.

"Jessie, I don't want any misunderstanding."

He paused, looked at Kate, and smiled. "There's no misunderstanding, Kate."

Jessie took her hand and led her to the general's table, where the congratulations came from all directions. Jessie stepped to the side, allowing the congratulations to reach Kate first.

General Rockey was one of the last to step away from Kate and slapped Jessie on the back. "Son. That was wonderful! Just wonderful. My thanks."

"Thank you, sir. It was an honor to play for you."

General Rockey moved back to his seat as Gunny Killeen approached with the grin of a proud father. "Fine playin', to be sure, lad. Couldn't be prouder if you was me own boy."

"Did you know that Kate was here, Paddy?"

The lines around the old salt's eyes deepened. "Well now, lad, there was a rumor, but I never put much stock in it. . . ."

Just behind Gunny Killeen, Sir Jerald Huxley gave Kate

a lingering kiss on the lips. Blood rushed to Jessie's ears and turned Paddy's words to garble. A few moments later Jessie excused himself with a gracious thanks to the general, then slipped away. At the elevator, someone tapped him on the shoulder. He turned to see Kate standing behind him. Her expression was hard to read, but it wasn't happy.

"I just don't think I'm cut out for the Marine Corps, Jessie."

"What?"

"I don't know if I'm ready to get involved with the Marine Corps again."

"What are you saying, Kate?"

"I watched my mother. She was married to the Marine Corps. She suffered alone most of her married life. I want a man who comes home after work, someone who's there to talk to when I need him! Not some jarhead warrior who spends his life one ricochet away from death."

"I'll quit."

Kate's eyes widened. "What?"

"I'll get out."

"Oh, Jessie! Don't!" Kate turned away.

"I'm telling you the truth. After this hitch, I'm out. This is my last cruise."

"You can't quit! I know you! You're just like O'Cleary and my father and Paddy. You'll never stop being a Marine. You've got Gunnery Sergeant Slate tattooed all over your future!"

"That's a bunch of bull! I'm finished after this one last hitch."

A faint, ironic smile crossed her pretty face. The band played a drumroll and she looked back over her shoulder. "I'm being paged."

"Kate, I'm telling you, after this cruise, I'm finished with the Marine Corps."

Kate paused for a moment to study his face. She touched his cheek and ran her fingers along his square jaw. Then she smiled.

"Let's just take it slow, Jessie. Let's see how things work out."

"How long are you going to be in China, Kate?"

"Just a couple of months. I'm not positive about our next destination. We should know soon."

"Where do you live?"

"We live over a tailor shop. Just down the street. There's a big sign in the window—"

" 'Worked for the British Army,' " Jessie said finishing Kate's sentence.

"Yes. You know where it is?"

He nodded, and smiled at the realization of just how involved the plan was to get him and Kate together.

"Jerald's family owns it," she added.

"I'll come by to see Charlie as soon as possible, if that's all right with you?"

"Yes, of course you can. I have to go." She turned and walked back into the Leopold Room. Jessie watched her as long as he could. She had a rear view that could keep a man awake at night, and tonight he wanted to remember.

CHAPTER SEVEN

Early the following morning, Jessie entered the tailor shop. His insides churned. Would Kate or Charlie be happy to see him, or would it turn out to be awkward? The Chinese tailor stood in his usual place behind a small counter. The room was hot, and the overhead fan didn't seem to help much. Even the old tailor was sweating.

"You get uniforms. Two days." He held up two fingers.

"Thanks. Hope they're done right. We got a big inspection coming, and if they get screwed up, I'll probably be riding shotgun on the An-Ping Railroad for the rest of my cruise."

The old man smiled and nodded, but Jessie had the feeling he hadn't understood a word.

"Big inspection, you say."

Jessie turned to see who was butting in on the conversation. He wasn't pleased. Sir Jerald Huxley stood at the foot of the stairs, wiping sweat from his brow with a handkerchief. He wore a white linen suit, white shirt, brown tie, and brown wing tips. He carried a white panama hat with a brown rim that matched his shoes and tie.

"Yeah. General inspection. Gotta keep the troops sharp and unhappy. Marine motto. 'Semper Fidelis.' Always Miserable."

65

" 'Semper Fidelis?' I thought that meant Always Faithful."

Jessie grinned and gave a nod. The guy had the wit of a tree stump. "You here to see Kate?" he asked.

"Just did, actually. Is that why you've made this appearance?"

"Yes, actually, 'tis," Jessie said mockingly.

Huxley forced a phony grin, then headed for the door. He stopped and looked back as he put his hat on.

"I say, Private. I do hope you won't make this a habit. Kate and I have an understanding. She told me about your unfortunate time together. Wartime romances are shallow at best, and I should think a gentleman would allow old wounds to remain closed."

"Maybe you should mind your own business, Jerald," Jessie said.

Huxley turned and left. Jessie headed for the stairs, wishing he'd said something wittier, anything but "mind your own business."

At the top of the stairs was a hallway, and at the end of the hall, a door, in front of which sat baby Charlie. A small bamboo fence blocked the hallway from the stairs. Jessie climbed over it, rushed down the hallway, and picked the little boy up. He immediately began hugging him and kissing him. Baby Charlie seemed stunned by the sudden attack, but so far did not object. Jessie held him out at arm's length.

"You're a Slate, all right. What a good-looking guy. I sure wish your grandmother could have seen you."

Jessie put the boy down and pulled out a bag of marbles.

"These are marbles, Charlie. I sent you some before, in the mail. Remember?"

The little blond boy's bright blue eyes opened wide as if he suddenly recognized something. He pointed at the marbles, then at Jessie. "Daddy?"

"Yes! It's me! Daddy!" Jessie's shout brought on a wave of emotion that he couldn't control. Tears welled up in his eyes as he grabbed up the little boy and squeezed him again.

The door behind Charlie opened and Kate peeked out with a head full of bobby pins. "Hey, what goes on out here?"

Jessie cleared his throat and tried to brush away the tears before Kate spotted them. "Nothing. Just a little man-to-man discussion going on."

"Are you okay, Jessie?"

"He knew me."

"He has a photo by his crib."

"Thanks, Kate."

Jessie smiled and wiped a tear away by brushing his cheek against Charlie's curly blond hair.

Kate touched the bobby pins in her hair and retied her pink silk robe. "I look a mess."

"You couldn't look bad if you tried, Kate."

"I'm just on my way to the club, Jessie. We're rehearsing a couple of new numbers."

"Oh, I was hoping we could go to church together."

"We already went this morning, early. I'd have loved that. I wish I'd known that you wanted to go."

"Maybe another time." He scanned the hallway. "So this is home?" he said. "You've been staying here since coming to China?"

"Yes. Home sweet home for now. I wanted to be close to Dad. His Standard Oil office is next door, so it was perfect, except for the fact that he's never there."

"Any plans yet? About going back to Nouméa?"

"We'll be here for one more month at the most. I don't think it's a good idea to stay, with the country becoming so violent."

Jessie's heart sank at the thought of them leaving, but he pretended to accept the news with an understanding nod.

"Jerald and some other friends are giving me a going-away party next month. Will you come?"

"Of course," Jessie said. "Say, how about some break-fast?"

"Oh, I'd love to, but I have to hurry for now. Have to get Charlie over to our baby-sitter's before I go to the club."

"Baby-sitter? I'd like to take the guy out on the town. If it's okay with you, Kate."

Kate appeared apprehensive. "Are you sure, Jessie?"

"Yes. I want to be with him, Kate. I saw a little carnival, Chinese-style. We can have some fun. He'll love it."

She smiled and nodded yes and closed the door, then opened it again. "Have him back by three, okay? Nap time."

Jessie saluted. "Aye aye, Mom."

Jessie had a wonderful day with his son, but just one day wasn't enough. With the help of Gunnery Sergeant Killeen, getting liberty passes proved a cinch. Each morning as Kate prepared to leave for the club, Jessie knocked on her door. When the door opened, he saluted sharply.

"Reporting for baby duty, ma'am." Then he handed Kate a bouquet of flowers, and Charlie would come running into his arms for hugs and kisses. At the end of the fourth day, at 1500 hours sharp, Jessie marched Charlie up the stairs of the tailor shop to Kate's apartment door. Charlie slapped the door three times and came to attention holding his newly acquired wooden rifle at port arms. Kate opened the door and started laughing. Charlie brought the rifle to left shoulder arms and saluted. "Charlie 'porting for duty, sir."

Kate burst out laughing, then pretended to be stern. "I was wondering what you've been doing with my son, PFC Slate. I should have known."

"We've had a grand time, Kate. I hate to see it end, even for a day."

"You can't come tomorrow?" She looked sad, and it pleased Jessie deep into his soul, filling him with hope.

"General inspection. Matter of fact, I have old Broken

Wing here with me to pick up our uniforms from the tailor downstairs for the big march in revue tomorrow."

"Broken Wing! I want to see that scoundrel."

"Him here," Broken Wing said from the top of the stairs.

Kate rushed forward and gave Broken Wing a big hug as he climbed over the baby fence at the top of the stairs. She kissed him on the cheek, and though the hall was dimly lit by a single dirty lightbulb, Jessie thought he saw the slightest hint of a grin crack Wing's granite face.

"So, what have you been doing with yourself, Mr. Wing?"

"He's been playing with Charlie and me, lately," Jessie said with a laugh.

"Yes," Kate said accusingly. "Just what have you two been teaching my baby, the manual of arms?"

"We have much fun," Wing said. "Fired A-2 machine gun today."

Charlie pretended to shoot his wooden rifle, making machine gun sounds.

"We rode horses yesterday," Jessie added.

"Bayonet practice," Wing said.

"Bayonet!" Kate exclaimed.

"No danger. We leave the scabbard on," Wing explained.

Kate looked horrified. Her face relaxed into an accusing frown. "You two are pulling my leg."

Jessie and Wing exchanged questioning expressions.

"You mean you really let my child fire a machine gun?"

"But don't worry, Kate," Jessie said soothingly. "We put ear muffs over his ears so it wouldn't hurt them."

"He liked throwing grenades better," Wing said.

Kate took a deep breath, as if she was having trouble breathing.

"Don't worry, Kate! They were practice grenades, not real ones."

"Yes, we threw the real ones for him," Wing said.

Kate looked pale.

"That isn't all we've been doing, Kate. We took Charlie

to the Santa Anna Ballroom and got some ice cream, and the Italians did sort of a little circus routine for him."

Kate seemed speechless for a couple of moments, then looked at the three faces before her and smiled in amusement. "It sounds like you boys have had a swell time," she said.

"Oh, we did, Kate!" Jessie said. "Now don't worry. I'd never let anything happen to Charlie. He just needed to have some boy-type fun. We had a ball."

"Okay. I'll take your word for it."

"Well, we have to get these uniforms back right away. I'll see you day after tomorrow, if it's okay with you."

"That sounds fine, Jessie. This time, I'll skip rehearsal and go with you guys. Sounds like you're having more fun than I am."

"That would be great. We'll take you to the pistol range."

Kate pinched the bridge of her nose and looked back at the smiling little boy. Jessie kissed Charlie good-bye, then moved to kiss Kate. She pulled away for a moment and his heart sank to his boots. Then, abruptly, she kissed him hard on the lips.

The kiss left Jessie in a blissful haze as he helped load the bagged-up uniforms onto the truck and drove back to base. His bliss lasted for the rest of the day and into his dreams that night.

The next morning, Jessie scrambled to get his clothes on in time for inspection. He rushed out of their quarters and headed for the main barracks, where Gunnery Sergeant Killeen and Captain Fitch were already waiting out front.

"About time, PFC Slate!" Captain Fitch shouted.

"Where's the uniforms, lad?" Gunny Killeen asked.

"Wing's bringing the truck around back, sir."

"Outstanding."

Ten minutes later, Able Company stood in line behind the truck as two lieutenants shouted out the name taped on each paper clothing bag. A Marine would then run forward, grab his uniform bag, and rush into the barracks to dress.

"Move it! Move it, Marines!"

"Hey, Sarge, this uniform—"

"Stow it, Marine! Too late now!"

"Inspection in fifteen minutes!"

The regimental band sounded exceptionally crisp as Able Company marched onto the parade ground. The sun was shining in a cool blue sky, and the smell of fall was in the air. It should have been a glorious morning, but impending doom was written on the faces of Able Company. Some men snickered with dread. Others used Jessie's and Wing's names in vain.

Envy, anger, and embarrassment spread like a fire across the faces of the rest of the regiment as they spotted Able Company in their new, pressed dress greens. That moment of envy, that sweet taste of momentary victory . . .

"Column left!"

"Column right!"

"Parade rest!"

Commands from barking sergeants echoed across the parade ground.

"Able Company! Attention!"

Captain Fitch marched along the first file of ramrod-straight Marines with the face of a man accepting death and determined to bring others with him. He stopped with a stomping right-face in front of Jessie and Broken Wing. His face was purple with rage. Large veins pulsated in his neck and formed a vee on his forehead. His lips quivered as he spoke.

"PFC Slate. PFC Wing." He spoke slowly.

"Sir."

"Does my Marine Corps remind you of the RAF? Or the British Army, maybe?" Rage grew with each syllable.

"No, sir."

"Showing up for a general inspection with our stripes

sewn on upside down is akin to urinating on the commandant's shoes!"

The cursing that followed would go down in Marine Corps lore. Captain Fitch wove a tapestry of profanity that any sergeant would have been proud to call his own, until suddenly, without warning, he stopped, nearly sagging in utter despair. He did an about-face and prepared for the inevitable. General Rockey and the various senior grade officers seemed unable to comprehend what they were seeing as they walked past Able Company, like men waiting for the end of a joke they did not understand. At one point General Rockey laughed and turned away. Jessie hoped desperately that this was a good sign. Maybe everyone would actually see this as a funny episode and no one need be blamed.

Eighteen hours later, Jessie and Broken Wing were attached to guard duty for thirty days on the An-Ping Railroad. No one said it was punishment. No one had to. Jessie tried to get word to Kate that seeing her would be impossible for the next month, but he wasn't sure she got the message.

Thirty miserable days later, with the weather getting downright cold, Jessie returned to the base to find an envelope and small black Bible waiting for him. He ripped open the letter, with Broken Wing hanging over his shoulder.

"It's from Kate."

Jessie put the letter to his nose and inhaled; the scent of lilac was strong. A grin spread across his face, and it felt good inside to just smile again.

Broken Wing gave a grunt and sat back against the wall. "Let me know if it is any of my business."

Jessie began to read to himself.

10/12/46

Dear Jessie,
     Charlie and I have passage on a ship that sails tonight.

I feel just terrible about saying good-bye like this, but I had hoped you would return from An-Ping duty in time for me to explain my sudden departure.

Dad has done a swell job for Standard. They offered him an office promotion in San Francisco, but he turned it down. He's decided to retire and fulfill a lifelong dream. He has put a down payment on a bed and breakfast in Wilmore, Kentucky. He wants me and Charlie to move in with him. I'll run the B&B while dad attends seminary at Asbury. The B&B is only a block away from the college.

I must return to New Caledonia and our Café la Rue Sans Issue. Dad asked me to take care of matters there while he goes to Kentucky. I will join him in the USA after selling the café. Don't know how long that will take. I'll send you our new address when we're settled. It seems that fate is against us sometimes, darling. I hope that you come see me and Charlie when your cruise is up. We'll be waiting in the land of mixed uniforms where no one is in charge. I know that your hitch should be over by sometime in 1950, so I've told Charlie that at the very least he'll see his father then.

See if you can stay out of trouble for two years, good-lookin'. Dad wants to give us the bed and breakfast when you get discharged.

I love you and I'm waiting, but not forever.

Kate

P.S. The Bible is from me and Charlie and Dad.

CHAPTER EIGHT

Nineteen forty-seven was a bad year for the Marine Corps and a bad year for PFC Jessie Slate. Broken Wing's orders got changed somehow, and he ended up at Pendleton for a duty station. Jessie got the Brooklyn Navy Yard. Saying good-bye to Wing was tough. Stateside duty was one continuous pain anyway, but without that goofy Navajo, it seemed even worse than normal. He passed many an hour wishing he could have finished up his career in China. When the Corps had suddenly been pulled out, the reasons were obvious. The only way the Nationalist government could be saved would be to wage a full-scale war against the Communists, and the American people wanted no part of that. So the Corps was brought home to a nation that had forgotten why it needed Marines.

When the outfit came back from Tientsin, the Marine Corps could not even pay the troops. On some bases the chow halls were out of food. The Corps was down to 70,000 men, 50,000 counting just effectuals.

The country was disarming at the fastest rate possible. The Corps was getting hit the hardest, thanks in part to the U.S. Army. Many men who stayed in after the war had rank, and the Corps was top-heavy. Budget cuts came with a new order, ALMAR, that was general and all-sweeping. Any Marine Master or Master Technical Sergeant who had a date of rank after said month in 1942 was reverted back in rank. Some officers were reduced to staff sergeants. A few took it in stride; some couldn't handle it.

Jessie's only goal was to find some decent duty for the rest of his enlistment, get out with an honorable discharge, marry Kate, and live happily ever after. Stateside duty was always bad, but if you were smart and lucky, you could make it livable. Scuttlebutt said that members of the Marine Rifle Team had a good deal going. Team shooters did not stand guard duty and got all the liberty time they could afford. Jessie fired High Expert and made the team.

He fired in the 1948 Wurgman Trophy Matches and then the Individual Matches in the East Coast Division. Life became bearable again. Each day's routine was the same, sixty rounds of M-1 in the morning and fifty rounds with the .45 caliber pistol in the afternoon, then liberty in New York City. It was wonderful. Then it ended, with orders for Camp Lejeune.

It would be a long bus ride to Lejeune. Jessie looked at his orders and the name of the officer he was to report to for the fifteenth time. Captain Fitch. Fitch had never forgiven him for the inspection fiasco. Jessie slammed the orders down on his footlocker, snatched up his khaki barracks cover by the bill, and headed for his last liberty call in New York.

He reached the main gate of the Brooklyn Navy Yard on Sands Street still muttering to himself in disbelief. A familiar voice hailed him from the guard shack.

"Jessie! Slate!"

Jessie paused and stared at the heavyset Marine for a moment, as if he wasn't sure the man was really there. It was one of the men from his old Paramarine unit.

"Sam? Sam Hill! You old sea dog!"

The big Navajo hadn't changed a bit. Big oval face, mournful pouches under both eyes, and looking sad even as he smiled.

Jessie ran forward and grabbed Sam in a headlock,

knocking his piss cutter to the deck. He rubbed the top of Sam's head with his knuckles, then released him.

"I can't believe it!"

"Long time," Sam said, laughing.

"How long's it been, Sam?"

"Since after Iwo Jima. Heard you were in China."

"Yeah, I was. With good old Broken Wing. He's in Pendleton now."

"Good man," Sam said.

"See any of the old Paramarines?"

"Oglethorpe."

"Yeah? So where you stationed?"

"Just signed up to train Korean Marines. That's why I'm here."

"What's a Korean Marine?"

"It is a promotion to corporal and away from stateside harassment."

"I'm a civilian in 1950, Sam. I promised Kate. That's it for me, I'm surveying out."

"You got back with Kate?"

"Well, not completely, but yes, as long as I stay out of trouble and as long as I promise to be a civilian in 1950."

"Really! That is a shock. But that still leaves you with over a year of stateside duty. Where's Kate now?"

"She's in New Caledonia, taking care of the café until they get it sold."

"Then what difference does it make where you spend the next year?"

"I got orders for Lejeune."

"That changes if you volunteer for Korea. If you're coming from the rifle team, you'll get Korea real quick. They want instructors!"

"I don't know, Sam."

"There will be a few fellas from the old outfit there. Remember Sergeant Rim?"

"That old bulldog! He's in Korea?"

"Yeah. The C.O. is an old Paramarine. That's why he wanted me to look you up."

"Gee. It does sound good. What's Korea like, anyway?" Sam grinned and gave a thumbs-up. "Rear echelon pull, my friend. Corporal pay will allow us to live like kings."

"Corporal?"

"Yes. But get this, we'll be sergeants to the K.M.'s. Acting sergeants, but officially Marine Corps corporals."

Jessie scratched the back of his neck and sighed with the decision. "A year with Fitch means brig time for sure."

"Fitch?"

Jessie shook his head and extended his hand to Sam. "I'm going to Korea for a year."

Chinhae, Korea, May 1950

Korea was an unknown land to most Americans. Before he got there, Jessie wasn't even sure where it was on a map. It was a rugged, mountainous country that could bake a man alive or freeze him into a solid block of ice. Korea had been cursed with powerful neighbors that took turns over centuries invading and torturing the stout little people. To the east was their most hated enemy, Japan. To the west was China. Korea's northeastern border nearly touches the Soviet Union. During the war, Korea had been a possession of Japan. The Japanese had used Korean men as slaves and Korean women as concubines for their military. When the Empire of Japan fell, Korea had been split in two along the 38th Parallel. The Soviets controlled the north and the United States had jurisdiction in the south.

The Russians turned the North Korean People's Army into a well-oiled machine, a machine that was extremely well-equipped. After building up the NKPA, the Russians pulled all of their own combat troops out of the north in January 1949. The United States built up a South Korean Army minus any heavy equipment, then pulled all American combat troops out of the south in June 1949. From every intelligence report, it was apparent that the Russians had left a much more powerful army in the north than the Americans had in the south. Scuttlebutt had it that the U.S. State Department did not trust the South Korean president, Syngman Rhee, and didn't want him to have offensive military capabilities.

The average Marine knew little of the political posturing, and as far as Jessie was concerned, none of the scuttlebutt mattered as long as he got his discharge on time. The Russians and the Americans left advisers when they pulled out their combat troops. The small detachment of Marines stationed at Chinhae were under the command of KMAG, the Korean Military Advisory Group. KMAG headquarters was in the ancient capital of Seoul. Chinhae was the home of the newly formed South Korean Marine Corps. Chinhae was not all that different from any other Marine Corps boot camp. It consisted of obstacle courses, firing ranges, chow halls, and drill fields. The big difference for most of the American Marines was that this time they got to play Senior Drill Instructor, accompanied by two Korean counterparts. All things considered, the last year of Korean duty had been extremely satisfying for Jessie. It provided the time to get reacquainted with good old Sergeant Rim and Corporal Sam Hill. He'd made some new Korean friends too, and been given the opportunity to undergo martial arts training with a famous Korean grand master, Kwan Jang Nim Dong Keun Park.

The last year had been one of the best in his life, Jessie thought contentedly. He picked up an envelope from his footlocker and glanced at a full-length mirror on the wall. He was pleased. He was in the best physical and mental shape of his entire life. He missed Kate and Charlie, but his time spent in Korea had actually brought them closer together through daily letters. He and Kate had spoken more thoroughly writing than either could have ever done aloud, and Jessie knew that Kate was his again.

The only real void in his life over the last year was that aggravating Navajo. It was embarrassing to admit, but there were times when he felt downright lonely without that stupid Indian around. Jessie unfolded the tattered letter from Broken Wing's wife and read it again.

Dear Jessie Slate,
   This is Bright Morning writing you. Broken Wing said he is quitting the Marine Corps. He is a terrible businessman. Jewelry store is no good. He is not happy. I am not happy. He was born warrior. Should stay warrior until old age. Come get. Good-bye from Bright Morning.

Sergeant Jessie Slate chuckled to himself and put the letter in his footlocker. He leaned over and grinned, to see his teeth in the reflection of his spit-shined low quarters. He gave one last buff with a soft rag and stood up. He took a last look in a full-length mirror, searching for any Irish pennants that might have escaped the first inspection. He spotted one and quickly snipped away the loose thread with a pair of scissors. He measured the distance from the rim of his pith helmet to the bridge of his nose, threw back his broad shoulders and attacked the door of the Quonset hut. Two square-jawed Korean drill instructors snapped to attention just outside the barracks door.

"Are your maggots ready, Sergeant Jae Sen?"

"Yes, sir, Sergeant Slate!"

"Are your scumbags ready for inspection, Corporal Dae Sung Lee?"

"The scumbags are ready for inspection, Sergeant Slate!"

"Lead the way, Marines."

"Aye aye, Sergeant." The two Koreans spoke as one. They did a smart about-face, and Sergeant Jessie Slate followed their lead toward two platoons of Korean recruits standing at parade rest on the drill field.

"Charrrrr yut!" A deep voice barked out the command, and 160 Korean recruits snapped to attention. The echo of

320 boots popping together resounded around the parade ground like a single shot. A surge of pride nearly brought a smile to Jessie Slate's granite face. But not yet. They would not be treated as fellow Marines until graduation, and that was a full six hours away. Slate, with a Korean counterpart on either side, marched up and faced the first Marine in formation.

"Preeeesennnt arms!"

The formation brought their M-1 rifles to present arms in perfect coordination. Sergeant Slate took the rifle from the stiff, young Korean recruit and twirled it around with the ease of a baton. He checked the bore, frowned, and handed the rifle to Sergeant Jae Sen. Sergeant Jae Sen repeated the snappy rifle inspection.

"Is this dust Marine Corps issue, Private Scumbag?" Sergeant Slate screamed into the young recruit's face at the top of his lungs. Sergeant Jae Sen handed the rifle to Corporal Dae Sung Lee, then rushed up to the offending recruit and flattened him with a forearm strike to the side of the head.

"You have disgraced the KMC!" Sergeant Jae Sen shouted over the dazed young recruit.

The inspection continued, with two similar incidents of violent discipline. Jessie had grown accustomed to Korean discipline after a year with these stout little men. At first the brutality had shocked him. Not that Parris Island was without some good licks, but not to the same extreme. They were building good Marines, though, and Jessie was proud that he had made his contribution. He also knew that good Marines were going to be needed. The Soviets were arming the North Koreans to the teeth. For the last four months, the North Koreans had been threatening an invasion. Not a day went by without a mortar barrage or a shower of leaflets informing the local population that the North Koreans would soon come across the 38th Parallel.

Jessie scanned the rows of strong young men, and he liked what he saw. But he feared for them, as did the other advisers. Without tanks, heavy artillery, or an air wing, these brave men had little chance if war came. America wasn't paying much attention. The pennant race was getting started, and Ted Williams was already looking great. That jackass Harry Truman was spending most of his time in Washington trying to help the Army brass get rid of the Marine Corps. They would have loved to disband the Corps if it weren't for those pesky little wars popping up all of the time. It seemed Washington was convinced that they could just scare the Reds away with bigger atomic bombs.

"Have your men ready for the run, Sergeant Jae Sen!" Jessie shouted. "They will fall out in full pack and 782 gear with canteens filled."

"Aye aye, Sergeant Slate!"

"Will you be running with us, Sergeant Slate?" Corporal Dae Sung Lee asked. "If I may suggest, Sergeant Slate, you will need strong *ki* for tomorrow's match." *Ki* was a word borrowed from the Japanese. It meant life force, or spirit.

The serious tone in Corporal Lee's voice seemed odd, Jessie thought. He gave the Korean a confident wink.

"Maybe you're right, Corporal. I could use a few extra hours in the *dojang*."

"You already spend more hours in the *dojang* than all other students," Sergeant Jae Sen said. "Do not become tired."

Sergeant Jessie Slate awoke to the light tapping at the bottom of the sliding, light-wood-framed, oiled-paper door. The air was cold, even for May in Chinhae, and though he knew that a straw mat would never actually be comfortable, the warmth of his thick wool Marine blanket made it bearable. The door slid open. A wave of cool air filled the large wood-floored room.

"Boo Sah Bumnim, Slate." Corporal Dae Sung Lee bowed, removed his sandals, and entered barefoot.

Jessie stood up stretching, yawned, and bowed.

"Student Lee. Good morning."

Corporal Lee bowed again. "Good morning Boo Sah Bumnim. You sleep *dojang* again."

"Yes, Grand Master Park is very kind to allow me this extra time in the *dojang*."

"Kwan Jangnim honors your martial spirit, Boo Sah Bumnim, Slate. He says you have the *ki* of the Hwa Rang Do."

"Ancient Tae Kyun, right?"

"The Hwa Rang united the three warring kingdoms into one kingdom with the power of the Hwa Rang Do. They conquered all enemy with Tae Kyun and named the new united kingdom Koryo."

"The form required for the first *dan*, correct?"

"Yes. This is where the name comes from."

"I've heard this all before, but sometimes it is difficult to understand the master's broken English and I end up retaining only bits and pieces."

"Yes, Boo Sah Bumnim. I constantly struggle with your language in much the same manner."

"Your English is beautiful, Student Lee."

Lee seemed embarrassed and a bit overwhelmed. He bowed twice. "I am deeply honored, Boo Sah Bumnim."

Jessie smiled, bowed again, and moved to the door. Corporal Lee began preparing two buckets of water. Jessie breathed and watched his breath float into the cold morning air. The mountaintop *dojang* was partially shrouded by misty gray clouds. The tiny village of Chinhae, which lay below, looked like a postcard. The only traffic was one small South Korean Army convoy made up of American trucks and jeeps.

"Boo Sah Bumnim, Slate. You are excited about going home on leave?"

"A little."

"It is difficult to think of anything except your match."

Slate turned to watch Corporal Dae Sung Lee drop in the yellow sticks of odorless soap. He picked up a stiff wooden brush and began brushing the floor on hands and knees in the prescribed manner, showing respect to the *dojang* with a humble spirit.

"To tell you the truth, I was really surprised when Kwanjangnim allowed me to volunteer to represent the school."

"Yes, it was a surprise to me also, only because you are not Korean."

"I hope that I do not dishonor the Ji Do Kwan."

"To lose to the Chang Moo Kwan would not bring dishonor, but finding forgiveness in Grand Master Dong Keun Park's eyes will be as one searching for the warmth on the mountain of Keum Kang in winter."

Jessie smiled and pretended to see the humor in Corporal Lee's analogy, but in his heart the mere mention of the word forgiveness was attached to the blood of Charlie Rose. That pain had lessened since that night at the Leopold Room, but the memory would always be there, attached eternally to a word that he still did not fully understand.

Jessie stared down blankly at the large mass of callus that had transformed the knuckles of his forefinger and middle finger into one huge knuckle. He walked over to the hemp-covered post, assumed the horse stance, and began his ritual of two thousand punches. When he finished, he bowed and moved to the three bamboo boxes sitting against the wall of the *dojang*. He bowed and bypassed the first box, filled with sand, and the second box, filled with river gravel. He knelt before the third, filled with crushed glass, and began his thousand punches. When he finished, his mind was clear again.

By ten A.M. the *dojang* was crowded with silent students from the two opposing schools. The Chang Moo Kwan students of Grand Master Jeong stood at attention against the portside wall, while Grand Master Dong Keun Park's Ji Do Kwan students assumed the same position on the starboard wall.

Grand Master Jeong bowed respectfully to Grand Master Park, then faced his students. *"Kyungye!"* he barked.

The Chang Moo Kwan class bowed.

Master Park faced his class. *"Kyungye!"*

The Ji Do Kwan class bowed.

"Boo Sah Bumnim, Slate!" Master Park shouted.

Jessie ran forward, snapped to attention, and bowed.

Grand Master Jeong looked surprised but not displeased at the sight of an American representative.

"Boo Sah Bumnim, Kim!" Grand Master Jeong shouted, and a stout-looking young Korean ran forward, snapped to attention, and bowed.

Jessie's heart began to flutter, and for the first time since playing the Irish pipes in the Leopold Room in Tientsin, he knew he had butterflies and had them bad. One of the masters barked a command and the two young men faced each other. Suddenly Jessie wondered why in the world he had volunteered for this.

"Charyut!"

"Kyungye!"

"Chunbe!"

"Sheajak!"

The stout Korean black belt charged forward with two quick punches aimed at Jessie's face, followed by a lightning quick front kick to the groin. The kick hit high, but still crumpled Jessie backward. He quickly rolled away from another onslaught and glanced over at Grand Master Jeong, expecting him to reprimand his student, but the master's expression didn't change. Jessie looked at Grand Master Park, but there was no hint of help coming.

Jessie sprang to his feet and avoided a series of spinning kicks, but was unable to avoid two hard punches to his right kidney that knocked him against the back wall of the *dojang.* Without looking back, he threw a weak back kick that managed to push his opponent away long enough for him to spin around and avoid a powerful, skipping side kick. A follow-up back fist knocked him against the wall.

Blood ran down his face from a gash over the right eye. Jessie moved away from the wall quickly and set up in a cat stance, then shifted to a fighting horse stance as the Korean black belt adjusted for distance. The Korean threw a fast roundhouse kick at Jessie's groin. Jessie came down hard with an elbow strike that sent a loud, sickening crack through the *dojang*. He immediately dropped to his left knee, with his back to the Korean, and spun 360 degrees, sweeping his opponent's feet from under him with his right leg in a classic iron broom. The Korean landed with a groan, the back of his head slapping against the hard wooden floor. His eyes rolled back until the whites were all that showed. He went limp.

Jessie stood up, stared down at his opponent, and bowed. The right trouser leg of the unconscious man's white *do bok* was soaked through with dark red blood from an obvious compound fracture of his tibia. No one spoke, but the anger on Grand Master Jeong's face said everything. He grunted at his unconscious fighter, then bowed respectfully to Jessie. Jessie responded instinctively. Grand Master Jeong pointed at the fallen black belt and barked something that Jessie did not understand. Four white-belt students rushed forward and picked the man up. The Chang Moo Kwan class bowed and filed out the *dojang*, each man bowing one final time at the door.

Jessie stood at attention in a slight state of shock, not fully understanding what had just taken place. He knew it would be a tough free-sparring session, but no one had bothered to explain that the Chang Moo Kwan black belt would be trying to kill him. Now it made sense. No wonder the other students were making such a big deal of the match.

Class ended after a strenuous workout. Students were not allowed to speak unless asked to by the master, so no one mentioned the contest until they were outside of the *dojang*. In the lovely garden overlooking Chinhae, Corporal Lee asked Jessie to wait. Soon the entire class formed a circle around Jessie and began to sing an unfamiliar song. They laughed as they sang, with arms locked around each other's shoulders.

"By your leave, Marine. Is this what you do up here all the time, Slate?" The familiar burly voice of Staff Sergeant Rim broke through the celebration. The Koreans stopped singing and someone broke open a jar of *kim chee,* a combination of cabbage, radishes, and burning-hot peppers. Another Korean produced a long, thin bottle of *soju,* a strong Korean liquor.

"What are you doing here, Staff Sergeant Rim?" Jessie shouted at the rugged Marine with the fireplug build.

"You and Sergeant Hill got your ride. You got a flight out of Kimpo in the morning."

"Out-Marine-Corps-standing!"

"So, what is this little song and dance? You hanging out with Korean beatniks, Slate?"

Jessie laughed and so did the Koreans, some of whom spoke bits of English.

"I think it was sort of a 'for he's a jolly good fellow,' Korean style."

Corporal Lee handed Jessie a small bowl of *kim chee* with chopsticks.

"Corporal Lee, why didn't you tell me my opponent would try to kill me?"

Dae Sung Lee looked surprised. "Combat," he said.

"Combat?" Jessie asked.

"As Kwan Jang Nim teaches, you win you live, you lose you die."

"Was that supposed to be to the death?"

"No. But if one should die, it would not have been . . ." he paused in search of the right word.

"A surprise," Jessie helped.

"Yes! It would not have been a surprise. Death is always a missed block away."

Jessie touched his very sore right kidney. "I'm ready for some *soju.*" He pretended to wipe sweat from his brow and the Koreans laughed. Then Jessie turned back to Sergeant Rim.

"So," he said. "Sam got leave too?"

"Affirmative. Says you and him are ready to pay that visit to Broken Wing?"

"Yes, sir. Bright Morning asked Sam to help out too. He had some back leave time built up. We both think it's the least we could do for Broken Wing," Jessie said with a sly wink.

"Broken Wing is one crazy Indian. Outstanding Marine. He's a fool for surveying out of the Corps. My God, he had the Silver Star, he'd be up for promotion eventually. I think the purge has just about run its course."

Jessie nodded solemnly. "I knew it was coming the last time I saw him. He's sort of hinted at it in his letters too. He was stringing his back leave together to give civilian life a try. When he didn't get promoted this last time, that did it."

"I dang sure agree with you and Sam that a man like Wing belongs in the Corps. He'll make one sorry civilian, and the same goes for you, Slate."

"You're half right, anyway, Staff Sergeant Rim. This is it for me. When this hitch is up, I'm through. But old Wing couldn't make it as a civilian."

Rim scratched thoughtfully at the horseshoe-shaped shrapnel scar on his cheek. "Now explain this to me, Slate. If Wing knows that you're hanging up the pack in a couple of months, then how in God's Marine Corps are you and Sam going to convince him to stay in?"

"That was easy. I lied. I told him that I re-upped."

Rim smiled and shook his head.

"It's for his own good," Jessie said emphatically.

"How did you get the colonel in on this, I mean how did the colonel get Wing's discharge papers?"

"He pulled some big strings after I read that pitiful letter from Bright Morning."

Rim frowned. "I read that letter, didn't I? Just said he was a lousy businessman or something like that."

Jessie grinned. "Not that letter, Sarge. Me and Sam wrote another one that gave a little more character to the situation. Like how Wing was contemplating suicide and that sort of thing."

"My God, Slate!" Rim exclaimed. His eyes widened and he shook his head. He started to speak but began snickering, then broke into a full-out belly laugh.

CHAPTER NINE

The short flight from Kimpo Airfield to Tokyo on a big four-engined C-54 was bumpy, with bad weather over the Sea of Japan. Jessie and Hill spent one night in a barracks near MacArthur's headquarters. The HQ was a sprawling gray structure called the Dai Ichi Building. Old MacArthur had become a resident king in Japan. Strangely enough, the Japanese people seemed to love the guy.

Jessie and Sam hung around the Dai Ichi Building for a few hours, hoping to catch a glimpse of good old Doug before their next hop to Guam, but to no avail. A two-hour rest in Guam gave them time to look up Gunnery Sergeant Paddy Francis Killeen, who had some pogue duty at the air base. Naturally, they had to toast the occasion before flying on to Hawaii. He woke up in a Navy brig, busted back to PFC. All Jessie could later remember of Hawaii was a terrible hangover and a sore jaw as he flew to San Diego aboard one of the big, new Boeing Stratocruisers. A bus ride to Pendleton to report in, then they were immediately off again by train. Destination Arizona.

The train ride took the better part of two days, but Jessie didn't mind gazing at the wide-open beauty of America. They traveled through Yuma to Prescott and on to Ash Fork and Flagstaff, through part of the Petrified Forest along the Rio Puerco before reaching Houck, a little frontier town as close to the town of Window Rock as the tracks would come.

Air brakes whooshed and a shrill whistle broke through the hot May air. A conductor called out.

"Comin' into Houck!"

Jessie looked out of the window. "This is a town?"

"Yes. Used to be forty, maybe fifty people here."

Stepping onto the station platform was like stepping back into the Old West. Besides an old dusty one-room train depot, there were four other wooden buildings. One had a handpainted sign that said GENERAL STORE. One said HOTEL; it was two stories. One said NAVAJO JEWELRY. The other had no sign.

Three chubby Navajo women stood beside the hissing train with two spotted ponies loaded down with colorful Indian blankets. Eight tourists from the trains piled out, stretched, and headed for the minitour of Houck, Arizona.

Sam and Jessie tagged along behind an older couple walking toward the Navajo jewelry store. The store had one long, thin show window in the front, which proudly displayed an assortment of rings, earrings, necklaces, and bracelets, all made of silver and some adorned with beautiful onyx and turquoise stones. Jessie let the older couple go in while he halted Sam.

"Let's drop our seabags out here."

"Okay."

"See if we can make him think we're just tourists."

Sam nodded and started to open the door just as another, older couple approached. A gray-haired lady who looked like Bess Truman, only fatter, and her skinny little husband, who looked like an older Stan Laurel, paused.

"Are you going to open the door, Arthur, or do I have to myself?" Fat Bess Truman's voice was deeper than the average man's voice, and her huffy attitude made Jessie dislike her instantly.

"Sorry, dear. I did not want to jump in front of these Marines."

"That's quite all right, sir, after you," Jessie said.

The old man smiled politely, but Fat Bess strutted by, obviously bothered by the episode, rearranging her gaudy diamond necklace as she passed. Jessie and Sam exchanged raised eyebrows and followed the couple into the small store.

The breeze from a standing fan in the corner nearest the door felt good. Sam nudged Jessie and nodded toward the back of the room. There stood Broken Wing, arms folded and a long Indian pipe in his mouth, staring down at a crude glass case. Just seeing that broad acne-scarred face brought a smile to Jessie. He pretended to shop for jewelry with Sam, keeping the other customers between himself and Broken Wing's line of sight.

"You." The Fat Bess lady pointed and wagged her finger at Broken Wing. "Yes, I'm speaking to you."

Broken Wing pointed to himself.

"Yes! Don't you even speak English?"

Broken Wing walked over to Fat Bess with his arms folded across the chest of his baggy overalls and his pipe pointing straight at her nose. His black hair had grown to an unmilitary length, and he wore a headband made of leather.

"I would like to purchase this ring. Now, I'll give two dollars for it and not a penny more."

"Okay."

"Young man?" another elderly lady called, and waved.

"Yes?"

"Don't you have anything more feminine, you know, something delicate?"

"I want this wrapped," Fat Bess growled.

Jessie and Sam exchanged frowns, crossed their arms impatiently and watched Broken Wing from across the room.

"If he don't put this old dame in her place soon, I'm gonna throw up right here, Sam."

"Leave room for a second puddle."

"Young Indian, I'm in a hurry. I'm starting to perspire in this closet you call a jewelry store."

"Tennnn-shun!" Jessie Slate shouted with the fervor of an accomplished drill instructor.

Broken Wing snapped to attention by reflex, while the tourists all stood startled with their mouths hanging open. Jessie and Sam marched briskly up to Broken Wing, stomping to a stop. Both of their faces nearly touched his.

"You call yourself a Marine, mister!" Jessie shouted, and snapped Broken Wing's headband.

"I suppose you're gonna lick this old squaw's feet if she gives you a tip!" Sam bellowed.

Fat Bess gasped in horror.

"I seen better haircuts on a civilian, Marine!" Jessie shouted.

"You couldn't join the Army with a haircut like that!" Sam added forcefully.

Wing's eyes widened with each outburst, then he relaxed from standing at attention.

"Where did you two come from?"

"Korea," Sam said.

"That's where the next war's gonna be, boy! That's where we're taking you!"

"Oh, no. I am a civilian. I sell jewelry."

Jessie scrunched up his handsome face as if he had just smelled something foul, then exchanged looks of utter disgust with Sam Hill. They looked scornfully at Broken Wing.

Fat Bess crossed her arms and began tapping her right foot impatiently. "Young Indian, I will wait no longer, and I will not stand here and be insulted. If you want my business, you had better move, and right now!"

"Be right with you, lady," Broken Wing mumbled.

"You gotta be kidding me, Wing!"

"Go away. I am earning a living."

"Sergeant Broken Wing, you are a disgrace to the Corps. Ain't he, Sam?"

"Quite revolting."

"Never even made sergeant," Broken Wing said.

"You are now," Sam Hill said.

"That's why we're here. Staff Sergeant Rim said he'd see to it you get promoted soon as you reenlisted. Got the colonel's okay."

"Rim?"

"Yep. He's in Korea too. Great duty."

"Ain't reenlisting."

"Yes, by God, you are, Marine!" Jessie growled.

"Nope."

"It should be quite obvious that this is a humiliating existence for a United States Marine," Sam said with chin up and shoulders back.

Broken Wing frowned at Sam. "Since when does Sam Hill talk like a professor?"

Jessie gave a scoffing wave at Sam. "That blasted Ogelthorpe's got Sam talking just like him."

"Ogelthorpe's in Korea?"

"Yep. We got a new C.O. Old Corps all the way. Colonel Cain. Served with my dad and Gunny O'Cleary in the Great War and China too."

"He was at Choisel," Sam said.

"Paramarine?"

Fat Bess cleared her throat as loud as she could. "Henry, take me away from these rude barbarians right this minute!"

"Sorry, lady. I get that ring for you right now."

"And when you're done with that, boy, me and Sam want our boondockers spit-shined."

"You can stow that in your galley, Slate!" Broken Wing barked.

Sam whistled and Jessie pretended to be shocked.

"Golly, Sam. That sounded like Marine talk, didn't it?"

"Facsimile."

Tkele-cho-gi," Wing said.

"As you were, Marine! If you're gonna call me a jackass, you do it in Marine Corps English."

"I'm leaving, Henry. These people are heathen savages."

"No," Broken Wing answered, quickly turning his attention toward the startled Fat Bess.

He pulled up the sleeve of his checkered flannel shirt and held up his hand so that the lady could see his silver-colored bracelet. He pointed to a cross engraved over Indian symbols.

"I am Christian," Broken Wing said plainly.

Jessie stared in disbelief for a moment, then realized that his mouth was in danger of catching flies. He closed his mouth and stepped closer to Broken Wing. He pulled up the sleeve of his dress khaki shirt, revealing his matching bracelet.

"You still wear it," Broken Wing said. His dark eyes seemed to soften with the memory.

"Of course I do," Jessie said matter-of-factly. He started to ask about the cross but decided to wait.

"Come, Henry." Fat Bess twirled around and headed out the door. Jessie watched them leave, then turned to Broken Wing.

"Poor old Henry."

"Yes. Evil squaw," Broken Wing said.

The other elderly couple looked at each other as if unsure of what to make of all that was happening, but judging by the grins on their faces, they were thoroughly enjoying the entire drama. Jessie pointed at them.

"You people are in luck today. This store is having a going-out-of-business sale, and I bet you can get everything for half price."

"I am not going out of business."

"Isn't this marvelous, Jim," the elderly lady commented with a bright smile. "It's just like listening to one of those wonderful radio shows."

"Yes, now that you mention it, dear, it does. . . ." The elderly gentleman's voice trailed off as he realized that Jessie, Sam, and Broken Wing were now quietly staring at him and his wife.

He cleared his throat. "Pardon us, we didn't mean to interrupt."

The old lady's eyes squinted behind very thick glasses. "Exactly where is Korea, young man? The papers are filled with news about Greece and the Middle East, but I don't recall reading about Korea."

"*A-nah-ne-dzin,*" Jessie grumbled in his best Navajo.

Broken Wing and Sam Hill looked at each other, then stared at Jessie incredulously until he felt uncomfortable and stammered out an answer.

"It's right beside Japan."

"Oh," she said, as if everything was now clear.

"Hear from Paddy?" Broken Wing asked.

"Killeen was on Guam the last I heard."

"Guam?"

"Yeah. You know Gunny Killeen, he hates stateside duty."

"Great man."

"Yes. Sure miss him."

Sam pulled an envelope out of his trouser pocket and handed it to Broken Wing. "Here. Sign."

"What is this?" he asked suspiciously.

"Enlistment papers."

"I am not enlisting. I am a civilian businessman."

Jessie forced a laugh. "Just sign the papers, Wing, and quit all the jaw-jackin'. You look stupid out of uniform and you darn well know it."

Broken Wing slapped the envelope into Jessie's chest. "No."

Jessie and Sam looked at each other with raised eyebrows.

"How's Swift Eagle and the little woman?"

"Boy is outstanding. Squaw is *a-nah-ne-dzin.*"

"What's she hostile about?"

"You.'

"Me!"

"You write troublesome letter, Slate."

Jessie glanced at Sam with a slight smirk, then turned an innocent, almost pleading face to Broken Wing. "But what did I write that troubled your wife?"

"You told her I should be in Marines for life."

Slate patted his bracelet. "Just trying to help a blood brother who happens to have made a grave mistake."

"And is living in disgrace," Sam added. "Marines are not salesmen."

"Disgrace?"

"It is when your blood brother is about to go to war while you hide out here on the reservation."

"I hear nothing about war!" Broken Wing growled.

Jessie held up both hands. "Hey! It's your life. You want to stay here with the squaws weaving blankets while the warriors take care of business, me and Sam understand. Right, Sam?"

"Conclusively. However, it should be pointed out that others could not be expected to understand."

"Obviously," Jessie agreed.

"Yes, of course," the old lady with the thick glasses mumbled in a concerned tone.

Broken Wing's eyes widened in rage. He pointed at the door. "Out!"

"Come, Martha. I guess we're not wanted," the old man said as he took his wife's hand. The train let loose a long, shrill whistle.

Broken Wing turned to the elderly couple. "Not you! You want to buy anything?"

"No. I'm afraid we have to be getting on that train also," the old man said.

"But I do so want to thank you for a most entertaining stop," the woman said. "I have thoroughly enjoyed this."

Broken Wing grunted and glared at Jessie and Sam. "Aren't you gone yet?"

Jessie pointed at himself. "Who? Us?"

"We have reservations at the hotel," Sam said with a sly grin.

"Yes. Didn't we tell you? We plan on spending our leave here with you."

"We can help you out."

"Yes. Out of business. Go away."

Jessie turned to the elderly people, shaking his head solemnly. "It would be hard for someone to believe that this is my blood brother speaking in such a way."

"To the man that named your very own son," Sam added glumly to Wing.

Martha put her hand over her heart and tilted her head sympathetically. "You named his son," she said, as if talking to a little boy.

"Yes, ma'am. Swift Eagle."

"What a fine name," she said.

Broken Wing groaned.

"I think so too, ma'am," Jessie said, with a hint of sadness in his tone.

Sam Hill laid a hand on Jessie's shoulder. "Especially when you realize that Sergeant Slate, here, saved the boy from a lifetime of humiliation."

"That is correct," Jessie agreed.

"*Beh-na-ali-tsoisi,*" Broken Wing mumbled.

"Let us shy away from cheap name-calling, Broken Wing," Jessie said in a supercilious tone. He turned back to the elderly couple to plead his case.

"Would you want to go through your entire life being called . . . what was it? Stinking Baby?"

"It was Walking Skunk!" Broken Wing blurted.

Jessie faced the elderly judges with hands extended. "See what I mean?"

"Sergeant Slate also saved his life," Sam added.

"Out. You two go away." Broken Wing pushed Jessie and Sam toward the door.

"Well, Martha. I certainly do not want to give such an ungrateful person our business."

"I concur, dear."

Sam Hill opened the door for the elderly couple to leave, and the two Marines followed them out of the door, with Broken Wing watching in a state of scornful disbelief.

Twenty-four hours later another train chugged into Houck with a loud whistle and a rumble that shook the tiny hotel room where Jessie and Sam had spent the night. Sam rolled off of his stale-smelling mattress. He sat up, stretched, and yawned. Jessie stood in his boxer shorts, staring out of the window. An evil grin crossed his face.

"What?" Sam asked. He got up and ambled over to the window to look. Below, a group of tourists filed off of the train and began to meander past the stores. One couple stopped in front of Broken Wing's store, pointed at jewelry in the long, narrow window front, then moved to the front door, where they paused and then walked away. A moment later a gray-haired gentleman did the same thing.

Jessie's evil grin widened.

"You put a Closed sign on the front door," Sam accused.

"Yes."

"Last night?"

"Yes."

"Outstanding."

"Thank you, Sam."

"I'm afraid that we don't have time to make a serious impact on his business. We really should be on the afternoon train if we don't want to get something beside a headache out of this twenty-day leave."

"I know."

"He'll come looking for us when he sees the sign."

"Yes. That's when we'll tell him that we're shoving off on the afternoon train."

"Train leaves at two P.M. Think that will give us enough time? He used to have a powerful tolerance."

"The Marines have landed and that situation is well in hand."

"How?"

Jessie pulled four long, thin bottles of clear liquid out of his seabag. Each bottle had Korean characters on a bright blue label. Jessie pointed at a nick in the label of one bottle. "This is our bottle. Plain water," he said.

"Outstanding."

"All we can do is give it our best effort, Sam."

Twenty minutes later the whistle blew again, and soon after that the train pulled away from Houck. Five minutes later there was an angry knock at the door of their hotel room. Jessie grinned at Sam, straightened his tie, and opened the door. Broken Wing's furrowed brow said it all.

"That's a horrible face to open a door to, Wing," Jessie said.

Wing held up the Closed sign. "I am not closed."

"Now, look, Wing. Major Cain is making it possible for a lot of the old Paramarines to serve together again."

"Yes," Sam said. "We're training the K.M.'s."

"K.M.'s?"

"Yeah, the Korean Marines," Jessie said.

"I don't want to train K.M.'s."

"Ah, sure you do! You got green blood, boy! You sure as crap ain't cut out to be no salesman!"

"Correct," Sam said.

Broken Wing balled up the Closed sign and dropped it on the floor. "No."

Jessie's shoulders sagged as he looked down at the balled-up piece of paper. He shook his head dejectedly, then lifted his eyes from the floor after a long, silent pause and turned to Sam.

"Well, can't say we didn't try."

Sam nodded solemnly, his oval face a picture of defeat.

"He was a good Marine and it was worth trying," Jessie said slowly.

"Yes, I concur," Sam said sadly.

"I am not dead. Just don't wanna be Marine."

Jessie smiled and slapped Broken Wing on the shoulder. "All right, old buddy. Come on in and say good-bye properly."

Jessie ushered Broken Wing in and closed the door behind him. Sam motioned to a cane chair. Sam and Jessie sat facing each other on their beds. Broken Wing pulled his chair up between the two of them and sat down.

"Yep. Guess this is it, Wing," Jessie said.

"You leave?"

Sam nodded. "Have to be on the afternoon train at two P.M. in order to reach Pendleton in time."

"The Corps is changing, Wing. Shoot, we live like kings in Korea now."

Sam smiled. "Luxury all the way."

"You speak with forked tongue."

"I always loved it when you said that Indian stuff, Wing," Jessie said.

"You got galley water coming out of your ears if you think I believe that luxury crap."

Jessie laughed and nodded at Sam. "He's right, Sam. No use trying to fool an old salt."

"No use," Sam said.

"Well, the least you could do for your own blood brother is have a couple of shippin' out drinks with me."

"Don't drink much no more," Broken Wing said sheepishly.

"What?" Sam asked in disbelief.

"Yeah and your mother was the king of the swab jockeys," Jessie scoffed.

"No. Not good to be drunk."

"Bible?" Jessie asked.

Broken Wing nodded.

"I wanted to ask you about that cross. What happened to the old Wind God and all of the little dirt drawings?"

"Have learned much, Slate."

"Okay. Let's drink to it."

"No. I have to quit drinking too much."

"Now hold on just a minute!" Jessie held up his hand. "What was Jesus' first miracle?"

"I know. But I drink too much."

"Oh! Well, me and Sam here will make sure that we don't overdo it."

"Of course," Sam said.

"Just a farewell drink. Maybe two."

"No bar in town," Broken Wing said.

"We're in luck! I just happened to bring back some *soju* from Korea for a souvenir."

"You could drink it all day and not become inebriated," Sam said with a confirming wink.

"Yeah, it's so weak the Korean whores drink more of it than the Marines do."

"I don't know."

"Ah, come on!" Jessie said. He pulled two bottles from his seabag. Sam took one.

"Here." Sam handed Broken Wing a bottle.

The lonely train whistle sounded over the clickety-clack of the big steel wheels as the smoking monster steamed through Holbrook, the county seat for the Hopi Indian Reservation. The conductor tapped on their compartment door and handed them a stack of newspapers.

Sam and Jessie spoke little of Broken Wing, other than to wonder if he would try to bayonet them when he awoke and discovered that he had reenlisted in the United States Marine Corps.

Oddly, when he finally did come to, he said not a word for two hours. Then he joined in the conversation as if nothing out of the ordinary had happened. From that day forward, Wing would always insist that reenlisting had been his idea from the start.

CHAPTER TEN

The big four-engine C-54, or R5D as the Marines called it, lumbered into the dark sky above Tokyo for the hour flight to Kimpo Airfield, near Seoul. Jessie found a spot to rest his head and quickly joined Sam and Wing by falling fast asleep. In his dreams, he fell directly into the arms of a beautiful redhead. He couldn't quite make out her face, but she seemed to be very familiar. She kept saying, "I love you," over and over. He pulled away to look at her face, and it was Kate staring back at him. Her piercing blue eyes glared at him with bitterness, but her caress thrilled him with passion as she pressed against him. He grinned and thought about her last letter. Just the thought of running a bed and breakfast with Kate and Charlie filled him with a sense of peace that transcended all worries.

A sharp pain opened his eyes, and he realized that his head had banged off of the bulkhead of the R5D like a billiard ball off a cushion.

"What the . . . !" someone shouted from the other side of the green-curtain cockpit door.

"Get us out of here!" another voice cried out. The engines roared with the strain of a full-throttled climb.

"What's going on?" Jessie shouted at Broken Wing. Wing shrugged and struggled to his feet. He moved toward the porthole.

"See anything?" Sam asked.

The curtain to the cockpit burst open and a graying, middle-aged copilot started yelling, "Grab a parachute off the wall! Kimpo's being strafed by Yak fighters!"

He yanked the curtain closed. The three Marines exchanged frozen stares for a moment, then scrambled for parachutes hanging on the bulkhead of the plane near a hatchway. Jessie fumbled with the straps of his until it fit properly, then rushed to a porthole. The morning sun glistened off a flashing silver North Korean Yak fighter as it streaked over the airfield below. Jessie knew the R5D was dead if the Communist fighters spotted it.

"How do you get this on?" Broken Wing asked casually.

Jessie twirled around to find the stone-faced Navajo yawning into his face.

"Turn around, you dope! Put your arms in! Now, tighten the harness in the crotch."

Wing yawned again and began to take the parachute off.

"What are you doing?"

"Don't need this."

"You do unless you plan on sproutin' wings, mister!"

"No."

"What do you mean, no."

"Not jumping. Don't need a 'chute."

"If we get shot down, you got to jump!"

"No."

"What do you mean, no!"

"Don't want to."

Jessie turned to Sam in exasperation. "Sam! Talk to this idiot!"

Sad-faced Sam looked away from the porthole at Jessie and Broken Wing, then rubbed his sleepy, mournful eyes.

"What?"

"You two better wake up!" Jessie barked angrily. "Unless I miss my guess, we just flew into a war!"

The R5D circled high above Kimpo for a few minutes,

then began to drop down. The copilot opened the curtain hatchway and leaned out.

"The airfield says it's all clear for now. We're going to try and land. Better get off the plane quick when we stop." He closed the curtain again.

The plane circled the airfield twice. Three burning American planes sent up billows of black smoke from the end of the pockmarked runway. The white administration building to the left of the runway was riddled with holes, and a group of people stood outside waving frantically at the R5D as it circled low over the field one last time.

A green flare shot into the bleak, rain-laden sky. The big transport leveled off, and the landing gear thumped as it lowered. Jessie's heart jumped. A moment later they touched down with a bounce that rattled through the tin bulkhead. The R5D stopped dangerously close to the burning wreckage at the end of the airstrip as a group of at least twenty people came running toward the plane, mostly Army officers, with five or six American civilians, men and women. The smoldering remains of an R4D were strewn along the edge of the field, as if the cargo plane had been dismissed and tossed in different directions. The pilot kept the engines running on the R5D while everyone but himself scampered out of the big double cargo doors and down a roll-up stairway that two Air Force enlisted men pushed up to the plane.

"You got room on that plane, Marine?" a stern-faced Army colonel shouted at Sam as he led the others down the stairway. The dour colonel was the nervous, officious type that years of pushing papers seem to produce.

Sam reached the bottom and saluted. "Yes, sir. Just us three, the crew, and some cargo aboard."

"Good!" He turned to the group of terrified faces behind him staring up anxiously at the sky, searching for Yak fighters. "Let's get on board! KMAG people first!"

He waved them forward.

"What's the word, Colonel?" Jessie asked.

"The Reds are pouring across the 38th Parallel with heavy Russian armor! The South Koreans are buggin' out!"

Jessie, Sam, and Broken Wing exchanged looks of apprehension. Jessie glanced at an American woman scampering up the stairway to the R5D and wished he could follow her, for more reasons than just typical Marine lust. Out of nowhere a vision of PFC Charlie Rose's big, happy face flashed into his mind.

"We're advisers to the K.M.'s, sir, and I've got some buddies still in Seoul and at Chinhae. I better go see if I can help."

The colonel's face froze for an instant. He blinked and regained composure.

"Very well, Marine, but you may be needed here. Report to Captain Rowles in the admin. building over there. He's putting together a platoon to try and defend the airstrip. He'll be the man burning documents."

"Sir, if we just leave our seabags on board, could you—"

"Yes. Yes. I'll see to it."

The colonel saluted, and the Marines returned the salute as he rushed up the stairs. Jessie expected to catch some saltwater from Sam and Broken Wing for wanting to stay, but they said nothing.

A few Air Force and Army personnel rushed about carrying filing cabinets and personal belongings, but for the most part Kimpo was engulfed in an eerie silence. The motors of the R5D revved up for takeoff as the three Marines reached the bullet-riddled administration building. A young Army captain rushed out of the building with an Army corporal close behind, both carrying bundles of folders, heading toward a small bonfire just beside the flagpole in the front yard.

"Captain Rowles!" Broken Wing yelled as they approached.

The Captain gave a quick glance, then tossed the files into the fire.

"Yeah!" he said briskly.

"A colonel told us to report to you. We're advisers to the K.M.'s, reporting back from leave. We need to get back to our unit but he said you may need us to defend the airfield."

"You heading for Seoul?"

"Yes, sir. We were supposed to meet the other Marines there before heading back to Chinhae."

"First reports from the South Koreans said the Reds took the city."

"The Reds took Seoul!" Jessie exclaimed.

Captain Rowles threw up his hands in disgust. "Well, that was the first word out, but we just got word from KMAG that Seoul is still in friendly hands."

"Sir," Jessie blurted, "we got buddies in Seoul, and some more of our guys were with the K.M.'s in Chinhae, so if it's all the same to you, we'd like to go to Seoul, then rejoin our outfit."

"The K.M.'s might be rushed to Uijongbu corridor. That's where the main Communist push was." He turned back to the bonfire for a moment, then faced the three Marines. "Look, if this last report is right and the Korean Military Advisory Group is heading back into Seoul to set up shop again, we'll probably have a convoy moving out in a few minutes."

"We would like to take off now, Captain," Broken Wing said.

"Yes, sir," Jessie added.

The captain shrugged, then motioned toward the administration building. "If you're going, you better get some weapons. Tell Sergeant Willis in there that I said to give you weapons and ammo."

"Think anyone else is heading that way, so we can hitch a ride?" Jessie asked.

"Transportation is no problem. Every civilian in Korea bugged out of here like their butts were on fire. Just look around. You'll find plenty of transportation."

He was right. They were even able to be picky. Three

Buicks, two Dodges, a Cadillac, and a LaSalle had been abandoned nearby. Most people just left the keys inside, but some idiots had taken the time to lock up their cars to keep the Commies out. Broken Wing insisted on taking the LaSalle and no one argued. Jessie drove.

The road to Seoul was an ugly sight. Fleeing refugees carrying everything they owned on their backs streamed away from the city. Terrified women lumbered along the side of the road with huge baskets on their heads and crying babies on their backs bound up papoose-style. South Korean soldiers moved in both directions using every mode of transportation available, from bikes and horses to camouflaged trucks. Some soldiers were obviously fleeing, while others were heading for the front.

Panic was etched on every Korean face. The mood seemed even more somber as they traveled farther west on the bleak, rainy road. It was only eight miles to Seoul, but progress was painfully slow, weaving between and around streams of Korean refugees until finally crossing the Han River Bridge. Vicious artillery duals rumbled like thunder beyond Seoul. They passed over a railroad track, which was straddled by a burning American truck. Just beyond that was a hospital. Wounded Korean soldiers lay on stretchers all around the outside of the building. Past Yangsan Railroad Station they turned right two blocks to the old Japanese Army headquarters, now the home of ROK, Republic of Korea staff officers working alongside the Americans of KMAG. Two artillery rounds whistled by overhead, exploding somewhere in the vicinity of the hospital. A makeshift perimeter of American soldiers, Marines, and even an Air Force man or two stood guard around the gloomy, sprawling gray-stone KMAG building. Jessie pulled into a small parking lot just beside a new, two-story building. Over the main entrance was a black and white sign, KMAG HQ. The deep bulldog voice of Staff Sergeant Rim was already shouting out a command.

"Get your sorry butts over here, Marines! Somebody found us another war!"

"Staff Sergeant Rim?" Jessie shouted with a laugh. He was instantly thankful that he'd come back.

The short, stocky old Marine looked happy to see them, or at least as happy as he was capable of looking. He had never quite been the same since Gunnery Sergeant Patrick O'Cleary died on Iwo Jima, but then neither had Jessie. He had loved O'Cleary like a father. Standing beside Rim was a tall, gangling American in civilian clothes with a thick moustache and a long, thin face.

"Thought you'd be back at Chinhae, Sergeant Rim," Jessie said as he extended his hand.

Sergeant Rim gave Jessie's hand a firm shake and laughed at Broken Wing. "So, you got this useless Navajo back in the Corps! Outstanding job, Marines!"

"Nope!" Broken Wing said with an indignant expression.

Sergeant Rim scratched at the horseshoe-shaped shrapnel scar on his cheek and turned pridefully to the gangling civilian beside him.

"These are your U.S. Marines, Mr. Chick. While every cockroach in Korea is heading south, these men came north. And these two went halfway around the world to keep this one—" He pointed an accusing finger at Broken Wing. "—from leaving the Corps."

"Nope," Broken Wing said arrogantly, with his arms crossed around his M-1 rifle.

"We're going to need Marines, Sergeant Rim, and plenty of them," Mr. Bob Chick said.

"Mr. Chick is a journalist with the *Chicago Daily News*."

"How do you do, gentlemen."

"You have any inside dope, Mr. Chick?" Jessie asked.

"Well, I can tell you this. The North Koreans ordered civilians to evacuate a two-mile stretch bordering the 38th Parallel. You know, of course, that they have been showering leaflets daily, threatening invasion, and mortaring Kaesong, and still nobody was prepared. You'd think

America would learn. Hitler told us what he was going to do. No one listened."

"How bad is it?" Sam Hill asked.

"Well, from what I've been able to gather from the KMAG brass, it seems that in the first few hours, the South Korean Army fought well. They retreated to prepared positions, took heavy casualties, but didn't break, but haven't been able to do anything against the heavy Russian tanks."

"Bazookas?" Broken Wing asked.

"First reports say that the 2.6 bazooka rounds just bounce off these monsters. The Reds came down the Uijongbu corridor north of Seoul. Two South Korean divisions out of the four seem to have folded up and run for it. But the big news is this: MacArthur has been given command."

"Wow! America's gonna fight?" Jessie asked.

"No one knows, but the Advisory Group had abandoned Seoul a few hours ago, and MacArthur told them to reenter the city and set up shop."

Jessie looked at the others. No one spoke but all of them knew what it would mean. It was fine to say, "We have to help Korea," but when it came time to die, they each knew who would be doing the dying. Jessie nudged Broken Wing.

"Remember what old Gunny O'Cleary would say?"

"No better way to die than to die a Marine."

"Where do you want us, Sergeant Rim?" Sam asked.

"We got a billet back there, but you won't be needing it. We're on line full-alert. If the Reds break through, we might have to bug out at any time."

"What makes you think that might happen, Sergeant?" Mr. Chick asked.

Sergeant Rim scratched at his horseshoe-shaped shrapnel scar. "Just a feeling."

Five hours later, lights began popping on throughout the KMAG headquarters building. Jessie wiped rain from his eyes and shivered. An officer raced out of the main door of the HQ and shouted.

"The Reds have broken through! Get ready to move out!"

Jessie grabbed his rifle and stood up from behind the makeshift bunker of sandbags and discarded filing cabinets. Suddenly, mortar rounds began exploding in the front yard of the KMAG HQ. Jessie slapped at the back of his neck. It was wet with blood from a shard of burning shrapnel. Broken Wing yanked him down until they were face-to-face.

"How bad?"

"Look." Jessie twisted so that Broken Wing could get a look.

"Too dark."

"Feel it."

Broken Wing touched the back of Jessie's neck and shoved him away in seeming disgust.

"What's that for?" Jessie snapped.

"Mosquito bite."

"I oughta bite you! I'm wounded, you useless—"

"Not much of a wound."

"You're jealous, aren't ya?"

Broken Wing took Jessie's left hand and placed it on the back of his head. Wing's short, bristling hair was wet and warm.

"You stupid, useless sister to a swab jockey!"

"What is it with you two?" Sam shouted over two nearby explosions.

"This idiot is wounded!"

"How bad, Wing?"

"Worse than mosquito bite," he said in his usual deadpan manner.

"Ankle too."

"What?"

The Navajo lifted his foot. The light was too dim to see clearly, but there appeared to be a quarter-sized piece of shrapnel sticking through his right shoe and into his foot just below the ankle.

Sergeant Rim ran from the HQ shouting, "Get the lead out, Marines!"

A series of mortar blasts walked up the street. The Sergeant dove for cover behind Jessie, Broken Wing, and Sam.

"Where we going?" Sam shouted back at Sergeant Rim.

"We're putting together a convoy! We have to make it to the Han River Bridge ASAP or we're gonna be sittin' in a POW camp! Go get that LaSalle you clowns came in and help form up a convoy out front! Now!"

Sergeant Rim jumped up and ran back across the lawn and into the KMAG HQ. Slowly, a ragtag convoy of staff cars, civilian cars, troop trucks, jeeps, and a couple of weapons carriers lined up in front and halfway around the two-story HQ. Sam found some sheets and ripped them into bandages for Broken Wing and Jessie while they waited for the word to move out.

Rain came down hard as the convoy moved out slowly, then picked up speed in a race to reach the only exit from Seoul. They roared past the gas plant, its tall stacks visible in flashes of shells bursting. Just past the hospital, the streets were beginning to fill with panicked civilians and ROK troops running from the front lines. Across the main railway track from Pusan was a small road that led to Inchon. At that junction, the traffic got thick with American troop trucks filled with fleeing Korean soldiers. Suddenly, horrific flames lit the black, rain-laden sky over the Han River, and in that instant of vision Jessie saw the mighty bridge collapse. Trucks filled with screaming soldiers plunged into the black water as another explosion ripped with white light across the river. For a moment it seemed as if the crowded road went completely silent in horror. A young U.S. Army lieutenant ran back along the convoy shouting into each vehicle, "They blew the bridge on their own men! Go back to KMAG!" As if unable to believe such a thing possible, no one in the odd little convoy of Americans made a move to turn around.

Finally, the lead jeep managed a U-turn in the panicking mob, and the other vehicles followed it. When they reached KMAG HQ, a group of fifty or sixty Americans, most of whom were officers in the Korean Military Advisory Group, huddled in the front yard of the building studying a map. The others remained in their idling vehicles praying that incoming artillery rounds would not find their mark. A few minutes passed before word went out that a search for another way to cross the Han River was to begin.

Six hours later, with the sun coming up, incoming artillery grew heavy and began to zero in on the convoy, which had stopped near the river. A few men searched the banks for a place to cross. Sergeant Rim strolled up to the LaSalle and lit a cigarette. He leaned in the passenger side window.

"You two stop bleeding yet?"

"Yeah, but we have to get Wing to a hospital, Gunny," Jessie said.

Sergeant Rim nodded and looked toward the river. "No way to save the vehicles. We'll have to leave 'em and swim for it."

Cracking small arms fire straightened Jessie's spine. "What's that all about, Gunny?" he asked.

"That's our well-trained South Koreans shooting at their own people or anyone else that has a boat they want."

"You're kidding!" Jessie said.

"Wish I was. We'll need some protection, if we can find a ferry or some small boats."

An hour later the Americans, along with a few Korean officers and enlisted men, made their way across the muddy river. Enlisted men hung onto the sides of small fishing boats while the high command rode inside. It didn't matter. The rain was so heavy that no one stayed dry. Jessie clawed his way up the muddy bank of the Han River and pulled Broken Wing after him. Broken Wing looked pale. A cheer rose up from the soaked band of tired Americans. Jessie and Broken Wing followed the skyward gaze of those around them. Silver-colored American fighter planes dove and strafed and bombed the city of Seoul like angry bees. Nearby, Koreans began to sing. Some even danced. Jessie turned to Broken Wing with a smile.

"Why smile?" Broken Wing asked grumpily.

"This will upset those Army generals who wanted to disband the Corps."

Broken Wing shook his head. "You think more like Gunny O'Cleary and Paddy Killeen every day."

Jessie laughed and felt good inside. That was probably the nicest compliment his stone-faced, emotionless blood brother had ever given him.

One thing became obvious. If South Korea was to hold against the Reds, it would take America to do it. All along the mountain trail leading to Suwon, Korean troops were dropping their weapons by the side of the road and running away. At one point, a Korean officer attached to KMAG pulled out his revolver and opened fire on his own retreating soldiers. The shots scared the crap out of everyone, but no one was hit.

It was nearly a twenty-mile walk to Suwon, and the long march took its toll on some of the soft, overweight HQ staff. Broken Wing's limp grew worse with every mile, but the head wound was the real worry. His bandage was red with fresh blood, and his eyes looked glassy.

"Quit groaning, will you!" Broken Wing spoke through clenched teeth.

"Sorry, but watching you walk is killing me."

Broken Wing turned and poked Jessie. He pointed with his M-1 toward the front of the column where Staff Sergeant Rim was halting a passing jeep.

"Bet I know what he's doing," Broken Wing mumbled. The Navajo looked pale and tired. He seemed to have trouble looking straight ahead, eyes on the ground most of the time as he plodded forward.

"What?" Jessie asked.

"Gettin' us a ride."

"Yeah. Great! I bet you're right, old Navajo-face."

Just then the sergeant stepped away from the jeep and saluted. The jeep peeled out in the mud and struggled up the mountain road.

"Said no," Broken Wing growled.

An angry flash of temper shot through Jessie and he found himself jogging forward to the front of the column until he came alongside Sergeant Rim.

"Sarge!"

Staff Sergeant Rim turned a tired glance toward Jessie. "Yeah, Slate."

"Broken Wing can barely walk and his head wound is still bleeding. He should have been in that jeep!"

"I asked 'em, Slate. They said they were sending transportation back."

"That could take hours! Did you tell them he had a head wound!"

"They were in a rush, Slate! They weren't ready to listen."

"You should have made them listen, Rim!"

"I tried."

"O'Cleary would have done more than try!" Jessie snapped.

Staff Sergeant Rim's bulldog face turned red and Jessie knew that he'd hit below the belt. Rim spit rainwater off his upper lip and pointed toward the back of the column with his thumb.

"Get to the rear, Marine."

Twenty minutes later another jeep overloaded with seven South Korean soldiers tried to drive past. Two senior American officers and a Korean civilian stopped the jeep near the rear of the column. Jessie watched as the angry soldiers slowly climbed out of their jeep. Three American officers, two South Korean officers, and the Korean civilian climbed in. The sloshing boots of Sergeant Rim raced past Jessie and Wing. He ran all the way back to the jeep just as it started moving forward. He stood in the middle of the road waving his M-1 and forced the driver to stop. He rushed to the passenger side of the mud-caked jeep and began talking and pointing toward Jessie and Broken Wing. Jessie couldn't hear the conversation, but judging from Rim's face, it was beginning to get intense. Then the sergeant's shout reached Jessie and Broken Wing.

"I repeat, I have wounded in need of transportation, sir!"

The officers in the jeep exchanged angry looks of frustration. Then a lieutenant colonel in the front seat turned and pointed at two majors in the back. They climbed out. Sergeant Rim saluted, and the stocky forty-year-old ran forward until he reached Jessie and Broken Wing.

"You two get on this jeep!"

"Not me, Sarge," Jessie said. "I ain't that bad."

"I said get on that jeep and get some medical treatment! That's an order, Slate! Now shut your mouth and get aboard!" With that, Rim turned to stop the approaching vehicle. They hopped on after a quick salute to the frowning officers and a nod to the smiling Korean.

Jessie saluted Rim as the jeep churned away through the mud. "Thanks, Sarge."

Rim signaled a thumbs-up, and Jessie felt bad for giving him such a hard time. The man was all Marine, and Jessie knew it. He hoped the salute would show his thanks and respect.

CHAPTER ELEVEN

The hour-long ride to Suwon was one harrowing slide after another as the jeep nearly tumbled off the mountain trail. The chilly rain killed any desire to talk after the first mile or so. Each man withdrew into silence, pulling his collar around his ears and balling up as much as possible against the wet cold.

Suwon, the temporary capital of South Korea, was a chaotic combination of panicked civilians, streams of refugees pouring in from Seoul, and disorganized military units. Someone guessed that there would be a sick bay up near the airstrip.

Two officers helped Broken Wing out of the jeep in front of a small olive-drab Quonset hut on the eastern edge of Suwon Airfield. Frantic Koreans and blood-splattered U.S. Army medical personnel rushed in and out of the tiny dispensary, carrying bandages and plasma bottles.

"You take it from here, Marine," an Army major said as he put Broken Wing's right arm around Jessie's shoulder.

"Yes, sir."

The two Army officers sprinted back to the jeep and peeled out as if they were under fire. A sharp pain stabbed at the back of Jessie's neck.

"Ow! Get your arm off my wound, stupid!"

"Mosquito bite," Broken Wing mumbled, then grimaced.

"Getting worse?"

"Yes."

Jessie felt fresh blood on the back of Broken Wing's neck. The Indian closed his eyes and went limp. Panic seized Jessie.

"Corpsman!"

An older, distinguished-looking man rushed out of the Quonset hut. He was tall and lean with salt-and-pepper hair. He shoved a shoulder under Broken Wing's left arm.

"I got him son, let's go!" His tone was reassuring, but he was heading around the dispensary. It began to rain harder.

"Where you going?" Jessie demanded.

"The dispensary is full. We have a first-aid tent out back with cots set up."

A large canvas tent behind the Quonset hut was over-flowing with wounded Koreans. A spare, small-boned Army medic with freckles hustled forward to help with Broken Wing.

"I got him, Chaplain. Let's get him to the rear of the tent. I just squeezed in three more cots."

The distinguished-looking chaplain nudged Jessie. "I'm Chaplain Scott. Are you wounded too?" His eyes looked like a road map of fatigue.

"Yes, sir. But not bad." Jessie pointed with his thumb at the back of his neck.

"That looks pretty nasty, Marine. Corporal Glenn, you better check this one out too."

"Yes, sir."

"Take care of my buddy first," Jessie said as they gently laid Broken Wing onto a wet, muddy canvas cot.

"What are you two doing here?" the chaplain asked. "I didn't know there were any Marines in Korea."

"We've been here for months, sir. We were training the K.M.'s down at Chinhae."

Glenn turned to work on Broken Wing.

"Where were you when you were wounded?" the chaplain asked.

"Seoul. What have you heard so far, Chaplain? What's the scuttlebutt?" Jessie asked as he watched the medic cut strips of gauze for Broken Wing's head wound.

"Last word we got was that the Reds managed to get tanks across the Han River and a column is heading straight down the road."

"Tanks!"

"Yes. Heavy Russian tanks."

"Has anybody confirmed that, Chaplain? 'Cuz we had to ferry across the Han ourselves. South Koreans blew the bridges out from under their own men. How could the Reds get tanks across?"

"They got across somehow."

Freckle-faced Glenn looked up from bandaging Broken Wing. "He's got a head wound, and I don't know how deep the shrapnel went. We don't have the equipment."

"Well, how bad does he look?"

"Stay calm. He's okay, but he needs more attention than we can give him. His ankle could be broken."

"Where's the doctor?"

"He's at Taejon." The medic turned to Jessie and began cleaning the back of his neck with a damp cold rag.

"We have a plane due in soon. I'll see if we can get him aboard," Chaplain Scott said.

Night came and the rain continued until rivulets wove under the cots and turned the tent floor into a slippery carpet of mud. Broken Wing awoke two or three times, usually when another one of the wounded screamed out. Finally, as the first gray shafts of morning streaked through small holes in the old tent, the gruff voice of Staff Sergeant Rim seemed to come from nowhere.

"Well, I see you two found your usual plank holder's duty!"

Jessie sat up and winced from the burning pain in the back of his neck. He grabbed at the wound and discovered fresh bandages. Glenn must have changed them during the night.

Fireplug Sergeant Rim was standing at the foot of the cot with his hands on his hips.

"Where'd you come from, Sarge?"

"We got in late last night."

"Where you staying?"

"Looks like we ain't."

"What?"

"Just got orders to keep going south to Taejon."

"That's eighty miles from here!"

"We got some trucks this time."

"Why Taejon?"

"Pretty big city, railway station. Maybe they plan on making it the staging area," he grumbled and shook his head. "How's the Wing doing?"

"Be quiet," Broken Wing griped and sat up stiffly.

"What's wrong with you anyway, Marine?" Rim pretended to bark at Broken Wing.

"Feels like bad torpedo juice in head."

Jessie scrunched up his face. "That bad? Remember what that stuff tasted like—"

"Be quiet." Broken Wing pointed and stared down the row of cots.

The chaplain and the medic were on their knees beside a wounded Korean soldier six cots away. The chaplain prayed quietly while Corporal Glenn swiped angrily at tears trickling down his face. They stood up and Glenn covered the dead Korean soldier's face with a wool blanket, then began immediately tending to another patient in the next cot.

"For a dogface, that medic is a good Joe," Jessie said.

"That right?" Rim asked.

"Him and the padre have been going nonstop all night. I'll tell you, Sarge, I'm impressed."

"Maybe we better ask him if you two can travel or not?"

"We can travel," Broken Wing grumbled through obvious pain.

"Yeah, I hear ya," Rim scoffed, and headed for the medic.

They spoke quietly together, glancing back at Slate and Wing with curious expressions. Staff Sergeant Rim finally nodded and walked back to face Jessie.

"Well, he says Wing better lay still for a couple of days before we start dragging him around Korea. You stay with him, Slate. One of you ain't worth crap without the other anyway."

"What are you going to do in Taejon?" Jessie asked.

"I don't know. I guess we're attached to KMAG until things get squared away."

"Heard anything about the K.M.'s?"

"Last thing I heard, they were still at Chinhae. That's where we'll head, if possible, but nothing's for sure right now. These KMAG officers don't know crap. Anyway, I better shove off."

Jessie laughed and gave him a thumbs-up. "See ya soon, Sarge."

"Semper Fi."

The morning drifted by slowly. Jessie sensed an air of nervous anticipation in the faces of the chaplain and medic and even some of the patients. Artillery off in the distance pounded like a great drum getting closer with each passing hour.

Broken Wing seemed stronger. At least he could sit up without wincing. At noon Glenn, the medic, entered the tent with a smile.

"That grin looks like good news, Corporal," Jessie shouted.

Glenn gave a thumbs-up and walked to the rear of the tent. "We got a transport landing in twenty minutes!"

"Outstanding!"

"Think you can help me with some of the litter cases, Slate?"

"You bet. Say the word."

"We better start carrying some of them out to the landing field now."

Jessie sat up and began lacing up his low quarters. "Sounds like it stopped raining."

"It has for now." The medic paused and scratched at his unshaven face. He glanced pensively at the roof of the tent. "Do you hear planes?"

The roar of planes above was getting clearer. Suddenly, a ripping explosion from the airfield made the canvas tent quiver as if from a powerful storm. The chaplain burst into the tent and shouted, "They're strafing the field!"

Immediately, the clatter of heavy machine-gun fire and what sounded like 20mm cannons was followed by another bomb blast. A piece of shrapnel slapped through the top of the tent, bringing down a ray of sunlight on Broken Wing's face. The enemy planes continued their attack for five or six minutes before breaking off. Acrid black smoke became thick from fires around the airfield. Jessie shook his head at Broken Wing. "I got a bad feeling about this."

"Yes. No plane ride out."

"That's my guess, old nickel-face."

Twenty minutes later their fears were all but confirmed. Word came down that the R3D had turned back due to enemy fighters in the area. From then until late into the night, Korean wounded trickled out of the tent. Those able to walk helped the more seriously wounded. Corporal Glenn tried to convince them all to stay, but it was no use. By mid-afternoon only Jessie, Broken Wing, and a young U.S. soldier with two broken legs from a jeep accident were left in the tent. The soldier was a kid named Andy Haslam from Wyoming. He wore a cowboy hat and sang the "Tumbleweed" song quietly to himself while he played solitaire. Corporal Glenn entered the tent with three canteens and a look of deep concern across his face. He dropped one canteen by Andy Haslam's cot and brought the other two to Jessie.

"Find out the scuttlebutt yet?" Jessie asked.

"The Koreans got word somehow that the Reds are surrounding Suwon. They say that the commies forded the Han with fifty tanks and they're close."

Jessie's stomach tightened from a sudden, undeniable grip of fear. He took a breath and faked a chuckle. "Real considerate of 'em to let us know, Glenn."

The freckle-faced medic did not smile.

"That's not the worst part. They took off because the word is out that the North Koreans are killing everyone, taking no prisoners."

Broken Wing sat up, holding his head with both hands. "I feel better."

"Yeah, right. You look like death," Jessie scoffed. He turned to Glenn. "How many of us are left, Corporal?"

"A couple of the KMAG officers. Most of them already took off for Taejon. We have three litter cases in the Quonset hut and you three in here."

"Some of those Koreans looked bad. How could they all just walk out?"

"You got me. Some of them headed for Taejon and some are hiding out on the local farms, I think."

"Corporal Glenn," Chaplain Scott called out from the other end of the tent.

"Yes, sir."

"We better start getting ready to go. A KMAG major just told me Suwon is surrounded."

"Well where are we supposed to go if it's surrounded?"

"They're hoping that we got another transport plane coming in."

Night came and the rescue plane did not show. Enemy Yak fighters strafed the airfield again, but it was obvious to everyone left in Suwon that no American plane was coming. At midnight on June 13 the motors of a convoy, consisting of every available remaining vehicle in Suwon, rumbled out of town, splashing past the dispensary through a steady rain. Jessie helped Corporal Glenn load the litter cases into the back of an old Dodge Army ambulance truck. Broken Wing seemed a lot better, but he couldn't walk on his swollen ankle.

The truck did not want to start. By the time it finally cranked over and they pulled away from Suwon, it was well past midnight. The rest of the American convoy was long gone. There would be no catching up. Jessie rode up front with the chaplain, while Corporal Glenn stayed in the back with the litter cases. The steady rain turned into a monsoon downpour, so keeping the ambulance on the muddy road got harder with each mile. After about ten miles Glenn shouted from the back of the ambulance, "We're gonna have to stop!"

Chaplain Scott frowned and glanced at Jessie. "Osan is just around this hill, PFC. Think the Reds are close behind?"

"Your guess is as good as mine, Chaplain." Jessie wiped at the condensation on the windshield and peered through the pouring rain ahead. "But we don't have a choice."

Somewhere around the bottom of the next hill lay the small village. The railroad went through it, paralleling the road to Pyongtaek ten miles farther south, then cutting through Chonan, where it forked. One fork led along the coast through Kunsan and down to the southwestern tip of Korea at Mokpo. The other fork followed the road to Taejon and eventually all the way to Pusan on the southeastern tip of Korea.

Chaplain Scott pointed at a narrow, overgrown road branching off of the main road. "I know the farmer who lives down this path. I helped him with his water buffalo once and his family was very grateful. We can stop there."

The road leading to the farmhouse was actually a grassy overgrown path. It was well-camouflaged by small trees and brush. Jessie turned to Chaplain Scott. "Is this wide enough for a truck?"

"It's gonna be now."

Two hundred yards down the trail the truck slid to a

muddy stop with headlights illuminating the porch of a Korean farmhouse. Jessie jumped out into an ankle-deep puddle, grabbed up his M-1, and cautiously reconned the house. It was dark and quiet except for some chickens that squawked at being disturbed. Jessie turned and rushed back to the truck. He jumped back into the cab and shook off the water like a dog.

"It's empty."

"Jenkins isn't doing well. Glenn thinks the bouncing might have started some internal bleeding."

"Which one is Jenkins?"

"The dark-haired soldier. Young lieutenant. He was seriously injured in the first attack on Suwon."

Jessie sighed. "Brother. Guess we'll have to stay put till daybreak."

"Yes. Anything to sleep on in there?"

"A couple of straw mats."

"We'll take shifts with Corporal Glenn. Why don't you two get some rest while I take the first watch."

And so it went. A tense but quiet night except for the pounding rain. Morning brought a sense of relief to everyone. The rain had subsided and birds chirped from nearby trees. It was already warm. By noon it would be steaming hot. Jessie sat up from the straw mat and stretched. His wounds had bled overnight and he felt stiff. He scratched at his crotch, then at his armpit.

"Oh no!"

Corporal Glenn jerked awake beside him. "What! What?"

"Fleas!"

"You scared me to death." He wiped sleep from his eyes and looked around. "Hey. It's daylight! No one woke me for my watch."

"Yeah, me either. I guess the chaplain let us sleep."

Glenn stretched and shook his head. "He's about the best Joe I ever met."

"He seems like a real nice fella."

"I was told that he saved the lives of more than fifty men when he was a POW in Germany."

"POW?"

"Yep. Got captured at the Battle of the Bulge."

Jessie stiffened, cocking his ear. "You hear that?" The sounds of war echoed from a distance.

"Yeah."

They jumped up and ran through the burlap door and onto the porch. Two navy blue American jets strafed the road, two miles to the south. Their engines left white com trails in the gray sky, and Jessie knew he was witnessing a bit of history.

"Wow! Will you look at that! Ain't that something," Glenn exclaimed.

"First time I've seen 'em in action," Jessie said.

"What are they?"

"F9F Panther jets," Jessie said.

"They must have taken off from Japan. Carriers, maybe?"

"I don't know."

"What do you think of that, Chaplain Scott?" Glenn asked.

The chaplain was sitting on the front bumper of the ambulance, staring into the sky. He turned slowly to face the two gawking enlisted men. "Actually, I've seen jets before in combat."

"You have?" Jessie asked, astounded at the statement.

"Where?" Glenn asked.

"France. Right at the end of the war, the Nazis were using the ME-210s. They couldn't stay in the air very long, but they made a couple of passes over us and headed for home. Scared us plenty. We didn't know what they were, at first." He turned back to watch the American jets make another run over the road.

"They can sure move," Jessie mused, still watching the white smoke trails.

"Have you boys noticed anything in particular about the bombing that's going on?"

"No," Glenn said.

"Oh, no!" Jessie cried out.

Broken Wing opened the back door of the ambulance and stuck his head out. "What's going on?"

"American jets are bombing the road south of us!" Jessie shouted.

"Exactly." Chaplain Scott sounded tired.

"You mean we're behind enemy lines?" Glenn asked haltingly. His freckled face became a mask of terror as the sudden barrage of artillery signaled the opening salvo of a nearby battle.

Jessie gave him a pat on the shoulder. "We'll be all right."

"We better get moving." Chaplain Scott's tone was ominous.

"How," Glenn asked, "if the Reds have the road? Unless we walk, we have to go by the road, and we can't possibly carry everyone." His voice cracked with the first hint of panic.

"Look!" Jessie pointed at artillery flashes coming from the ridges just north of Osan.

"What about Jenkins?" Glenn asked.

Chaplain Scott paused thoughtfully. "He is breathing easier, but God only knows what a bouncing truck will cause."

"We got no choice," Jessie said.

"But that battle is between us and Osan," Glenn blurted.

Chaplain Scott sat against the bumper of the truck. He appeared to be contemplating his mud-caked leggings. His kind face was lined with fatigue. "We'll have to wait and pray that our guys win that battle."

They exchanged serious glances, but no one spoke.

Somebody pulled some C-rations, frankfurters and beans, from the truck. They took turns standing watch about one hundred yards down the narrow farm road, not daring to get any closer to the main road. The heavy guns ceased firing around noon. By three in the afternoon the distinctive burps of Chinese machine guns were the only sounds coming from Osan. It was common knowledge that the Russians and Chinese were supplying North Korea. Words were unnecessary. The concern etched on each man's face spoke for him. An hour after all firing had ceased, Chaplain Scott climbed in behind the wheel.

The drive down the narrow trail to the main road was quiet. It was as if each man wanted a few moments alone. Fear brought on memories of Kate and baby Charlie until Jessie had to shake his head to ready himself for possible action as they neared the main road. The chaplain stopped a few hundred feet away, still camouflaged by brush and small trees.

"PFC Slate, maybe you better scout ahead."

"Good idea, Chaplain."

Jessie climbed out of the cab and flipped his M-1 off safety. He rushed forward, crouching, until the road was in sight. His heart pounded out fear. Memories from Bougainville flashed through his mind. He found himself thinking about old Corporal DiCicca and wondering how he was doing on one leg. Legs. He thought about Kate's legs and smiled. Wonder if it's normal to be thinking of gams before you get your brains blown out? he mused.

Jessie shook his head, took a deep breath, and moved closer to the road. Suddenly, he dropped to his stomach as the unmistakable rumble of a big diesel engine broke the silence. Jessie low-crawled to the edge of the main road and looked back toward Suwon. Nothing. He looked south toward the village of Osan. The 88mm barrel of a behemoth thirty-eight-ton Soviet T-34 tank bounced up and down slightly as the monster clamored around the bend a couple of hundred yards away. Jessie flattened out under brush and watched in horror as a second tank appeared. Behind the tanks came two columns of infantry walking in the ditches on both sides of the muddy road. Many were carrying Chinese submachine guns and camouflaged with leafy branches tied to their backs.

He had seen enough. He crawled backward until it was safe to get up and run to the ambulance. The sprint winded him by the time he reached Corporal Glenn and Chaplain Scott, who were anxiously waiting in front of the Dodge.

Jessie handed Glenn the rifle and grabbed both his own knees. He heaved for air as he spoke. "Reds. Two columns of North Koreans with tanks. I think they're pulling back."

"Hey! Maybe our guys are coming this way for a change!" Glenn said excitedly.

Chaplain Scott looked Jessie in the eye. "Think we should pull back to the farmhouse?"

"They might hear the ambulance start up. If it backfires again, we're dead."

"Well." Chaplain Scott removed his helmet and scratched at his graying hair. "Guess we just have to sit still."

"We better pray that they stay on the main road," Jessie cautioned.

Chaplain Scott smiled. "Excellent idea." He turned, walked a few feet away, and knelt down to pray. Jessie shook his head. Some people sure were literal about these things.

One nervous hour passed with no sign of the enemy. Rain began to fall again. It was just as well, Jessie thought wistfully. It could hide the sound of their motor.

"What do you think, Slate?" Chaplain Scott asked as he finished off the last bite of C-ration peaches.

"Let's move out. I'll scout ahead a couple of hundred yards in front. If you hear shooting, slam that Dodge into reverse and try to hide out back at the farm."

"God be with you, Slate."

Jessie smiled and signaled a thumbs-up. "I better say 'bye to my brother, just in case."

"Brother?"

"We've been blood brothers since Bougainville. I named

his kid. If you get a chance, you should talk to him. Broken Wing turned Christian recently."

"That's wonderful!"

Jessie shrugged. "If you say so."

He headed for the back of the ambulance. The doors were swung open and Wing's head was hanging out looking into the rainy sky. His mouth was open.

"Why don't you use a canteen, stupid?"

"Milk is better straight from cow."

"I'm gonna scout ahead. They've had plenty of time to pass us by now."

"Okay."

" 'Bye."

" 'Bye."

"That all you have to say?"

Wing stared at Slate upside down for a few moments then raised one eyebrow as if a thought had come to him.

"Good . . . bye."

"Have I told you what an irritating human being you are?"

Broken Wing's expression was as inadequate as always, and it was especially meager at a time like this. Sometimes Jessie wondered why he cared about this goofy Indian anyway. Then he'd remember Bougainville and Iwo. He shook his head and turned to walk away.

"Jess," Broken Wing said.

Jessie turned back. Wing had pulled his sleeve down, revealing his bracelet. He gave a thumbs-up. Jessie did the same. A couple of minutes down the narrow, overgrown trail he heard the Dodge's engine crank up.

The afternoon sky was dark with rolling rain clouds. The soggy ground sucked at his boots with each step. He reached the main road, stopped and took a deep breath. His heartbeat picked up speed as he stepped onto the muddy Taejon highway like a man walking on eggs. The giant tracks of the Russian tank were already turning into canals in the downpour. No sign of movement. Hearing anything over the pounding rain would be difficult. That could be good or bad, Jessie thought as he started walking cautiously south toward Osan. Each step felt heavier than the last, though Jessie knew it was as much his dread that weighed him down as it was the mud.

The rain let up a bit, enough to see Osan spread out in a valley below. Small fires burned here and there throughout the town. It appeared abandoned, but that did not mean there would be no snipers. He shoved the fear out of his mind and picked up his pace. The ridges and slopes north of Osan were littered with American dead. Water-filled ditches along both sides of the road looked red. Fifty yards farther on, Jessie saw why. Lying facedown with their hands tied behind their backs, twenty-two U.S. soldiers had been shot in the back of the head.

Jessie continued down the road. At every step his heart filled with a rage such as he'd never felt before. He stopped at the outskirts of Osan and waited for what felt like a long time before the ambulance pulled up beside him. He climbed back into the truck cab. The chaplain stared straight ahead.

"What took so long?"

Chaplain Scott held out his right hand. It was full of dog tags. Jessie stared at them, then started to speak. He wanted to tell this kindhearted man that he was a fool for wasting even one minute, but he couldn't say it.

"Slate?"

"Yes, sir."

"There's no easy way to tell you," he said, measuring his pauses carefully. "Here." He handed Jessie two dog tags that he had in his left hand, separate from the others.

"What's this?" Jessie asked, not really wanting to know. He took the two dog tags, held them in his palm and read the names. *Hill, Sam . . . PFC . . . USMC . . . Blood type . . . Rim, Cyrus . . . Sgt . . . USMC . . .* Jessie's chin dropped to his chest. He felt as if someone had kicked all of the air from him. He forced himself to inhale.

"Does Broken Wing know?" Jessie asked solemnly.

"Yes."

Jessie put the two sets of dog tags around his neck.

"They will pay," he said quietly, and repeated it over and over to himself as they drove through the smoldering, abandoned town of Osan.

CHAPTER TWELVE

The ride to Pyongtaek was quiet and hot, but for some reason, Jessie felt so cold he wrapped himself in a blanket. His wounds burned, but the rest of him froze.

Nine miles out of Osan, just north of Pyongtaek, they came upon another grizzly scene. Two South Korean soldiers lay in firing positions behind the body of a dead horse. Their heads had been blown off. But one, a lieutenant, still clung to his rifle. Just beyond that lay the naked bodies of fifteen men, hands tied behind their backs, a gunshot in the back of each man's head.

Pyongtaek lay between Osan and Chonan, along the main road leading from Suwon to Taejon. It was a typical small Korean town: a few buildings and a few hundred shacks with small rice paddy farms surrounded by rugged, barren hills. Like Osan, Pyongtaek had been abandoned.

Just south of the town Corporal Glenn shouted the truck to a stop. Jessie jumped out and ran around to the back. He yanked open one door and found Corporal Glenn frantically pounding on Jenkins's chest. Jessie and the others watched in awe as the young medic worked feverishly for a full ten minutes, then stopped one last time to check a pulse and listen with his ear against the chest of Lieutenant Jenkins. Glenn sighed deeply and laid his forehead against Jenkins's chest.

"Our Gracious Heavenly Father . . ."

Jessie felt a nudge from Broken Wing as Chaplain Scott began to pray. Jessie bowed his head.

"We ask that your grace be poured out upon this wonderful young man's family, Father. Protect his two daughters with your holy angels. Be with his lovely wife, Pam . . ."

Jessie's mind floated back to Nouméa, back to his own son and Kate. I'm getting married and leaving the Corps this time, he thought, no matter what. My enlistment is up in a couple of months and I'm out.

They buried Jenkins on the side of the road in a muddy, shallow grave and marked it with some stones and an American helmet on top.

"I think I saw movement," Broken Wing said as the medic, Chaplain Scott, and Jessie came back toward the ambulance.

"Where?"

"In Pyongtaek."

Chaplain Scott ran to the cab. "Let's get!"

Two miles outside of Pyongtaek the chaplain slowed to drive around three blackened, smoldering American trucks. Along both sides of the road lay the mangled bodies of Korean refugees who had been caught in a strafing. More bodies were spread around the rice paddies on both sides of the road, but it seemed that most had tried in vain to find cover in the ditches, from which now rose the steaming stench of death.

"This is horrible," the chaplain mumbled, his tender eyes nearly in tears at the carnage.

"I didn't even see any YAKs, did you?" Jessie asked.

"No. I believe this was done by our own planes. . . ." The chaplain's voice trailed off.

Darkness fell like a heavy blanket. Realization of just how desperate the Korean situation was had become clear. Jessie's heart weighed heavy with despair. They were losing this war and losing badly. God only knew what was waiting at Chonan.

"I wonder if America knows how bad things are," Jessie mumbled to himself.

Chaplain Scott shook his head.

"We should be pretty close by now," Jessie said.

"Chonan's just around this bend."

"Pull over, Chaplain!" Corporal Glenn yelled.

Chaplain Scott downshifted to a stop at the edge of Chonan. He looked back over his shoulder. "What is it?"

"We have to stop! The bumping is going to kill this man back here! He's having a seizure!"

Chaplain Scott bowed his head and mouthed a silent prayer that probably lasted no more than a few seconds but felt like an hour to Jessie. He opened his eyes, shoved the truck into gear, and started forward.

"Look for the best place to hole up, PFC."

Chonan was a dark and eerie collection of rickety wooden houses that wouldn't qualify as a slum back home. It looked totally deserted, but it was impossible to tell for sure. Jessie rolled the window down and readied his M-1 for firing.

"How's that one look, Slate?"

Chaplain Scott squinted and pointed at a fairly well-built wooden structure in the headlights ahead.

"Good as any, I guess," Jessie said.

"Think we should stay out here on the main street, or find a place back down one of these side streets?"

"Good thought. I vote for hiding. How close behind do you think they are?"

The chaplain looked at Jessie with a cold expression of concern that brought on a rush of anxiety. There was no need to speak of it anymore. The chaplain turned down a slightly flooded side street and stopped in front of the sturdiest building. The thatched roof looked well-constructed, more so, anyway, than the houses around it.

Jessie opened the ambulance door, stepped onto the running board and looked back. "Sit still, I'll check it out. Back up and put the headlights on this shack."

Jessie ran through the downpour and bounded onto a slippery porch. He kicked open the door and jumped back out of sight. There was no sound from inside.

"Anybody here? We're Americans!"

The one-room shack was empty. They carried the litter cases in and laid them on the floor. The tumbleweed cowboy from Wyoming, Andy Haslam, asked to be propped up in a corner to play solitaire. The others slept. Chaplain Scott broke up C-ration boxes to start a fire in a crude stone fireplace. The rain eased up during the night, but by daybreak the deluge pounding against the corrugated roof made it hard to hear.

Corporal Glenn pumped some plasma into one of the litter cases. The young, wounded soldier looked pale and struggled to breathe. Something about the kid reminded Jessie of Charlie Rose. Corporal Glenn hung a plasma bottle on a hook above the man and walked over to the chaplain.

"How's he look?"

The medic shook his head. "Not good."

"Think we can move him?"

"No way. Not yet."

The chaplain grunted and looked at the wood-plank floor. Jessie patted the chaplain on the shoulder, grabbed up a poncho and the M-1.

"Well, if we're going to hole up here for a while, we better get some eyes out there."

"Me too," Broken Wing said, trying to stand.

Jessie pushed him back down, "Oh, shut up." He turned to the chaplain. "We got any chow?"

"Yes. There is a case of C-rations in the back of the ambulance. I'll relieve you in three hours."

Jessie huddled under the dry porch of a small shack on the edge of town, nibbling on beans and franks and staring down the muddy road leading back to Suwon. Two hundred meters down, the road veered off in a bend around a mountain. He could see no farther than the bend and knew that if the Reds suddenly appeared, it was going to be a close race to get back, load the wounded, and get out of town. The three hours passed like three days. Nothing showed on the road. Chaplain Scott relieved Jessie. Three hours after that, Jessie relieved the chaplain for his second shift.

By dusk the rain had subsided to a drizzle, and the sun actually poked through the clouds for a few moments. The sky was blue in the south toward Taejon. Blue sky brought on a memory of the sky over New Caledonia. Jessie turned back toward the road leading north and tried to see Kate's face. God, what I'd give to be with her right now, he thought with a sigh. The hazy sun dropped below the mountains. Jessie thought about his son Charlie and wondered if the boy ever thought about him. Old Jeremiah would tell the boy his dad was a Marine, and therefore not all bad. The thought made Jessie smile.

His smile melted into a frozen stare as he searched for the cause of a low, distant rumble that stuck in his ear and grew louder. His stiff, cold, wet hands ached from a white-knuckle grip on his M-1. The frightening rumble began to vibrate the ground. Movement caught his eye at the bend in the road. Suddenly the long gray 88mm barrel of the giant thirty-eight-ton Russian T-34 moved slowly into view. North Korean soldiers, branches sticking out of their packs and helmets for camouflage, flanked the tank. They carried short-barreled burp guns and crouched as they moved cautiously forward. Jessie's heart felt as though it had stopped. Then, without warning, it began pounding against his jacket like a sledgehammer. He jerked himself free from his terrified stare and flattened onto his stomach. He quickly low-crawled off the porch and around the corner of the house, then jumped to his feet and sprinted through the ankle-deep water. Overwhelming fear pushed his feet faster than he could ever remember running, so fast that he slid right past the ambulance, then scrambled back to the door of their shack. He burst through the door already shouting, "Reds! Get 'em loaded! Now!"

No one spoke. Corporal Glenn and Chaplain Scott

snatched up the nearest litter and headed for the ambulance. Jessie pulled Broken Wing up, shoved a shoulder under one arm and headed out the door with Broken Wing hopping on one foot.

Jessie helped Wing into the rear of the ambulance, then turned and shouted, "Crank it up, Chaplain! I'll help the medic!"

Chaplain Scott waved and ran around to the driver's side. Jessie and Corporal Glenn ran back for Andy Haslam, the cowboy. The ambulance engine whined as they lifted the stretcher into the back. Andy started singing the "Tumble-weed" song again, his voice squeaking with anxious nerves. Smoke coughed from the tailpipe as the engine kicked over, then died. Chaplain Scott tried again, with the same result. Corporal Glenn paused at the door of the shack and looked back at the ambulance with terror in his eyes. The engine starter turned over again, but there was still no ignition. The young medic glanced at Jessie, wide-eyed with fear.

"The battery?"

Jessie turned toward the end of the street where he knew that the first North Koreans would soon appear when they began their search of Chonan.

"Hit it again, Chaplain!" Jessie shouted.

The chaplain's boot came down hard on the starter. The engine whined twice, then fell silent. Jessie's pounding heart fell silent too. His fixed stare froze on the corner at the end of the narrow street, waiting to see the first North Korean.

"What now?" Corporal Glenn asked in a voice that sounded far too calm.

Jessie forced a chuckle. "Maybe that tank I saw can give us a jump."

No one even smiled. Chaplain Scott and Glenn ran to the back of the ambulance. They stood gawking at the end of the street.

Jessie slapped himself on the thigh hard. "Let's push!"

Jessie moved to the front, opening the driver-side door so he could push and steer. The heavy Dodge began to roll forward slowly. The other two pushed from behind. Jessie stopped, ran to the back, and opened the door.

"Wing! Come on!" Jessie helped Broken Wing up front and into the driver's seat. "You drive so I can push!"

Broken Wing nodded weakly.

Jessie slung his rifle over his shoulder and joined Chaplain Scott and Corporal Glenn. Traction in the mud was slightly better than ice, but the panic seemed to give the men more than natural strength as they rolled the truck faster and faster until they were jogging. Jessie could feel the blood rushing to his ears. The sound of planes overhead bent back the necks of the three struggling men. A squadron of four dark blue Marine Corsairs with big, beautiful, white stars on their gull-shaped wings broke formation, each following the other, tipping their wings and nosing down into a dive toward Chonan.

"Yeeeiii! Get 'em, Corsairs! Get 'em!" Corporal Glenn shouted.

Rockets streaked from the lead plane like Fourth of July sparklers. Cracking explosions resounded from the edge of the city. Return tracers shot into the gray sky.

"Let's push!" Jessie shouted.

"We can't push all the way to Taejon, Slate!" Corporal Glenn answered sharply.

"It'll be dark in a few minutes. Let's just get out of town."

Broken Wing steered the ambulance left around a corner and toward the main road again. They slowed at the corner and Broken Wing applied the brakes. Jessie ran forward to peek around the corner of what looked to be an abandoned restaurant. Two hundred meters away the big Russian tank had pulled off of the road and under the cover of some trees. No soldiers were visible. Jessie leaned back, away from the corner, and turned quickly, bumping heads with Broken Wing, hanging over his shoulder.

"God! I hate when you do that!"

Broken Wing replied with his usual dull, expressionless stare. "Better go now," he mumbled.

"Yeah." Jessie helped the hobbling Indian back to the ambulance and ran around behind to push.

"Chaplain, Glenn, a commie tank is at the end of the street, and I'm sure there's some troops too. But this will be our only chance to get these wounded men out of here."

Both men took deep breaths.

"Ready?"

"Wait a second," Chaplain Scott said. He bowed his head.

"Dear Lord, we ask Your protection. Shield us from the enemy, O Lord. Into Your loving hands we put our lives. Amen."

The chaplain opened his eyes and looked at Jessie.

"One."

"Two."

"Three!"

They shoved the heavy truck with more strength than Jessie thought they had. Broken Wing steered around the corner just as a Corsair ripped by overhead, strafing the enemy tank at the end of the street. He pushed until his heart felt like exploding. Each muddy step got harder. He glanced at Glenn, the veins in the medic's neck bright blue against his pale skin. On the other side of Glenn the chaplain's eyes were closed and he seemed ready to drop. Still no enemy fire. The faint sound of an airplane getting closer lifted Jessie's eyes from the mud. He peered around the ambulance to the southern sky. A dark blue Corsair was heading straight at them, treetop level above the road leading out of Chonan. Jessie stopped pushing and jumped away from the ambulance. He waved his arms frantically. The single-seat Marine fighter roared just overhead, firing 20mm cannons at the tank. Jessie gasped, then hustled back to pushing the ambulance. Another thirty yards brought them to the end of town. There, the road began to descend, and they picked up speed until the three pushers were jogging behind the old

Dodge. Broken Wing popped the clutch; the engine sputtered, then died.

"There's a bend at the foot of this hill with tree cover!" Chaplain Scott shouted.

Jessie's heart hammered out a throbbing beat. Fear gripped his mind and he expected a bullet to scream through the back of his head with each step. He could hear the planes making another pass.

"Think they can tell we're Americans?" Glenn's words came through gasps for breath.

"They must. Otherwise, we'd be dead."

An eternity later the ambulance rolled around the bend in the road at the foot of the hill and behind the cover of trees. Corporal Glenn eased up.

"No! Don't stop pushing!" Jessie barked.

Glenn leaned into the task again. They reached another slight downhill run and gave it all they had to pick up more speed. Broken Wing popped the clutch, but the engine would not fire. The downhill run took them another thousand yards before the chaplain collapsed into a heap on the muddy road. Jessie and Glenn fell to their knees. Wing popped the clutch again, and again the engine sputtered and died. Jessie's lungs burned like they hadn't burned since winning the Charleston High relays. Fatigue brought on a flood of memories. Headlines in the Charleston *Gazette*, "Native West Virginian, Sergeant Jack Slate, Dies Heroically on USS *Panay*." Kate's face flashed across his weary mind, and for a moment he could smell her lilac perfume.

"We can't go much farther," Chaplain Scott said, coughing out his words.

The chaplain was gaunt, his eyes flat. He looked like a man having a heart attack. For the first time Jessie wondered how old he was. Forty, maybe even fifty.

Corporal Glenn struggled to his feet and spat. "What are we going to do?" he asked. "We can't push it through this mud."

Jessie got to his feet and looked around. To their right

the terrain dropped steeply down into fields of rice paddies stretching across a narrow valley. Left of the road rugged mountains rose straight up. There was only one way to Taejon, and this miserable mountain road was it.

"We don't have a choice, gentlemen," Jessie said.

"Think there's any way we can drag the stretchers, Glenn?" The chaplain's tone said that he already knew the answer.

Glenn shook his head. "Not without killing two of those men."

"I'm gonna move ahead," Jessie said, "see what we got."

"If there's a hill to climb, don't even tell me," Glenn said with a smile.

Jessie went to the cab of the Dodge. Broken Wing's eyes were closed. The bandage around his head was red with new blood.

"I'm gonna scout ahead."

"Think they take prisoners?" Wing asked dryly.

"Quit trying to cheer me up."

"I'm hungry. Want a drink too."

"I'll see if I can find a bar up here."

"Least you could do."

Jessie smiled. That sounded more like his crazy Navajo. He turned and headed south down the road. Just around the next bend the road started going slightly downhill again. His hopes rose. He walked faster for two hundred yards and around another bend in the twisting mountain road. The road continued its downhill slope for another three hundred yards. But there, at the foot of the long slope, Jessie's hope faded. His shoulders sagged at the sight of a steep uphill climb. He knew they could never push the Dodge up that hill. For an instant the thought of dying seemed very real. He shoved the thought out of his mind quickly, turned and jogged back to the others. Overhead, Corsairs broke off their attack and headed for home as Jessie rounded the bend to find himself facing the hope-filled eyes of Corporal Glenn and Chaplain Scott.

He shook his head. "It don't look good. We can go downhill for a little ways, but that's it."

Chaplain Scott bowed his head for a moment as if in prayer, then looked up. "Well, let's get as far as we can."

"I agree." Jessie said.

"Broken Wing!" Chaplain Scott called.

"Yes, sir."

"If we can get up enough momentum, put it in second and pop it good."

"Aye aye, Chaplain."

"I'm ready," Glenn said.

"Let's go," Jessie said.

They pushed with every ounce of strength to get the truck rolling. Once around the first bend, the grade started gradually downhill and they picked up speed. Two hundred yards farther, they rounded the second bend and picked up even more speed. Finally Broken Wing shouted, "Get ready!"

"Come on, baby!" Jessie pleaded.

Chaplain Scott fell onto his stomach hard.

"Ready!" Wing yelled.

He popped the clutch and the old Dodge lurched, the engine rumbled for one heart-stopping moment, then went silent. Broken Wing braked the truck to a stop. Corporal Glenn picked himself up off the ground and looked at Jessie with a pale expression of fading hope. Jessie looked past the ambulance. He tried to spit an acrid taste from his mouth but there wasn't enough saliva. There was still another two hundred yards or so of downhill run.

"Ready?"

"What?" Glenn sounded angry.

"We got one more chance. Let's push with everything."

The three men gave tight-lipped nods as they leaned against the back of the Dodge, exchanging one last determined glance at each other as they dug in for the effort.

"Ready, Wing?" Jessie shouted.

"Ready."

"One. Two. Three!"

They pushed, groaning and grunting; they knew their lives depended upon the effort. Broken Wing waited until the last possible moment. Finally, the shout came.

"Get ready!"

The three pushers shoved against the bumper with their last gasp of strength, falling forward onto bleeding hands and knees in utter exhaustion. A loud backfire choked gray smoke from the exhaust pipe. The engine coughed and fell silent as the truck rolled to the bottom of the incline and stopped. The three men stayed on their hands and knees for a few moments. It seemed impossible that it could end like this. Jessie struggled to his feet and gave a forlorn gaze back up the road.

"How much time do you think we have?" Glenn's disheartened tone said that he did not really want to know the answer.

Jessie shrugged, and sighed wistfully. "Maybe they'll stop at Chonan for a while before . . ." His words trailed off as he turned and surveyed the terrain. Four small, barren hills surrounded them. It was an indefensible position, even if there was something to defend it with.

The hot June sun dipped beneath rolling black clouds as night approached, with every man watching the hills around them. Jessie checked the extra ammo clips in his pockets for the umpteenth time and glanced pensively again at his watch. Far away, artillery echoed through the hills like distant thunder. Chaplain Scott walked forward holding a steaming canteen cup.

"How's it look?" he asked as he knelt beside the large rock Jessie sat on.

"So far so good."

The chaplain nudged Jessie with the canteen cup. "Have some."

"Thanks."

"Look, PFC. Slate. I've been thinking about what we're gonna do if they do come down that road."

"Yes, sir. Me too."

"The Lord promises wisdom to any of His children that ask. Do you believe that, PFC Slate?"

"Never gave it much thought," Jessie said, and he didn't want to think about it now either.

"Well, I believe it. I've prayed about this situation that we find ourselves in, and I've made a decision." His voice took on an official tone, and for the first time since they met at Suwon, Jessie was forced to recognize that Chaplain Scott was also Major Scott.

"I'm staying with the wounded. Corporal Glenn is too."

"Of course, sir. So am I."

"No."

"What do you mean, Chaplain?"

"The litter cases can't possibly make it."

"I know that."

"Your friend Broken Wing might be able to make it on foot with your help."

Jessie opened his mouth to object.

"No. Hear me out, PFC. Since I am ranking officer here, I've decided that the best thing for all of us is for you to try to get out and at least let the world, our families, know what happened to us."

"Now wait a minute, Chaplain—"

"I'm making that an order, PFC. The wounded will need Corporal Glenn to keep them alive, even in a POW camp, and he'll need my help."

"I'm not sure, Chaplain." A flood of emotions surged through Jessie.

"I've been a POW before, son. It might be where the Lord wants me."

"I can't abandon these men."

"I know. I'd feel the same. But you have to see that I'm making good sense. If they do kill prisoners, then you'll be saving Broken Wing's life."

"Yes, sir. I guess." A million doubts raced through Jessie's mind. He looked back toward the mountain road, grayish-colored now as daylight began fading. The chaplain slapped Jessie's shoulder and stood up.

"Just a contingency plan. Let's pray it won't be necessary."

"Yes, sir."

Jessie sat for a few minutes after the chaplain went back to the ambulance. He hoped desperately that it would not come to that, but suddenly automatic fire from a Chinese burp gun chattered from the road at the top of the hill. Jessie jumped to his feet and took aim at a dim silhouette now crouching in the center of the road. He squeezed the trigger just as more enemy fire spit down from the hill on his right. A bullet whined off a rock by his foot. Muzzle flashes blinked from the road and hill.

Jessie turned and ran back to the truck. The litter cases were on the ground beside the ambulance. Corporal Glenn stood beside them like a frightened animal, staring wide-eyed at the hills. Bullets whined off of the tire rims and thudded into the earth all around. A strange sound clattered like cymbals from the distance. Whistles blew amidst the chatter of burp guns. The maniacal screams of North Koreans resounded from their right.

Chaplain Scott ran from behind the Dodge, grabbed Jessie by the shoulders and shouted, "Now! Go! Now!"

"What?"

"Slate! It's your only chance." The chaplain's voice lowered and his eyes became steady. He smiled. Jessie's heart throbbed against his chest and terror gripped him as never before. He couldn't move.

"PFC Slate, get Broken Wing and head for Taejon. That's an order. God be with you." The calm in the chaplain's voice hushed the storm of panic raging through Jessie's mind.

The chaplain's eyes were peaceful in a way that seemed

to transcend the chaos all around them. He gave Jessie a shove.

"Go, son. My Lord is with me. Save Broken Wing. It is your duty."

Jessie could not find the words necessary. He snapped off a salute and held it until the chaplain smiled faintly, then returned the salute.

Jessie rushed over to Broken Wing, lying beside the other litter cases. He yanked the Navajo to his feet and scanned the terrified faces of the other wounded. They were looking up like little children begging to come along.

"PFC," Andy Haslam said, holding out a photo of his girl. His eyes were swelled up with tears. He said no more as Jessie grabbed the photo and shoved it in his pocket.

"I'll let her know, Andy," Jessie said, then shoved a shoulder under Broken Wing's left arm and hurried into the brush.

The shouts of oncoming Reds sounded closer. Jessie scrambled up the hill, half dragging Broken Wing along. They moved to the right side of the road under cover of thick brush, all the while clawing higher as fast as possible. Burp guns rattled from below as the North Koreans swarmed down on the ambulance. Broken Wing stumbled and groaned out loud.

"Get down," Jessie whispered. They dropped to their knees in waist-high brush and looked back at the scene below.

Chaplain Scott was on his knees beside Andy, the cowboy, a few feet from the ambulance. The first North Korean approached cautiously. Corporal Glenn stood beside the Dodge with hands raised as a group of ten North Koreans, most carrying burp guns, ran toward him. Suddenly they opened fire on Glenn. He crumpled to the ground. One of the men on the litters sat up and screamed, "No!"

A North Korean charged at him with a fixed bayonet. His scream continued as the Korean drove the bayonet through him, pushing him back and pinning him to the ground. The Korean pulled the bayonet out and ran him through again. Two Koreans with burp guns walked up to Chaplain Scott and Andy and opened fire. One Korean smiled as Chaplain Scott fell forward without a word.

Jessie and Broken Wing exchanged looks of horror. More hate welled up inside Jessie than he had ever felt in his life.

"Can you make it?"

Wing nodded his head yes.

"Let's sit tight for a couple of minutes till it's darker."

The chatter of more burp guns below told them the Koreans were murdering the other wounded Americans. They sat still for a couple of minutes. Night engulfed the ambulance, and it was no longer visible. Korean voices echoed through the hills, but they didn't seem to be moving forward, at least not for now.

Jessie grabbed Broken Wing's arm and helped him up. They struggled on over the crest of the hill, staying in the brush for a mile or so before risking the road. They walked all night, only pausing when one or the other collapsed.

CHAPTER THIRTEEN

By morning, hunger and fatigue had brought on a feeling of hopelessness. With each step forward came the urge to look back. Jessie's wound burned on the back of his neck like acid frying into his flesh, but he knew Broken Wing's pain had to be much worse. The Indian would rarely groan, but his face was twisted in pain.

"That chaplain . . ." Jessie said.

"Yes."

"He ordered me to try to escape with you."

"Yes."

"A braver man I've never seen."

"Yes. Wise and courageous."

"He should have been a Marine chaplain."

"Or a Navajo."

"We have to write their families."

"Yes. His family will be very proud. A great Christian warrior."

"If we live through this one, buddy, I'm gonna divorce the Corps and marry Kate."

Broken Wing looked at Jessie and paused as if pondering him dubiously.

Jessie glowered at Wing. "Well, what's that look for?" he barked.

Broken Wing shook his head.

"I hate when you do that, Wing!"

"Then not be a stupid man."

"I'm not a stupid man."

"Kate has form of God's mountain and God's river."

Jessie paused and looked at Broken Wing with a squint, as if the sun were hurting his eyes. "Just what the crap does that mean, you Navajo eight ball?"

"Great tom-toms. Perfect curves. You are stupid."

"God, she is beautiful, isn't she?" Jessie said sadly. Then he smiled and nudged Broken Wing to start moving again. They limped a few feet before Jessie stopped. "She probably doesn't want to marry me."

"I fix."

"What?"

Broken Wing looked at the road ahead. "I fix."

"What do you mean?"

"I fix."

"Yeah, you'll fix. You're probably dying right now, stupid."

"Am not."

"Sure you are."

"Nope."

"Well, even if you aren't, the Reds are probably going to catch us soon and kill you."

Wing's broad, brooding face took on a pensive expression.

"Oh, good grief, Wing, don't start thinking! You'll worry yourself to death."

"Should have stayed in jewelry business," the Navajo grunted, and started forward again.

Jessie stopped, gritted his teeth, and scratched hard at his crotch.

"These fleas are killing me!"

"Yes."

"I haven't seen you scratching!" Jessie snapped accusingly.

"No."

"Well?"

"Navajo hide work better."

Jessie scrutinized the Indian's expressionless face out of the corner of his eye as they continued to walk. Jessie stopped and shifted Broken Wing's weight around his neck and shoulder. He scratched the side of his head as another squad of fleas attacked.

"Wing?"

"Huh?"

"You remember when we got dropped off those trucks on Hilo, right before we hit Iwo Jima?"

"No."

"Yeah, you do. Remember the long survival march across that desert? They only gave us one canteen so we'd learn to make the water last."

"Yep."

"And we were all dying and Ogelthorpe gave up and sat down."

"Yep."

"And you gold-brickin' Navajos couldn't understand why the white man was so weak and needed so much water."

"Yep."

"We were told not to touch those plants."

"Yep."

"You were drinking water out of those plants!"

Wing nodded in recognition of the fact.

"You kept telling us that Navajos didn't need as much water."

One corner of Wing's mouth lifted slightly. It would equal an all-out belly laugh on a normal human, and Jessie knew it.

"That was low, Wing."

Broken Wing's nod was just barely an acceptance of guilt. Jessie looked accusingly at the Indian Marine.

"Now fess up. What's keeping the fleas off you?"

Broken Wing's eyebrows pinched together.

"Come on, out with it!"

Wing grunted and reached for the inside pocket of his dress green jacket. He pulled out a small gray can of flea powder. He held it protectively for a moment, then handed it over like a kid giving up his candy to an angry teacher.

"You rotten swab jockey. I hope you're ashamed. . . . Blood brother . . . I named your son . . . sister to a swab jockey . . . If it wasn't for me, you'd be a civilian, for God's sake. Some thanks . . ."

Three hours later Jessie had run out of guilt-inducing remarks and the two staggered silently along the mountain road. Near the top of a steep incline Broken Wing suddenly gripped Jessie's shoulder. He turned his right ear toward the crest of the road ahead.

"Get off road!" Broken Wing said as he pulled Jessie toward scrub brush and dwarf trees to the right side.

They flattened out in the wet brush. Jessie gripped the M-1 and aimed at the crest of the hill. He nudged Broken Wing. "Should I fire if it's Reds?"

"Don't know."

A shiver of panic ran down Jessie's spine. "Well, they don't take prisoners, buddy."

Wing looked hard at Jessie. His piercing black eyes said all that needed to be said. Jessie turned back to the road with his finger gently touching the trigger. That familiar empty sensation of suspense gnawed at the pit of his stomach. He suddenly felt very hungry. A moment later the round shape of an American helmet bobbing up and down appeared on the crest of the hill. Jessie exhaled as his chin dropped to the butt of the rifle. He looked at Wing. Broken Wing's eyes were closed in prayer, and for an instant Jessie felt as though he were intruding. Soon two columns of American GIs walking along the ditches on both sides of the road came over the hill. Jessie got to his knees and waved. "Hey, GI! How 'bout a lift?"

The lead soldiers dropped to their knees, aiming in Jessie's direction.

He held up his hands, waving. "We're Americans!"

"Hold your fire!" A young officer ran forward with his arm raised.

Jessie helped Broken Wing to his feet and they hobbled back onto the road.

"Marines?" the officer said in disbelief.

"Yes, sir. Attached to KMAG. We're advisers to the K.M.'s."

The tall man began to laugh out loud as he turned back to his halted column and waved someone forward. "Sergeant Mendez."

A chunky, round-faced sergeant hustled forward.

"Yes, sir, Major Kurt."

The handsome young major had a contagious smile and good-natured laugh. Jessie instantly liked the guy, even though he was a doggie.

"Forgive my laughing, Marines, but about—"

"I'll be MacArthur's mother!" the sergeant blurted, his eyes bulging in an unbelieving stare at Jessie's uniform.

The major looked at the sergeant and laughed again, then turned back to the two Marines.

"About five minutes ago Sergeant Mendez here was just griping about you guys. He just finished saying, 'Why ain't those glory-hound Marines over here in Korea? They're supposed to be the first in.'"

The major chuckled again, and the sergeant just shook his head in disbelief.

"Well, what are you doing out here?" Sergeant Mendez asked.

"We just got back from a thirty-day leave and were trying to report back to our K.M. unit."

"We got nicked in Seoul."

"You two were in Seoul?" Sergeant Mendez asked.

"Yeah," Jessie said. "Where are you guys comin' from?"

The major nodded back at the two columns of soldiers kneeling in the ditches along the road.

"I'm leading two infantry platoons from the 34th Regiment, 24th Division, to scout out Chonan. The 24th Division is forming up at Taejon right now, and HQ says we didn't need to pull back that far south. They want me to check Chonan, see if we can't stop the Reds there. If so, the rest of the division will move up."

"We just came from there," Broken Wing said.

"How's it look?"

Jessie shook his head. "Reds hold the town, Major. We've been running from 'em with some wounded out of Suwon. They massacred our guys north of Osan."

"I know." The major looked around. "Where are the others? Your wounded?"

"All dead. The gooks murdered them while they lay in their litters."

"Killed a chaplain and a medic too," Broken Wing said. "They don't take prisoners."

The major and sergeant exchanged angry glances.

"We saw at least one Russian T-34, Major. Could be more."

"I was afraid of that," the major said.

"Those 2.6 bazooka's just bounce right off the T-34. At least that's what we've been told, Major," Sergeant Mendez put in.

"I think the 2.6 will work, sir." Jessie said. "They have to be fired at close range, twenty-five to fifty yards, and the impact can't be less than a forty-five-degree angle or they just bounce off. Still, it would be nice to have the new 3.5s."

"The 2.6s are all we have. These troops aren't ready for war any more than their equipment." The young major's voice rang with disgust.

"Where they coming from?" Broken Wing asked.

"Anywhere the Army can find a warm body," Sergeant Mendez growled.

"Most of them are from Japan. They're throwing clerks and typists and every man they can find into this. Half of these boys haven't fired a weapon in over a year."

"How about tanks, Major?" Broken Wing asked.

"I guess they're on the way from somewhere, but they're not in Korea. MacArthur committed troops with Truman's okay. We just have to hold on until America can mobilize. That's the orders I have."

"Sounds like cannon fodder to me, sir," Jessie said.

The young officer gazed back at his baby-faced troops. "Well, we have to hope that the North Koreans will change their minds when they see that America has entered the war."

"They do not bluff, sir," Broken Wing warned.

Major Kurt nodded but didn't answer. He turned to Sergeant Mendez. "Get these Marines a medic and tell the men we move out in five."

The medic was as green as the rest of Major Kurt's men. He ran forward, took one look at the bloody bandage around Wing's head, and gleefully dove into his work.

The first probe at the back of Broken Wing's head brought an angry response from the testy Navajo. "What are you doing?" he barked.

"Quiet, PFC. If I can get this shrapnel out, would you mind if I keep it . . . sort of as a souvenir?"

Broken Wing turned on the greenhorn with a murderous glare. Jessie laid a calming hand on Wing's shoulder.

"No, Wing. They might need this kid in a few minutes."

Broken Wing relaxed slowly. "Just bandage it," he said.

A few minutes later the medic had Wing hooked up to a bottle of plasma and lying flat. Major Kurt said something to Sergeant Mendez and walked over to the wounded Marines. He looked down at Broken Wing.

"The doc says you need to lay still for a bit before you move anymore."

"Yes, sir."

"We're moving out. I've got a jeep and another medic ready to take you back to Taejon. But Doc says you should lay still for a couple of hours before getting bounced over this pothole called a road."

"Think he is right," Broken Wing said with his eyes closed.

"Good luck, Major," Jessie said.

"Thanks. Let's hope they think the whole U.S. Army is in Korea and head back north."

The major chuckled and gave a thumbs-up, then headed back to the road.

"Move out!"

A couple of hours later the Army medic helped Broken Wing onto a stretcher lying across the back of his jeep. Jessie sat up front. Sounds of heavy firing from the direction of Chonan began echoing clearly through the Korean hills. Broken Wing lifted his head from the stretcher to listen, then fell back.

The drive to Taejon was slow. The medic did everything he could to lessen the jarring bumps, but nothing worked except going slower and slower, until walking would have been just as efficient. An hour down the road, a long column of American soldiers appeared. They were moving fast. Almost double time. The jeep stopped near the point of the long column and an older officer ran forward.

"You men from the 34th?" he asked.

"No, sir," Jessie answered. "We're Marines."

"Marines? Where did you come from?"

"We were attached to KMAG, sir. We're advisers to the K.M.'s."

"I'm Lieutenant Colonel Backus."

The medic gave a salute. "I'm with the 34th, sir. Major Kurt told me to take these men to Taejon."

"We heard what sounded like a pretty heavy firefight, Colonel," Jessie said.

"Do you have any idea of the enemy strength, Marine?"

"Not really, sir. We did see at least one tank at Chonan, and I'd guess it was at least a company's worth of Reds that caught up to the eight of us two miles south of Chonan."

"Where's the rest of your group?"

"Murdered," Jessie said. "Bayoneted in their litter cases as they lay pleading for their lives."

The colonel's face grew taut.

"Shot Chaplain Scott as he prayed over the wounded," Broken Wing said.

"The chaplain ordered me to help PFC Wing here and try to make a getaway."

"There was nothing we could do," Broken Wing said.

The lieutenant colonel's eyes welled up with tears and anger. "Bill Scott was the finest man I've ever known. I couldn't imagine him dying any other way. Thank you, men. I'll see that his family gets the word."

Jessie searched deep into one pocket and pulled out the girl's photo. He handed it to the colonel. "Here, sir. One of the wounded soldiers gave me this. Private Andy Haslam. Maybe you would have the pull to find her."

The colonel took the photo and put it in his pocket. He looked grim and resolute.

"What have you heard from Major Kurt, sir?" the medic asked.

"He's dead. They must be in pretty serious trouble. The man who radioed for help was a corporal."

The young medic turned to Jessie with a pale, determined expression. "Are you well enough to drive back alone?"

"Take off, Corporal. We'll be fine."

"Lieutenant Colonel Backus. Request to come with you, sir."

The lieutenant colonel looked at Broken Wing for a moment, then at Jessie. "Can you make it?"

"Yes, sir. Let the man do what he has to do."

"Fall in, soldier."

With that, the lieutenant colonel turned and waved the long column forward. Jessie sat still on the side of the narrow road until the relief battalion of the 34th Regiment had passed. He cranked up the engine and drove about a mile before he had to pull over again as two small columns of ammo trucks hauling 105mm guns sludged by.

It was nearly dark when Jessie stopped the jeep in front of a small Army aid station beside the road, just outside a quiet village. The station was chaotic with activity. Wounded soldiers were everywhere. A row of stretchers with dead Americans covered by ponchos lay beside the main tent. Four smaller tents had been thrown up around the big tent, and they all looked crowded. Jessie helped Broken Wing out of the jeep. An Army medic spotted them and came forward to put an arm under Broken Wing.

"Where you from, 34th?"

"No. We're Marines."

The medic took another look at their uniforms. "Marines?"

"Yeah, we're attached to the K.M.'s. What's the situation?"

"Bad. Real bad. We got a couple of stretchers you can camp on till a doctor gets to you. You'll have to lay outside, though."

It was the next morning when Jessie felt the first tug at his blood-soaked bandage. His neck burned like someone was putting out cigarettes on it.

"Hold still, Marine. You got a pretty good infection here."

Jessie opened his eyes. A middle-aged man in a blood-splattered smock had rolled him onto his side and was cutting away the crusty bandage.

"How's my buddy, Doc? The Navajo Marine?"

"You'll both be fine in two or three weeks."

"Where is he?"

"Got him in the big tent. Had to cut some steel out of his head."

"He'll be okay?"

"Yes, if we don't get overrun."

"That bad?"

"That bad."

Twenty-four hours later the aid station packed up in a hurry and moved south toward Taejon along the rugged, mountainous road. No one was sure of the date anymore, but it was in the middle of July. The days ran together, each one hot and miserable, except for those that were hot, *wet*, and miserable. Wounded men were forced to lie on stretchers in the rain, covered by ponchos when possible. Jessie's infected wound and the medication to treat it kept him drowsy. Someone laid a poncho over him and he slept again.

He opened his eyes. A tent roof was over him. Rain slapped against it, and occasional thunder that made the canvas quiver.

"Move it!"

"Get that equipment in the corner!"

"Corporal Rowles! You and Barnes get that patient with the head wound first!"

"Yes, sir."

Jessie tried to sit up, but a hand pushed him back down. His whole body ached with fever and fatigue. He felt incredibly weak.

"Where are they now?" a nearby voice asked.

A sudden spray of machine-gun fire hit something just outside of the tent. Jessie's heart jumped against his chest.

"Does that answer your question, pal?" someone shouted.

Jessie rolled left and blinked away the blur of drug-induced sleep. A soldier with both arms bandaged all the way to his shoulders lay in a cot beside him. He had a cap beside him with a lieutenant's bar. The soldier was very young and his eyes were frightened.

"Hey, Lieutenant, what's up?" Jessie asked. "Where am I?"

"A clearing platoon. Taejon. Medical Company 34th Infantry." He spoke in quick spurts, his frightened, dark eyes searching the chaotic tent with each verbal burst. He had curly brown hair, long, lean features, and a stomach like a washboard. Jessie blinked his eyes. He had a pounding headache.

"What day is this, Lieutenant?"

"I don't know. Nineteenth, I think."

"What's going on?"

"We set up to defend Taejon."

"The 24th Division?"

"Yeah. I'm Lieutenant Millini. First Battalion, 34th Infantry. We're about half strength."

"Half?"

"Yeah. Third Battalion's even worse. Got mauled. Out of five companies, they just formed up what was left into one understrength company."

A huge explosion shook the tent. Jessie shot up.

"How long have I been here?" he shouted at a medic rushing past.

The medic didn't answer him immediately, but instead looked at Jessie for an instant and shouted to someone outside of the tent. "Hey, the Marine with the fever made it!" He looked back at Jessie. "You've been out for a few days. Your wound got infected bad."

"Where's my buddy?"

"Don't know," he said as he rushed out of the tent.

Jessie turned back to Millini. "What's our situation, Lieutenant?"

"We got the 21st Infantry holding a blocking position south of Taejon. But they were below half strength when they set in."

"Isn't there a big river around Taejon?"

Lieutenant Millini sat up, staring straight ahead like a man in shock. "Kum River," he said. "We blew the bridges. Somehow they forded the river in strength. No way to stop them. Only two officers left in the regiment yesterday."

Someone on the outside of the tent began shouting. "Hey! There's a tank at the end of the street! Tank!"

"Yeah, I see it!" another man yelled. "We got a tank coming!"

"Is it ours?" someone yelled.

Raking machine-gun fire ripped gaping holes through the tent walls. Jessie rolled off his cot and scrambled out through the tent flap. He scanned the area. The aid station sat at a junction where three roads came together. Four ambulances were parked in a semicircle with motors running. Litters with badly wounded men lay everywhere. He crawled on hands and knees toward a row of litter cases lying nearby and checked the faces of each man. Broken Wing was not among them.

An earsplitting explosion flattened Jessie onto his stomach. Medics scrambled for cover and weapons. Jessie brushed debris off himself and looked down the road to his right. One hundred yards away a Russian T-34 tank straddled the road. White flame shot from its cannon. A ripping blast struck behind Jessie. He pulled his face out of the red dirt and looked back. His tent was a scattered pile of flaming canvas. Jessie pushed to his feet and ran back. Lieutenant Millini lay in the rubble, his left leg on fire, but there was no agony on his face or life in his chilling, dead stare.

"Get that bazooka over here!" a panicky voice shouted.

A soldier ran past the burning tent carrying a bazooka and a single round. Jessied pulled his gaze away from the dead lieutenant and watched as the soldier dove to the side of the road. He loaded the round, checked behind him, and fired. The back blast was vicious. All eyes strained, each man praying for a hit. The bazooka round landed square on the turret with a sharp blast that did little more than burn paint from the monster. The tank fired again, and again debris exploded over the area. The tank's engine rumbled and black smoke blew from its exhaust. Jessie cringed. The beast was coming, and there was no way to stop it. Abruptly, without explanation, the tank spun around and headed back down the road.

"Wonder why he didn't roll over us?"

Jessie turned to see who was talking. A wounded soldier on a litter had his eyes glued to the retreating tank. His head shook like an old man losing control. Nineteen at the most, Jessie thought.

"He's waiting for infantry, kid. To cover his flanks."

The soldier looked at Jessie for an instant, then nodded as if a light of comprehension had been turned on.

"Get 'em loaded! Let's get out of here now!" a medic shouted with all of his might.

Someone tugged on Jessie's arm. "Can you sit up, pal?"

Jessie turned around to face a soldier with a nose like Jimmy Durante. "Yeah, think so." He took a step, then felt woozy and staggered back.

"Hop in that ambulance! Grab a rifle and ride shotgun! Help me with this litter first!"

Jessie took a deep breath and forced himself to follow the medic to the row of wounded on the ground nearby. They loaded two stretchers into the back of the ambulance. Jessie squatted to lift the third. Everything went gray and began to spin. He felt himself falling forward onto all fours.

"Hurry up!" someone yelled.

"I need a hand over here!" The medic shouted.

Jessie shook the cobwebs from his brain and struggled to his feet. The stench of burning flesh was strong. He felt sick. He turned away and began to vomit, belching up the kind of bile that forms only in an empty, terrified stomach. Flies had covered the brown vomit before it finished splashing to the ground.

"Can you ride shotgun?"

Jessie shivered, then felt better. He nodded.

"Hop in the cab. Jones will help me load them."

"Where's the rifle?"

"In the cab. You going to be okay enough to hit a gook?"

"With my eyes closed I shoot better than anyone in the Army."

The medic turned away as if he hadn't heard the wise-crack. "Hey! Somebody get the lieutenant's dog tags!"

A few minutes later the tiny convoy of three jeeps, a quarter-ton truck, and four ambulances pulled out. A jeep with two stretchers wired down where the passenger seat should have been led the way. Jessie's driver drove their ambulance in the second spot behind the lead jeep.

Jessie checked the M-1 rifle to make sure it was loaded and put the barrel out the window. "Where we going?" he asked.

"Pusan. Wherever that is."

"You don't know?" Jessie asked.

"Look, Mac, I've only been in this stinking country for a week!"

"If that's the case, maybe we better let me lead this convoy. I think I can get us to Pusan."

A sniper round slapped through the hood of the ambulance. They raced along a deserted street littered with everything from dead animals to a burning DeSoto. The convoy skirted around the carcass of a large, dead, headless mule. The head of the mule was still harnessed to an old wooden cart, separate from the body. The lead jeep turned down a side street as a burst of machine-gun fire came from up ahead. The convoy went a block and turned left then slid to a halt, the lead jeep stopping just a few feet from the rear end of a Russian T-34 tank.

"My God!" the medic with the Durante nose shouted as he slammed the ambulance into reverse and peeled out.

Miraculously, the tank never spotted them. The convoy reversed direction and found a route around the T-34. Two blocks down and left again, the convoy again squealed to a halt. A burning, overturned quarter-ton truck blocked the way. Four dead GIs, still gripping their weapons, were scattered around it. The lead driver jumped out and checked each man, snatching dog tags as he went from body to body. He ran back, slammed his jeep into gear, and sped around the burning truck.

The road ahead was littered with grenades, electrical wire, and debris of all kinds. They raced through a series of back streets until they finally stumbled onto the main street again.

The road south looked clear, but North Korean troops were firing down on them at will from the mountains around the city. Each vehicle in the convoy floored it for a mile. Suddenly, an enemy machine gun opened fire from the window of a three-story building. The lead jeep swerved out of control and the driver fell back dead, his head exploding like a broken watermelon. The jeep crashed into a pole, sending the two wounded men flying like rag dolls into the side of a building. Gunfire erupted from all sides. Bullets smacked through the cab of the truck.

Jessie gritted his teeth and opened fire on a man in white shooting from a second-story window. The man dove back. The driver stomped the gas pedal while Jessie opened fire on another enemy soldier leaning from another window with a burp gun. Glass exploded from four quick rounds and the soldier fell back. Jessie gasped for breath, his heart pounding. Two blocks later the incoming fire subsided.

"Can you see if the others made it?" the medic asked.

Jessie leaned out to look back. They all seemed to be there. "Looks okay."

"If we can get far enough south, maybe we can make it to the First Cav lines."

"Step on it."

"Oh, my God." The medic's mumble was more like a groan. Jessie looked up. The road ahead was a gruesome scene. A convoy of at least twenty wrecked vehicles was scattered, burning, along the road. American soldiers lay dead all over. Black smoke choked the air for a quarter mile, providing cover for their escape, but it was hard to see it as a blessing.

Once beyond the city the medic stopped the ambulance along the side of the road on a hill overlooking Taejon. It was like looking back down on Hell. Here and there Jessie could see small pockets of Americans hopelessly surrounded. Long columns of North Korean soldiers and tanks could be seen entering Taejon from two directions.

Three of the wounded in the ambulances had been killed by bullets, and one medic was severely wounded. The medic with the Durante nose put a tight bandage on the back of Jessie's neck and they started off again. The wound was not serious, but it hurt, and it kept hurting. Ten miles later one of the ambulances gave out. The convoy stopped while a couple of the men tried to fix it. Somebody said a bullet went through the radiator. Two hours later they started off again. Four miles later they stopped again. The medic who had been wounded was dying.

The convoy spent the night along the side of the Taejon to Pusan road. Small columns of tired, defeated soldiers straggled past. No one knew how far back the enemy was. Common sense said they would have to stop and secure Taejon before pushing south, but you could not keep from looking over your shoulder.

The next morning the convoy had swollen to fifteen vehicles as more Americans escaped Taejon. The number of wounded had also grown and progress was slow. Every mile or two some wounded or dying soldier needed aid that could not be given in a bumping vehicle. It took four long, hot days to reach the railway station at Taegu. There the wounded were put aboard trains for the trip south to Pusan.

A South Korean soldier helped Jessie aboard the filthy passenger car. Stretchers lay across the backs of wooden benches. The stench of blood and urine filled the hot car. Soft groans followed one lone medic rushing about futilely trying to tend to all of the pain. Jessie found a place in the aisle to sit, leaned his head against the edge of a stretcher, and fell asleep wondering about Broken Wing.

CHAPTER FOURTEEN

On August 2, 1950, the First Provisional Marine Brigade landed at Pusan. It was to be an advance unit of the First Marine Division and was actually the Fifth Marine Regiment reinforced. It was the best the Corps had. The Marines swaggered off the gangplank with the usual Marine Corps attitude that said, "Show us the little turds that are causing all the trouble. We'll kick their butts and get home before Christmas."

Word of their arrival spread through Pusan like a gasoline fire. Doc Seals got a medic to drive Jessie to the dock just to watch the jarheads debark. A Korean band, made up mostly of children, showed up to play a marching song, an odd combination of the Marine hymn and "Stars and Stripes Forever." A lot of Korean schoolchildren brought flowers for the occasion. All in all, the dock area was festive.

Jessie sat in the jeep with the medic and tried not to show his excitement, but the sight of those cocky jarheads landing gave him goose bumps from head to toe. His wound was much better, but Doc Seals had insisted on no walking around. Jessie figured it would be a while before he saw action again.

Two days later he was transferred to a naval aid station in Pusan. Reports of the fighting came in steadily, along with the first dead Marines. But scuttlebutt said that the Corps was helping the Pusan Perimeter to hold, and the brigade had gone on the attack at a place called Ch'angch'on. It was the first offense of any kind for the American side.

12 AUGUST 1950

At 0630 the 1st Battalion passed through the 3rd Battalion and continued the advance as far as Ch'angch'on. Fifty enemy-abandoned motorcycles with sidecars, twenty Russian-built Ford jeeps, and numerous quantities of small arms were passed, burning or camouflaged beside the road, all having been abandoned by the enemy as the result of rapid movement of the brigade and air strikes.

SPECIAL ACTION REPORT, 5th MARINES

The North Koreans had finally gotten a bloody nose. But before the brigade could finish the job at Ch'angch'on, they were ordered to pull back to a place called Miryang by rail and truck. North Korea's elite division, the Fourth "Seoul," had broken through the Pusan Perimeter at a place called the Naktong Bulge. Army units at the Naktong could not stop the onslaught.

By August 15, Jessie's wound had healed with no sign of infection. It was time to rejoin the fight, and though Jessie knew his duty and wanted to do his part, he was scared. He was temporarily attached to D Company of the First Battalion of the First Provisional Marine Brigade as a replacement BAR man. It would be just like old times, packing around the Browning automatic rifle.

The only thing missing was that dumb Navajo. He seemed to have vanished from the face of the earth. Jessie had written Bright Morning and Kate numerous letters, but so far there was no answer. The only thing he knew for sure was that Broken Wing was not in any of the aid stations in Pusan. He was either in Japan or lying dead somewhere in Taejon.

By the time Jessie disembarked from the train at Miryang, any gung ho feelings he had mustered were replaced by an anxious stomach and butterflies the size of seagulls. From the depot, a two-mile ride in the back of an ammo truck brought him to the brigade encampment under a grove of clean-smelling pine trees along the bank of a cold blue river near a blown bridge. Naked Marines dove from the bridge like a bunch of kids playing hooky from school as Jessie and other replacements piled off of the truck. He found his way to the First Battalion HQ. A sergeant major was leaning over the shoulder of a corporal at a typewriter. Jessie knew him at once.

"Sergeant Major Erwin!"

The sergeant major stood up in surprise and twirled his silver handlebar moustache. He was bald on top, gray on the sides. Tattoos of the eagle, globe, and anchor on each Popeye forearm seemed to have grown even larger since Taku Bar.

"Slate, you old seadog!" he boomed. "How in God's own Marine Corps are you!"

"How ya been, Sergeant Major?" Jessie asked, extending his hand. Sergeant Major Erwin grasped it and shook it firmly.

"All right for an old man, Slate. How 'bout yourself?"

"Outstanding, sir."

Erwin yanked open a bottom drawer of his desk and lifted out a red and green cigar box, laid it on his desk, opened it and smiled. He held the box out with the lid open.

"Have one. You'll never guess where I liberated these in a million years. They're the best Cuban cigars made."

"Nicaragua with Gunny Killeen," Jessie guessed as he grabbed a cigar and ran it by his nose.

"Nope, guess again."

"Haiti with Gunny O'Cleary," Jessie said.

"Nope." The old man sat back and laughed.

"Philippines?" Jessie guessed.

"Nope. Took these off a dead kraut!"

"German?"

"Yep. After the fight on the Canal, the Corps sent me and about a dozen other Paramarines to England to help train some limey parachutists. That's how I missed the Choisel raid."

They spent a few minutes enjoying old memories, then Erwin said, "Come on, let's meet your platoon leader."

Second Lieutenant Perkins, first platoon, Dog Company, seemed like a good Joe. The sergeant major said he had won the Silver Star on Okinawa as a corporal. He had a wife and two girls. He was a handsome guy, about thirty years old, with reddish-brown hair, a strong chin, and a quick smile. Jessie liked him right away.

"Permission to introduce Slate to his squad, Lieutenant?"

"Of course, Sergeant Major. Anything you want," Lieutenant Perkins said.

Jessie felt honored. Reporting into a new company was never comfortable, but it was especially uncomfortable during war. You were probably replacing somebody's pal who had been killed or wounded, and nobody was going to trust you until you proved yourself in combat. Jessie understood this. He'd felt the same way in the Pacific and in China. That did not make him feel any more comfortable as Sergeant Major Erwin led him toward his new platoon and squad. He stopped in front of a half-dozen shirtless Marines sweating under a pine tree.

"Listen up! Second squad. Got a new boot here, probably ain't worth a private's pay, but here he is anyway."

Jessie was surprised by the sergeant major's remark. He turned to face the men who were all sitting up to examine the new replacement. He could not believe his eyes. There, big as a man mountain, was Christopher Diez LaBeau. His matinee-idol looks had not changed since they first met up at Camp Gillespie in 1942. He had cold black hair and cornflower-blue eyes and was built like Tarzan. Jessie hadn't seen LaBeau since Iwo Jima.

"You big Cajun goldbrick! What are you doing here?"

"Slate!" LaBeau shouted, sprang to his feet, and ran forward with his hand out. "I heard you were dead a dozen times."

"I thought you got out of the Corps in 'forty-five."

They clasped hands and he and LaBeau traded slaps on the back. "Yeah, I did. Worked on oil rigs for a bit, not too far from my home there in Baton Rouge. Hard work. So I tell myself, 'LaBeau, the war's over. The Corps might be a good place to relax.' And somebody told me that they were discharging all the Yankees out of the Corps."

A couple of the other men began laughing.

"Where's the Wingman, Slate?"

A hollow feeling in the pit of Jessie's stomach began to ache. He shook his head. "Don't know yet, Chris. We got separated in Taejon."

"You been here awhile?"

"Yeah. We were training the K.M.'s. We've been here since the day it started. Wing got hit in Seoul. I got hit too, but not bad. His was worse, a head wound."

"Bet a month's pay that crazy Wing will turn up. When's your cruise over?"

"Forty days."

The other men groaned with envy. Sergeant Major Erwin laughed an evil laugh. Jessie turned a scowl toward the sergeant.

"What's so funny?"

"You can put that rice on hold, Marine. You ain't going nowhere till this war's over."

Sergeant Erwin turned to the men.

"Slate will be your new BAR man. He's no recruit, lads. You're bloody lucky to have him. Introduce yourselves and saddle up. After chow, we're moving by motor to the Naktong River. Seems the Army can't live without us."

The men gave a collective groan. A short, dark-haired, muscular Marine stood up and extended a hand to Jessie. "Welcome aboard. I'm Sergeant Rosett, squad leader." He turned toward a gaunt-looking man beside him. "This is PFC Murray. He'll be your partner on the BAR. That's Sands and Skeeter over there."

A couple of the other men nodded and went back to writing letters. They could have been brothers, both tan and blond with round faces and sunburned cheeks.

"Where's my piece?" PFC Murray asked. He was bony, with a high-bridged nose and washed-out brown eyes.

"Get over to supply and requisition a rifle," Sergeant Major Erwin ordered. "Better hurry, Marines. We have some special chow cooking down at the mess area."

"It's too hot to be hungry," somebody griped.

"What's next, Sergeant Major?" a tall, lean, red-haired kid asked as he put his shirt back on.

"Chow."

"No. I mean, where's the outfit going? What's up at the Naktong River?" He sounded anxious with excitement, which seemed odd since there was very little to be excited about at the moment.

"Gather 'round, mates."

The sergeant major searched the equipment lying about and found a bayonet. He squatted down and started drawing in the dirt. The squad huddled around him quietly, putting everything else aside for the moment.

"It's looking like this, lads. The skipper tells me the press is calling this the Pusan Perimeter, and that pretty much sums it up. The Army got itself pushed all the way to here." He drew a rough picture of Korea, then scratched a semicircle around the little part that the army occupied. "We got nothing more than a toehold. This rectangular area is all we have left, about fifty by a hundred miles. This is east, and the line of defense ends at the Sea of Japan, so they'll not be flanking us. The southern boundary would be the Korea Strait, and they'll not be flanking us that way either. ROK divisions holding the mountains here are in a good position. The Eighth Army is holding this line here." He drew along the line that marked a portion of the perimeter running south. "This would be the Naktong River, wide and deep, they tell me. The enemy is trying to break through all along this line by crossing the river and attacking where the Army line is thin. Our job is to—"

"Play fireman," the red-headed kid grumbled.

At 0400 word came and the Marines stumbled aboard trucks in the dim moonlight. The road was rough and Jessie felt fidgety.

"Hey, Slate."

Someone nudged him. It was PFC Murray. His long, thin face was outlined by a quarter moon.

"Yeah."

"If I get wounded today, write my wife. Tell her I'm okay?" He spoke in quick, nervous bursts and his washed-out brown eyes darted back and forth.

"Yeah sure, Murray. But don't get yourself killed. I hate writing letters."

"Nope. Won't get killed now," Murray said assuredly.

The truck convoy stopped and off-loaded the Marines. The company gunny rushed by the column spreading the word. "Prepare for a forced march. Move it."

The march was probably eight to ten miles. The company left the road and climbed up a steep hill. They set in along the slope near the top. Their hill was part of a sprawling mountain range that curved around a large rice paddy below. At the other end of the paddy was a higher ridge in the same mountain range. D Company was up there. Must have been a nice little farm before the war, Jessie thought. Some poor sap trying to get away from it all with the wife and kids. That's what he ought to do, he told himself. Him and Kate and a little bed and breakfast. Yeah. He liked it.

Someone rustled the brush behind Jessie's position.

"Sergeant Rosett, tell your men to gather 'round."

The short, wide sergeant stood barking, "First squad, get over here!"

The lieutenant began drawing in the dirt with a bayonet

as the men scooted closer. He seemed edgy at first. Jessie wondered what the guy must be feeling. A bad decision by a lieutenant could get a lot of men killed.

"Now listen up. This is the river, here, and this stubby thumb formed by the bend in the river is called the Naktong Bulge. This bulge is bound on three sides by the river. Got it? The inland border is the valley out there." He looked up at the tired faces. "You follow me?" No one spoke, but some men nodded. He rubbed his strong chin hard with his dirty palm. He looked and sounded tense. He scratched a line in the dirt through the bulge.

"Now, this line is Yongspan Road. Comes from the east, reaches the bulge, the stubby thumb, and stops at the tip of the thumb. The bulge itself is a natural fortress of mountains. These two hills here guarding the road are called Finger Ridge and Hill 207. There's a village here in the gully by 207 called Tugok. I think it's abandoned, but I'm not sure. It's Army responsibility. Directly east, here, is Obong-ni Ridge. That is our objective. Stand by."

The lieutenant stood and moved toward the next squad. The men continued staring at the dirt map after Lieutenant Perkins was gone.

"Any questions?" Sergeant Rosett asked. No one spoke. Jessie started to ask a question but decided not to. Didn't matter anyway, he thought. No matter how long he studied a map, be it a dirt map or the real thing, he just couldn't quite figure them out. He hated maps.

CHAPTER FIFTEEN

Jessie stared pensively as the first gray shafts of sunlight crept over Obong-ni Ridge. It looked like a sea monster spread along the river's edge. It was a series of hills growing taller, with gullies dropping between some and a spiny ridge connecting others.

"Looks like it's starting," Murray said dryly. He pointed at a flight of dark blue Corsairs sweeping in low over the distant hills.

One by one they ripped in over the rice paddy and dropped 500-pound bombs on the crest of the sprawling ridge. They swept in again, this time delivering napalm. The planes left and artillery whistled low overhead like passing freight trains. The mountain erupted. Artillery fire was terrifying, but it looked inaccurate. Some rounds completely missed the ridge. A few minutes later the artillery ceased and a formation of Marines started sweeping across the rice paddies below, walking straight toward the enemy hill that had been pounded.

Suddenly, enemy fire struck the Marines on the paddy. It was coming from the other flank, which was supposed to be secured by an Army outfit. Men all along the ridgeline began cursing the Army as they watched fellow Marines being cut down. By the time they reached the foot of the enemy hill, they had lost twenty percent of the first and second platoons. Navy Corpsmen ran in under intense enemy fire, again and again retrieving fallen Marines. Their bravery sent goose bumps down Jessie's spine.

"Lay some fire on that enemy ridgeline!" a deep voice bellowed from somewhere nearby, and Jessie aimed the BAR at targets he couldn't see. He opened fire into the brush and trees. The attacking platoons rushed up the hill in teams. From Jessie's vantage point, he could see small explosions erupting all around the attackers. The gooks were rolling grenades down on top of them. The Marine advance halted about halfway up. The intense fire looked accurate. It was hard to tell where it was all coming from. Another barrage of American artillery ripped by low overhead. The enemy ridgeline began to explode as if small volcanoes were erupting and tearing it apart. When the artillery ceased, the Marines began the assault again. They started rolling back down the hill like limp dolls. The assault halted.

A few minutes passed, then D Company watched in helpless agony as the two platoons began attacking yet again. Artillery fire roared overhead and phosphorus shells exploded like white-hot lava along the enemy hilltop. More Marine units swept across the rice paddies below. Again enemy fire from the supposedly secured left flank began to cut the Marines down.

"Saddle up!" Lieutenant Perkins bellowed.

"Next batter up!" some wise guy shouted nearby.

Jessie looked around. Sergeant Rosett was with Lieutenant Perkins. They came forward and waved the men to follow. The platoon moved along to the end of the ridge, then down into a gully and across a road that Jessie had not known was there. A burned-out Russian tank sat in the road, and beyond that was a small village. They crossed the road and walked into a stand of pine trees. A loud, irritating buzz caught everyone's attention. Four dead soldiers lay among the trees. One was cut clean in half and millions of flies were feasting on his separate halves.

The hill grew steep quickly. The Marines climbed past a heavy .30 caliber machine gun that was firing up at the ridge, but no one could see the target. The air was thick with gunpowder. Dark blue Corsairs swooped above in a strafing run that rained empty shell casings down on the advancing Marines. Somebody cursed, burned by the casings.

"Think you can wait for a Corpsman?" a Marine replied sarcastically.

Soon the crest of the hill was in sight. Up ahead Marines were flattened out behind a small rock wall that some farmer had, thankfully, built many years ago. Enemy machine guns opened fire. Somebody shouted for a Corpsman.

"We got wounded over here!"

Jessie scrambled forward to the wall, crawling over two dead Marines. Men were diving for any available cover. Jessie reached the wall and peeked over. Fifteen yards uphill a young, blood-splattered Marine was trying to drag two others back to the wall. Jessie jumped over the wall to help him. At that instant an enemy machine gun riddled all three Marines with bullets. The enemy gun kept pouring lead into the men, while Jessie could do nothing but lay in the dirt and watch. The enemy gun stopped firing. Streams of blood ran downhill from the dead Marines.

Dirt kicked up in front of Jessie's face. He searched for the enemy. Nothing. He rolled back toward the wall and scrambled over it. Whining bullets ricocheted off the stones, sending chills down his spine. He felt something wet and warm running down his right leg and knew he'd just wet his pants. Anger shot through him like a bullet. He jumped to his knees, lifting the BAR over the wall as he yanked back the bolt, cocking the action, and sent a twenty-round magazine into the ridge above. Still nothing, except brush, rocks, and trees. He ducked down and the rock wall sang with enemy bullets bouncing off it.

"Move out! Move out!" somebody shouted, and the men slowly crawled over the wall and proceeded uphill. Enemy fire rained down. Four Marines dropped in a bloody heap.

"Pull back!" an angry voice screamed over the chaos. "Corpsman!"

The men fell back again, flattening out behind any cover possible. No one moved.

"Listen up!" Perkins shouted. "A squad reached the crest of that part of the ridgeline to our right!"

They huddled under fire for what felt like only a few minutes, though the sun had dropped significantly in that time. Suddenly, Lieutenant Perkins charged uphill, screaming, "Attack! Charge!"

The wounded were left behind the wall as those still able started the attack again. Jessie slapped Murray's helmet and scrambled over the wall behind LaBeau. Heavy Marine artillery whistled overhead, then slammed into the hilltop with frightening velocity. The ferocious barrage suppressed the incoming fire, and, slowly but surely, what was left of the platoon reached the top. Fire teams charged over the crest of the ridgeline.

The men dove into abandoned enemy trench lines and foxholes. Jessie's heart pounded out blood and adrenaline until it sounded like drums in both ears. Sickening sights were all around. Naked, bloating flesh and ghastly white faces of dead American soldiers lay scattered about the area. Most of the dead Koreans were fresh kills. The men set about frantically throwing the enemy corpses over the edge of the hill. The dead Americans were laid out in a row; somebody covered the most gruesome of them with ponchos. Heavy fighting erupted at the southern end of the ridgeline.

"Slate!" Sergeant Rosett shouted, and waved from twenty feet away.

Jessie turned away from shoveling out pieces of a dead North Korean from his fighting hole. "Yeah, Sarge."

"The lieutenant's badly wounded. I'll need you to help the Corpsman take him back to the aid station."

"Aid station?"

"Yeah. Be back before the sun sets!"

"Aye aye."

"Slate, better leave the BAR with Murray."

"Right." Jessie turned to Murray, who was cleaning the debris from a foxhole to Jessie's left. "Hear that, Murray?"

"Yeah, take my rifle. Good luck. If you see any grenades laying around, you better bring 'em back."

"Right."

Jessie followed Sergeant Rosett back to where Lieutenant Perkins had fallen. A boyish-looking Corpsman was working feverishly on him. The lieutenant's stomach was torn open; the jagged skin along the wound looked like the work of a ripsaw. They rigged a stretcher with two small tree limbs and a poncho for the long, grueling hike back to the aid station. Twice they dropped the stretcher as sniper rounds hit close by.

Lieutenant Perkins looked dead by the time they reached the road, along which dead and wounded Marines waited to be picked up and taken to the aid station a mile away. A flurry of activity greeted Jessie and the Corpsman as they lumbered up to the group of four tents housing the aid station. Sweat-drenched men rushed in and out of tents shouting orders and complaining. A short, middle-aged man with graying hair pointed at Jessie. His hand was dripping with blood.

"Stomach wound?" His dungarees were splattered with blood.

"Yes, sir," the Corpsman answered.

"Get him into that tent!" He pointed at a tent fifteen yards behind them. His eyes looked wild with fear and fatigue. "Hurry! We may have to evacuate any minute!"

"What?" Jessie barked.

"Tanks! Enemy tanks are comin' down the road! We just got the word."

Jessie and the Corpsman exchanged a wide-eyed glance, then rushed over to the tent. They laid Lieutenant Perkins down gently on a bloody, hardwood table in the center of the canvas operating room. A doctor began cutting his clothes away. Jessie knew as he turned to the Corpsman that the lieutenant wouldn't make it. He tugged on the Corpsman's sleeve.

"We better get moving, Doc."

"Yeah. But what about the tanks?" He sounded like he had a cold. His quiet green eyes were tearing up.

"Don't know. How could they get tanks around our flank and onto that road without the Corsairs spotting them and killing 'em?"

They started back down the road that led to the killing ground known as the Naktong Bulge. Half a mile later they came upon three American trucks that sat abandoned in a row, blocking the road.

"I don't like the looks of this," Jessie mumbled.

He glanced at the baby-faced Corpsman as if waiting for him to say more.

The Corpsman shrugged and wiped at his pug nose with his sleeve. "My name is Brad. Brad Cummings. I'm from Michigan. Lansing. Got a dog named Dog and a cat named Fido. Play tennis and had a scholarship to play in college, but I wanted to see the world."

Jessie's eyebrows pinched together as he studied the face of Brad Cummings. He was a calm kid, considering what he'd just been through. "Are you okay?"

"Oh, sure. I'm fine. I would just really hate to die around people who don't know me. So we can keep moving now . . . now that you know me."

Jessie blinked away a dozen questions and tried to focus his attention back on the road ahead. They moved past the trucks cautiously, but no one seemed to be around. About two hundred yards later Jessie paused at what sounded like the clattering of a powerful machine. They both turned to look back in the direction of the aid station. An M-26 Pershing tank had rolled up behind the trucks. One of the tank crew climbed out, ran to the trucks, and soon got one started up. He drove it as far off the road as possible, then went to work moving the second truck.

Jessie tugged at the Corpsman's sleeve. "We better get moving."

"Right behind you."

They picked up the pace, jogging around the bend in the road. Another fifty yards on, the road bent again, with slight slopes on either side covered with small pines and brush. Jessie stopped in his tracks from the grip of a strong hand on the back of his shirt.

"What's that sound?" the Corpsman asked.

The rumble from the bend in the road ahead was frightening. Even though the sun had set, there was enough light to see dust kicking up into the air. Vibration from a very heavy vehicle sent shock waves up Jessie's legs.

The muzzle of a tank cannon bobbed up and down as the giant came around the bend twenty-five yards away.

"Tank!"

"Get down, you idiots!" someone shouted from the brush-covered slope on the left side of the road. A Marine was frantically waving Jessie and the Corpsman back.

Jessie pulled the Corpsman and ran for the side of the road. They ended their sprint with a headlong dive into a ditch. Jessie peeked up. The monstrous Russian tank came slowly. Everything was quiet except the clamoring engine. Suddenly, bright flashes appeared at the bazooka team's position on the slope. Two 3.5 rockets ripped into the side of the enemy tank with loud bams that sent fire and pieces of metal smacking into the leaves and brush above Jessie and the Corpsman. Jessie cringed lower, then rose to watch the next event.

A third rocket shot into the wheels of the monster as the turret swiveled and all of the tank's guns began firing. Then two 75mm recoilless rifles opened fire, tearing gaping holes clean through the steel monster, as if it were made of tin. The enemy tank began to burn, sending up plumes of black smoke. A tank crewman tried to escape from the turret hatch, and gunfire erupted from both sides of the road. The tanker fell dead.

A couple of Marines on the slope near the rocket team began to cheer, but the cheer fell silent as the nose of another T-34 rounded the bend in the road. The second tank moved around the burning hulk of the first just as an American M-26 Pershing moved into position, blocking the road about a hundred yards away. The Pershing fired first, and the Russian tank rocked from a hit that tore off a large piece of steel on the right front. A second shot from the Pershing smashed through the T-34's turret. The smoking enemy tank was dead.

Less than a minute later a third T-34 rumbled around the bend and into the black smoke from the two burning wrecks blocking the road. The instant the third tank moved past the wreckage, it came under fire from everything in sight. The recoilless rifles sent rounds into it at the same time the Pershing blasted away, while the rocket teams did the same. It was quickly over. Somewhere men cheered. Jessie and the Corpsman joined in.

It quieted down again and everyone waited to see if any of the tank crewmen would try to escape. Jessie felt no sorrow for them. He kept thinking of how many untrained American soldiers had been massacred by these tanks at Taejon and Chonan and Suwon and every town in between. How many guys tried to stop these monsters with those useless 2.6 rockets that bounced off like rocks thrown by kids. After a few moments a hatch opened on the last tank and two North Koreans scrambled out. Jessie opened fire, joining in a barrage that cut the tankers down in a hailstorm of lead. They fell riddled beside their burning tank.

Incoming artillery rounds whistled overhead. Explosions followed back down the road. The Corpsman nudged Jessie.

"It'll be dark soon."

"Yeah."

"Think we better try and get back to the platoon."

"Yeah. If there's no more tanks coming down this way."

They climbed out of the ditch cautiously and made their

way around the burning hulks. Thirty minutes later they reached that portion of the ridge where what was left of the third platoon was set in a rectangular perimeter.

" 'Bout time!" Sergeant Rosett shouted from the C.P. area on the crest of the ridge.

"Me and Brad saw a tank battle, Sarge. It was right out of a movie!" Jessie exclaimed.

"Killed three T-34s!" the Corpsman added.

"Slate, go find Murray and get that BAR ready. We control about half of Obong-ni—"

"You mean this place has a name?" the Corpsman said sarcastically.

"Let's hope we don't make the name too famous. We'll be getting hit tonight to be sure. We're at less than half strength. I don't think there's half a dozen officers left in the regiment."

"That bad?" the Corpsman asked.

"I'm in command of the platoon. We got orders to hold. The C.P.'s over here, Brad. Got a couple of wounded for you to look at."

The short, wide sergeant wiped sweat from his dark eyes and looked at Jessie.

"The BAR is back there on the ridge where we're tied in by fire to B Company."

Jessie signaled a thumbs-up and made his way along a well-worn path that followed the crest of the ridgeline until he spotted a couple of helmets in a fighting hole.

"Hey, Sands. Where's the BAR?"

"Over there, Slate." Private Sands pointed toward a three-foot-tall mound of red dirt.

On the left side of the mound was a good-sized hole, probably four by four. In it sat Murray, with the BAR propped on bipod legs and pointing south. The field of fire wasn't very good, but it was too late to move.

"Murray!"

"Yo."

"Comin' in." Jessie dropped down into the fighting hole and handed Murray the carbine. "How's it look?"

"Bad. I hear the gooks still hold the high part of Obong-ni." He pointed south to where the spine of the ridge dipped and rose. The two companies had linked up there, and part of B Company was on the slope beneath the ridgeline.

"Man. This is a lousy position to try and hold," Jessie grumbled.

"You can say that again."

"How many grenades you got, Murray?"

He pointed at four lying beside five magazines of BAR ammo.

"I got three," Jessie said, placing them beside the BAR.

"Did the lieutenant make it?"

"I don't think so."

"I really liked that guy." Murray's words were barely audible. He sounded tired.

"Why don't you sleep. I'll stand first watch."

"Sounds good."

Murray slumped into one corner of the big foxhole. The sun was completely gone now, and Obong-ni Ridge disappeared in the blackness. Jessie's eyes strained to see movement, but it was too dark.

"Slate."

"Yeah."

"How long you been in the Corps?"

"Since 'forty-two."

"How many guys have you known who had premonitions? You know, guys who thought they were going to die."

"I don't know. A few."

"Did they die?"

"I guess a couple did. A couple didn't." Jessie tried to sound cool to the idea, but in his heart he did think there was something to premonitions.

Murray sat up straight. "Listen, I know it sounds crazy,

but from the moment I boarded ship I knew that I wasn't going home."

"Don't talk like that, Murray!"

"No. It's okay now, Slate. It had me plenty worried, I don't mind admitting."

"But not now?"

"I still get scared. But I've never prayed so much in my life, and it's really helped. Funny. I was raised in a church-going family and all, but I always just went through the motions. I used to think that Jonah and Moby Dick were from the same story." Murray laughed quietly.

"So what's changed?"

"Me. I've changed. I prayed for a sign from God that would make me know that He's hearing me."

Jessie glanced back at the bony Marine and snickered. "Everywhere I go I keep running into people talking about divine providence. It gets a little spooky. Especially when they start claiming God sends them signs."

"He does use signs. I stumbled across a verse, first verse I ever memorized in my life.

"For I know the plans I have for you,
declares the Lord,
Plans to prosper you and not to harm you,
a hope and a future.

"That verse is just stuck in my mind. I think about it all day, even when I try not to. Then I got a letter while we were at Miryang. I'm gonna be a dad."

"Wow, congratulations, Murray. I got a little boy myself. He's beautiful." Jessie tried to brush away a sudden sense of sadness.

"See what I mean? It's a sign. A hope and a future."

"Sure looks that way, Murray," Jessie said, but he felt like he was blowing wind. If there was a God and He really loved people, he hadn't noticed many signs of it lately—not in this war. Or the last, for that matter.

Jessie woke Murray around midnight to take over the watch, then leaned back and fell into a restless trance. Before long, a bright light followed by a loud explosion overhead shook him awake. A 51mm illumination round exploded bluish light over Obong-ni Ridge like a miniature sun popping out of the black sky.

Jessie sat up wide-eyed. The entire ridgeline burst into small arms fire. A series of explosions ripped all along the ridge. Murray opened fire at men coming down at them from higher up. At the same time, a squad of North Koreans charged uphill toward them on Jessie's right flank. Jessie grabbed the BAR and opened fire. One of the Koreans fell back as the others paused and threw grenades. Jessie and Murray ducked down. Five quick explosions ripped the earth just below their position.

Someone to their left screamed in agony. Jessie knew it was a Marine. He peeked over the edge of the foxhole again. A group of Koreans slightly downhill and to Jessie's right jumped up in unison, tossed grenades at Marine positions along the ridgeline, then ducked down. An instant after the explosion, another squad just behind the first stood up with burp guns and charged forward, firing. Murray pulled the pin on a grenade and tossed it downhill. The explosion brought screams. Jessie opened fire as another squad stood to throw grenades at Marine positions on the right. He fired until the vibration stopped. Two enemy soldiers fell back. The illumination round burned out with a frying sound overhead. The ridge was engulfed in blackness and gunfire. Jessie shoved in another twenty-round magazine of .30 caliber ammo and took aim at the muzzle flash of a burp gun ten yards away. Murray pulled the pin on another grenade and let loose. Before the first explosion, he had another pin pulled. He tossed the grenade to their left. The white explosion brought more screams. Something thudded into the ground close by.

"Incoming!"

Jessie ducked his head, but the explosion from the enemy

grenade blew his helmet off. His ears were ringing. He looked up in time to see a shadowy figure emerge above them. The white flash from the enemy soldier's burp gun blinded Jessie. Murray fired at the same moment. The Korean fell back. Jessie jumped up and, still standing in the hole, fired the BAR from the hip. He could see nothing, but someone fell in the weeds just in front of their foxhole. He ducked back down and felt for another magazine like a blind man as he tried to fight off a wave of panic.

"Murray! Ammo!"

The sound of men running past the foxhole sent a shiver through Jessie. The strong smell of garlic permeated the hot air. Koreans carried garlic. The ridge was in chaos. Muzzle flashes spit from the black hillside like thousands of lightning bugs. Another series of grenades went off like a string of firecrackers along the crest of the ridge. The sound of men scuffling in the brush behind Jessie told him they were being overrun. Burp guns rattled off automatic bursts all around the ridgeline until Jessie wasn't sure where they were attacking from. He found a grenade, pulled the pin, and tossed it out in front of the foxhole. The explosion brought an agonizing scream. He lifted his head to fire into the blackness just as something thudded to the earth nearby. He ducked down, covering his head with his hands and grimacing so hard he could hear his teeth grind before the numbing blast slammed him to the deck of the foxhole. Bits of steel and dirt and rocks stung his back like a hundred hot stickpins poking him all at once.

Jessie opened his eyes. He was on his stomach and his head was throbbing. Every part of his body ached and burned. An illumination round burst in the air above. He blinked to regain vision and rolled over slowly. The blur of an enemy soldier rushed past the foxhole. Another Korean leapt over the foxhole and kept going. Jessie was seized by a sudden violent fear. He lay still, listening to the horror of men dying and killing all over Obong-ni Ridge. Finally the illumination round burned out. He pushed to his knees and peeked out of the hole. He could hear groups of Koreans speaking nearby. He felt for Murray again, touched a boot and shook it hard.

"Murray," he whispered.

He shook the boot again, harder. "Murray." He felt for Murray's hand. It was limp. He checked for a pulse but could feel none.

Jessie grabbed the BAR and crawled out of the hole on his stomach with the heavy weapon in front of him. He crawled toward what he guessed was the northern slope of the ridge, until he reached a sudden drop-off that had him tumbling downhill head over heels. He crashed into the trunk of a tree that smelled of pine and wondered how far he'd fallen. A burst of gunfire splintered chips of wood into his face.

"You get him?" a voice called out from the darkness.

"Don't fire! It's me! Slate! A Marine!"

"Hold your fire over there."

"All right, come on in real slow."

Jessie began to crawl downhill. The terrain leveled off a few feet later. He had no idea where he was. Another illumination round bathed the terrain in a flickering, delusive light. He could see a line of Marine positions to his right.

"Over here," a voice called from his left.

Jessie moved toward a helmet sticking out of a hole. He flattened out beside the hole.

"Who you with, Mac?"

"Dog Company," Jessie whispered as the illumination round began to burn off.

"Well, you're with Baker now. Better stay put. Just heard we might counterattack."

Jessie's back burned with tiny shrapnel bites that felt more like thorn pricks than wounds but were irritating just the same, especially with sweat seeping into them.

"What's that?" The Marine in the foxhole beside Jessie put his rifle to his shoulder and aimed at something crashing downhill through the brush.

"Psst. Baker Company?" a familiar voice called from the darkness.

"Over here," Jessie said.

A moment later an illumination round burst over Obong-ni Ridge. Murray's blood-splattered face emerged from the brush as he staggered toward Jessie's position. Jessie pushed to his feet and ran forward, grabbed Murray by the arm, pulled him back, then shoved him down beside the foxhole.

"I checked you! I was sure that you were dead."

"I guess I was knocked out. Don't remember a thing."

"You wounded?"

"No. A few shrapnel cuts."

"How'd you get here?"

"I just got up and walked down the hill."

Jessie started to speak, but what was there to say? Murray was one lucky jarhead.

The sounds of gunfire and grenades erupted on the top of the ridge to their right. The blinking of muzzles over the ridge was interspersed with large, bright flashes from grenades and a new barrage of mortars.

"Listen up!" someone bellowed.

"Pass the word over there. Stay put till daybreak," a deep voice called from the dark hillside to Jessie's left.

"Thank God," the man in the foxhole mumbled, then lifted up and called to his right, "Pass the word! Stay put till daybreak."

No one slept for the remainder of the night, and three hours later the first gray shafts of sunlight lit the horizon. A squat-looking lieutenant moved along the line of Marines burrowed into the hillside.

"Get ready to move," he ordered as he ran past, hunched-over and breathing hard.

A moment later a barrage of mortar fire ripped into the ridgeline thirty yards above and straight ahead. The barrage lasted for ten minutes, and a chilling scream followed al-

most immediately after the last round. Someone let loose
with a maniacal howl, then yelled, "Charge!"

"Gung ho!"

The ridgeline erupted with gunfire as Jessie scrambled to
his feet and let loose a fully automatic burst of fire from the
BAR. Bullets slapped through the leaves and whined off of
rocks. He knew that this charge was suicide. He'd die going up a hill that no one in America had ever heard of.

A vision of Kate flashed through his mind.

Murray ran uphill past Jessie, his face a mask of dried
blood from shrapnel wounds in his forehead. An American-
style grenade landed to their front and rolled downhill toward them. Murray shouted and dove to the ground. Jessie
hit the dirt face first, gritting his teeth and covering his helmet with both hands. The explosion blew him back downhill. He opened his eyes, and he was staring at the gray sky
above. He shook his head and felt for wounds, but he
seemed to be okay. Sitting up, he searched for his BAR. It
lay a few feet uphill. He crawled up after it. A spray of
machine-gun fire ripped the earth in front of Jessie so close
that dirt stung his eyes, and he flattened out with both
hands outstretched, gripping the BAR.

"Slate! You hit?"

Jessie peeked up from under his helmet. Murray was uphill a good fifteen yards, flattened out behind a charred tree
stump.

"Charge!"

"Charge!"

"Charge!" Somewhere along the slope a crazy Marine let
loose a bloodcurdling scream and men sprang forward
again in the uphill run.

Again the ridgeline erupted in gunfire as lead poured
down upon the crumbling line of Marines. The charge
halted as three more Americans were blown back downhill.

"Charge!" The scream came once more, and to Jessie's
right front, the squat lieutenant ran a zigzag course toward
the ridge again.

Jessie scrambled to his feet and sprinted forward. A rush of adrenaline pushed his feet faster, and he heard himself screaming. Another grenade came hurdling toward them from the crest above. Jessie flattened out.

"Grenade! Murray!"

The explosion came from behind them, blowing Jessie forward and covering him with debris. He scrambled to his feet again, grabbed up his BAR and charged.

A North Korean hiding behind a thick bush just this side of the ridgeline stood to run back up and over the ridge. Murray opened fire with three quick shots from his M-1, and the Korean fell forward on his face. A second Korean rushed to aid the first and grabbed him by his jacket. He began pulling his comrade back up the ridgeline. Jessie stopped and shot from the hip. His first round hit low. He walked the next five shots up the back of the wounded Korean and into the face of his rescuer. The man's head exploded as he fell back, still clutching his comrade.

Jessie paused, pulled a grenade from his trouser pocket, yanked the pin and lofted it over the crest of the ridgeline. The explosion brought a loud groan, and pieces of clothing blew into the air above. He charged forward again, finally scampering over the crest.

The terrain flattened out for twenty or thirty yards before plunging downhill on the western slope leading toward the Naktong River. North Koreans were in a full-out run trying to make it to the western slope. Jessie opened fire, as did every Marine reaching the top. Three Reds fell in a clump from a hail of Marine fire, but many others dove over the edge in a falling, running, tumbling escape down the steep slope. Marines rushed to the edge and fired downhill. The Corps took great pride in marksmanship. From boot camp on, each Marine knew that there were no better marksmen in the world, but Jessie had never seen it proven so thoroughly as at this moment. With nearly every shot, an enemy soldier tumbled forward dead, until the slope below was littered with dead Communists.

"Cease fire!"

"Hold your fire!"

When the firing ceased, the men stared at the carnage below until the squat lieutenant began shouting orders. The
top of the ridge was littered with dead Koreans and dead
Marines from the night before. Many of the Marines had
been bayoneted.

"Make sure each man is identified! I want the bodies laid
out over here on the double! And cover 'em up!"

Jessie and Murray walked over to their foxhole of the
night before. To the left of their position in another foxhole,
two Marines lay dead. It looked as if they had been killed
in their sleep. Each was curled up under a bloody poncho
full of bayonet holes. Seeing young dead Marines was sickening, but knowing they died because someone fell asleep
on watch made it even worse. Murray fell to his knees at
the edge of the foxhole with the two dead Marines. Jessie
lifted the ponchos from their faces and Murray began sobbing. It was Sands and Skeeter. The two blond Marines
looked like brothers even in death.

"I'll take care of 'em, Murray. Go over there and sit
down."

Murray got to his feet and walked away like a drunk.
Jessie called to another Marine nearby, and the two of them
carried the dead men to the assigned area. A row of nine
dead Marines was laid under some torn canvas tent covers.
Corsairs appeared overhead. Their gull wings tipped and
they dove down at the scarred ridge, sweeping past in a
brutal strafing run at the river's edge. The screams of enemy troops could be heard clearly. Some of the Koreans
tried to swim the river. Marine snipers had a field day from
the high ground.

Another fierce battle erupted on Hill 147. A few minutes
later word came that the third platoon of B Company
caught over 150 Reds in an orderly retreat, marching down
the slope in a column of fours. The orderly retreat had

turned into a panicked rout as Marine firepower cut into
their ranks unopposed.

"Hear that?" Brad Cummings, the Corpsman, mumbled
as he walked past Jessie with a handful of dog tags.

A furious barrage of artillery, mortars, and 500-pound
bombs from swooping Corsairs sent up a deafening cacophony of explosions echoing through the valleys and off the
hills. The earth vibrated.

"Sounds big."

"Yeah. I just came from the C.P. Percy, the radioman, got
word they caught hundreds of gooks massing at the river's
edge. It's a turkey shoot down there and—" The Corpsman
stopped in mid-sentence as a dark blue Marine Corsair
flashed past overhead with all guns blazing. Jessie dove for
cover as the 20mm cannons and .50 caliber machine guns
raked up the slope and over the ridge. Marines screamed
angrily at the plane climbing away high into the gray sky.

The Corpsman pulled his face from the dirt. He looked
pale with fright, breathing in gasps.

"You okay?" Jessie asked, then spat dirt from his mouth
and glanced toward the sky. The Corsair circled high above,
then dove down at the Naktong River with guns blazing.

"I'm okay. But you ain't." The Corpsman's voice was
low and still choked with fear.

"What?" Jessie asked. He pushed up onto all fours, and
a sharp, burning sensation stabbed deep into his back like
a dagger. He fell to his knees again. His ankle would not
support his weight.

"Better let me take a look at your back," the Corpsman
said.

"Am I hit?"

"You got a piece of wood sticking in you."

"I think my ankle's broke too, Doc."

The Corpsman picked up a large rock by Jessie's foot.
"Look. I think a 20mm round from that Corsair blew this
rock into your ankle and splintered off a chunk of tree."

Jessie grimaced from the pain that now shot from the

middle of his back up to his neck. He reached over his shoulder but could not touch the wound. He bent his left arm back under and behind him until he touched a rough piece of splintered wood sticking out just to the left of his spine.

"How big is it, Doc?"

"It's at least five inches long. I tell ya, this is really unusual. You get wounded twice and ain't even touched by metal." The Corpsman began to laugh.

"I'm glad you're getting such a chuckle out of this." Jessie's words came through gritting teeth.

"Hold still, I'm pulling this tree out of your back."

Jessie heard himself groan, and his body lurched as Brad pulled on the piece of wood hard enough to lift him slightly up.

"Air might have come out of this hole. I didn't think it went that deep, but you might have punctured a lung."

Jessie felt faint. From the heat more than the pain. Hobbling to the aid station seemed to take forever but every step away from Bloody Ridge felt like another step away from death. By late afternoon he found himself in the back of a stifling ambulance with six other groaning men. The others had more serious looking wounds than his own.

"Slow down before you kill these men!" someone bellowed.

A burst of automatic weapons fire sounded close by. A man riding shotgun opened fire with an M-1 out of the window.

The driver shouted back over his shoulder. "I slow down, we all die!"

Another burst of fire shot out of the surrounding hills, and a loud crack tore a hole in the side of the ambulance just above Jessie's knees. A blond Marine on a litter beside Jessie went limp. A bullet had entered the man's left temple and there was a clean, round hole just beside the ear.

Jessie wiped at torrents of sweat draining into his eyes and held on to the litter above him to brace himself for each pothole in the bombed-out road. The firing ceased and the ambulance slowed to a bearable speed. Jessie closed his eyes and plunged into a fitful sleep.

"You got him, Jack?" a voice said.

"Got him."

Jessie opened his eyes. He wiped at puddles of salty sweat that had formed around his eyes and mouth. It was night. A hissing locomotive sounded close.

"Hey. Where am I?"

"Calm down, Marine. We got you now. You're going to be okay." The guy had a New England accent. "We're loading you onto the Purple Heart Special for a ride back to Pusan."

Somebody stuck a morphine needle into Jessie's arm. He closed his eyes again. Sometime later a voice called out "Miryang!" The train stopped for a moment. Jessie could see that many of the men around him were in bad shape. He tried to sleep, but the groans of dying Marines felt more torturous than his own pain. Finally, fatigue and morphine won. He dozed off to a gray sleep.

The sound of an engine woke Jessie. He found himself being carried onto a plane. He looked up into an Army medic's straining face.

"Where you taking me?"

"Well, some of the guys are getting hoisted aboard hospital ships, and others are getting treated here in Pusan, but the real lucky ones with the right tag on 'em, like you, get to fly out of this armpit and back to Japan."

Jessie knew that he was not hurt that badly, but Paddy Killeen didn't raise a fool. A nice rest in Japan sounded like a trip to heaven. He smiled contentedly. His war was over, and he was going to enjoy this flight. He sighed and inhaled deeply. "Can you smell that, medic? That clean, fresh scent?"

The medic frowned.

Jessie smiled, "That's the sweet aroma of honorable discharge, pal."

CHAPTER SIXTEEN

It was only 120 miles across the Korean Strait, but it was like landing on another planet. A real bed, real hot food, a pillow and clean sheets. It was just too wonderful to be true. For the first time in ages Jessie felt clean. After two weeks he felt human again. He'd gained back some weight.

The news from Pusan was coming in via wounded Marines, two-week-old newspapers, and the letters some of the fellas were already getting from home. For the first time since the war had started, the news was hopeful.

The brigade had done its job and the Pusan Perimeter was holding. The North Korean Fourth "Seoul" Division had been flattened and shoved back across the Naktong River. What was left of it hid in the hills west of the Naktong Bulge. Prisoners taken after the battle verified that the enemy division lost all of its heavy equipment and had only a few hundred survivors in each regiment.

Scuttlebutt reports like that could do nothing but lift the spirits of every wounded Marine in Yokosuka. It was no small matter to them that the North Korean Army had been pitching a shutout until they met the Corps. One newspaper reported that captured documents verified the NKPA awareness of it. The Reds were advising all units to avoid contact with Americans wearing yellow leggings. American Marines. Pride was never in short supply where the Marines

were concerned, but even hardened old salts found it difficult not to gloat over such reports.

Jessie was working on his thirteenth letter in the last ten
days.

My Darling Kate and Charlie,

I know that I've said this in all my letters, but thank
God you and Charlie and Jeremiah finally sold the café
and are in the good old USA.

I still have not received any other letters that you may
have sent. If you mailed them to KMAG HQ in Seoul or
at Chinhae, I might never see them.

News from the war is better. The Pusan Perimeter is
holding, thanks to the brigade—that's the Fifth Regiment
reinforced. We knocked the Reds back across the
Naktong River, kicked their butt good, but just got word
that they came back. Same spot, the Naktong Bulge. The
brigade went in again. The O.D. here in Yokosuka just
posted the results, and you'd think we just got the score
from the World Series from all the cheering.

The brigade received orders to pull back on September
5. Scuttlebutt says a big amphibious landing is about to
happen. It's the worst kept secret in Korea. New casualties
arriving at the hospital from Korea already had a name for
it: "Operation Common Knowledge."

Now don't worry, honey. I'm through with the Marine
Corps. This landing is going to happen without me. I'm
sure I can go back to the States, get surveyed out, and
then it's me and you and Charlie. I'm already beginning
to feel like a civilian innkeeper.

There's only one loose thread now. I have no idea
what happened to Broken Wing after Taejon. I've written
Bright Morning, but no reply. I'm terribly worried.

I love you and miss you both.

Love, Jessie

P.S. Wounds are healing up fine. Should be heading

home soon! And my seabag caught up with me. Got my Irish pipes back!

He sealed the letter into an envelope and handed it to a nurse, then fell back grinning with his eyes closed. He felt he could almost touch Kate.

"Look stupid when sleeping too."

Jessie opened his eyes. He blinked at the vision above him. The acne-scarred cheekbones looked even more pitted than usual. Broken Wing's broad, brooding face stared down at him with absolutely no sign of emotion. Jessie blinked again and rubbed his eyes. The Navajo face was still there. He reached up and twanged the Indian's prominent nose.

"Ouch!"

"It *is* you!"

"Yes."

"You ain't dead!"

"No."

Jessie sat up and grabbed the Indian in a headlock. He hugged him and started laughing. Broken Wing grunted and straightened up as if his Indian dignity had been ruffled.

"Look," Wing said, and he pointed to Gunnery Sergeant Paddy Francis Killeen, who stood behind him, his arms folded and a pipe in his mouth, as if he were posing for a portrait.

"Paddy! Where'd you come from? It's great to see you." Jessie clasped the gunny's hand with both of his.

"And so 'tis to see you, laddie. Now why would you be laying about like this when there's a fine war to be fought?"

Jessie laughed.

Paddy pointed toward the ward doors with his pipe. "I've just been talking to your doctors, Slate, and joyous you'll be to hear that I've obtained your release from this awful place."

Jessie laughed. The edges of Wing's mouth came up. Jessie stopped laughing.

"What are you smiling about? You only smile when something is wrong."

"Here." Broken Wing handed Jessie a piece of paper.

Uniform and Equipment for Embarkation (1) Individual arms and equipment. (2) Utility with steel helmet camouflage cover, green side out, and leggings. (3) Field Transport Pack with following minimum content: 1 belt, web, trouser, w/o buckle; 1 buckle, metal, trouser, belt: 1 cap, utility; 1 coat, utility; 2 drawers, cotton, pr; 1 trouser, winter service; 2 trousers, utility; 2 undershirts, cotton; 1 razor, w/blades; 1 soap box, w/soap; 1 toothbrush, w/case; 1 comb; 1 soap, shaving; 1 toothpaste; 1 mirror; 1 handkerchief; 1 legging laces; 1 towel; 1 sewing kit; 1 sleeping bag, w/blankets.

ADMINISTRATIVE PLAN NUMBER 3-50
1st MARINE DIVISION

Jessie looked up from reading the paper and grinned. "This is hilarious, Gunny."

"Thought so too," Broken Wing said.

"Where you been, anyway? You stupid Indian, you scared me half to death! You're too stupid to write! You should have gotten word to me where you were!"

"Was just at NAS Itami. Felt good too. Now I am with the Seventh Marines. Do not feel as good."

"Nurse!" Paddy Killeen called to a young Navy nurse walking past with a tray full of pills.

"Yes, Gunnery Sergeant," she said pleasantly.

"The lad here will be needin' his things. Be a good lass and help us get to movin', will ya darlin'?"

"But he can't just get up and leave, Gunnery Sergeant."

"Aye, it's true enough, 'tis, but the lad here has a war to tend to, darlin'."

"But I don't have that authority ..."

"She doesn't have that authority, Gunny," Jessie agreed.

"Aye, but the boy's orders are being cut as we speak."

"What!" Jessie shouted. "No! I'm going home! I'm getting married! I'm a civilian in ten days!"

Paddy Killeen's thick neck grew as veins suddenly appeared. "Listen up, son of Jack Slate! Approximately seventy percent of the men hitting this beach, very soon, have come from the bloody reserves. When they formed the brigade they took every able-bodied regular west of the Mississippi. That didn't leave a full canteen for the First and Seventh regiments. And now they steal another five hundred Marines from us!"

"What? How?"

"Some bloody fool in Washington has just pushed through an order to have every Marine under the age of eighteen taken out of combat. They snatched five hundred seventeen-year-olds. Already some of the lads old enough to be hitting that beach have only a few summer meetings under their belts, not even boot camp!"

"I don't buy that, Paddy. They'd never send Marines into combat without even putting them through boot camp."

"And is it a liar you'll be calling me, PFC?" Paddy Killeen's eyes narrowed.

"Of course not, Paddy, but—"

"I need veterans! And you two are volunteering!"

Jessie pinched the bridge of his nose and closed his eyes. There was really no decision to make. He knew that if he said no, it would haunt him forever. He owed it to Wing. He owed it to Paddy. And he owed it to Charlie Rose. He slumped back in resignation and looked into the battle-aged eyes of the Irishman, wondering if he would ever see Kate and his son again. Jessie swung his legs from the bed and stood up. He grimaced from pain in his ankle.

"Ah, 'tis only your feelings that hurt. And how bad is this little pinprick, anyway?"

"They thought I had a lung punctured, but it ain't. It's my ankle that's giving me the most trouble."

"Nothing a good shot of Irish whiskey would not cure, right PFC Wing?"

Wing grinned without showing teeth.

Jessie glared accusingly at Broken Wing. "How in the world did you get out of Taejon?"

"Truck."

"Truck?"

"Truck."

"That's it? That's all of the details?"

Broken Wing lifted his chin as if a sudden wave of nobleness had swept over him. "Grass grows too slow for dog with quick eyes."

"He's a pearl," Gunny said, pondering studiously.

"Oh, brother! Don't try sounding like an Indian now."

"Pearls of wisdom, laddie," Gunny Killeen said thoughtfully.

"Don't fall for that garbage, Paddy! He just throws stuff like that out when he wants to confuse people. What he really means is that he was probably unconscious and does not have the slightest idea how he got out of Taejon."

Jessie and Paddy Killeen looked at Wing. Broken Wing stared back for a moment with his vacuous face hanging out, then he turned and walked toward the doors mumbling something about Custer.

Jessie smirked. "By the way," he said, "who's the skipper of the outfit?"

"Captain Fitch," Paddy said with an evil smile.

Jessie groaned.

"Don't worry, Slate. He's forgiven you for Tientsin.

Jessie groaned again.

Twenty-four hours later, Jessie followed Killeen and Broken Wing up the gangplank of the AKA Okinogin like a man going to prison. Memories of that first beach landing filled Jessie's heart as he made his way to the crowded 1st platoon troop compartment area. The bunks were in tiers of five and, as always, there was barely enough room to scratch your back without scratching someone else's. Packs, helmets, and weapons lay everywhere.

The clatter of dice sounded from a bulkhead. A static-filled radio blared, "This is the Honshu Hayride! Country music from your Armed Forces Radio Service!"

"One of the new lads brought one of them Trans Oceanic Radios," Gunny said as he stepped over and around clothing and equipment.

"Them bums is bigger bums than any other bums in the National League!"

Jessie stopped cold. The nasal quality of the shouting baseball critic was like hearing a ghost. He looked questioningly at Broken Wing.

"Aldo Perelli? From Bouganville?"

Wing nodded.

"And Stukowski" Wing said. "They joined up together. They stayed in the reserves. First to be called up. Still fight constantly."

"Brooklyn couldn't come up with bat boys for the Cards, Perelli!" A big, strong blond Marine with huge arms was pointing down at a smallish, banana-nosed Marine with jet-black receding hair.

"Read it and weep, Stukowski!"

Aldo Perelli and big Ski. Jessie dropped his gear and stood with arms folded. He couldn't believe his eyes or ears. Nothing had changed, the two old Paramarines were still bickering. Poor Ski didn't have a chance, as always. Perelli spit words out like a machine gun. Good old Stukowski was still about two words too slow. They were an odd twosome, joined by a love for baseball. Ski was from Newark, played Single A farm team for the Yankees for a bit; he was playing for the Padres in the Pacific Coast League when Pearl Harbor was attacked. Perelli used to work for the biggest bookie in New York and was a used car salesman.

"Ski! Perelli!" Jessie shouted.

The two Marines looked up, then ran over and started

pounding Slate on both shoulders. The four old salts went up on deck, where Wing produced a fifth of whiskey. Perelli prodded Jessie, "Hey, Slate. You ever get back with your wife? Last thing I remember about you was that Dear John you got just before we hit Iwo."

Jessie twinged with a slight pain from the memory, then glared at Gunny Killeen. "We're getting married again if I can ever get a divorce from the Marine Corps."

"You had a kid, didn't you, Slate?" Ski asked.

"Sure do," Jessie beamed. "Charlie Rose Slate."

"That's right! You named him after old Rose," Perelli said.

"I liked that guy," Ski said.

"Yeah," Jessie said quietly. "He was the best."

Perelli grabbed the bottle and took a swig.

"I remember you always working on jewelry, Chief."

"Me too," Ski said. "I remember you carving those bracelets out of that P-51 that went down on Bougainville after ol' Slate saved your life."

Broken Wing and Slate held out their right arms and pulled up their sleeves.

"You still wear 'em!" Ski exclaimed, pointing.

Wing tried to take Jessie's bracelet off. Jessie yanked his arm away.

"Yeah but not for long if this goldbrick keeps hounding me about it."

"I engraved it. I change it. Make it right," Broken Wing said defiantly.

"I don't understand John 3:16 and you ain't touching my bracelet."

"What's he want with your bracelet, Slate?" Perelli asked.

"He want's to put John 3:16 on it instead of my Wind God stuff."

The men chuckled.

"As well he should!" Killeen shouted. "And we'll be drinkin' to it, lads!"

* * *

The First Battalion, Seventh Marines proved a formida-
ble group. Most of the East Coast Rifle Team, men Jessie
had served with in the Brooklyn or Philadelphia navy
yards, were with 1/7. They were the best shots in the
Corps. Many of the reserves called up were WWII veterans
and old China hands. Some of the PFCs, veterans who had
left the Corps during the terrible purge of '47, had more
hash marks than senior officers and NCOs. The leadership
of the Seventh Marine Regiment was just as outstanding as
the Pusan Brigade had been, and the First Marine Regiment
was led by Chesty Puller, a living legend in the Corps. The
strange combination of nearly civilian kids and legitimate
old salts was striking at times. On the deck of the *Oka-
nogin*, old salts exchanged memories of Guadalcanal,
China, hot-blooded women, and slop chutes around the
globe, while young recruits asked each other where they
had gone to high school and exchanged gripes about Mom,
Dad, teachers, and football coaches.

The division was to be MacArthur's big left hook to the
flank of the North Korean People's Army at Inchon, just below the 38th Parallel and only a few miles from Seoul. In
three days 260 ships converged. Some came straight from
the U.S., some from Japan. Everybody was a bit nervous about the landing. There was no lack of confidence, but
conditions were tricky. One briefing officer said the tide-
water often dropped thirty feet, and there was a sixteen-foot
seawall to be scaled by ladders. The objective would have to
be reached and secured quickly or the division could be
stranded in the open muddy flats as the tides fell.

The Reds seemed stunned by the sudden appearance of
thousands of Marines on hundreds of ships attacking at a
point that no sane person thought they would. The Fifth
Marines, formerly the First Marine Provisional Brigade, had
done a job on Inchon just as they had at Pusan.

Some of the young Navy coxwains panicked at times,
some missed their designated landing zones, and for a

while platoon and company commanders had a totally confused mess on their hands. It got worse when a beached U.S. Navy LST opened fire at Marines on the beach with 40mm and 20mm cannons. But for the most part the landing went well, considering the speed at which it had been put together.

A couple of units got into some pretty loud fighting, but the North Koreans, caught off guard, abandoned the beachhead. Prisoners revealed that their commanders had pulled back into the city with a "stand or die" order. They were being told by Russia to turn Seoul into another Stalingrad. Seoul was the cultural heart of Korea since the 1300s. The potential for heavy casualties was a serious concern.

When the Seventh Marine Regiment landed, it practically ran all the way to the Han River after watching the USS *Missouri*'s sixteen-inch guns pound a large hill just on the other side of the river.

When Jessie's squad reached the crest of the target hill to take up covering positions for a first platoon movement, men stopped and stared in disbelief at the sight before them. A row of fifteen dead North Korean soldiers lay in their positions along the barren ridge of the hill. Their uniforms were new and bloodless. Not a mark on them. They had all died from the concussion of one of Big Mo's sixteen-inch shells.

Doc Klemawesch stood over the bodies in deep thought, plucking at his long Groucho Marx eyebrows and humming "Shave and haircut . . . two bits."

Doc Klemawesch was a typical Corpsman, always seeming to march on the port side while the rest of the world marched on the starboard. Doc K. was tall and thin, like a bayonet. The line of his short hair was very black against the white of his forehead. He was thirty years old and a former barber who had once given Tyrone Power a haircut in California.

Jessie helped set the light .30 caliber machine gun up in one of the enemy trench lines, and watched two old salts,

Perelli and a Hopi Indian named Welcome Joseph Snow-water, pick over the bodies for souvenirs. Welcome Joseph found a box of strange-looking Russian rations and a pair of glasses nearly as thick as his own. Perelli found a wallet with some family photos and a wad of North Korean script.

"Slate!" Gunny Killeen shouted from a position at the end of the ridge. He stood with Lieutenant Mitchell, who was spying out something with binoculars. The lieutenant took aim with a rifle and fired, then cursed. The gunny waved. "On the double!"

Jessie grabbed up his rifle and ran to the gunny.

"Here." Gunny Killeen handed him a Springfield 1903-A4 with Unertl scope sights. The sniper scope was nearly as long as the barrel.

"Yes, sir. What a beauty, Paddy. Where'd you get it?"

"A lad who didn't come back. The lieutenant found it."

Lieutenant Mitchell lowered his binoculars and faced Jessie. "Slate, Paddy tells me you fired in the 'forty-seven Wurgman Trophy Matches."

"Yes, sir. And the Individual Matches in the East Coast Division. Fired High Expert at Philadelphia Navy Yard in 'forty-seven."

"That's what he was doing here with the ROKs, sir. Lad speaks the lingo too."

"Here, take a look, PFC. Between those two hills." Lieutenant Mitchell handed Jessie the binoculars.

"I can see them, sir," Jessie said without looking through the binoculars.

"Probably a thousand yards."

"That's my guess, sir."

"Can you hit something that far?"

"Six hundred yards was our average distance for team shooters, sir."

The stern-faced lieutenant grunted and stepped aside. "Have at it, PFC. Get that officer who's pointing at the head of the column on the right."

One thousand yards away a company of North Koreans was forming into columns with platoon guides holding red flags. Jessie dropped to a sitting position.

"The sights are off, PFC Slate," Lieutenant Mitchell said coolly. "I tried and couldn't hit a thing."

"Yes, sir. You have to zero in by matching the crosshairs on something at around three hundred yards, like the corner of that building down there beside the road." Jessie aimed as he spoke. He put the crosshairs on the cornerstone at the top right of a gray two-story block building. "Then you take the bolt out." Jessie pulled out the bolt as he spoke. "Look down the barrel from the chamber side of the Springfield and imagine crosshairs across the end of the muzzle. Until you actually fire them for a bit, this will put you within inches of your true dope. There, that oughta have it about right."

Jessie dropped into a prone position and took aim while Lieutenant Mitchell observed through the binoculars. Jessie brought his breathing under control and zeroed in on the North Korean officer who was standing with hands on hips. He put the crosshairs square in the center of the man's back and squeezed off a round. The kick was solid against Jessie's cheek and shoulder. The enemy officer dropped onto his face. Jessie pulled back the bolt and loaded another round, took aim at one of the platoon guides holding a red flag. He squeezed off another round. The man fell back. Still the columns of enemy troops stood in their ranks, as if oblivious to what was happening.

"My God! That's Marine Corps shooting! Look at 'em, Gunny! They're just standing there! Keep firing, Slate."

Jessie squeezed off another round, and a second man with a red flag dropped. Jessie loaded and aimed. A fourth Korean dropped. Then the man directly behind him dropped. The round had gone through both. Jessie continued to fire as quickly as he could reload. Unbelievably, the North Koreans stood their ranks until a squad's worth of men had dropped. Finally, they broke ranks, scrambling for cover. But even then the targets of opportunity were overwhelming. Jessie fired and loaded and fired and loaded until his jaw was swollen from the recoil. His shoulder ached. The targets finally disappeared. Jessie lowered his rifle and tried to shake the ringing from his ears. His hands were quivering. He glanced up at the lieutenant, who was staring back in awe. Gunny Killeen stood with arms folded like a proud daddy. Jessie stood up and handed the rifle back to the lieutenant.

Lieutenant Mitchell laughed out loud. "Keep it Marine! It's yours, mister."

A wave of pride swept over Jessie as the men around the immediate area gave a cheer.

"And you should hear the lad play the pipes, sir."

"He's the one with the bagpipes?"

"Aye, that he'd be, sir. A present from me, meself."

Lieutenant Mitchell chuckled and turned to look around. "Where's the radioman? Tell him to get the 300 radio set up."

Jessie walked back over to the squad of gawking Marines. After the backslaps were over, he sat down with a can of fruit cocktail. He wondered how many men he had just killed, and he wondered why he did not feel worse. Broken Wing sat beside him quietly.

The next day Able Company Seventh Marines moved toward the outskirts of town. Meanwhile, the Fifth Marine Regiment fought through the Peking Gap, along a double-tracked railroad and down a dirt and gravel highway. Movement was slow but steady as each objective was knocked out until the Marines entered Seoul City on September 22. There they came across a squad of Marines from the First Regiment who had blown a bank vault open. Korean script bulged from the pockets of the dirty, tired Marines. Jessie wondered why they would bother. There was nothing left in Korea to buy.

The Army's Seventh Division broke across the Han as the First Marine Regiment knifed through the city in house-to-house fighting. The battle for Seoul was won. Trapped between the Inchon attack and a breakout by the American and Republic of Korea troops at the Pusan Perimeter, the North Korean People's Army was broken and running for its life after a few weeks of extremely bitter fighting. To the average Joe in the average squad of soldiers or Marines, the war was nearly over. Scuttlebutt had the whole division going home before Thanksgiving. In October the men were put on a convoy of trucks and taken to the new First Marine Division assembly area at Inchon.

The Marines were billeted in the Jinsin Electrical Works. Jessie finished his tenth letter in four days to Kate and Charlie and sealed the dirty envelope as Paddy Killeen's booming voice echoed through the cavernous electrical works. "All right, Marines, saddle up! Prepare to board! Draw your winter gear on the dock!"

"*Winter* gear?" someone screamed.

CHAPTER SEVENTEEN

When the Seventh Marines marched up the gangplanks of the LSTs at Inchon for the landing at Wonsan, it started off that same combination of thrill and fear that every assault brought on. This time there was an added sense of doubt because no one could believe that the war was not over. As Jessie reached the top of the gangplank, he knew that this trip would be different. Each Marine paused and did a double take as they stepped aboard. The crew was Japanese, which did not go over well with men who had lost buddies in the Pacific. Sergeant Stelzel spat at the deck in disgust as he came on board.

"Weren't we shootin' these guys a while back?"

"They can't drive an LST no worse than the squids!" Perelli quipped.

"Just the same, I'd rather see some bluejackets steering this floating coffin!"

"The war with Japan is over; they're friends now," a Private Cole chipped in.

The burly veteran jumped close enough to the Canadian kid to touch noses. "You ever cut a Marine down from a tree after the Japs cut his eyes out and stuck his peter in his mouth, kid?"

The young red-haired boy swallowed and looked at the deck. "No, sir, Sergeant."

"You speak when you've earned the right."

"Yes, sir, Sergeant."

Nerves got no better. The Reds mined the waters around Wonsan, and by the time the few mine sweepers available could do their job, a simple operation had turned into two weeks of misery. Soon everyone on board was sick with dysentery, along with some other strange epidemic. The short voyage had become a typical Marine ordeal. Men were put on short rations. Quarters were cramped and miserable. Doc K., the Corpsman who seemed to have the personality of a mad scientist, was the only man aboard who looked happy. He cooked up one alien concoction after another and gleefully tested them on puking Marines. He loved needles but no one was sure what good the shots did. Adding insult to misery, when the First Division finally hit the beach at Wonsan, the Marine Air Wing was already there, along with American and ROK forces that had gone overland. But by far the greatest humiliation came when the Marines discovered that Marilyn Maxwell and Bob Hope were doing a USO show as the assault troops were trying to land.

Chesty Puller's First Marine Regiment boarded gondola cars for a train ride to Kojo. The Seventh Marines boarded trucks for a ride north, and the Fifth Marines followed, relieving the I ROK Corps in the vicinity of Fusen Reservoir. Nothing seemed unusual as the 2½-ton trucks, in convoy, started up a one-lane paved road.

"We'll be home for Christmas. Bet you a convertible Packard," Perelli said confidently as he shivered from the first touch of frost blowing in from Manchuria.

The road was known as the MSR, or Main Supply Route. If it had another name, no one in the ranks knew what it was. The forty-three-mile trek from Hungnam to Chinhung-ni was through relatively level country, but it began to get hilly just north of Majon-dong. From Chinhung-ni to Koto-ri the highway became a treacherous one-lane dirt-and-gravel road. From Koto-ri to Hagaru the

MSR rises like a snake of ice for three thousand feet. Rugged rock cliffs on one side of the narrow road, and deep, dread-inducing chasms on the other. The corkscrew road of icy dirt was just wide enough for a 2½-ton truck, and no one was anxious to hang over the side for a look.

The weather turned colder as the First Marine Division started the attack north. A couple of days into the move the Seventh was put on alert. Chesty Puller's First Marines got in a serious fight. Information picked up via intercepted radio message revealed that they had been attacked by a thousand to twelve hundred enemy troops. Twenty-three Marines had been killed. Enemy dead were estimated at over two hundred. That seemed like a good-sized fight, considering most of the North Korean Army was dead. The word was that only a few small pockets of the NKPA were left intact.

No one doubted that the North Korean Army was nearly finished, but persistent rumors about the Chinese entering the war left many of the men with an uneasy feeling. That uneasy feeling became more profound when an advanced patrol reported in with a few captured Chinese soldiers. The rumors grew as Korean civilians along the way reported that large groups of Chinese had passed through their villages.

The First Regiment got hit again on Halloween, and Jessie could not ignore the eerie feeling that there was something more than frost in the cold Manchurian wind as October drew to a close.

It was 0400 on a freezing morning when the harsh nudge of a boot awakened Jessie, though it did not motivate him enough to stick his face out of his sleeping bag and into the icy wind.

"Saddle up! Out of the rack, Marines!"

"Move it! Move it!"

"Leave everything except your rifles and cartridge belts."

Jessie groaned aloud and sat up stiff. It was cold and dark. "God. Why didn't I stay in Japan?"

"Where we going, Sarge?" Welcome Joseph squeaked.

"Up the road, place call Sudong-ni."

Broken Wing mumbled something in Navajo as he began to roll up his sleeping bag.

"I'm not leaving my Irish pipes here unprotected, Sarge."

"Everything will be guarded, Slate. Move it. We got vehicles on the way."

"Sure we do," someone said sarcastically.

By the time the first warming shafts of sunlight broke from over the purple mountains that towered above the steep road, Able Company was moving slowly north in fifty straining jeeps. Sometime later the jeeps stopped and the men piled out. Then came the order to double-time, and no one complained. Running warmed the bones. Wounded ROK soldiers from the First ROK Division were walking back down the road as the Marines ran forward. The ROK men stopped and saluted the Marines as they went past. It gave Jessie goose bumps of pride, but every man in Able now wondered what they were running into.

They reached a level spot in the road that led through a clearing. Immediately, incoming fire rained down from mountain ridgelines above. The company attacked up steep slopes and battled the enemy at long range.

A runner went from position to position, relaying the word for first platoon to pull back. Not until then did Jessie notice that the sun had dropped behind the mountains and the temperature had fallen drastically.

The platoon moved back down to the road, then marched around a bend to waiting trucks, which carried cold weather parkas, shoe packs, and the rest of their gear. The shoe packs were fitted out in the darkness by swapping back and forth until the men could find a fit. More ammo was issued and the shivering men marched back up the road. The platoon moved onto a high ridge overlooking Sudong Valley. The climb was twice as hard with a full transport pack, entrenching shovel, canteens, C-rations, and enough ammo to save Fay Wray. The Irish pipes did not weigh much, but even an extra pound or two could be felt at times like this.

Jessie wondered if being the regimental pipes player was
worth the honor.

At the top of Hill 552, Able Company dug in. The earth
was so rocky it felt like shoveling into a parking lot. Five
hundred feet below, an ancient railroad paralleled the dirt-
and-gravel road that led north to the village of Sudong-ni.

Jessie nudged Broken Wing. "Wing, I can't stay awake
anymore. Take over."

Broken Wing's head popped out of his parka. He felt for
his helmet and brushed off the frost. Jessie leaned back in
their shallow foxhole, wishing they could have scratched
out a deeper hole in the frozen ground.

Suddenly, the clatter of tanks echoed up from the valley
below. A staccato of explosions down in the valley brought
Jessie to a sitting position. From their ridge each white explosion could be seen as well as felt. Then, as if in a
strange dream, a blast of bugles erupted from the valley
floor. Another blast of bugles called from enemy positions
in nearby hills, sending a chill of fear through Jessie as he
gripped his Springfield rifle. Flares shot up from the valley
and arched across the black winter sky, then popped into
tiny red suns. The eerie flickering light revealed hundreds
and hundreds of enemy soldiers sweeping out of the hills
and against the First Battalion positions in the valley and
along the ridges.

"Jessie!" Wing shouted, his dark eyes like saucers as he
jerked around, firing from the hip with his M-1. Two
screaming men fell silent ten feet away. Jessie raised the
Springfield and fired at another quilted uniform. The man
shouted something in Chinese as he fell back. Jessie tasted
blood and knew that he'd bitten his lip. Another flare
popped open in the dark sky. A Chinese bugle wailed. A
line of soldiers dressed in white rushed forward to within
twenty yards of the perimeter. An officer blew a shrill whistle and the Chinese stopped, threw grenades, then ducked
down as Marines in every foxhole opened fire. Sheets of
lead ripped into the enemy skirmish line. A water-cooled,

.30 caliber machine gun opened up and seemed to fire for five minutes straight. Light from the flares burned out and blackness engulfed the chaos. Enemy grenades thudded to the frozen ground all around.

Jessie sprang from the shallow hole and kicked two concussion grenades down the slope. The thudding sound of two more grenades hitting the ground sounded close to his side. He kicked wildly in that direction and felt his boots make contact with the grenades. Ripping explosions sent up blinding flashes all over the perimeter. Men screamed in agony, only to have their voices swallowed up in a cacophony of explosions and gunfire.

Another flare popped above. Hundreds of shadowy Chinese emerged from the black hillside in skirmish lines, and came forward in neat rows firing submachine guns. The big .30 caliber raked back and forth, killing groups of Chinese with every sweep, but as soon as one row of skirmishers fell, another took their place.

Jessie fired and loaded as fast as his frozen hands could work. A Chinese grenade exploded to the left, blowing his helmet off. He rubbed his eyes and tried to focus. He felt dazed, his vision blurred with tears, but sheer terror made his cold fingers work to reload and fire. Each shot was on target even when the flares dimmed. It was like firing point-blank into a crowd. He felt for his grenades, pulled the pin, and threw. He grabbed another, pulled the pin, and threw. Screams told him he'd hit pay dirt. A flare came up from the valley. A platoon's worth of Chinese stood up twenty-five yards away and threw grenades. Jessie fired. Broken Wing swiped madly at the frozen ground around their foxhole, then grabbed Jessie around the neck and yanked him down. A series of dizzying explosions tore into the cold earth, showering the perimeter with rocks, pig iron, and a horrible odor that spread in clouds of red smoke.

"Gas!" a panicked voice screamed.

"It's gas!" another Marine shouted.

"No it ain't, you stupid recruit!" Sergeant Stelzel's voice boomed, settling the issue.

"Jessie!" Broken Wing barked.

Jessie looked up as Broken Wing fired three shots into a bundled-up Chinese soldier charging with a bayonet straight toward him. The soldier dropped onto his long rifle and started groaning.

A squad of Chinese charged out of the black night, emerging into view twenty feet away. A bugler led them, blasting the same three notes over and over as they screamed, "You die tonight, Marine!" Jessie loaded and fired. The bugler stopped in mid-note. Somewhere to the right, two Marines cheered insanely for a moment. The .30 caliber raked the enemy squad like a scythe, then it jammed and the gunner let out a curse.

Broken Wing leaned back in the hole and began kicking at his M-1. "It's frozen!" He threw it to the ground and felt for his entrenching shovel like a frightened blind man.

"You got an extra weapon?" an angry voice shouted through the chaos.

Jessie glanced left. A hunched-over Marine was shouting, "Carbine won't eject! They're frozen!" A flare popped open. At that instant, a blast of fire from a Chinese burp gun hit the hunched-over Marine. Pieces of his frost-covered parka exploded away from the man, then he fell. Jessie fired at an enemy soldier walking forward in a crouch. In the white light, the man's face splattered with blood, then he fell back and rolled into a line of Chinese who were moving slowly forward, as if too frozen to do more than shuffle.

It was too late to reload. From his right Jessie caught the blur of two Marines running toward a line of Chinese, one with a bayonet charge and the other with his entrenching shovel drawn back like a club in one hand. The first group of Chinese paused in disbelief. The Marine with the M-1 reached the Chinese first, ramming his bayonet into the groin of a startled soldier as he stumbled forward on the icy slope. The soldier gave a horrible scream, clutching at the rifle as he fell back. The other Chinese shot the Marine, then began clubbing him. The first Marine's buddy reached the slaughter with a blood-chilling howl, swinging his entrenching shovel like a madman. The shovel glistened in the light of white and red flares. Mortar rounds began falling on the enemy. Screams rose from the slopes below. The Marine wielding the entrenching shovel swung until the five Chinese were sprawled and writhing in the snow.

"Cover me!" Jessie shouted, and gave Wing the Springfield. He forced himself from the foxhole and ran, falling, crawling, and sliding, out to the Marine with the entrenching tool, who was now struggling to drag his buddy back inside the perimeter.

"Give me a hand!" the Marine shouted as he slipped to his knees.

Jessie recognized the voice. It was Stukowski.

"I'm comin', Ski!"

Jessie slid in beside Ski, grabbed the wounded man's parka hood and began dragging. The light of a flare revealed the bloody face of a man Jessie didn't recognize. He kept asking for his mom. A sick, ominous feeling gripped Jessie's heart. They pulled the Marine back to the perimeter. The fighting subsided. Jessie turned to big Stukowski who was still holding onto his entrenching shovel. His eyes huge in the phosphorescent light, he turned away and screamed, "Corpsman!"

"You okay, Ski?" Jessie shouted into his face.

"My BAR won't eject! It froze! Same with Perelli's carbine! I got nothing to fight with! This guy came over to help me while Perelli searched for weapons!"

Jessie looked around. Dead Chinese littered the area. He rushed over to one of the bodies. The man was still gurgling as Jessie pried his frozen hand away from an old Thompson submachine gun. Jessie tossed it to Stukowski as a Marine trudged forward from the center of the perimeter.

"Who needs a Corpsman?" Doc K. stood perfectly up-right as if there were no war going on.

"Here, Doc! Hurry!"

Doc K. jogged to the wounded Marine and knelt down. From the dark slope whistles blew, then a bugle.

"This guy's dead," Doc K. said, then ran toward another call for a Corpsman.

Chinese skirmishers stood and ran up the slope. A series of ear-splitting explosions rattled off like a string of fire-crackers on the north side of the perimeter. A fierce shoot-out erupted from the valley below, but Jessie had no time to watch the show as the line of Chinese rushed forward, stopped, and threw grenades. They exploded in batches. One man cried out in angry pain.

Jessie lifted his face from the frozen ground. White flares streaked up from the valley floor as 81mm illumination rounds lit the entire valley and ridgelines in blue light. The hills seemed to be moving. Jessie squinted and blinked to refocus his eyes. He shuddered as he realized that thou-sands of Chinese troops were moving into the valley and along the ridges. Suddenly, thirty yards away, another line of skirmishers ran forward firing burp guns and Thompson submachine guns. A Marine .30 caliber on Jessie's left cut loose.

Jessie stood in a crouch, his legs quaking with fear. He ran for the foxhole as Broken Wing fired and loaded as fast as possible. Jessie dove for the foxhole. Bullets tore through his parka hood by his left ear. Broken Wing dropped the Springfield and started throwing grenades. The first one didn't detonate.

"Loosen the spoon! They're frozen!" Jessie screamed as he fumbled to fix his bayonet on the end of the Springfield. He shoved in another .03 round, worked the bolt, and fired point-blank into a startled Chinese soldier ten feet away. Another Chinese charged with a high off-the-shoulder thrust that Jessie parried past his face with more reflex than skill. Jessie rose up and drove his bayonet into the bundled-up soldier. The man gave a great groan as he tumbled backward, rolling down the slope with the wind knocked out of him. The bayonet thrust had not penetrated the man's quilted clothes.

Jessie threw the rifle down, dropped to his hands and knees, and felt through the scattered gear for his entrenching shovel. He felt the wooden handle and came up ready to swing, but there were only dead men to the front. A series of bugle blasts shattered the momentary lull. Then the blaring was joined by the shrill of whistles somewhere to their rear.

"PFC Slate!"

"Slate! You over there?"

"Yeah! I'm here, Gunny!"

"Captain Fitch wants you! Bring your pipes!"

"What? You out of your mind?" Jessie shouted toward the voice coming from behind him. A flare went off and he could see a Marine twenty feet back, hunched over and waving him to follow.

"That's an order, Marine!"

He couldn't believe his ears. For an instant he wondered if he were in shock or hallucinating. He grabbed his pack and pulled out the pipes, gave Wing a pat on the helmet and ran after the gunny. The entire perimeter was aglow with 81mm illumination rounds, but clouds of foul smoke from dozens of Chinese grenades hovered like thick patches of red fog. Even with the illumination rounds, he could not see more than a few feet ahead in some directions. The blast of Chinese bugles continued, closer and louder.

"This way!" Gunny Killeen waved at Jessie, then disappeared through a patch of cordite smoke. Jessie followed him. He broke through the fog and found himself at the crest of the ridge with Marine positions drawing a line up the icy slope across the crest of the rocky ridge, down about twenty yards on the other side, and then back toward his end of the triangle-shaped perimeter.

"Got him, Captain! And a proper answer it'll be to those sorry gook fish horns."

"Outstanding! Slate, get to playing!"

Jessie gawked at Captain Fitch in utter disbelief.

"I said play, Marine!"

Jessie stood upright and tried to wet his lips. He removed his glove, rubbed the lip of the blowpipes with his hand, then put his lips to the frozen mouthpiece. The stinging cold burned as he tried fingering the holes through a five-second practice chanter, then broke into "Pi Brocht of O'Donnell Dau."

Marines along the frozen ridge cheered. He blew with all his might until he could no longer hear the bugles and whistles. He finished the tune and began again. A sharp white-hot explosion blinded Jessie. He felt himself flying backward.

"Corpsman!"

He could hear air. Something cold was touching his throat, and he felt the parka around his neck. Something sharp was stuck in the parka. A shiver of panic raced through Jessie. Air was coming from the sharp tube sticking in his parka. Then someone grabbed up a handful of his parka and began dragging him.

"I got ya buddy. Stay calm."

The Corpsman dragged him to a row of dead and wounded Marines laying on their backs, covered with canvas. A second Corpsman leaned over, searching for wounds, as the first one rushed off to the shouts for Corpsman.

"Where you hit, Marine?" Doc K. asked.

Jessie pointed at his throat.

"What are you holding there?" The Corpsman held up what was left of Jessie's bagpipes. Jessie moaned. Doc K. hunched over to hide the beam of his flashlight. "Looks like you tried to give yourself a tracheotomy with this blowpipe. Hurt anywhere else?"

Jessie shook his head no.

"You're not bad." He yanked the blowpipe free. "You're cut, but not deep." The Corpsman pulled the parka open. Cold air numbed Jessie's neck immediately. "Sit up." He began wrapping a bandage around Jessie's neck. The other Corpsman dragged up a crying man as Doc K. finished the bandage. "You can fight. Get back on line. I'll give you a shot later if you're still alive."

Jessie struggled to his feet, then dropped to his stomach as a string of greenish-yellow tracers shot through the perimeter. He stood to a crouch and ran for his foxhole, mumbling aloud, "Please God, let Wing be okay." He felt relieved that he could still speak. Warm, thick blood ran down the back of his throat. He gagged and spat.

"Wing!"

"Over here."

"Get down, idiot!" an angry voice bellowed from nearby.

"Wing!"

"Down here!"

Jessie ran for the sound of Wing's voice. An illumination round burst light over the valley floor and onto the surrounding ridges. Jessie spotted Wing and made a dash toward him. He dove into the hole as a burp gun opened fire from the dark slope.

"Heard you play," Wing said. "Heard wind bag stop. Dead, I figured."

Jessie ignored Broken Wing and readied his spare ammunition. The battlefield became deadly silent. Occasional groans wafted through the freezing wind from the dying who littered the landscape like so many large rocks covering a hillside. Bitter, freezing wind howled, blowing against parka hoods and under helmets. They stared ahead, wide-eyed, and waited for daylight.

Daybreak brought some of the most gruesome scenes that Jessie had yet witnessed. The dead were all around, inside and outside the perimeter. Chinese lay in pools of frozen red ice. Some had crawled as much as fifty yards with

their brown-colored bowels trailing behind them. All frozen
stiff. A sudden commotion around the ridge turned every
man's eyes to the valley below.

"Wonder if this is the start of World War Three." Jessie
spoke but it sounded like someone else.

"Slate. You still alive?" someone called.

"Pass the word, Captain wants Slate and the scope."

Jessie looked around. Ski and Perelli sat huddled over a
dead Marine's body twenty feet away.

"Ski. You call me?"

Ski didn't look up, just shook his head no.

"Slate! Skipper wants you!"

Jessie grabbed the Springfield and his extra ammo and
sprinted across the perimeter. Men were in a line of positions overlooking the valley floor as he approached Captain
Fitch.

"Slate, take a look through that scope." Captain Fitch
pointed down at the tracks by the road where people were
moving about. Jessie removed the canvas cover from the
Unertl scope and sighted in. Groups of blue-quilted Chinese
soldiers were actually forming in ranks. It seemed too insane to be possible.

"What in the world are they doing?"

"Forming—"

"I can see that, Slate! But that's nuts!"

"Maybe they think we're all dead, sir."

"They're marching out, sir!" an excited Marine nearby
shouted and pointed.

"Get to work! Machine guns on line over here!"

The long columns of Chinese began marching, four
abreast, north down the railroad tracks. In an instant Marines from all around the valley opened fire. Jessie shot as
fast as he could load. From somewhere below, a water-
cooled .30 caliber started firing and didn't stop for a long
time. They fell like dominoes. Not a single jam. Suddenly,
a flight of Corsairs swept into the valley one at a time, raking the enemy column with murderous fire. Then a Corsair

dropped a canister of napalm. Even from a distance the heat could be felt and the screams heard. Surviving Chinese scrambled up a slope on the other side of the road. Jessie fired, shoved a round in the well, chambered it, put the crosshairs on a target, squeezed the trigger, and repeated the procedure. A Chinese soldier tumbled down the slope with nearly every shot. Jessie fired until his shoulder ached, his jaw was swollen, and he was out of ammunition.

When it was finally over, an edgy silence covered the valley, interrupted sporadically by a single shot or a spotter plane above. Most of the men seemed speechless. Some were in shock. They just slumped in foxholes, exhausted, and stared blankly into space.

By noon the wounded were marched or carried off the hill. Trucks showed up and took the men back to an aid station at Hungnam. Dead Marines were placed in lines along the road, only their boots showing under canvas tarps.

Jessie leaned against a pale, unconscious man from Baker Company who had no left arm. He fell asleep.

Hungnam, November 25

Jessie sat up and straddled his cot. He began his daily ritual of playing solitaire. Word came down that Marines with two Purple Hearts did not have to return to the front. It was an odd but contented sensation knowing that your war was over. He worried about Broken Wing, yet longed to see Kate and Charlie so bad that he tried to think of nothing but them. Kate and Charlie were his only escape from the ugly, vivid scenes that continually crept into his mind.

"Slate!"

Jessie placed a red ten of diamonds on a black jack of clubs, then looked up. A shirtless Lieutenant Mitchell stood over him with an angry scowl.

"What are you doing here, Slate?"

"Going home, sir. I got three Purple Hearts since landing at Seoul and—"

"Get your butt out of that rack and follow me to the basement and grab some dead men's gear that fits!"

"But I'm, wow—" Jessie stopped short and pointed at two ugly bullet holes in Lieutenant Mitchell's ribs just under his right pectoral muscle. The holes were dark red. Each hole had a painful-looking black and blue circle around it. "That looks bad, Lieutenant."

He glanced down and shook his head. "It'll be okay. Burp gun. The .45 slugs must have bounced off something and got stuck between the ribs."

"You getting them taken out?"

"Don't have time, Slate. The regiment needs every man."

Lieutenant Mitchell was the finest officer Jessie had ever served with. Always fair. Totally honest, and completely dedicated to his men and his Corps.

"You wounded worse than this, Slate?" he asked with a commanding tone.

"No, sir."

"Get up and follow me. We got a ride waiting." With that, Lieutenant Mitchell turned and headed for the basement. Jessie followed like a man sleepwalking, hoping that he would wake up.

CHAPTER EIGHTEEN

The town of Hagaru sits at the southern tip of the Chosin Reservoir. Two roads branch off both sides of the reservoir from Hagaru. Hagaru was battered by bombing because it was a communications center for the NKPA, but it was still a lot more to look at than Koto-ri or Chinhung-ni. It was fourteen miles from Hagaru, sitting at the foot of the Chosin Reservoir, to Yudam-ni on the western side of the reservoir. Between the two was Toktong Pass, four thousand feet up from Hagaru, strikingly eerie, with dark gorges and craggy cliffs. Fox Company Seventh Marines was holding the pass. The road drops from Toktong Pass to a wide valley where Yudam-ni sits surrounded by menacing ridgelines with fourteen-hundred foot peaks.

When the trucks carrying resupplies and replacements finally pulled into the wide, flat valley of Yudam-ni, the weather was bitterly cold. At the far end of the valley, Marine Corsairs were diving and bombing a large hill with everything they had: napalm, rockets, and 20mm cannon. It was quite a show. Somebody said it was the Seventh Marine Regiment in a little shootout, but when the second wave of Corsairs began bombing the purple mountains at the end of the valley, a shivering replacement spoke up.

"Just how big is the Chinese Army?"

West of the main road, called the MSR, an engineer

company was working overtime to carve a runway out of the frozen valley floor. Cold weather gear had been issued at Wonsan, but no one in the outfit had imagined the temperature dropping so suddenly. The biting cold penetrated layers of clothing like no cold Jessie had ever experienced.

The Fifth Marines set up positions on the east side of the Chosin Reservoir, while the Seventh Regiment were on the west. The cold weather gear was proving to be less than perfect in the subzero temperatures. The boots drew the most gripes. The good old boondockers had been replaced by a new "Mickey Mouse" cold weather boot that had a dead air space in a felt liner, which would keep your feet warm if you stood still. Twenty-mile patrols were another matter. Feet sweated and the felt liners turned to ice. It seemed like half the platoon was suffering from frostbite. The parkas worked as well as could be expected, but the plain, obvious fact was that human beings were never meant to exist in that kind of cold.

Able Company was on a hill west of the reservoir. Jessie finally finished the climb to join them just as a patrol from first platoon was heading off.

"Hey, Slate's back!" Stukowski called out. Jessie gave a tired wave at the line of bundled-up and shivering Marines.

By nightfall the temperature on the snow-covered mountain was unbearable. Men huddled in groups inside sleeping bags, peeking out only if they had to.

"They said it's thirty-one below zero," a stuttering Doc K. said as he shuffled by each position around the icy mountain. "Protect your feet. It's thirty-one below."

"Who was that idiot?" Perelli grumbled.

"Corpsman," Ski said.

"So knowing the temperature is supposed to help!"

"Quit your bellyaching, Perelli."

"What's that gurgling noise?" Jessie asked.

Jessie peeked out of the top of his sleeping bag. Broken Wing was sitting up, still inside his sleeping bag with his head barely exposed.

"What are you doing?"

"Nothing."

"I heard you make a funny noise."

"Warming up."

"You drinking something?"

"Hate cold."

"Did you find some booze, Wing? How could you?"

"Could be tending sheep."

Jessie scooted across the ice until he was leaning against a clump of sleeping bag that was Broken Wing.

"Did you?" Jessie asked quietly, forcing his head up out of the warm sleeping bag. Cold air burned his face.

Broken Wing's bag shifted as he maneuvered around, then he whispered, "Here. Don't spill."

Slowly a shivering glove holding a quart-size juice can rose from the top of the sleeping bag like a hand coming up out of a grave in a monster movie. The moon was bright enough to see the can of Donald Duck grapefruit juice. Jessie pulled off his right wool glove.

"Grapefruit juice?" He snatched the can and ducked back down into his own sleeping bag. His fingers were numb. He put them in his mouth to bring back feeling. Jessie maneuvered to let some moonlight shine through the top of his bag. He studied the red, blue, and yellow picture of Donald Duck, then took a drink of the slushy substance. His eyes teared instantly at the criminal flavor. He took a deep breath of the frozen air to relieve the trauma to his senses. It burned like hot coals and tasted like a gasoline slush. Jessie tried to speak, but his voice couldn't function. He tried again.

"Wing. Wing."

"Hmm."

"Where'd you get it?"

"Liberated sick bay alky from Yudam-ni aid station."

"How'd you keep it from freezing?"

"Win Scott."

"Win Scott?"

"Win Scott."

"Heavy machine guns?"

"The water cooled .50s do not work."

"What do you mean?"

"Water freezes."

"Yeah. So?"

"Sergeant Gilley stole antifreeze from truck supply convoy."

"He's using antifreeze in the water-cooled machine guns?"

"Yes."

Jessie took another drink and gasped from the pungent, nearly suffocating odor. No doubt about it—he felt something that could pass for warmth, but it felt warm the way acid might feel just before frying your skin.

"So what has this got to do with—oh, no! Have you got me drinking antifreeze?"

"Sound like papoose."

"I oughtta stick a grenade up your Navajo butt!"

"A-nah-ne-dzin."

"Not friendly! I'll tell you what's not friendly. Poisoning me is called *a-nah-ne-dzin.* Here. Take this crap back."

Jessie closed the top of his bag, tucked it under his head as a pillow, and curled up in a fetal position. He pulled his extra pair of socks from his pocket, removed his gloves, and with stiff fingers opened his parka. He fumbled with the buttons on the first of his two flannel shirts, pulled up both long john shirts, and stuck his socks against his chest. It was the only hope of keeping them dry and unfrozen for the move that was sure to come. Frozen feet meant your chances for survival dropped, and every Marine in the First Division knew it. He buttoned up again and tried to warm the sleeping bag with his breath. A dreadful chill penetrated the down bag, numbing Jessie into a strange, uncomfortable sleep.

The toe end of a boot struck Jessie in the tailbone. "Saddle up. Everybody out of the rack. Get moving."

Jessie peeked out of his down bag. Biting cold hurt his face. He yanked his head back inside.

"Listen up and listen good, lads. You got ten minutes to get formed up. And keep it quiet."

Jessie peeked out again. The cold stung his flesh like angry bees.

"What's it like out, Gunny?" a muffled voice asked from nearby.

"Bright with stars, lads. A good sign. If a star is in the Manchurian sky at night, it means clear weather in the morn and the wing-wipers can earn their pay. Make sure you're wearing your firing mittens, the one with the trigger finger. The colonel's got a notion that something's afoot, and Able Company will be finding out on the double."

A sudden loud pop close by was followed by a shout, "Corpsman! Corpsman!"

Jessie scrambled from his sleeping bag as Gunny Killeen slid in beside a Marine writhing in pain nearby. Paddy checked the man over, then slapped him across the top of his parka hood. He stood up beside the Marine and kicked him hard in the rear end, then turned and motioned for a Corpsman who was on the way.

"All right, now listen up, jarheads! We're going to need every man here, and this is the third casualty in two days from a frozen C-ration can exploding. You will punch a hole in the can before opening! The next Marine wounded by a frozen pea through his throat will have it extracted from his ass by my bayonet! Is that clear, Marines!"

Jessie couldn't tell who the guy was, and no one spoke of it as they began to move in a column around the icy mountain. Footing was nearly impossible. Forty-five minutes later the call to halt was whispered back through the column of freezing men. Jessie fell back into a pile of snow beside the ice-covered stump of a fallen tree. Sweat turned to ice the moment the air touched it, and stopping for even a moment caused the legs to go numb.

"Why'd we stop?" a snow-covered Marine whispered

from a clump of frozen brush to Jessie's left. It was too cold to comment.

A few minutes later the word came back to move out again. One Marine helping a buddy slipped and fell to Jessie's right. Jessie and Wing went over to help them up while another Marine stuck out his rifle for them to grab to keep them from sliding down the icy slope.

"You okay, Mac?" Jessie asked as he lifted one of the men up.

"Thanks, mate."

"We're moving."

The company column paused at the top of a steep slope while the lead platoon filed on down the mountain. A burst of gunfire startled everyone. Men dropped to the snow and prepared to fire, but all of the action was at the bottom of the snowy slope, and there was nothing to do but watch the show. Only muzzle flashes and white grenade explosions were visible, but it was obvious that a sharp fight was going on.

The battle did not last long. It ended as abruptly as it had started. Helmets turned to pass the word.

"Get a squad turned around."

"Cover the rear."

"We got wounded coming up."

Details came in whispered phrases as Able headed back to the base camp at Yudam-ni. Lieutenant Mitchell was dead, killed leading a counterattack and holding off the Chinese nearly single-handedly while wounded Marines were rescued.

"Should have seen him. All Marine."

"He must have killed thirty of 'em!"

"He'll get the Medal of Honor," Killeen mumbled to Jessie as he shuffled past him in the column.

Jessie thought back to the hospital at Hamhung, the bullets in Mitchell's ribs and the leadership in his battle-hardened eyes. No doubt he had died a hero. It was only proper for a man like him. A Marine like him. At Yudam-ni the wounded and dead were dropped off at an aid station at the edge of the frozen valley. Immediately someone shouted those hated words, "Saddle up! Able Company!"

"Gunny Killeen! Get those men moving!"

"Aye aye, Skipper!"

"Make sure every man is out of the warming tents!"

"Charlie Company's surrounded. We gotta move it, lads!"

"Squad leaders! Make sure every man has 170 rounds, cartridge belt, two bandoliers, and four grenades! And every other man carries a sixty-millimeter mortar round! And every other man carries a tin of machine-gun ammo! Is that clear?" Paddy finished barking out commands as he hurried past Jessie, then paused to look around.

"What you looking for, Paddy?" Jessie asked.

"Ah, Slate, it's no weather for a man in need of making a head call! Four inches of clothing and a half-inch penis! Now that's some shot, lad!"

Jessie laughed out a cloud of vapor. Paddy rushed over behind a warming tent. Men went only when it could no longer be avoided. It meant certain frostbite if it turned into a long procedure.

Broken Wing picked up a tin of machine-gun ammo and tried to fit his glove through the handle. He groaned.

"This is looking serious," Jessie griped.

"Hunting dinosaur again."

"That Corpsman with the thermometer said it was thirty below," Welcome Joseph squealed. "Gotta be twice that cold with a twenty-mile-an-hour wind."

"Gotta be . . ." Jessie's lips were too numb to pronounce his words. They felt the way they did after seeing a dentist.

No one knew where they were going. Up snow-covered mountains, marching until all feeling from the knees down was gone. There was a sense of urgency in the pace of the march. Jessie was dying for a drink, but every canteen was split, frozen solid. He tried to scoop up some snow and let it melt in his mouth, but it did not help. The column finally reached the top of an immense mountain and trudged along a spiny ridge in knee-deep snow with heads bowed against the increasingly icy wind.

Broken Wing paused just ahead of Jessie and cocked his ear to listen for something that Jessie could not hear.

"What's up?" Jessie whispered into the angry wind.

Wing lowered his head and continued on.

Jessie trudged forward to catch up. He poked Wing in the back. "What's up?"

"Hear bugles somewhere."

Jessie felt too cold to be very frightened as he scanned the wintry terrain. It was like being on top of the world. Ice-covered mountain peaks stretched for as far as he could see in the bright moonlit night. He lowered his head against the blustering wind to hide his face. His eyes teared from the icy gale and the tears turned solid on his flesh. Sweat from the long march covered him. He felt almost desperate to open his parka, but he didn't dare.

Somebody nudged Jessie's shoulder. He peeked up from the hunched-over march, letting the wind bite his face again just long enough to see who it was.

"Go over that ridge and be the flank guard."

Jessie could not see the man's face, but it sounded like Stelzel. He nodded and followed four other Marines moving uphill and over the ridge of snow just above them. They paused to let Jessie catch up, and he trudged on past them.

"Take the point, Slate," a Marine called to Jessie as he stooped to fix something on his shoe pack.

Jessie fought his way up the slope against the wind, poking his finger out of the firing mitten as he climbed up and over the top.

CHAPTER NINETEEN

It looked clear, just mountains and valleys of undisturbed snow. He led the tiny column of four downhill about twenty yards, then along the slope, trying to parallel the direction of the main column. The terrain leveled out slightly where two mountain masses joined. Jessie glanced back to make sure the others were keeping up. They were twenty yards back.

He worked his way around a huge snowbank built up on a gentle slope, and stopped with rifle ready. The muffled but distinct chatter of Chinese voices wafted through the icy wind. Jessie turned and waved for the others to halt, then turned back to find himself facing a Chinese soldier no more than ten feet away.

Breath smoked from the man's nose and mouth. The ears of his furry hat were pinned up, and Jessie could see his face plainly in the bright moonlight. Jessie raised his rifle and fired point-blank before the Chinese soldier could lift his burp gun. Blue-white sparks flew from his ears like a man being electrocuted as he fell backward.

Suddenly, gunfire erupted from all directions. Something hit Jessie in the hip with the force of a sledgehammer, knocking him to his knees. He looked down. His parka and cartridge belt were on fire. He rolled wildly in the snow until the flames were gone, then struggled to his feet and grabbed up his Springfield. A Chinese soldier a few feet away was aiming at him with a rifle. It was jammed. Frozen. The Chinese soldier lowered the rifle and hammered at the bolt with his fist, then charged Jessie with a shoulder-height bayonet thrust. Jessie turned his back as he dropped to his left knee, going under the bayonet thrust. He spun on the knee with his right leg out in an "iron broom" foot sweep that took the soldier off his feet and onto his back. Jessie struck at the man's throat as hard as he could with the knife edge of his gloved hand. Something cracked. He jumped up and stomped him with all of his might in the groin. Bullets sang by his ears and he could hear them flattening into the frozen ground.

"Come on!" somebody shouted.

Jessie turned back to the other Marines. Only two were standing. The other two were on their faces in the snow. The two standing Marines grabbed the boots of the downed men and started dragging them. Jessie ran back to them and seized the arms of one of the wounded.

They struggled up the slope, stopping twice to throw grenades. At the ridgeline, a squad of Marines met them and helped carry the wounded men back into a hasty perimeter being formed against the incoming fire.

"Get that .30 cal working!" Gunny Killeen shouted toward a position to Jessie's left and slightly above him on the ridgeline.

The perimeter was forming on a moderate incline that ran downhill from the top at a thirty-degree grade for a couple of hundred yards, then fell sharply to a snowy gorge a thousand feet below. Beyond that gorge, faraway flares shot into the dark sky, lighting the white mountains surrounding Yudam-ni Valley and the endless reservoir. Bugles sounded. Whistles echoed. Red flares shot into the night sky ahead.

Hundreds of white-clad Chinese swept over the crest of an adjoining hilltop about two hundred yards north. They ran screaming down the gentle white slope of the hill, then up a forty-degree grade to Able Company's position.

"Incoming!"

The first mortar round hit the ridge to Jessie's right front, blowing ice, snow, and rocks into the air. The second round hit a three-man machine-gun team as they were setting up.

"Corpsman!"

Jessie ran for the machine-gun position, reaching it just as the Corpsman did. A young PFC sat up, fumbling with his entrails, which were pouring through a gaping, bloody slit in the stomach of his parka. "My intestines are slipping through my fingers."

"Get that .30 working!" someone shouted.

Jessie forced his eyes from the dying Marine and jumped behind the machine gun, dropped his rifle, pulled the cocking lever and fired. It was impossible to miss. Across the smooth, white gully the entire slope straight ahead looked to be moving. Jessie felt someone slide in beside him, but he couldn't look away from the screaming onslaught racing at them.

"Opened a new tin!"

"Broken Wing?" Jessie shouted over the chatter of the machine gun.

"Don't melt the barrel!"

Jessie ceased fire for an instant, then opened fire again.

"Ammo!"

Broken Wing fed another belt into the machine gun straight from the tin. Jessie opened up again. Red tracers streaked into Chinese troops. Enemy soldiers tumbled down the slope like snowballs, but as one fell, another ran over the crest of the hill to take his place. Another mortar round landed close by, then another sucked through the air with cringing speed. Something smacked hard against Jessie's helmet, but he kept firing. Suddenly the gun jammed. He pulled back on the bolt and released it, then fired again. Still jammed. He tapped the cover, pulled the belt to the right, held his left hand at the point where the cartridges entered the feedway. He pulled the bolt to the rear again and released it. He aimed and pulled the trigger. A burst of fire shot from the machine gun. Jessie worked the .30 back and forth on the tripod, sweeping the slope with deadly accuracy, but still they came across the snowy gully. Another flare shot into the sky, revealing at least a hundred Chinese troops charging up the Marine slope, firing burp guns and Thompson submachine guns. The .30 caliber jammed again.

"Barrel's burned out!" Broken Wing shouted as he began to remove it.

"Grenades!" Gunny Killeen's voice shouted into Jessie's ear from close range.

Jessie turned to see the gunny finish dragging up a box of grenades. He wanted to ask where they came from, but the gunny was already heading for a new position. Jessie grabbed up two grenades from the wooden box. They were yellow and the date printed on them in black said 1917 issue.

"These things are from World War One!"

"Throw!"

Jessie pulled the pin and tapped the spoon to loosen the ice. He heaved and waited. A loud bang and bright flash was followed by screams. He pulled the pin on the second grenade and repeated the procedure, getting the same result. A Chinese soldier rose up ten yards away and shot a burst from a submachine gun. Someone behind Jessie groaned. A Marine to their left put four shots into the enemy soldier, sending him backward.

"No time, Wing! Start throwing grenades!"

Broken Wing dropped the old barrel into the snow and snatched up two handfuls of grenades. They threw until nothing in front of them was moving. Jessie's arm ached. Finally someone behind them started shouting.

"Cease fire!"

"Cease fire!"

"Let's get that barrel on!" Jessie yelled at Wing.

"Corpsman!" another Marine shouted from a position to Jessie's left.

"Wing! Get the barrel on!" Jessie yelled again, then turned to Broken Wing, who was on his back with his gloved hands over his face.

"Wing! Wing! You hit?"

Another flare shot over the frozen peaks, spreading light over the white terrain. Jessie could see dark red blood oozing between Wing's gloved fingers.

"Corpsman!" Jessie shrieked, and pulled Wing's hands away.

The Indian's face was a mask of blood, but his eyes were open and he looked strangely calm. Jessie wiped blood away with his glove. More blood oozed from a dark, round hole in Wing's jaw. Pieces of his jawbone were sticking through the skin where the bullet had exited.

"Shot through the jaw, buddy. You're gonna be okay."

"Gonna be ugly," Wing mumbled as he tried to sit up.

Jessie forced a laugh. "Who you kidding? It'll probably be an improvement."

"Tkele-cho-gi."

"Yeah, same to you, pal. Corpsman!"

Doc K. slid in beside them like a man stealing second base. He took one look at Broken Wing and pulled a morphine cylinder from his mouth, removed the plastic cover, and shoved a hypodermic into Broken Wing's forearm. He pulled a bandage from his satchel and tossed it to Jessie.

"Wrap him." With that the Corpsman was up and running toward another wounded Marine.

Suddenly, the shrill whistles of Chinese officers broke the momentary silence. Another flare arched across the black sky. Jessie wrapped the bandage around Broken Wing's face as he stared in horror at the slope of the hill across the gully before them. It looked like a human avalanche rolling down the mountain slope. Broken Wing tugged on Jessie's arm.

"Leave mouth open to spit blood. Gagging." Broken Wing's words were gargled.

"There. How's that?"

He nodded.

Jessie tied it off, leaving a gap for Broken Wing to spit blood, then fumbled with frozen hands to put the spare barrel on the .30 caliber machine gun.

Captain Fitch ran along the line shouting, "Hold your fire until I give the word!"

"Hold your fire!"

He ran past Jessie and Wing. "Let's see some of that marksmanship, Slate!"

"Captain! I need a weapon that works!" someone yelled out.

"Take that dead man's M-1 and pitch that carbine!"

"Ready! Fire!"

Every able-bodied man opened fire at the human wave of Chinese rushing across the snow-covered terrain. Maniacal screams from both sides filled the frozen air. Bullets sang by Jessie's ears like irritating mosquitoes. He fought the urge to bury his face in the snow and continued to fire.

"Load!" Jessie shouted as Wing shoved in another belt of ammo from an open tin box.

Jessie yanked back on the bolt and let it slam forward. The machine gun fired without pulling the trigger, and Jessie knew it was overheated, but there was no time or chance to lay off the trigger. A new line of skirmishers climbed over the bodies of their fallen comrades in an insane screaming charge, only to be cut down like ripened wheat by a scythe of lead. One soldier rose up out of a stack of dead men and heaved something. Jessie fired into the man's pale face and he fell dead. A numbing explosion flipped Jessie's legs into the air. He landed on his back and knew that his ankle was broken. He rolled over, got behind the machine gun again, and opened fire, but the stack of dead men was catching most of the bullets. He grabbed up grenades, pulled the pins, and threw as fast as he could. A flare shot above the battlefield.

Broken Wing scrambled out on all fours to the stack of dead men twenty yards in front of the machine gun and began yanking away the bodies to clear a field of fire. Suddenly, a Chinese soldier emerged from behind the wall of dead men and drove a bayonet through Broken Wing's back. He put his canvas tennis shoe against Wing and shoved to pull the bayonet out.

Jessie let out an unearthly scream, then shot the Chinese soldier a dozen times, firing even after the man's head was blown into a hundred pieces.

A faraway whistle stuck in his ear, growing shrill then sucking past and crashing into the Chinese horde like a thunderbolt. The enemy attack broke under the American artillery as the frozen earth erupted in fire and shrapnel. What was left of the Chinese troops began trudging away. Jessie continued to fire, along with every Marine still able.

"Cease fire!"

"Cease fire!"

"Dig in!"

"Who fired that shot?"

"Gooks, Captain!"

"Dig in!"

"You can't dig into rock!"

"Second squad! How many men you got left?"

"Ain't no second squad, Sarge!"

"Corpsman!" Jessie screamed over the chaos.

"Third squad! Sound off!"

"We got six men left!"

"Second platoon! Get a head count!"

"Corpsman! Over here!" Jessie wailed as he crawled out to Broken Wing and lifted his head from the snow.

"Wing! Wing!" Jessie shouted, and shook Broken Wing hard.

The Navajo opened his eyes. He had that thousand-yard

stare that Jessie had seen so many times before. The stare that sees death.

"Bad day," Wing rasped with a weak cough, then spat a mouthful of dark red blood onto the white snow. His head fell back and his eyes closed.

Jessie turned away and screamed, "Corpsman!"

Calls for Corpsmen came from every part of the perimeter. Somewhere a Marine called pathetically for his mom, then cried out in agony and went silent.

Jessie grabbed Broken Wing's parka hood and began dragging him back to the machine gun. Stukowski, with one limp arm dangling, ran forward to help. He latched onto Wing's left arm with his good hand and dragged the Navajo back to the .30 caliber, then disappeared. Jessie lifted Wing's head and shouted into his face.

"Wing! Open your eyes!"

Broken Wing did not move. Jessie turned and again shouted frantically, "Corpsman!"

"Dig in!" an angry voice barked down at Jessie as he cradled Broken Wing's head in his hands. Jessie's tears froze to his eyelashes when he looked up into the bitter wind to see Sergeant Stelzel anxiously guarding over him, his M-1 ready to fire.

"Put him down, Slate. He's finished."

"No, he's not!" Jessie screamed out in a sudden, violent rage.

"Well, let the Corpsman do his work. Dig in if you plan on saving him!"

Jessie glanced at his own ankle and saw blood. The cold had frozen it and, strangely, there was very little pain, but the loss of blood could send him into shock, and he knew it. Stelzel slapped Jessie hard, knocking his helmet off his head. For an instant he felt dizzy from the blow, then a surge of anger brought him to his senses.

"I said lay the man down and prepare your position, Marine!" Stelzel screamed.

Jessie nodded.

He lay Broken Wing onto his side to allow the blood to drain from his mouth.

"Stay that way, Broken Wing, so you don't strangle on your own blood."

Broken Wing did not answer. Jessie got to his knees.

"I'll be back to feed the machine gun in a minute," Sergeant Stelzel said as he rushed toward the next position.

A flare shot into the sky from the Chinese positions, and again the sound of a fish horn playing those same three notes began echoing through the mountaintops. They were coming. Jessie scrambled out to the stack of dead Chinese and grabbed one by his quilted jacket. He dragged the dead man across the snow and ice and placed him in front of the machine gun. He crawled back out, grabbed another Chinese soldier, dragged him back to the position and rolled him on top of the first. He crawled out again, and when he yanked on the collar of a bleeding soldier, the man groaned out loud. Jessie froze for a moment, then dragged the man back to the machine-gun position. Over and over, like a madman, he repeated the gruesome task. He lifted the last body on top of two others, finishing his human bunker with three corpses stacked on each side of the machine gun. He fell back in the snow and tried to catch his breath and stared at the trail of brown intestines and blood leading to his stack of human sandbags. He stared up at the light of white flares drifting down under tiny parachutes and wondered if he would ever be sane again. He turned as Doc K. ran up behind him, huffing with fatigue. Whistles sounded from the icy mountains.

"Doc! It's Broken Wing! Bayoneted clean through!"

Doc Klemawesch dropped down to his knees beside Broken Wing, pulled his ice-caked parka back and put his ear to Wing's nose. Jessie felt himself stop breathing as he waited for the word. Doc K. looked up, his eyes wild with fatigue, adrenaline, and terror.

"Still alive!"

The Corpsman hoisted Broken Wing over his shoulder in

a fireman's carry and lumbered back toward the center of the perimeter.

"Here they come!" Captain Fitch stood, defiantly yelling out across the Marine lines. "Make every shot count!"

Jessie turned and shouted, "I need an assistant gunner over here!"

A few seconds later Perelli slid in beside Jessie.

"Open a tin of ammo! Hurry!"

Artillery rounds whistled overhead, blasting into the surrounding slopes like a series of sharp volcanoes. Enemy machine guns opened fire, spraying streams of green tracers into Marine positions. Bullets cracked into the frozen human bunker. Perelli shoved Jessie down, then screamed out, "Help! I'm hit! I'm hit!"

"Where you hit?" Jessie shouted over the growing racket of incoming and outgoing fire.

"My eye!" he screamed. He jerked wildly on the icy ground, clutching at his face with both hands.

Jessie held the writhing Marine still by putting his knees on Perelli's chest. He yanked his gloved hands from his face, then rolled his head left to get light from a drifting flare onto the wound.

"Something's sticking out of your eye! Don't move!" Jessie pulled off his right firing mitten, worked his frozen fingers to get feeling in them, then gripped a four-inch-long, thin, white object sticking through the closed right eyelid.

"Hold on, Perelli! Hold on!" Jessie yanked back.

Perelli screamed and clutched at his bleeding eye. Jessie glanced at the object for an instant and knew immediately what it was. A sliver of human bone that had splintered away from their bunker of dead Chinese.

"It's out! Make your way back to the C.P. and get it bandaged!"

Perelli crawled away, clutching his right eye.

"Get that gun working!" someone shouted from Jessie's right.

Jessie rolled back into position and tried to squeeze the

trigger, but his fingers were stiff and his flesh stuck to the metal of the machine gun. He snatched up his glove, put it on, worked his bleeding fingers and gripped the trigger. Another human wave swept down the slope to his front and rolled across the small gully toward the Marine perimeter. It was like shooting into a flock of sheep.

Jessie fired until his ears rang and his body vibrated. When the gun went silent, he yanked open the feed cover, pulled a tin of ammo closer, and loaded a belt of bullets. He pulled back the bolt and started firing. Chinese continued to charge. The machine gun was all that was keeping the Marine line from being breached. Enemy concussion and pig-iron grenades flew into the Marine perimeter as fast as American grenades flew out.

A clump of Chinese grenades tied together landed behind Jessie. He turned away from the screaming onslaught and reached back with his left hand while continuing to squeeze the trigger with his right. He stretched as far as possible, swiping frantically to knock the grenades away, but they were out of his reach. He closed his eyes and waited to die.

"Keep firing, lad!"

Jessie opened his eyes. A Marine dove on top of the grenades, still shouting, "Keep firing, lad!"

"No! No!" Jessie screamed and turned away to shield his face from the blast. The deafening explosion blew Jessie onto his side, but he clung to the trigger, traversing the .30 caliber machine gun, squeezing out a sheet of lead that staggered the Chinese charge. He sat up, gripping the machine gun with all of his strength, raking deadly fire back and forth and back and forth again. American artillery and mortars slammed into the Chinese remnants as they tried to crawl away.

"Cease fire!"

"Cease fire!"

"I said cease fire!"

The call resounded around the Marine positions with hurried shouts. Jessie released the trigger and sat stunned.

Sweat gushed in torrents from every pore. He stared into the snowy field of death, wanting desperately to turn and find Paddy alive. It was hopeless. His heart sank deep into his guts with utter despair. He knew his Irish father was gone.

"Paddy!" His mournful wail drowned out all other sound, echoing through frozen gorges and off ice-covered mountains until it seemed that the baleful howl had shrieked into heaven itself. He sagged onto hands and knees under the mountainous weight of his sorrow.

An eerie silence fell over the white battlefield. Here and there stacks of men burned like human cordwood. Jessie tried to move, but felt too stiff with cold and too weak from loss of blood. His head reeling, he gave a bewildered glance down at his ankle. A pool of red ice lay around his foot. Clouds of cordite drifted over the snowcapped mountain. Foul-smelling red smoke from the Chinese grenades hovered over the gully like fog. A low, continuous, barely audible chorus of dying men groaning out their final sounds drifted through the icy wind. One by one the groans softened, then stopped as men froze to death.

Sunrise revealed a scene straight out of hell. Bodies of ice, frozen in every conceivable position of death, littered the barren landscape. Marines met the new day with dull stares, wondering why they were still alive. Some were in huddles praying.

"Hey, Slate."

Jessie turned to see the squat shape of a bundled-up Marine holding a canteen and empty ammo tin. His heavy green sweater was pulled up to his nose and his parka was pulled down to his eyebrows, but Jessie knew those Coke-bottle thick glasses could be no one other than Welcome Joseph Snowwater. Blood and brains were splattered in frozen clumps on his coat sleeves.

"Gotta have coffee, Slate."

"Yeah, me too. Come on over and help me with the jacket."

"My fingers won't work," he said.

"Frostbite?"

"They've turned black. I know that I'm going to loose them."

"Yeah. Maybe," Jessie said. His voice sounded monotone.

He drained the antifreeze from the .30 caliber water-cooled machine gun and packed the jacket with snow and ice. Jessie fired off a ten-round burst to heat the water, then drained it into canteen cups with C-ration coffee packets. No one spoke. The entire perimeter was strangely quiet. Hot coffee warmed Jessie's insides, and with the new warmth came feeling. He stared down at his mangled ankle as the pain suddenly increased until a gray, warm sleep forced his eyes to close and he knew that he was fainting.

"Corpsman!"

Jessie opened his mouth with the help of someone's hand. Someone spooned in a mouthful of fruit cocktail. He swallowed and tried to open his eyes, but moisture on his lashes had frozen his eyes shut.

"Sorry it can't be more, mate, but this is the only thing that ain't frozen."

The sound of engines was all around. A plane whipped by low overhead. Jessie tried to wipe at the ice on his eyes, but his arms were pinned down.

"Where am I?"

"Yudam-ni. We're heading south in a minute. Down the MSR."

"South?"

"Yeah. Scuttlebutt has it there's six Chinese divisions around us. We've taken over four thousand casualties."

"Quit moving around, Marine. You're tearing open my wound!" someone with a Boston accent yelled from above Jessie. Jessie scrunched up his face and forced open his eyes. They burned from a sudden rush of sunlight coming through the back end of the canvas-topped truck.

The truck hit a pothole and men groaned. Jessie tried to move his arms again, but there was no use. He looked around and realized that he was at the bottom of a stack of wounded men, some on litters and others just in blankets. The wounded were stacked in all angles in an effort to fit as many as possible into the back of the 2½-ton truck. The truck stopped. Something dripped onto his forehead and ran into his eyes. Jessie freed his right hand and wiped at his eyes with his glove. He looked down at his glove. Blood. Somebody called out angrily, "Hey, Corpsman!"

"Yeah."

"This guy is dead. Better move him."

Jessie watched as two Marines and a Corpsman struggled to pull the dead Marine from the stack of wounded. They tied the dead man over the hood of the next truck in the long column of vehicles pulling out of Yudam-ni Valley and away from the Chosin Reservoir. The bundled-up body looked like a deer being brought back from a hunting trip. Jessie closed his eyes. Men outside the truck applauded a bombing run by a flight of Corsairs somewhere close by.

"Anybody in here from Able One/Seven?" Jessie called out.

"Think these guys up front are, but they're either sleeping or dead."

"Does one of them look like an Indian?" Jessie asked as his stomach fluttered with expectancy.

"Sorry, Mac. Can't see their faces."

"Anybody here from Charlie Company?" another Marine asked.

"I am," a weak voice said.

"You know a guy named Collins? Big guy. Played tackle for Quantico?"

"Yeah. Forget him. Got his ticket punched yesterday."

"How 'bout a sergeant named Fowler?" another man asked.

"We lost ninety men yesterday," the weak voice said.

"I heard a guy at HQ say we annihilated two entire divisions."

"How many Chinese can there be?" a tired voice asked in a dry monotone that had less emotion that a cough.

"Not as many as yesterday," another tired voice answered.

No one else spoke. Jessie's body ached to move, but with even the slightest movement the man lying across him groaned out in pain. He moved his face away from the dripping blood and fell asleep to the sound of a battle in progress to the left side of the MSR. The column stopped and started dozens of times as Chinese roadblocks were blasted open and each hill and ridgeline along the fourteen miles of torture between Yudam-ni and Hagaru was cleared with constant help from the wing wipers above.

Jessie opened his eyes as the weight above him lessened. He tried to speak, but didn't seem to have the energy. Two Marines lifted a man off Jessie and carried him away while two more half lifted and half rolled Jessie onto a stretcher.

"Where am I?" he mumbled. His lips were numb with cold and he did not think that the men had heard him.

"Hagaru. Hang on, buddy. Don't give up. You're gonna make it. We're fighting our way out of this like Marines."

Jessie lifted his head to look around. The cow pasture that sat beside the dirty little village of Hagaru did not make much of an airstrip, but it could not have been more beautiful if it had been La Guardia.

"They're flying us out?" Jessie asked with a newfound zeal.

"No. Sorry, pal, the last gooney bird just took off. We have to truck it to Koto-ri. Eleven more miles."

The saucer-shaped plateau of Hagaru sat surrounded by purple hills with white caps that looked like a cone-shaped wall around the decrepit village. Tracer rounds shot from hill to hill in spurts of green and red, and Jessie knew that the Chinese would try to trap the two Marine regiments in Hagaru if they could. On the other side of the MSR, a de-

tachment of MPs had hundreds of Chinese prisoners encir-
cled. Three big American tanks opened fire at a nearby hilltop.

They carried Jessie to a scrubby-looking shack. Someone
had covered the floor with hay. The shack was filled with
wounded, but there would be no complaints, Jessie thought
with a smile, as the litter bearers laid him inside, out of the
perilously cold wind. A Catholic chaplain was administer-
ing last rites to a dead Marine in one corner of the room.
He finished and covered the man's face with a blanket, then
stooped by another man and began.

"No," the wounded man said with a wave of his hand.

"It's okay, Marine," the chaplain said.

"I'm not Catholic, Chaplain."

"That's okay, son."

The chaplain held the man's hand until his labored
breathing ceased. The chaplain covered the man's face with
a towel, then stood up and walked toward the door. Jessie
watched and wanted to cry, but could not. He clutched at
the chaplain's leg as the chaplain stepped between him and
another man.

"Can I help you, Marine?"

"Chaplain. My buddy, Broken Wing, is around here somewhere. I gotta know if he's okay!" Jessie's voice cracked.

The chaplain stooped down on one knee. He had a kind
face with dark brown eyes and pouches of fatigue under
each. He was small and pale and compact-looking.

"What's his name?"

"Broken Wing. PFC Broken Wing. Able Company, First
Battalion, Seventh Marines."

"I'll see what I can do, Marine."

"He was hurt bad, Chaplain. Real bad."

"If he's here, I'll find him. What's your name, Marine?"

"Slate, Jessie Slate. PFC."

The chaplain stood up and left through an open doorway.
Jessie stared at the tent stove set up in the center of the
straw-covered floor until he fell asleep. Warmth covered

him. It had to be a dream, but the warmth was wonderful, dream or no dream. Pain shot from his ankle as it began to thaw and it was no use fighting it, the pain was waking him. He opened his eyes. The flaming light of a raging orange fire stung them shut. Bullets ripped through the shack with smacking sounds. Enemy tracer rounds flashed through the tiny building of wood and straw, starting new fires. Yellow flames licked at Jessie's feet and the smell of hair being singed away caused him to shield his face with his gloved hands. He grabbed the boots of a man beside him and began dragging the man toward the door. Someone was screaming in agony. Jessie pulled the man outside and collapsed on his back.

"Just great," someone nearby growled.

Jessie opened his eyes to see a Marine kneeling over the man he had dragged from the burning building.

"You saved a dead one, Mac."

Jessie fell back, shivering from the cold, and waited for help. When he opened his eyes again, it was black. Something stung his face. He moved to touch it and discovered that he was under a canvas tarp. Someone was beside him. He pushed the tarp away from his face. It was daylight. He glanced to his left as he jerked on the tarp, revealing a row of gray faces frozen in death.

"I'm alive! Don't leave me here! I'm alive! I'm still alive!"

Boots ran toward him. "Calm down! It's okay. Calm down!" an unfamiliar voice called out.

Jessie turned to see a freckle-faced boy leaning over him.

"I got you, Marine. It's okay. Here, have a drink of grapefruit juice."

The man helped Jessie sit up as he put a blue and yellow can of Donald Duck grapefruit juice to his mouth. It tasted cold with chunks of ice, but sweet and refreshing like nothing had ever tasted before in his life.

"Hey, Mac! This one wasn't dead. Help me get him on that jeep."

CHAPTER TWENTY

The eleven corkscrew miles from Hagaru to Koto-ri were a bloody life and death struggle as every able-bodied man in the two Marine regiments, along with a unit of British Royal Marine Commandoes and a decimated U.S. Army battalion, fought through each gorge, around every hairpin curve, and across log causeways where elevation dropped up to three thousand feet in a matter of three miles. The First Marine Regiment under Chesty Puller was dug in a perimeter around a three-thousand-foot sheet of ice being used as an airstrip at Koto-ri. Everyone knew that it would be the last chance to fly out the critically wounded. Otherwise, it was a treacherous sixty-mile journey by truck to Hamhung, eight miles more to Hungnam.

F-4U Corsairs and Australian P-51s bombed and strafed Chinese positions in wave after wave while cargo planes dropped desperately needed supplies as Marines fought their way south. Remarkably, the weather held, but on December 6 the umbrella of Air Force, Navy, and Marine aircraft was replaced by an umbrella of snow. Somebody gave Jessie an M-1 and told him to get ready to use it as the tattered regiments rolled into Koto-ri in a snowstorm. Twice he used the body of another wounded Marine stretched across the back of the jeep on a litter as a rifle rest to aim and fire at Chinese snipers on the ridges above the MSR.

With each shot the wounded man would grunt and ask, "Get him?"

"Think so," Jessie said.

"Good, now get off me."

The convoy rolled to a stop near the airstrip and the wounded were lined up along the narrow, icy dirt road. Someone placed a tarp over them to protect them from the snow. The tarp was brittle and hurt if it touched your flesh. The sound of someone shuffling nearby opened Jessie's eyes. For the first time he realized that pain was coming from his back. He wondered how bad the wound was. Suddenly someone lifted the frozen tarp and blinding snow whipped it away from the wounded with a crack.

"Grab that tarp!" someone yelled out.

"Is there a PFC Slate here?" a familiar-sounding voice called through the howling wind.

"I'm Slate!" Blowing ice stung Jessie's face and eyes.

"I'm the chaplain!" the man shouted as he hunched over Jessie, trying to protect his face from the howling blizzard.

"Broken Wing! You found him!"

"Don't get your hopes up, Marine! He doesn't look good. I can take you to him! He's with some wounded in a tent beside the airstrip!"

"Bring me to him! Please!"

The chaplain bent down and lifted Jessie over his shoulder in a fireman's carry. He fought his way against the whipping windstorm for a good twenty yards before he had to stop. He lowered Jessie onto a snowbank and sank to the ground. His breath steamed and he coughed.

"Can you walk at all?"

"Yes. I'll crawl if I have to! Just take me to him!"

The chaplain tried to shield his face as he shouted through the wind. "He's in a warming tent! Not far!"

"Let's go!" Jessie yelled back, and fought to get to his feet. He fell.

The chaplain lifted Jessie over his shoulder and struggled on. The blinding snow was too thick to see in any direction.

"How do you know where you're going?" Jessie shouted.

"I'm guessing!"

Soon the chaplain lowered Jessie to the snow-covered ground and dragged him by the arms through a tent flap. The immediate warmth of a tent stove hit Jessie's face and feeling began to slowly come back to his frozen flesh. The tent was filled with bullet holes, which whistled with icy wind. Men with fresh lung wounds lay heaving, fighting for each breath. Some groaned, others stared straight up with chalk-white faces.

"He's over here," the chaplain said quietly.

Jessie crawled around wounded men until he reached the chaplain. Wing was in a sleeping bag. Jessie pulled the top of the bag away from his face and gasped at the sight. Frozen blood covered Broken Wing's bandaged face from the bridge of his nose to his lower neck.

"Wing. Can you hear me? It's Jessie."

Broken Wing's mouth hole moved. An eyebrow twitched, and Jessie heard himself sigh.

"Wing! Can you hear me?"

"Da-tsi," came a barely audible Navajo sound that filled Jessie's heart with joy.

"What did he say?" the chaplain asked.

Jessie looked up at the chaplain in the dim stove light and wiped at tears.

"He said 'maybe.' "

Jessie cradled Broken Wing's head for what felt like a long time and tried to warm the Indian with his own body heat.

"We can't stay here any longer, son," the chaplain finally said.

"I won't leave him!" Jessie sobbed.

"These men are tagged for the first flight out. You can't stay here."

"I won't leave him!" Jessie growled through clenched teeth, like a crazed dog.

A weak tug at his sleeve brought him out of his rage. He looked down at Broken Wing's trembling hand, then at his face. He was trying to speak but seemed unable. Jessie lowered his ear to the Indian's mouth hole in the bloody bandage.

"Say it again, Broken Wing."

"Pray, Jessie." The words were labored and burning with pain. Jessie collapsed onto Broken Wing's chest and sobbed uncontrollably. He felt someone lifting him up by his elbows and was too weak to fight any longer. They brought him to a new group of wounded Marines and lay him beside a small fire, which the men had started with old grenade crates. He stared up at the snow-choked sky, listening to other Marines, futilely trying to warm themselves by the fire.

"Without air cover we're dead," one Marine mumbled as he looked into the snowy black sky.

Some men tried to change the subject.

"Hey, Al. Remember that dame in San Diego?"

"Yeah. This blizzard reminds me of her. It ain't going away."

Jessie thought of Kate and Charlie. He longed to be with them once more, but had no faith that he ever would. How much he loved them both. How could he have let himself be convinced to give them up for this lousy war?

"If the transports can't land tomorrow, half those wounded won't make it to Hamhung," someone said in a hushed tone.

"God! Just one lousy star." One star would mean clear skies tomorrow. The blinding snowstorm showed no sign of abating.

"You ain't gonna see a star tonight. Not through this soup."

"It can't keep this up. Can it?" someone asked from the other side of the fire.

Bone-piercing wind blasted the thick snow against flesh like pieces of rock.

"Get the wounded inside the warming tents!" a deep voice shouted from the dark airstrip of ice.

Two Marines slung their rifles and grabbed up Jessie. They carried him to a warming tent and dropped him hard onto the frozen ground. The men inside the dimly lit tent seemed tense.

After a while a Marine wearing a furry cap with a first lieutenant's silver bar on it poked his head through the tent flap and shouted, "We're breaking out of Koto-ri tomorrow!"

"Without air cover?" someone shouted back.

"With or without! We wait any longer and we ain't going nowhere, mister!"

"What about the transports, sir?"

"Forget it. The gooney birds can't fly and can't land in this soup."

Jessie's heart felt as though it had fallen through his stomach. Broken Wing would die if he did not get evacuated now. The Navajo's words haunted Jessie as he tried to warm himself with his own breath. Wing was going to die.

"Listen up!" a tall Marine with a deep voice bellowed. "The skipper has asked the men to pray for a star!"

Jessie looked up and wiped away a tear.

"Did everybody hear what I said? The skipper has ordered every man to pray for clear skies. Pray for a star."

It was the strangest order Jessie had ever heard. The normally wisecracking Marines remained silent. His eyes and mind were open. In one corner of the tent he heard a familiar voice. The man was praying aloud.

"Murray? Is that PFC Murray? Rick Murray from Bloody Ridge?"

"Yes. I'm over here."

Jessie crawled around the sprawled out men until he reached Murray sitting with hands clasped and a blood-soaked bandage around his chest.

"Slate! God! It's good to see you!"

"Murray. Pray with me. I'm not too good at this."

Murray sat up straighter. He looked hard into Jessie's eyes and finally gave a slow nod. He bowed his head and began to pray quietly.

"O dear God, you know our situation.
Save the division, Lord.
Give us a sign of clear weather, O Lord.
A star."

Murray stopped speaking but remained bowed. Jessie repeated the prayer in his mind, then prayed aloud.

"Jesus, please save that stupid Indian.
I love him, God—"

Jessie's voice cracked. He suddenly felt overwhelmed with fatigue and despair. How could he believe God cared about him or Wing or anyone else at a time like this? God had left them to perish. He covered his face with his hands and stayed that way for a long time. When he lifted his head, Murray looked as if he were still praying. He was thankful for the dim light as he crawled back to his blanket. He did not want to look Murray in the eyes.

He fell into a fitful, exhausted doze the moment his head hit the ground. Visions of Kate and Paddy and Charlie Rose Slate and O'Cleary and Bright Morning and his dad all ran together, until only the face of his old Kentucky friend, PFC Charlie Rose, was clear.

"A star! A star!"

"God! That there's a miracle we're seeing!"

"Hey, there's a star out here!"

"Look up there! Can you believe that?"

"Yeeehii!"

Jessie sat up like a shot and tried to shake off the dream. He shook his head to clear the fog. Was he still dreaming?

He looked at the top of the tent. It fluttered wildly in the brutal wind. Snow blew through the front flap and under the edges of the canvas walls. Jessie crawled over and around the bodies until he was outside. He tried to shield his eyes from the painful, blasting snow. Marines stood huddled in small groups, pointing toward the southern sky. Jessie squinted, lifting his lined, bearded face into the fierce blizzard.

A star hung over the southwest corner of the First Marine Division perimeter. It was impossible, but there it was, like a light beaming through the eye of a hurricane. Some men cheered hysterically. Others stood, gaping as if seeing the face of God. And somehow, Jessie no longer cared about the cold or the pain from his wounds. He sat huddled and shivering and staring in wonder at the star over Koto-Ri.

December 7, 1950.

CHAPTER TWENTY-ONE

"Jessie! Jessie!" Kate called from the mailbox hanging on the gate post of her freshly painted white picket fence.

Jessie poked his head out the window of his upstairs room in the giant old Victorian-style house and waved. "Be right there, honey." He dabbed on some aftershave, then grabbed a clean shirt from his suitcase. He hustled down the one-hundred-year-old, oak-wood staircase, taking two steps at a time, and shoved through the screen door. Kate hummed the Marine hymn on the big green porch swing as she studied a postcard. Jessie plopped down beside her and kissed her on the cheek.

"He'll be here tonight," she said excitedly.

Jessie snatched the postcard. "That quick?"

"Yes. It says that he's on his way to Jungle Warfare School at Camp Pendleton. He'll be here on the fifth and leave the next morning. Think he can find us?"

Jessie laughed. "If he finds Wilmore, I'll wager that he finds Main Street. And if he can't find the Scott Station bed and breakfast, then this is one jarhead that reads a compass worse than I ever did."

"I guess you'll be in heaven, having a young Marine to talk to."

"I've enjoyed talking with your dad too. But I'll admit, I'm anxious to see this kid."

Jessie sighed nostalgically and faked a smile at Kate. Someone tugged on his sleeve.

"Dad."

"Yeah, Charlie. How's my boy this morning?" Jessie lifted his ten-year-old wonder onto his lap.

"Is your friend coming?"

"Yep. He sure is, but he's not really a friend. I mean, I've never met the young man. His uncle was my friend. Gunnery Sergeant Paddy Francis Killeen. A great man, son. He saved your daddy's life."

"And his nephew is a Marine?"

"Yes. So it seems. PFC Timmy Francis Killeen."

The handsome young Marine touched his mouth with a checkered napkin and smiled. "It's a wonderful cook you are, Mrs. Slate. I mean Miss Kate."

Kate smiled and stood up from the table. The young PFC stood politely. "You have to be a decent cook to run a bed and breakfast. Now stay seated while I brew up some coffee. And Charlie Rose, I think you have some homework to do, young man."

"Ah, Mom! I wanna hear about Gunny O'Cleary and Gunny Killeen! I wanna hear about the war!"

"If you had done your work instead of watching the Lone Ranger—"

"Ah, Mom!"

"You heard Mom's orders, Private Slate. Give your dad a kiss and hit the books."

"Ahhh. Grown-ups have all the fun." Charlie shook hands with Timmy, ran around the table, kissed his dad, and left the dining room.

"He's a fine boy you have, sir."

"Thank you, Timmy. But I can take no credit for that. Kate has raised him alone, with the help of her father, since they opened this place." Jessie Slate glanced down, seemingly embarrassed. He looked at Timmy. "Now that I'm retired . . . if things work out and we get remarried . . ." He paused and glanced toward the kitchen. "Well now, tell me, how did you find me?"

"Easy enough, sir. My uncle had written about you and your Navajo friend many times. I went through some of the old letters, and the last time I was on leave I contacted a friend at the Veterans Administration. He found you for me via the post office."

"Well, I'm glad he did, Tim. You know, I loved your uncle like my own dad."

"The feeling was mutual, sir. He called you his illegitimate son on more than one occasion."

Jessie laughed out loud and remembered. He fought off an empty sensation in the pit of his stomach that always followed talk of the Corps.

"God, I miss him, Timmy. A great man. A great Marine."

"Yes, sir. Sergeant Broken Wing has often spoken the same words, sir."

"Broken Wing! You know Broken Wing?"

"True enough, sir. Not a finer Marine in the group, sir."

"I can't believe it! Kate! Timmy here has met Broken Wing."

"You're kidding!" she yelled from the kitchen.

"I did not only meet him, sir. Extremely proud I am to say I'll be serving under him."

"Serving under him? Where? What duty station?"

"I don't want to appear an alarmist, sir, but . . ."

"Just speak up, son. What's the scuttlebutt?"

"Seems we're about to be in a bit of a fight."

"Shooting war?"

"Advisers to the South Vietnamese Marines, sir."

"They have Marines?"

"We're seeing to it, sir. The Communists are pouring over the 17th Parallel, sometimes with Chinese advisers."

"Well, the Russians are the big bankers, son. The Vietnamese and Chinese hate each other and have hated each other for over a thousand years. It won't be the Chinese helping them."

Timmy's bright inquisitive eyes were filled with awe.

"Your understanding is clearly superior to mine, Mr. Slate. A shame it is, sir, that we don't have more men like yourself and Sergeant Wing to lead us into battle." His tone was nearly reverent. Timmy's green eyes and freckles made him look even younger than he was.

"Battle?" Kate stood frowning in the doorway between the kitchen and dining room, holding a silver tray filled with coffee and cookies.

"You're not old enough to go into battle, Timmy," Kate said with a condescending smile.

"Of course he is, Kate."

Kate's blue eyes filled with sudden anger. "He's barely older than Charlie!"

"I'm a full seventeen, Miss Kate."

"They're going in as advisers, Kate."

Kate set the tray of coffee down and looked solemnly at Timmy. "Are they all this young?" she asked, quiet concern now evident in her soft, beautiful eyes.

"I was the same age when we hit Vella Lavella, Kate."

Kate's flashing eyes turned on Jessie. "Yes. And you've nearly been killed a dozen times."

"You're right. The only reason I'm not dead is—"

"Jesus Christ! That's the only reason, Jessie Slate! And prayer."

"You're right, Kate! Jesus Christ! God made sergeants! And sergeants keep kids like this alive!"

Kate's face looked suddenly pale, almost ashen. She blinked as if seeing a ghost and took a step back. Her mouth was open slightly, but words were not forming. Jessie's heart fluttered with adrenaline and his face felt warm. Kate's eyes turned cold. She excused herself. The men sat silent for an awkward moment.

"I apologize, sir. If I've spoken out of turn—"

"No. Not at all, Timmy. You were caught by 'friendly fire,' son. It's a private matter."

Kate returned a bit later, less effusive, but polite, as always.

The rest of the night went by pleasantly. Charlie was allowed to sit and listen after much begging. Jeremiah came home from Asbury Seminary classes about four P.M. Stories of the Devil Dogs of WWI were passed on to the young Marine. Timmy and Charlie couldn't hear enough about Gunny Killeen or Broken Wing. A bottle of Irish whiskey found its way into the sitting room, enhancing even the oldest memories. Kate brought out the Irish pipes and laughter followed until it was finally time for taps.

Saying good-bye to Timmy the next morning was hard. Jessie and Kate watched his old Chevy go down Main Street and turn right at the only stoplight in Wilmore. He drove past Asbury College, the IGA, and out of sight.

PFC Timmy Killeen pulled into Sandy's Motel on the outskirts of Wilmore. He parked the Chevy in front of Room 7, got out, and knocked on the door. The door opened immediately.

"Outstanding. Mission accomplished?" Broken Wing asked.

"Aye aye, Sergeant. Couldn't have gone better if I'd had a leprechaun in me pocket!"

"And he never asked why Gunny Killeen had not mentioned you?"

The young Marine made a smooth motion with his hand. "Slid right by them with barely a question."

"Outstanding, PFC O'Rourke." Broken Wing shook O'Rourke's hand, slapped him on the back.

Broken Wing placed the room key on the dresser. He hoisted his seabag over his left shoulder, scanned the room one last time, and walked out to the car. He loaded his seabag in the trunk.

"You drive first."

"Yes, sir, Sergeant."

"Long way to Camp Pendleton," Broken Wing said as he climbed in the passenger side, then leaned back and pulled his piss cutter down over one eye to sleep.

O'Rourke started up the car, pulled away from the motel, and headed down Route 68 toward Lexington.

"California, here we come."

"Job well done," Broken Wing said.

"I don't know, Sergeant Wing. I think the man needs one last push to actually reenlist."

"Yes." Broken Wing smiled.

"Daddy! Dad! Hey, Dad!" Charlie Rose Slate slammed the screen door of the big Victorian house and ran up the stairway, waving a small brown package. Just hearing his son's voice filled Jessie with joy.

Jessie opened the door of his bedroom. "Don't wake the other guest, son," he cautioned as he snatched the boy up and kissed him.

"It's from Uncle Broken Wing! It's postmarked Vietnam!"

"Really!" Kate said, standing in the doorway. Her hair was up and she wore a blue apron. The aroma of a country breakfast filled the old house.

"Can I have the stamp?"

"Let me open it, son," Jessie said.

"Ahh, I wanna open it, Dad."

Jessie laughed and set the box down. "Okay, you open it."

Charlie Rose ripped at the package as if it contained gold.

"Easy, Charlie. It might be breakable," Kate warned.

Charlie paused as he broke through the taped-up end of the small, square box.

"Well, what is it?" Kate asked excitedly.

The boy yanked the silver-colored object out of the bag and held it up.

"It's a bracelet! Just like Dad's!" He squinted. "But this

one says, 'John 3:16.' I know that verse, Dad! . . . 'For God
so loved the world that He gave His only begotten son, so
that whoever believeth in Him will not perish, but have
everlasting life.' "

Jessie's heart stopped beating. He haltingly took the box
from his son's hand and searched inside. He pulled out a
small piece of paper smudged with dirt. He unfolded the
paper and read aloud.

"Brother. May not make it back. If bad happens do not
want bracelet to end up with some office pogue. If so, be
sure it reaches my son, Swift Eagle. Semper Fi."

Jessie stared at the note for what felt like a long time. He
swallowed back a lump of emotion in his throat, then
slowly turned a pleading face to Kate. Kate's eyes were already misty and red. One large single tear meandered down
her cheek. She forced a smile that had no feeling and
walked away.

CHAPTER TWENTY-TWO
U.S.S. *Ogden*, South China Sea

"Enter and be recognized!"

Jessie Slate and Broken Wing opened the door to a cramped little office. They stepped in, came to attention and saluted.

"Gunnery Sergeant Slate reporting for duty, sir!"

"Gunnery Sergeant Wing reporting for duty, sir!"

Captain Volke, a stern-faced, middle-aged officer sat in a swivel chair reading a report. He glanced up, waving a return salute. "You landed over an hour ago, Marines. Why are you just now reporting in?"

"We—" Broken Wing began.

"Got lost, Captain," Jessie finished.

"Got lost?"

"Yes, sir."

"See that you don't get lost again, Marines."

"Aye aye, sir," Jessie said.

"I know your records, gentlemen, and I know how much trouble you two can cause. I still can't believe they put you together again. Just don't think you're pulling any crap in my outfit."

"Crap, sir?" Jessie said innocently.

"You heard me, Slate! I run a tight ship, mister! I'll have you two swabbing decks if there's one single incident. I am completely familiar with your combat record, but you'll get no favored treatment here, Sergeants. You will work by the numbers, just like every Marine in my command! Do I make myself clear?"

"Yes, sir."

"Yes, sir."

"Good. Then we will get along just fine. Now go introduce yourselves to your platoon leader."

"We're both in the same platoon, sir?" Jessie asked.

"Yes. Temporarily." He pointed at Broken Wing. "You will probably be working naval and fixed-wing communications for Operation Daring Endeavor during the brief time you're both on board. You will be briefed at the appropriate time. Now get down to your squad bay lockers. Get a new issue of utilities. You stink. Dismissed."

"Thank you, sir." Jessie found it difficult to form the words through his clenched teeth. They saluted, did an about-face and left the office. The reason they stank, Jessie thought angrily, was because they'd just come in from the bush, where they'd spent months advising a unit of Korean Marines and engaging the enemy.

"You already cause trouble," Wing groaned.

"Me!"

"You."

"I didn't do a bloody thing!"

Wing scratched at his stomach. *"A-chi yeh-hes."*

"Oh shut up. Intestines don't itch. Is that guy a jackass or what!"

"Cha-le-gai."

"Calling him a squid is being kind." This was it, Jessie thought. A few more weeks and he would retire and never have to see the likes of that kind of character again. At least not in a uniform. He'd seen enough of them over his years in the Corps—in Vietnam, Haiti, Lebanon, the Dominican Republic—every war produced its petty, office-pogue, bureaucratic jerks.

"He hates you," Wing said.

"Why would he hate me?"

"Maybe he thinks that you are stupid."

"I should have left you on Bougainville," Jessie wise-cracked, but he knew what was bothering Wing. Swift Eagle, Wing's son, was serving in this platoon—in fact had served under him a few months before—and Wing didn't want to bring the boy any more problems than he needed. Being a grunt was hard enough without having a father around with a reputation as a troublemaker.

Two other newcomers to the ship, Gonzales and Justice, joined them while they were being issued lockers. The four were led to a large ward room where about thirty Marines were in the process of cleaning their weapons. They had their rifles in various stages of disassembly. They even had their magazines apart. Morale was high, judging from all the jaw-jacking going on. A lieutenant spotted them as they entered the room. He approached, already saluting as if they were the officers. They came to attention and saluted.

"Gunny Slate and Gunny Wing?" he asked quickly, turning the salute into a handshake.

"Yes, sir," they answered.

"I'm First Lieutenant Kutler. You've been assigned to Echo Two/Seven, first platoon. I'm platoon leader. Did you meet the C.O.?"

"Yes, sir. We met him." Jessie's tone told the story.

The lieutenant smiled. "He's not that bad."

"Strange welcome he gave us, Lieutenant," Broken Wing said.

"Well, I think he's just overcompensating."

"Oh, no," Jessie moaned.

"First command?" Wing asked.

The lieutenant nodded as if admitting something he didn't want to admit.

"Has he ever been in the bush, Lieutenant?" Jessie asked hesitantly.

The lieutenant shook his head slowly.

Jessie's shoulders sagged with dread as he exchanged a discouraged glance with Wing. He turned to the lieutenant again. "Pleasure to meet you, Lieutenant Kutler," he said.

The lieutenant had a nice smile but was not a handsome man. He had a big fleshy face and dark brown eyes that seemed tiny under one long, bushy eyebrow connected between his eyes in an almost straight line.

"The honor's all mine, Gunnery Sergeants," he said. "I've heard about you two from the old salts, and I'm just flat-out happy to have you aboard."

"Thank you, sir. Hope we don't disappoint you. Evidently, somebody has been spreading an awful lot of scuttlebutt about us."

"From what I hear, the colonel must have served with you two on Bougainville, or maybe it was in China or Korea. Anyway, he's a fan of yours."

"What's his name, Lieutenant?"

"Lieutenant Colonel Rockey."

"Lieutenant colonel?" Jessie exclaimed.

"Couldn't be," Broken Wing said.

"How old is he?"

"Look's about thirty-five to forty, my guess."

Jessie turned to Wing. "Did General Rockey have a son?"

Wing shrugged.

"That must be it. The general's son is the regimental commander. It's unbelievable."

"How well do you know the colonel, Gunny?" Kutler asked.

"Don't know him at all, Lieutenant. Do you Wing?"

"No."

"Well, he sure know's a lot about you two."

"We knew his father. The general was one outstanding Marine. A Marine's general all the way. Where did his son come from?"

"Eleventh Marines."

"Eleventh?"

Lieutenant Kutler shrugged as if he didn't understand either.

"A cannon-cocker. How did an artillery officer get command of a grunt regiment?"

First Lieutenant Kutler rolled his eyes and shrugged. "I guess your daddy being a three-star doesn't hurt."

Jessie whistled. "That sure doesn't sound like something General Rockey would pull. He was one fine Marine."

"A man will do just about anything for his own son, Gunny. I can't say I wouldn't do the same thing."

"Yes," Broken Wing said.

"I'll tell you the truth, Gunnery Sergeants. So far, he's done one fine job, and you'll hear very few complaints about the old man's performance."

"If he's anything like his father, that doesn't surprise me a bit, Lieutenant." Jessie turned to Wing. "Remember when he kept us from getting the ax in China?"

"Is that when you two tried to raise the Irish flag over the British Consulate on St. Patrick's Day?"

Jessie and Wing stared at the young first lieutenant as if he'd just stolen something. A couple of Marines nearby started laughing, and it was obvious the conversation was being enjoyed by the entire platoon.

"How could you know a thing like that, Lieutenant?" Jessie asked.

"Sort of part of the legend about you two, I guess. I can't remember who it was told me that one, but it was just too colorful to forget."

"Six months in the brig were not colorful," Wing said with an accusing look at Slate.

"Now wait a minute, Wing, I don't remember you arguing the need to raise that flag."

"Yes."

"Yes what?"

"Yes."

"Are you saying that it wasn't as much your doing as mine?"

"Yes."

"What about Bougainville?"

"Bougainville?"

"Yeah. Bougainville. Remember how you had to have booze so bad that you came up with that brilliant idea of digging up Jap stiffs to trade souveniers to the bluejackets for torpedo juice!"

Wing said nothing, but looked insulted. The rest of the men in the ward room had stopped cleaning weapons and were watching and listening. Jessie suddenly felt like he was bragging, and he did not like it. He cleared his throat.

"Well. Those things were a long time ago."

"Bougainville. Is that where you shot down the Jap zero after the crew on a 40mm were wiped out?"

"Ancient history," Slate said.

First Lieutenant Kutler turned around to face the men. "First platoon, I know that some of you have already had the pleasure of serving with Gunnery Sergeant Slate here in Vietnam. But for those who have not met him or Gunnery Sergeant Wing, I'd like you to meet them now." He turned back to the two gunnery sergeants. "Gentlemen, we are sincerely honored to serve with the two of you. Attennnnnhut!"

The platoon snapped to attention as Lieutenant Kutler saluted the gunnery sergeants. This was above and beyond respect usually granted to any NCO. Jessie Slate felt his face flush with pride and embarrassment as he returned the platoon salute.

The room fell silent in expectation as Broken Wing stepped toward one particular Marine who looked exactly like him, but was bigger by a few inches and a good thirty pounds. The two men paused for a moment face-to-face, then clasped hands, gripping each other's wrists instead of shaking hands. They stayed that way for a while just staring. Broken Wing and Swift Eagle. Father and son.

Jessie thought of his own son and was envious. An overwhelming urge to write Charlie came over him. I'll write a letter tonight, he thought.

Broken Wing and Swift Eagle released their grip and Swift Eagle strode over to Jessie.

"Good to have you back, sir."

"Thanks, Corporal. How are the men?"

"Fine, Gunny. Took a couple of casualties, but no KIAs."

"Yeah, that's what Mouth and Blaine were saying. We brought you a couple of new grunts." Slate turned to Lieutenant Kutler. "Sir, this is PFC Justice ... what was your last name, boot?"

"Pimkin, Gunny. PFC Justice Pimkin."

"And this other one is PFC Gonzales."

"What is your MOS, Marines?" Lieutenant Kutler asked.

"Military Occupational Specialty 0311, sir," Gonzales answered.

"Riflemen. Crap, we needed some 0331s. We keep losing machine gunners."

Lieutenant Kutler turned to look for someone in the first row of Marines cleaning weapons. "Morse!"

"Yes, sir!"

"You get 'em."

"Aye aye, sir!"

"You two will be in Lance Corporal Barry Morse's squad. First squad, first platoon, Echo Company, Second Battalion, Seventh Marine Regiment. You got that?"

"Yes, sir," Gonzales answered.

Lieutenant Kutler looked directly at Justice, waiting for an answer. "Well?"

"I think so, sir, but I'm nervous as a virgin bride in a feather bed."

Lieutenant Kutler smiled and turned to Lance Corporal Barry Morse. Barry was a short, stocky, M-79 blooper man who seemed to match his weapon perfectly. Word was he could arch that M-79 40mm round onto the face of a dime at a hundred meters.

"Good to see you, Gunny," Barry said with a wave to Slate.

"You look different, Morse. What's changed?"

He rubbed his chin. "Beard. They made me shave it off when we came back aboard."

"Yeah, that's it. You had some facial hair there, Marine."

"Yes sir, Gunny. I suffered in boot camp, believe me." He turned to Broken Wing. "Honor to meet you, Gunny."

Wing nodded but said nothing. Swift Eagle stood beside him silently.

"You two better get clean while you can, Gunnery Sergeants. We never know when we'll get the word. Better get on down to supply, get your new issue and prepare yourselves," Lieutenant Kutler said knowingly.

"Yes, sir."

"Now if I understand the orders correctly, you, Gunny Slate, will be with us until your tour is up in a couple of weeks?"

"Yes, sir."

"And Gunny Wing is just here to work out communications between us and the K.M.'s for Operation Endeavor?"

"Yes, sir," Wing said.

"Welcome aboard. Better get moving."

Jessie and Wing saluted, "Aye aye, sir."

They left their weapons on one of the tables and made their way to the supply room, where a black corporal tossed out a new issue of jungles.

"What size boots?" the supply corporal asked.

"Don't need boots," Jessie said.

"Me either," Wing said.

The supply corporal leaned over a counter and stared at the boots that now appeared as brown moccasins molded to each man's feet.

"Them's salty boondockers, bros."

"Just breaking 'em in now, son," Jessie said with a smile.

They made their way to the head area and began to undress. Broken Wing stepped close as Slate dropped his pack and canteens on the floor. Wing held out his arm and pulled up his sleeve, revealing the tarnished old bracelet on his left wrist.

Slate smiled and pulled the sleeve of his jungle jacket up. Wing took Slate's wrist and checked the inscription. He grunted his displeasure.

"Oh, shut up. I like my wind-god drawing, so just shut up."

"Must change."

"No."

"Yes."

"No."

"Yes. Must."

"Will you forget it!"

"No."

"You know, Wing you can be like a pit bull that just won't let go of something."

"I made bracelet. I want it changed."

"No."

"Yes."

"No."

"Change bracelet."

"No. I like the wind-god stuff. It's sort of a conversation piece."

"Idolatry."

Slate smiled. "Let me see yours."

Broken Wing showed him his bracelet. The cross and John 3:16 were tarnished but clear.

"It doesn't look too bad but the wind-god stuff look's neater."

"I fix."

"I'll change it if I ever figure out what John 3:16 means."

This time Wing blinked to catch up with the conversation. "Make bet."

"What kind of bet?"

"Bet you re-up."

"Not a chance. Seventeen days and a wake up, bro. I'm history. I'm so short I can walk under the commandant's door."

"Bet."

"Okay, wise guy. You're on. What's the bet?"

"You will re-up. I will change bracelet. You will understand. I sleep better."

Slate forced a laugh and pointed at Broken Wing.

"You're on. If I re-up, you can change anything you want."

The jungle utilities were caked hard with dried sweat and any number of body fluids. It was like peeling off dirty skin. Taking off the trousers was almost unnecessary. They were split from stem to stern anyway. They both threw the tattered clothes into a GI can, but not the boots. The boots were worn out by civilized standards, but worn boots were a status symbol in Vietnam. New boots meant you were a new guy, and nobody wanted to look like a new guy. A regular Marine bush outfit would stay out for as much as ninety days at a time before coming back for new clothes, ammo, and one hot meal before going right back out. You would never look like a new guy for more than a day or two, but the Battalion Landing Team Marines would complete a short operation, fly back to the ship, and get new jungles regularly, so the only part of the uniform that said you were a salt was the boots.

The shower was warm and clean and soothing. Slate closed his eyes and nearly fell asleep. He wondered if his body could ever really be clean again after being in the Vietnamese jungle. If so, certainly not the same kind of clean. It had taken two years to get clean of the various jungle parasites and diseases after Japan surrendered, and he never spent nearly the same amount of time in those jungles as this new 'Nam Corps was spending in this jungle.

He finished rinsing the Life Buoy from his hair, stepped out of the shower, and took a deep breath.

"Whooo! What's that stench, Wing?"

"Us."

"Oh. Yeah. You're right. God, it's weird how you can't smell yourself until you're clean."

"Close the lid on that can," Wing said with a frown.

Jessie found the lid and shut the stink of their old jungles inside the can, but it still permeated the room. He stretched and felt light, as if he'd been weighed down with slime. He slapped Broken Wing on the back. "First stop, ship's barber."

"Mail call."

Twenty minutes later Jessie exhaled contentedly, leaning back in the barber chair with his hands behind his head. The barber finished cleaning up the white sidewalls, then started in on the moustache.

"As you were, seaman," Jessie said, balking. "No one under Commandant Chapman touches the 'stach."

"Yes sir, Gunny."

Jessie looked in the mirror, rubbing the shaved area above his ears. "White sidewalls look clean?" Broken Wing grunted. "Well, Wing, this could be one of my last military haircuts. Maybe I'll let my hair get a little longer when I get out. What do ya think?"

"Must hurry or miss mail call," Broken Wing said.

"Food first, Gunnery Sergeant Wing."

Jessie watched as the barber finished up Broken Wing, then they headed for the chow hall. Chow was top-notch on-board ship. Far superior to regular Marine mess. Sometimes it took a few days to get used to eating off plates and using knives and forks, depending on how long you'd been out in the bush. Warm food took a man's stomach a bit of getting used to also. Your taste buds would change and everything tasted bland, not that Marine Corps chow wasn't bland on its own. Probably because it was hot food, Jessie decided. It looked so good, you couldn't keep from gorging yourself, but it never failed to give a man the runs for the first day or two until the stomach could adjust. About the time it would adjust, you'd find yourself back in the bush. Then you'd have to get used to C-rats and water unfit for any living thing. The water could give you dysentery, since sometimes even the halazone tablets couldn't kill everything in jungle water.

After chow they walked around the ship. Jessie reflected that she was one busy lady. A beehive of activity at every turn. The *Ogden* seemed to get even bigger as you wandered about. They headed for the platoons' quarters amidship. It was cramped with cots in tiers just like the old transport ships.

"Man, does this bring back memories," Jessie mumbled as they stooped through the hatchway.

A group of Marines were playing back-alley poker between two rows of cots. A little black Marine and a big black Marine were jawing at each other over a hand. Four other Marines were playing craps against a bulkhead. PFC Gonzales sat on the top of a tier of cots with his legs hanging over, strumming a guitar and sounding darn good. Another Latin-looking Marine sat across the aisle from him on the top cot, playing another guitar. A few men lay in their racks writing letters or reading old ones.

Broken Wing stepped inside the hatch. He stood still beside Jessie for a few moments just watching and listening.

"Yes," Broken Wing said, as if reading Jessie's mind.

"It's amazing isn't it, old buddy," Jessie said quietly. "I can hear O'Cleary or Paddy Killeen tellin' the lads about the old Corps."

"And those vicious battles in Haiti with Charlemagne."

"Nicaragua. Now there was a real war, lads."

They chuckled, but it rang empty with a hint of sadness.

"Sometimes, Wing—"

"Yes. I miss them too."

Slate cleared his throat and threw his shoulders back a bit. "No better way to die . . ."

"Than to die a Marine."

"And as our 'Nam Corps would say—" Jessie began.

"There it is, bro."

They laughed again, and the laugh felt better. PFC Gonzales and his friend began the most beautiful rendition of "Guantanamera" that Jessie had ever heard. It was so beautiful that the Marines stopped jabbering and became serene.

He nudged Broken Wing and pointed at a big Marine playing cards. "That's Big Moose. Carries an M-14. He's nervous."

Big Moose hid his hand of back-alley and leaned against a bulkhead. He was probably six-four and a solid 220, and looked like he should have been playing center on somebody's basketball team. He had a sorry-looking face, deep-set dark eyes, and a long nose. He had a nasty habit of spitting when he was nervous, as Jessie remembered.

Moose carried an M-14. The Corps had just switched over to the new M-16s, and nobody quite trusted the things. The men called 'em Matty Mattels. At about six or seven pounds, and made out of plastic, they sure as crap felt like toys. Word was they jammed easy. They fired a 5.6 round, and it was supposed to tumble end over end so that when it hit Charlie Cong, the round would sometimes follow bone structure. Scuttlebutt said you could hit Charlie in the foot and the round might come out of his elbow or the top of his head if you were lucky. The Army had been using the weapon for a while, and the Corps would get their rejects as always. The older version of the rifle was actually called an AR-15, but they looked the same. Since no one completely trusted the M-16, at least one man in each squad would still carry the M-14. It was heavier but dependable, and accurate at long range, which Matty Mattel was not. It fired a 7.62 round that could knock down a cow. Moose was an M-14 man for the first platoon.

"Only man bigger than Moose is Pollock, by an inch." Jessie was unimpressed with the kid. "Not sure how good of a Marine he is," he said, pointing at the big farm boy from Wisconsin.

"Gunners any good?" Wing asked.

"The platoon has a couple of two-man machine-gun

teams. That thin black Marine over there is Sally. His side-kick and A-gunner is a short Marine named Pale because he looks so white beside Sally. I don't see him right now. The other gun team is a funny pair. I didn't know their real names, the platoon just called 'em Tall and Fat." Jessie pointed them out. They were sitting on a top bunk side by side. They were an odd-looking pair. Tall wasn't all that tall, but his face was so long and thin that it gave you the impression that he was tall. Fat was not all that fat; as a matter of fact, there were no truly fat men in the Corps, and certainly no fat grunts. Fat was just short with round fea-tures, his most globular feature being his face. They looked like Laurel and Hardy faces pasted on nearly normal bod-ies. Tall was a shy, quiet kid from Omaha, and Fat was a sleepy sort of boy from Georgia.

"They're a good group of lads, Gunny Wing," Jessie said, quietly observing the platoon and enjoying the im-promptu entertainment. "I pulled that last operation in An Hoa Valley with 'em."

"Good."

"Swift Eagle is the best Marine in the group."

"You are prejudice," Wing said.

"Better believe it."

"He is good?"

"He's outstanding."

Broken Wing nodded.

"Isn't there a rule about fathers and sons or brothers be-ing in the same outfit or something? Remember when the five brothers went down on that ship—right after we met, I think?"

"The Sullivans."

"Yeah. That was them."

"Yes."

"Yes, there is a regulation?"

"Yes."

"Why hasn't somebody said something?"

"Different name."

"Oh yeah. No last name."

"It is okay if you are not in the same combat unit, I think."

"Well, you'll be going back to the Koreans soon, I suppose."

"Yes."

Static followed by the boatswain's whistle sounded over the ship's intercom just as Gonzales finished his song.

"Now hear this . . . The movie tonight is *Ice Station Zebra*. Starting time 1900 hours. That is all."

Broken Wing checked his watch. "Want to see."

"You do?"

"Yes."

Jessie was surprised to see the Navajo show interest in something without prodding. It was a pleasant surprise.

"Time check."

"Eighteen thirty. Too late for mail. Closed."

"Let's dee-dee-mow. Want to get Swift Eagle?"

He nodded yes.

"Good. Hope they got some popcorn. Squids always got good stuff." Jessie turned to the squad bay. "Corporal Swift Eagle! Front and center! Move it! Move it! Move it!"

The platoon jumped at the command and the call was relayed through the squad bay.

"Chief!"

"Hey, get the Chief!"

"Where's the Chief?"

"Hurry up, Chief. Gunny looks ticked off."

Swift Eagle hustled from the back of the crowded quarters, stepping over and around Marines and equipment until he stood at attention in front of the two old salts. He was a spectacular specimen of what an American Marine and a Navajo Indian should look like. A solid six feet, with the lean, muscular features of a well-trained Marine. His dark skin, piercing black eyes, long straight nose, and high cheekbones, combined with his father's dauntless expression, impressed anyone who looked at him.

"Corporal Swift Eagle reporting as ordered, Gunny."

"Prepare to advance to the flicks. Take the point."

"Aye aye, Gunny."

The Marines had free run of the ship except for "officer country," and they did not have to pull too many useless details. The swabbies got all the chip and paint details as well as the cooking and cleaning. The Marines got to rest and prepare for the inevitable word to board choppers. The hanger deck doubled as the theater. *Ice Station Zebra* was no four-star flick, but Ernest Borgnine always acted like he should have been a Marine sergeant, and Jessie liked the guy. It was a good time. Somebody came up with popcorn, and for a couple of hours everyone enjoyed seeing something besides Marine green and Vietnam.

The next day the first platoon was ordered to draw Class II ammunition for fan-firing their weapons off the fantail of the ship. Each time the men came in from the bush, they had to unload their magazines and any old brass into big bins. That was a real plus for the BLT. A regular bush unit rarely got the chance to swap out all of their old ammo, grenades, 40mm's, and claymore mines for brand new ammo that had not been in and out of jungle rain or rivers. The Navy threw over all sorts of garbage as targets, then stood by to watch. They got a big kick out of it. After fan-firing weapons, Jessie and Wing went belowdecks to clean them thoroughly, then headed back to their quarters.

"Mail call," Broken Wing muttered again.

"No. I'm going to the room and sleep," Jessie said with a pretend yawn. Broken Wing grunted something in Navajo and walked off with Swift Eagle.

Jessie was happy for them, but sometimes envy got the best of him. He caught himself constantly thinking of his son, wondering what might have been had he stayed a civilian. Maybe he would still have Kate. He never heard from her anymore, but Charlie wrote him back once in a while. He tried to write the boy at least once a week. What a strange life he'd chosen for himself, he thought. He loved the Corps and felt nearly as gung ho now as he had in 1943. There were many things he would change if he could, but being a Marine was not one of them. No matter how many ways he looked at it, there was no other life he could live. Kate had finally realized that. And he knew that he could not ask her to be a Marine widow for the rest of her life. Never knowing where her man was, never knowing when the telegram might come. She had desperately wanted a home with a man who was there for breakfast and supper. There was no blame, only pain. If only Charlie could understand that it did not mean his father did not love him or care about him more than anything, Jessie thought. He dropped the pad and pencil and leaned back against his pillow as Broken Wing came in the door.

"Ah, good. You write a letter. Let us go to the mail room."

"All right. What is it that you're not saying, Injun?"

Broken Wing gave his phony "Who me?" look, and Jessie knew he was close to finally getting an answer.

"Don't just sit there with your Navajo face hanging out. What have you heard?"

"A-chi yeh-hes."

"Yeah, well mine are starting to itch too. Now out with it."

"Not supposed to tell. You should hear this from someone else."

"What?" A small tinge of fear fluttered in his heart, and for just a moment Jessie worried that the news was bad.

"Mother of your son writes mother of mine."

"Kate?"

"Yes."

"And?"

"She and Bright Morning exchange letters often."

"So what is it?"

"Charlie Rose is in-country."

"What? What are you talking about?"

"Charlie Rose Slate will be landing in Da Nang. Maybe already."

Jessie stood up from his bunk and tried to gather his thoughts. "How? He's in college at the University of Florida."

"No. He was ROTC and now is a butter-bar lieutenant with the First Marine Division."

Jessie fell back against his bunk like some invisible force had shoved him. He felt light-headed, dizzy. Vented air was cool on his tonsils, and he knew that his mouth was open. He swallowed.

"When did you say he landed?"

"Not sure."

"Could he be . . . how close?"

"He could be in Da Nang."

Jessie turned and walked out of the room like a zombie. He stopped at the door and looked back. "Why wouldn't Kate tell me this?"

"Check mail, stupid. That is why I did not want to speak until you heard from her."

Jessie turned and headed for the ship's mail room. He grabbed a passing sailor to get directions. A few minutes later he stood in front of a Navy chief and wasn't sure how he got there. His heart fluttered as the Navy chief thumbed through a stack of mail.

"Yeah, here you go, Gunny." He pulled a white envelope from the stack and handed it to Jessie. "Gunnery Sergeant Jessie Slate."

Jessie took the letter, found the nearest stairs and made his way to the flight deck. A million thoughts scrambled through his brain until, by the time he found a spot alone near the fantail, his thinking had become chaos. He ripped open the envelope and unfolded the letter.

Dear Jessie,

I don't know where this might find you, but I won't delay in telling you why I'm writing. Our son has joined the Marines without telling me. I assume he has not told you. I knew he was in ROTC, but being ignorant of the program, I took his word that he would just use it to help pay for college and go another direction. He evidently was in some Marine program, Platoon Leadership or something like that. I still don't have all of the details. I knew he was at Quantico, but he told me it was just part of the program and the courses there were part of the regular curriculum. When he finally told me the truth, we had a good cry. Just like you, he thought he was protecting me from being hurt.

He came home last month for his first leave. He looks beautiful, though I know he would die if he heard me say so. He is still such a little boy. He seemed more serious than usual, but I did not know why. He had orders for Vietnam, but again he did not know how to tell me, so he said nothing. I got a letter from him telling me that he would be in Vietnam by September 25. I was furious, and I was never more brokenhearted in my life. I've had time to make myself think more clearly about it all since then, and I realize that he is just like you. Be that good or bad, it is true.

I hate the Marine Corps like some women might hate a female rival. It has always felt like another woman trying to steal the men that I love. My father. My husband. And now my only son.

I'm worried sick. All we hear about is the Tet Offensive. Every night on television they show the number of men who died that day. Why are they not trying to win this war? Can you find Charlie Rose? He is in the First Marine Division. That is all I know for now.

Jessie, I have never forgotten your words when you tried in vain to explain your sense of responsibility to the kid Marines. You said a sergeant's job was to keep those kids alive long enough to become salts. Well, if you're so bloody good at keeping our boys alive while killing the enemy, then you find our son and you make him the best

Marine that ever lived, and you bring him home, Jessie. If he dies, I'll die too.

Kate

Jessie's head fell back against the bulkhead with a clunk but he felt nothing. A vision from the ship's morgue of all of those boys with blackened feet crept into his mind, and he shivered with a sudden dread that reached to the innermost parts of his heart.

"You do not look good."

Jessie looked up, startled. Broken Wing stared down at him with his deadpan, acne-scarred Indian face. But his eyes said that he was there to help.

"My God! Wing!"

"Jesus."

"No! I mean, don't sneak up on a man like that!"

"Letter from Kate."

Jessie blew out hard and his chin dropped. "Yeah."

"You must find son."

"Yes. I have to. That stupid kid!" He slammed the letter against the deck.

"Yes. Like father."

"Ah, shut up!"

Wing squatted down on one knee. Jessie handed him the letter without taking his fixed stare off of his own tattered jungle boots. Wing read silently for a few moments then grunted.

"Yes."

"Yes what?"

"Girl sees pattern of stupid also."

"Sometimes, Wing, you really get on my nerves."

"Yes."

"Yes what?"

"Yes. Nerves cause *a-chi yeh-hes*."

They sat together against the bulkhead for a while before Wing spoke.

"Rockey."

"What?"

"Go see the skipper."

"Why?"

"He will allow you to visit son. You will teach him."

"Maybe the kid has a good MOS. Maybe he's going to be stationed in Da Nang the whole tour."

Wing looked at Jessie with a stare that made him squirm.

"All right, all right. I'm dreaming."

"See the skipper."

"I don't know, Wing. The kid probably hates me. He won't even write me."

"Stupid."

"Shut up."

"Come." Wing stood up.

"Where?"

"Skipper."

"That jerk Captain Volke ain't gonna let me just waltz off the ship to visit my kid. I can't just go over his head to the skipper. You ever heard of the chain of command?"

Wing grabbed up the letter and read outloud, " 'Find him and make him the best Marine that ever lived. Bring him home alive.' " Wing dropped the letter and kicked Jessie's boot. "If you do not try, you will never forgive yourself."

"I know. Let's go."

They made their way back to officer country. The senior officers had regular cabins. A Marine MP stood guard outside the old man's door. He was a big strong lad with a hard-set jaw and an unfriendly expression that was all Marine. Broken Wing approached him first.

"Gunnery Sergeants Wing and Slate to see the colonel."

"Is the colonel expecting you, Gunny?"

"No, Corporal."

"Take it through channels, Gunny."

"No."

The corporal looked down at the shorter Broken Wing with a question on his face.

"You heard him, Corporal," Jessie said. "Now slap that bulkhead."

"I can't do that, Gunny. I'll get busted for sure. The colonel gave orders—"

"I'll take full responsibility, Corporal," Jessie interrupted.

"And I'll see that you get it, Gunnery Sergeant." He turned toward the door and glanced back at the gunnery sergeants. "It's your necks, not mine."

"There it is, Marine," Jessie said.

The corporal slapped above the door three times hard. An instant later the door was yanked open and a short stocky Marine in his khakis and bare feet stood with an unlit cigar hanging out of his mouth, glaring at Jessie and Wing with an angry scowl.

"Didn't I give orders—" He stopped and studied the lapel chevrons on the two gunnery sergeants. "Your name Slate?"

"Yes, sir." Jessie snapped to attention and saluted.

"And you got to be Gunnery Sergeant Broken Wing."

"Yes, sir." Broken Wing snapped to attention and saluted.

"As you were, Corporal. Come in Marines. I've been waiting to meet you two."

A rush of hope filled Jessie as he entered the cabin behind Broken Wing and the colonel. The colonel's cabin was typical Marine. Spartan all the way. A single eight-by-ten, black and white photo of his father the general and Chiang Kai-shek hung on one wall alone. On another wall was a photo of the colonel with Chesty Puller taken in Korea. Colonel Rockey was the spittin' image of his daddy. If he had half the balls of the old man, Jessie thought, he'd be an outstanding Marine. He moved around behind a large oak desk and sat down.

"Sit down, men," he said, motioning to two chairs. He yanked open a bottom drawer and produced a quart bottle of Irish whiskey. He leaned over again, produced two Navy coffee cups and a metal canteen cup, and slammed them onto the desk like an old-time bartender.

"Well, pour 'em, Sergeant," he said gruffly, then leaned over and pulled a box of cigars out of the bottom drawer. "You men know where these came from?" he asked with a twinkle in his eye.

"No, sir," Jessie said.

"An old friend of yours."

Broken Wing stared at the box of cigars, then straightened in his chair as if he'd been stuck with a cattle prod. "The sergeant major? Sergeant Major Erwin, sir?"

The colonel blinked with surprise, then appeared satisfied that Wing had known.

"There it is, Gunny Wing."

"How in the world did you know that, Wing?" Jessie asked.

"You having trouble with that bottle, Gunny Slate?" the colonel asked with a friendly growl.

"No, sir," Jessie said as he snatched up the quart and began to pour generous portions into each cup. "Sergeant Major Erwin. That old warhorse. Why he must be—"

"Sixty-six years young, Gunnery Sergeant," Colonel Rockey said as he picked up the canteen cup and held it out.

"To the sergeant major and the Corps."

"Aye aye, sir!" Jessie shouted as he snatched up a coffee cup and stood to attention, with Wing only a reflex behind. The colonel slowly stood up also, and the men clinked cups while staring hard into each other's eyes. They drank back the Irish whiskey in a single gulp and slapped their cups to the desktop. Jessie's hit first. The colonel looked at him for a quiet moment then burst out laughing. A good, hearty, contagious laugh, the kind that made men live longer.

"The sergeant major, is he well, sir?" Broken Wing asked.

"That he is, Marine. What a man! What a Marine."

"Yes, sir."

"He speaks no higher of any Marine than you, Sergeant Wing."

"Thank you, sir."

"You were on the Canal together, right?"

"Yes, sir."

"And the general speaks the same way about you, Slate. You and Broken Wing and Gunny Killeen."

"May I, sir?" Jessie reached for the bottle.

"Storm the beach, Marine."

"Aye aye, sir." Jessie grabbed the bottle and poured three more healthy portions. He took his cup and stood up, holding it out in a toast.

"To Gunnery Sergeant Paddy Francis Killeen. Marine. Friend. Father. Hero."

"Here, here!" Colonel Rockey stood up again, grabbed his cup and clinked with Broken Wing and Jessie. "And to the regimental bagpipes player of the Seventh Marine Regiment."

Once again they downed the drinks in one gulp, slamming them to the desk, and once again Jessie was first. The colonel laughed out loud.

"The general told me about the time you two had in China at the Leopold Room. Said you were the only real Marines in the place."

Jessie shrugged. "He's right."

The colonel laughed his hearty laugh and poured another round.

"The general, sir. How's the old bulldog?"

The colonel's face saddened as he paused before answering. "He died last spring. Long bout with cancer."

"I'm sincerely sorry to hear that, sir. Please accept my condolences."

"Thank you, Gunny. He would have preferred to die in battle. But I got to spend a lot of time with him during the illness. He could go on for hours about the old Corps. I could listen for hours and never tire of it. It brought us closer than we had ever been."

"To the general." Broken Wing held out his cup. The

others clinked cups and downed their drinks in one gulp. No one slammed down their cup.

"Hard footsteps to follow in, men," the colonel said.

"No doubt, sir."

"I'm just a bit younger than you men. Missed Korea for the most part, got there for the end. Spent my life trying to catch up to the adventure. Been hearing about you two and Killeen and O'Cleary and a hundred others since I was a kid." He stopped and poured another round, then sat down. Jessie and Wing sat down too. "You still play the pipes, Gunny Slate?"

"Yes, sir."

"If I'm not mistaken, you are probably still on record somewhere as the regimental bagpipes player."

"Yes, sir."

"I want you to play for me some time, Gunnery Sergeant."

"Aye aye, sir. Be honored to, sir."

"Where do you keep them?"

"With my seabag, sir. Stateside uniforms. I hope they're here on board, but they may still be in Phu Bai."

"Yes. I would like to hear the old Corps sound. Do the lads good too."

"Sir. I won't beat around about it. I have a request."

"You've been in this Marine Corps longer than I have, Gunnery Sergeant," Colonel Rockey's tone rang official, and Jessie felt his chances dwindle. "You know what the chain of command is."

Jessie felt himself slump. There was no way that jerk Captain Volke would help. He would have to go AWOL again and get busted again, and even then there was no guarantee he could see his son long enough to make a difference.

He took a deep breath and tried to speak calmly, but he knew the intensity in his heart would show through. "Sir, I've been keeping boot Marines alive through three wars. My son is a butter-bar grunt lieutenant. He just got in-country. I want the chance to break him in. I request permission to join him for two weeks, just two weeks to teach him what I've been teaching Marines for a quarter century, sir."

"Put it through channels, Gunnery Sergeant!"

Anger roared through Jessie Slate and he felt himself flush red.

"Sir! The gunnery sergeant requests permission to use his R and R vacationing with another outfit, sir!"

"Don't press it, mister! You get away with an awful lot because of that Medal of Honor, but don't push too far or you'll be wearing that CMH in the brig, Sergeant!"

"Sir! You can take this CMH—"

Colonel Rockey slammed his fist on the desktop and stood up. "Stow it, Marine!" He bellowed like an angry drill instructor.

"Sir," Broken Wing said sharply as he handed the colonel the letter from Kate. Jessie froze.

The colonel took the letter, still glaring at Jessie. He glanced down at it and began to read it to himself. It was hard to tell from his expression just what he was thinking. He sighed aloud once, then grunted as he finished and looked up at Jessie.

Jessie cleared his throat, still standing at attention. "I'm sorry, sir. I had no intention of letting you read that letter."

"Good thing I did, Gunny. Not that it excuses your blatant disregard for regulations." The colonel sat down, leaned back in his chair, and scratched his chin. He pulled his unlit cigar from his mouth and shook his head. "I don't see how we can do anything about this, Gunny. You know about the Sullivan act, or whatever that Navy regulation is called that forbids family members on the same ship. Well, the Corps frowns on putting family members in the same combat unit."

"Yes, sir. Sir, I have some R and R time built up. What if I was to take an in-country R and R?"

"Go on."

"Well, sir, I could put in for China Beach or a little rest on Freedom Hill."

"Do you know who the boy's with, Slate?"

"No, sir. I was hoping you could find that out for me."

Colonel Rockey grunted. "All right, let's say we find out where he is and you take an in-country R and R. Then what?"

A ray of hope began to shine through the anger in Jessie's heart. He tried to clear his mind; he had to make this good.

"Well, sir. I'll go see him. Just be a visiting platoon sergeant or company gunny lent out to advise his outfit on marking trails or spotting booby traps. Two weeks with him, sir. That's all I ask."

"I don't know, Slate. Trying to explain a Marine using his R and R to fight with another regiment might be tough, even with your reputation."

"I can make a difference, sir."

"You don't think there's some sergeant out there already doing that job?"

"Of course there is, sir, but—"

"Colonel, how many sergeants out there have been grunts through three wars?" Broken Wing said dryly.

The colonel stared at Broken Wing for a few seconds before finally shrugging. "Not too many, Gunny."

"I'll cause no trouble, sir," Jessie assured him.

The colonel seemed to be wavering. "You're asking me to stick my neck out a long way, Gunnery Sergeant."

"Sir, I'll take full responsibility for my actions. The Corps has been using me to advise and drill and train for twenty years. Let me just advise and train one more time. Technically, I would not be in his unit. I could just be temporarily attached as an adviser."

"Adviser?"

"Yes, sir."

"In what exactly?"

"Anything, sir."

"Booby traps." Broken Wing said.

"And weapons," Jessie added.

"Communications. F.O. Naval."

"Hand-to-hand combat, sir. I've taught everywhere from Lebanon to Haiti."

The colonel chewed on his cigar, then took another drink. He slapped the cup down and shook his head no. "No. There is just no way we can do this, Gunny."

"Why, sir?" Jessie's voice cracked with anger and forced restraint.

"Because you ain't gonna be here in two weeks, Marine! Your tour is over, mister. You are due for a discharge, if my information is correct?"

Gunnery Sergeant Jessie Slate took a step backward. He was stunned. He had completely forgotten. He looked at the deck for a moment to regain his composure, then stared Colonel Rockey straight in the eye.

"Request permission to re-up, sir!" He barked it out like a boot on a Parris Island drill field as he snapped to attention.

Colonel Rockey was already pulling papers from the top desk drawer. He laid them on the desk along with a ballpoint pen. "Sign this."

Broken Wing was trying to remove the bracelet from Jessie's wrist. Jessie watched him take the bracelet off like a man in a stupor. He stepped forward and signed the papers. Colonel Rockey checked the signature and looked at Broken Wing. The laugh began and continued for a full two minutes. Jessie stood silently, shaking his head in disbelief.

"That will be all, gentlemen. And Slate, I'll see if I can find out where he is. But no promises."

"Aye aye, sir," Jessie said. His hopes rose. Deep down he knew that the colonel was going to come through.

The colonel gave them the bottle to take with them. They drank in their cabin while Broken Wing carved on Jessie's old tin bracelet. Broken Wing had a habit of singing an Indian chant when he was happy, and, as Jessie saw it, when

Wing was really happy, he got a stupid look on his face. He did not smile or grin, but his eyelids sort of dropped, as if he felt so good he was ready to fall asleep. Jessie drank and stared at Wing's drooping expression and listened to the Indian chant. The red lights were on aboard the ship and taps was playing. Jessie leaned back and regarded the ceiling above his bunk for a long time before the spinning stopped enough to let him sleep, but that stupid chant stayed in his head all night.

Three hard knocks on the bulkhead sounded like thunder. Maybe he was on the inside of a drum, Jessie thought, but who would be so cruel as to hit it with a baseball bat? He opened one eye. It hurt. He closed it and tried the other eye. He surveyed the room through a spinning blur. Three more jarring hits of thunder rattled his eardrums, sending out shock waves of pain.

"What the crap is that?"

"Gunny Slate!"

"Affirmative!" Jessie shouted, and it felt like someone had driven a bayonet through his head. He gripped his ears with both hands, grimaced, and fought back an urge to puke. He belched and groaned.

"Colonel Rockey says your taxi's waiting."

Jessie opened both eyes. "What?"

"The colonel says your R and R to the Fifth Regiment, First Marine Division, came through. Don't ask me what that means. If that's the best R and R you can get, bro, you must have ticked somebody off real bad!"

Jessie sat up in his rack. The room began to spin out of control.

"Gunny!"

"All right, all right. Cease fire."

"You got a chopper waiting on deck right now, with rotors going! Saddle up!"

"Affirmative!"

"Oh, and the colonel says you owe him big-time for this.

He's got an assignment waiting for you with some CAG unit!"

"CAG?"

"Yes sir, Gunny. Says you will volunteer for it the moment you step back onboard! He wants me to make sure that is perfectly clear, Gunny."

"It's clear, Marine. Tell the colonel I volunteer. God, I hate to think what it might be, but I volunteer."

CHAPTER TWENTY-THREE

The prop wash had never sounded so harsh nor the vibration so turbulent. He tried to make himself sober up, but it didn't work. He looked down and saw a set of orders in a big manila envelope. Who handed me that? he thought. The fuzz in his brain had clouded everything except one thought. He was going to see his son, who was now in the Fifth Marine Regiment of the First Marine Division. It didn't seem possible. He shook his head and laughed, then flinched from the shooting pains of a throbbing headache. What a way to see him for the first time in years. How many years had it been? Three? Could it be four? Let's see, high school graduation . . . Christmas leave . . . when was that?

"We're getting near An Hoa, Gunny!" a door gunner shouted from the open hatch.

Jessie stared at the gunner for a moment then looked around the inside of the chopper. "This is a Huey."

The door gunner pretended to whistle and shook his head. "Man, that must have been some party! Do the squids have slop chutes on those ships, bro?"

Jessie pinched the bridge of his nose to ease another headache. He crawled over to the gunner and looked out the open hatch. The Huey gunship banked slightly with a loud popping noise. In the distance he could see an ugly brown spot on a luscious patchwork quilt of hundreds of shades of green. There were mountains in the distance, but the combat base sat in An Hoa Valley. It was the usual rear area for a grunt outfit. The medium-size village of An Hoa sat on the outskirts of the base, which was surrounded by rolls of concertina wire and spotted with sandbag gun bunkers. There was a tent area where the grunts would stay when they came in out of the bush for a night to get resupplies. Jessie could see a few more permanent structures; one would be a chow hall, maybe an officers' mess and an officers' quarters, and at least two slop chutes, one for the men and one for the officers. A battery of 155s and 105s and what might be some big 175s sat very close to the airstrip, which could accommodate the big C-130s. There were also chopper pads of corrugated steel.

All in all, it was pretty typical. The chopper began to circle down, and nervous anticipation gripped Jessie's stomach. He loved his son so much, but knew that Charlie Rose had always been bitter about not having him around like other dads. How could a kid not be hurt by that? Every kid needs a dad, he thought. But his own dad was a Marine, and he still loved him and was proud of him and wasn't bitter. At least he didn't think he was.

"Stand by, Gunny!"

The chopper kicked up a lot of dust as it settled to the corrugated steel landing pad. Jessie signaled a thumbs-up to the pilot as he jumped out the open hatch with his 782 gear. He hit the ground and belched up a mouthful of bile. He spat it out and fought back the need to vomit, then walked toward a waving Marine sitting in a jeep at the edge of the pad.

"Gunny Slate!"

Jessie sent a thumbs-up and headed for the jeep as the chopper lifted off.

"Hop in, Gunny."

Jessie threw his pack and shotgun into the back of the jeep and climbed in slowly. The corporal was one of those chipper characters, which was okay with Jessie normally, but not when a man was near death with hangover. He peeled out, slamming Jessie against the back of his seat.

"Whoa! Slow it down, Marine!"

The corporal lifted his foot from the gas pedal. The jeep still felt like a bucking bronco over the potholed dirt streets of the combat base. He rounded a corner with too tight a turn, and Jessie held on for life. It was typical driving for kid Marines, most of whom had never owned a car as civilians. Soon as they got a chance to drive military jeeps, they went crazy.

"Man, Gunny, you must have some rear echelon pull."

"Why do say that, Corporal?"

"The place is in a bit of a stir over you being here."

"Why's that?"

"Don't have the division commander showing up for a gunnery sergeant every day. Laying out orders for you to be given a chopper and just about carte blanche."

Jessie forced the fog from his brain and tried to focus in on the corporal.

"Now slow down, kid. What are you talking about?"

"General Perkins flew in here about an hour ago with a light colonel and a major."

"Who?"

"General Perkins. Division commander. Don't you know him?"

"Not sure," Jessie mumbled. "I know he just took over the First."

"You don't know him personally?"

"When you've been in the Corps as long as I have, boot, you sort of know everybody a little bit. I'm just not sure right now."

"He sure knows you, Sarge."

Jessie tugged at his ear and thought. The name rang a bell, but it was hard to think clearly. The Marine Corps was small compared to the Army or Navy. After a few years, you couldn't begin a new duty station without running into some old friend. It was like a big family for career Marines.

"Says you saved his life at some place called Bloody Ridge."

"Bloody Ridge?" Jessie straightened in his seat at the name of that hellhole.

"Where's Bloody Ridge, Gunny?"

"You ought to know that, Corporal!" Jessie barked angrily.

"Sorry, sir."

"There wouldn't be any South Korea right now if it were not for the Fifth Marine Regiment holding at Bloody Ridge. You're in the Fifth Marines if I'm not mistaken!"

"Yes, sir!"

"Every Marine in the Fifth Regiment should know where Bloody Ridge was, mister."

"Yes, sir."

The corporal turned down a dusty street with rows of tents on each side. A column of about fifty dirty, ragged, mean-looking Marines marched past in the opposite direction. Their faces were haggard, shoulders slumped with fatigue, and Jessie knew they had just come from the bush after ninety days out. He felt conspicuously clean as they passed, most of the men too tired to notice the jeep or who was in it.

"That's two platoons of Dyin' Delta, Gunny."

"How long they been out?"

"Three months."

"Are you the company clerk?"

"Yes, sir. Delta Company."

"You get any new butter bars in recently?"

"Yes, sir."

"What's his name?"

"Well, we got two. There's Slate ... Hey, we got one named Slate! Are you related, Gunny?"

"Yes. Where is he?"

"He just came in yesterday. He took over the second platoon. Their lieutenant stepped on a 155 a couple days ago."

A quiver of anxiety gripped Jessie, and he tried to ignore it. Somehow he had to think of Charlie Rose as just another Marine. He couldn't treat it any other way or they were both in trouble. It had to be strictly professional.

The corporal pulled up in front of one of the few permanent structures at An Hoa. The building had plywood walls halfway up, with the rest of the building made of screen and corrugated steel roof. A hand-painted sign out front said 5TH MARINE REGIMENT HQ. It was lined in front with softball-size rocks that had been painted white. Jessie took a deep breath as the jeep stopped. Meeting a general while he was too drunk to see straight was not the way he would have planned this. He climbed out of the jeep with his pack and pump shotgun and ambled toward the screen door of the HQ.

Halfway up the rock-lined sidewalk the screen door flew open and a Marine in starched utilities stepped down the two wooden steps. Jessie stopped, recognized a star on the Marine's soft cover, snapped to attention, and, shifting his pack to his left hand, saluted with the right. The general returned it as he came forward smiling. There was something familiar about the man.

"Slate. Jessie Slate."

"Yes, sir."

The general extended his hand and Jessie shook it, then belched up a foul whiskey burp. Jessie's eyes opened wide with terror and embarrassment. He wanted to vanish.

"Colonel Rockey told me you were suffering today, if he was any judge of that Irish whiskey he had." General Perkins laughed out loud and then slapped Jessie on the shoulder. They were about the same size, around six feet even. The general would have to be considered one of those dashing types, Jessie thought, but if first impressions were worth anything, he didn't seem to act as if he were better than anybody. A real Joe.

"So do you remember me yet, Gunny?"

"I might if I could think clear, sir. But right now my own name-rank-and-serial-number might be tough."

The general laughed again. "You remember a young butter-bar lieutenant that you and a Corpsman carried off Bloody Ridge in 1950?"

Jessie straightend with sudden recognition. He couldn't believe his eyes. It was like seeing a ghost. "Yes, sir," he mumbled as is he were in shock. He grabbed the general's hand and shook it violently. "I can't believe it! I was positive you were dead. It didn't look like there was any way you were gonna make it, sir. Not a chance in a hundred."

Perkins smiled and nodded. "It was about that close. If you hadn't hustled to that aid station the way you did, I would not be here right now, and that is a certainty, Sergeant."

"Outstanding! I just can't believe it! You had two kids, didn't you, sir?"

"Still do, Sergeant. They're both grown up now and I'm a grandpa."

"I always worried about those little kids growing up without their dad. What a great surprise. And now you're a general." Jessie smiled and wanted to laugh but thought better of it.

"Thank you, Gunny. Now come on in out of this sun for a minute and let's talk."

"Yes, sir."

Jessie followed the general back to the HQ, where a lieutenant colonel and two majors stood waiting. One stern-faced major held the screen door open as they entered. Jessie saluted them as he passed.

"Right there," General Perkins said, pointing to a corner of the tiny room. "Drop anchor."

"Yes, sir." Jessie dropped his gear in the corner, the general pointed to a chair, and he sat.

"Gentlemen, would you excuse us for a bit."

The officers saluted, then left. General Perkins sat facing

Jessie. He produced a cigar and matches from his breast pocket and handed them to him.

"Thank you, sir." Jessie lit up.

The general looked much as he had when he was thirty years old and a young mustang lieutenant. He was a little heavier, of course, with some battle lines around the eyes; just like his own, Jessie thought.

"So Rockey tells me you got a young butter bar in the First that needs some guidance."

"Yes, sir. I know it's an unusual request, sir. It is an unusual circumstance."

"I won't change his orders for you."

"No, sir. I would not ask that."

"Good."

"I just want the chance to break him in."

"Fair enough, Gunny."

"Thank you, sir. Now the problem is, will he take to it?"

"What do you mean?"

"Well, sir, to tell you the truth I think the boy's bitter toward me for choosing the Marine Corps over him and his mother."

The general leaned back. He blew a smoke ring and nodded. "Well, Gunny, can't say I haven't seen that situation before."

"I wouldn't blame the lad if he hated me, sir. I wasn't there for his college graduation. I wasn't with him for his first haircut or his driving test at sixteen. If I was him, I'd hate getting stuck with a Marine for a father."

"He doesn't hate you, Gunny, or he wouldn't be in the Corps. He was saying exactly that when he joined the Corps. The boy is a Marine now. When he realizes who his father is and what kind of Marine you've been during the last three wars, he'll come around. He will see all too soon that being a Marine is no easy job."

"General, I can't tell you how much I appreciate this chance to break the lad in. I know it's pushing regulations a bit, but if I hadn't gotten the chance and something happened to the boy . . ."

"I understand. I told Colonel Rockey about a situation we have with one of our CAP units. Combined Action Platoon. It's in the First Combined Action Group. Are you familiar with the CAG operation, Gunnery Sergeant?"

"No, sir. Not really. I've heard a little about the program. They work out of villages. Train the Vietnamese Popular Forces."

"That's only part of their role, Gunny. In some areas they're crucial for blocking routes of infiltration for entire provinces. Sort of like a village-size listening post."

"Yes, sir."

"I'm going to let you go out there and break in this boot lieutenant, Gunnery Sergeant Slate."

"Thank you, sir."

"But in return you will volunteer for the CAG program. And you will be dropped into a fairly ugly and crucial situation."

"Yes, sir."

"You understand the importance. I cannot order you to volunteer for this assignment, but I *am* ordering you to volunteer for the assignment."

"Yes, sir. I volunteer, sir."

"Might be a couple of months before you get back to the Seventh Marines Battalion Landing Team." The general pulled some orders out of his cargo pocket and unfolded them on the desk. He handed Jessie a pen. "Sign these, Gunny. These are your temporary transfer orders into the CAG from the Seventh BLT. Once you clean up the situation, you'll be sent back to the Seventh."

"Yes, sir." Jessie quickly signed the papers and handed the pen back to the general.

"Better take a cigar for the road," General Perkins said as he handed Jessie another cigar.

"Thank you, sir."

"Ever think of Bloody Ridge, Gunny?"

"Yes, sir. I'll never forget it even if I want to."

"We stopped 'em cold, didn't we?"

"There it is, sir."

Jessie's admiration for the man increased when the general snatched up his helmet and one of the new lightweight Army flak jackets.

"Saddle up, Gunny. Let's go see that boy of yours."

Jessie stood up, then paused. "Sir?"

"Saddle up. I'm taking you out personally to see the Marine Corps' newest Slate."

"Yes, sir." Slate grabbed up his web gear and tried not to act too surprised. One-star generals were not in the habit of flying into the bush.

They drove back to the An Hoa landing strip, where the general's Huey was waiting with the rotors already whirling. The chopper had a dog sitting in a soup bowl painted on the nose.

Twenty minutes later the Huey began to circle a barren hilltop amidst a sea of green jungle. They swept down on the rocky hilltop with a perimeter of Marines around the crest. Green smoke swirled up and scattered like vanishing fog under the rotors.

Jessie felt his stomach doing flip-flops as the Huey bounced to the ground. The general was the first one out of the hatch. He walked like the hill was his and everyone else a mere guest. Jessie moved past the door gunner and started to jump out of the chopper but a violent belch erupted from the pit of his stomach and he found himself hanging out of the hatch vomiting up whiskey and cigar. He could hear someone laughing, and he guessed it to be the general because others started laughing also. He groaned and sat still for a moment with his legs dangling out of the open hatch above a puddle of puke on and around one of the chopper skids.

Gathering himself together, Jessie followed the general. A baby-faced marine with a black lieutenant bar inked on his camouflaged helmet cover walked forward, with his radioman, close behind, carrying a PRC-25. The young lieutenant's bright blue eyes opened wide when he spotted the star on the general's soft cover hat. He snapped to attention and saluted sharply.

"Good grief! Lieutenant! You don't salute in the bush! Don't they teach you idiots anything at Quantico?"

"I'm sorry, sir! I—I—I never expected to see a general out here, sir. It threw me. Won't happen again, sir."

The general studied the lieutenant's handsome face for a few moments. "One stupid mistake will cost you and your men their lives out here, Lieutenant Slate."

"Yes, sir," he answered still standing at attention with his eyes straight ahead.

"I brought the best man in the Marine Corps out here to help you not make that kind of stupid mistake. You understand me?"

"Yes, sir."

"Well, I suggest you say a proper hello to that Marine who's going to all this trouble to keep you alive."

"Yes, sir," he said without moving.

"Well? Say hello to your gunnery sergeant, Marine."

Charlie Rose Slate blinked a couple of times, then relaxed from attention. What was happening seemed to be sinking in slowly. He leaned to look around the general and stared straight into his father's steel-gray eyes.

"Dad?" Charlie Rose sounded like a man in shock. His voice squeaked.

"Son."

"What are you doing here? Are you drunk? You reek of booze!"

"I'm here to break you in. And yes, I'm drunk."

Charlie Rose Slate stared for a moment openmouthed, seemingly stunned into silence. Jessie laughed and stepped forward to give his son the biggest bear hug he could muster. Charlie Rose didn't give much of a hug in return. Jessie released his son and stepped back to look at him.

"I'm your platoon sergeant for two weeks."

Charlie Rose said nothing for a moment. Jessie braced himself for an angry response. He wouldn't blame the kid if he told him to take a flyin' leap. Sometimes it felt like they barely knew each other.

A smile broke across his son's handsome face and he extended his hand. "That's great, Dad. I could use some advice."

Jessie gripped his hand and felt better than he had in a long time, and even the hangover did not hurt as much. General Perkins walked around the perimeter chatting with each man in the platoon for a moment or two, then signaled a thumbs-up as he boarded the Huey gunship.

"Pick his brain, Lieutenant!" General Perkins shouted as the chopper lifted off.

"Aye aye, sir!" Charlie Rose Slate shouted back with a thumbs-up.

"The C.P.'s over here, Dad."

"Better call me Gunny in front of the men, son."

"Better call me Lieutenant."

Jessie smiled. "Won't be easy."

They walked to the center of the perimeter, where a Corpsman was treating one of the men for jungle rot on his foot. They sat down just out of hearing range and faced each other.

"How long you been in-country?"

"What?"

"When did you get in-country?"

"In-country? You mean in Vietnam or out here in the field?"

Jessie smile and nodded. "Son, you're one boot butter-bar lieutenant."

"I know. Give me a break, Dad. I only got here yesterday."

"So you don't even know your men yet?"

"No. Not really. Well a couple. The Corpsman is Doc Sickle and the radioman is M.G. Kelly."

"Don't get to know them too well. It clouds your judgment."

"I don't know how I can do that. I never felt like I needed a friend more in my life."

"Let's say you know this Marine, he has two kids at home, so you don't put him on point, but he's your best pointman and because he's not out there when you need him you walk into an ambush and lose half your platoon."

"Okay."

"Don't get me wrong, you can't help getting to know them after a while, but don't rush into it until you're accustomed to seeing them die."

Charlie Rose Slate looked at his father as if he'd said something foul, and Jessie understood.

"Take those dog tags off your neck and tie them into your bootlaces. If you step on a boody trap, your boots usually stay together in one piece, and that way they can identify your body." Jessie paused. A cold chill ran down his spine. He'd said the same words to a thousand boot Marines without blinking, but this time there was no denying the first hint of fear gripping his gut. He forced his face to hide the apprehension and went on with the indoctrination. "Get your rifle."

Charlie Rose walked over beside the Corpsman, picked up his rifle, and brought it back. He sat down, looking intent.

"Don't ever leave your weapon that far away, Lieutenant Slate."

Charlie Rose smiled. "Okay, Gunny, sir."

"How many rounds you got in that clip?"

"Twenty. What it holds."

"And I suppose you have that many rounds in each clip?"

"Yes."

"It weakens the spring in your magazine. Take two rounds out of each magazine. Do it now."

"Why didn't somebody in training teach us this?"

Jessie stared at his son's dog tags, ignoring the question. "Get hold of a marker and blacken those dog tags. They catch some moonlight or sunlight, and the gooks see it ten miles away."

Charlie started removing M-16 rounds from his magazine.

"You write Mom yet?"

"No."

"Do it as soon as you get the chance. Got any writing gear?"

"Yes."

"Keep it in plastic and stick it inside your steel pot under the helmet liner. That's the only way to keep it dry. You might want to keep your crap paper there too." Jessie reached over and snatched a grenade off Charlie's cartridge belt. "Carry your frags there, but tear holes in your flak jacket. When a man gets killed, you want a quick place to hang his frags. You stick the spoons in the hole, that way they're easier to get to. You bent the pin on this one, did you bend all of them?"

"Yep."

"Good. When you're cutting through the jungle with a machete or just breaking a path, the branches get caught in one of those pins and you're blown to bits and you won't know why till God tells you face-to-face."

Charlie pulled another round from his fourth magazine. He looked nervous. He had his mother's eyes and they sparkled when he was intense. "I'm scared a little, Dad." His tone was serious

"So am I, son."

"I mean not all of the time. Part of me feels so excited that I'm afraid I can't control my bladder. You know what I mean?"

"Gunny O'Cleary and Gunny Killeen used to say, 'There's no better way to die than to die a Marine, and you ain't really living anyway until your life is on the line.' "

Charlie Rose Slate shook his head and grinned the way

he did when he was ten years old. "It's hard to believe we're sitting here on this hilltop in the middle of a war together."

"I know. When your mom's letter came telling me what you'd done I couldn't believe it. Why didn't you . . ."

"What? Talk to you about it? This is the most we've talked since I was eleven."

Jessie's shoulders sagged. For one miserable instant he felt like a complete failure as a father. There was nothing he could say or do to change the fact that he'd chosen the Corps over a normal family life. Explaining the past was like spitting into a monsoon and expecting to make a difference. His son had suffered consequences, and no amount of rationalization or lame excuses would change it.

"I guess I haven't been much of a dad, son. But no father loves their boy any more than I do. There's nothing I wouldn't do to buy back some of those lost years."

"Nothing? All you had to do is quit the Corps."

Jessie swallowed back a lump in his throat and knew that his son could never possibly understand. He pointed at Charlie's canteens. "You put your halazone tablets in each canteen?"

"Yeah."

"Take your salt tabs regularly or you'll get heat exhaustion. Make sure your men do too. Keep on the Corpsman about it. A casualty from heat exhaustion is the same as getting a man wounded. You'll have to tell the world your position when the medevac shows up."

"Okay."

"Take that helmet off regularly. The heat will fry your brain. You get spacey, and the lieutenant cannot afford to be anything but on top of the situation."

"Got it," Charlie said as he rechecked the pins on his grenades.

"When you write Mom, tell her to send you packs of Kool-Aid. Kills the taste of the water, and the heat won't ruin it. And don't ever take your boots off at night. But make sure you take 'em off in the day whenever possible. You'll probably get jungle rot anyway, but you must take care of your feet. Have the Corpsman tend to even small cuts, and try to get some Mercurochrome to carry with you. Dab it on every cut. Even the smallest nick will get infected within hours." Jessie searched through his pack and pulled out a small brown bottle. "Here, Lieutenant. Take it."

"What is it?"

"Hydrogen peroxide. Put it on every cut as soon as it happens."

"Okay, Dad." Charlie's tone softened and for a moment he sounded like the little boy who used to cling crying to his father when it was time for him to leave.

"Let me see your oil."

"What?"

"Your gun oil!" Jessie barked as a surge of impatience struck him. He was beginning to realize just how boot his son really was. Fear shot through his heart.

Charlie Rose glared at his father for a moment, then searched through his pack. He handed over the small green plastic bottle of oil. Jessie took it and stared at it. Rage filled his mind, and he could not hide it from Charlie. He dropped the bottle in the dirt, pulled out his K-Bar knife and stabbed through the oil, pinning it to the ground.

"What are you doing?"

"This is oil for the M-14! It's too thick. You use this on the M-16, the bolt swells, the rifle jams, and you die, Marine."

"Wrong oil?" Charlie Rose muttered in disbelief as he watched Jessie search through his pack again.

"Here." Slate handed Charlie a smaller bottle of higher grade gun oil.

"Thanks," Charlie said. He looked shaken.

"Miss cleaning it and the 16 will jam on you. Keep oil on it every single day. In one day's time that rifle can rust in this miserable climate. Rust will kill you. You got that?"

"Yeah, Gunny, I'm listening. Go on."

"When we're humpin' the bush, you have to notice everything. I mean everything, Lieutenant. Stay off trails whenever possible. If you have no choice and you must move along a trail, watch for size, shape, and color. Three of anything together approximately the same size shape or color is a marker."

"Marker?"

"Yes. This is how the gooks tell each other that a trail is booby-trapped. Sometimes they won't be the same size. For instance, let's say you're humpin' a trail. Up ahead you see a fallen tree and beside it or real close you see two smaller logs or maybe just big sticks that are nearly the same shape. Don't take another step."

Charlie shook his head but did not speak. Jessie stared into his son's eyes to make sure he was concentrating. He had his mother's beautiful blue eyes, and like Kate's, they were a window into his soul. Concern or fury would show in them clearly. Jessie wanted to take it slower, but there wouldn't be time. Charlie Rose would either grasp it or die.

"Listen up. Another marker they use is this: one large object beside a small object of the exact same shape."

"I'm not sure I understand." Charlie's face was already showing the strain, and Jessie could see it. His baby boy would look years older in just a few short months. Sadness gripped his heart for a moment, but he pushed it away. Too late to do anything but teach this Marine every possible way to stay alive.

"Okay, now listen. Let's say we're moving up a trail or a footpath and you see something like this." Jessie looked around the rocky hilltop until he saw what he wanted. He jumped up and grabbed a rock about the size of a golf ball. He scouted around on the ground until he found a larger rock, the size of a softball that was similar in shape. He walked back to Charlie and laid them side by side at his feet.

"Now you're walking up a trail and you see this lying there. You will get off that trail. Don't take another step."

"How can you possibly see that in the middle of the jungle?"

"You train yourself, Marine."

"Seems impossible."

"No, it's not. But you have to concentrate every second. And when you go back to the world, you'll have to work just as hard to make yourself stop concentrating."

"That hasn't been easy, has it, Dad?"

"No. And for many reasons the strain is more severe in 'Nam than it was in the Pacific or Korea."

"Why?"

"It goes on and on. You're nearly always night-fighting. Half the time you're not sure who the enemy is. For thirteen months you'll be under the heaviest stress a man can be under. But you let your concentration drift, and you miss seeing that one trip wire or ambush."

"I'll concentrate for thirteen months." Charlie sounded determined.

"Now pay attention. If you see three sticks or limbs or three marks on a tree, it can mean a couple of things—either it's a marked trail for enemy troops to follow or it's booby-trapped."

"How do you know?"

"A couple of ways you find out. One way is to ambush the path or trail. I found a trail marked like that right here in the Arizona Territory, near Dodge City. We decided it was marked for enemy troops coming across from Laos and through An Hoa Valley. We ambushed it with twenty Marines. The first night, a reinforced company of NVA, with helmets and packs and heavy weapons, marched right by our noses."

"You open up?"

"Of course not, Lieutenant! I'm still here, if you'll notice. Don't commit suicide for you and your men if you can avoid it. We let 'em pass and I called in some 155s and Puff the Magic Dragon."

"Puff the Magic Dragon?"

"A C-47 with miniguns and loaded with ammo. Thousands of rounds per minute. Tracers come out of the sky like a two-foot-wide golden arrow and with a god-awful sound. It rains lead."

"Yeah, I've heard about it. Covers every square inch of a football field in just a few minutes."

"Yep. The other way you find out about the trail marks is to know your A.O. And it won't hurt to get acquainted with the locals."

"How can I know my Area of Operations when I just got here?" Charlie's tone rang with frustration.

"If there are any villages in your A.O. make sure you go through them. Search them. Find any weapons, real weapons like AKs or material for booby traps. Then you burn the hooch where you find it. But make sure your Corpsman treats the people who need care. You will find every infection known to man. Show the village chief respect. Hand out some C-rats."

"Okay."

"Stay cool no matter what happens, Lieutenant."

Charlie nodded but did not speak.

"Have you checked your compass?"

"Got it right here." Charlie slapped his cargo pocket.

"Have you pulled it out and actually checked it to see if it works?"

"No. I got issued my gear and I just assumed—"

"Never! Don't assume anything, Marine. That compass has probably seen more action than me."

"Well, from what the general said, you must still work okay."

Jessie grinned and wanted badly to give his boy a big hug, but knew he couldn't. "Yeah, you're sounding like a butter bar all right. Now pull the compass out and check it. If it's off when you use the azimuth to call in an arty strike, you could kill your whole platoon. Let's see your map and go over your A.O."

Jessie reached into his other pocket and pulled out a map wrapped in plastic. He studied the map for a moment, then looked at his boy. He knew that he wasn't concealing the concern he was feeling. It was written across his brow.

"What is it, Dad?"

"Why did'n't you tell me you were joining the Corps, Charlie?" Jessie growled, and pinched the bridge of his nose. He suddenly remembered his hangover.

"Tell you I was joining the Corps? Dad, you've been gone most of my life. You're in Lebanon or the Dominican Republic or Guantanamo or training Korean Marines. You've been nothing but bad handwriting on dirty Marine Corps stationery to me and Mom for my whole life."

Jessie felt like someone had kicked him in the groin. "Well, you should have told your mom at least! She hasn't been in Lebanon."

"Confide in her like you always did, huh?"

Jessie looked at his handsome son and saw more of himself than he wanted to see. Charlie was right. He had no business questioning the kid on his decision when he had never been around to help him make one. He looked down at the map.

"Your area of operations is called the Arizona Territory."

"Yes."

"Talk to anybody about it yet?"

"A corporal in the third squad named Ferguson said it was a hot spot. Sounds like a good place to start kicking some butt and taking some names."

Jessie looked up and grunted. The kid was already talking like a frigging Marine. "Do you even know what that means?"

"What do you mean?"

"Kicking butt and taking names."

"I guess I do."

"It means killing so many of the enemy that you take

their unit designation off the map. Last I heard, you had the 308th NVA moving into An Hoa. If you can kill so many of them that there is no 308th NVA Regiment, then you've taken a name."

Charlie nodded.

"I'm going to try to tell you as much as I can about An Hoa Valley so that you know what you're up against. This valley is a natural supply route for the North Vietnamese Army coming off the Ho Chi Minh Trail and across the Laotian border."

"Why don't we attack the trail? Cut it off right at the head?"

Jessie groaned with exasperation.

Charlie shrugged. "Well, don't you think that's the smart way? It's the way we're trained to do it. Every tactics class I've had from ROTC to OCS disputes what we're doing here. I just wish somebody in Washington would let the Marines run the war."

"There it is, son! You're starting to sound just like an old Vietnam salt. But in the words of the great Gunnery Sergeant Paddy Francis Killeen, 'You'll be wishin' in one hand, lad . . . and you'll be defecating in the other, and see which one fills up first.' "

Charlie chuckled. It felt good to Jessie to see his boy laugh. "Well, go on, Gunnery Sergeant. Fill me in on An Hoa Valley."

"Affirmative, Lieutenant Slate. I guess you've already heard about Tet?"

"The Tet Offensive? Yes. That's all you hear about back home."

"Yes, well, if our media is up to par, then you're hearing a bunch of nonsense. We kicked some butt and we kicked it hard. I'm hearing numbers like three entire NVA divisions killed. They got clobbered good so far, but this is the second part of their Tet Offensive and now they're trying a new avenue of approach. An Hoa Valley."

"With Da Nang as the ultimate target."

"Right. The Laos-Vietnam border region is some of the most rugged mountains and jungle in the world. They can come out of those triple canopy jungles with an entire battalion without anyone spotting them. And you can find yourself up against a battalion of NVA with these seventeen Marines and no one close enough to help in time. Your only hope will be that radio. You got to know where you are at all times. You have to know how to drop a 175 round on a tree trunk from twenty miles away."

Charlie whistled. "What about the valley itself?"

"An Hoa is just as bad as the mountains, or worse. Knee-deep mud, leech-infested rice paddies, fields of waist-level elephant grass that could hide a regiment. It has some small rolling hills. Every inch of it is a maze of booby traps."

"Arizona Territory?"

"Parts of it look like Arizona. Like this part we're in now. Small rolling hills covered with rocks and brush. It also has a place called Dodge City."

"I saw that on the map. That's part of my A.O."

"I know. Right here." Jessie pointed at the map on the ground. "The enemy is shifting their main effort in I Corps to the central provinces."

"So I'm in the hottest spot in 'Nam right now. I mean we should see some real action, right?" He sounded excited, and it sent a chill through Jessie.

"Yes, son. You will see action."

Charlie slapped his dad on the shoulder. "Well, don't sound so down about it. That's what I'm here for."

"Well, I'm here to see that you don't go home in a green plastic bag. You go slow. You learn the ropes. You listen to every old salt you meet."

"I'm listening, Dad. Just don't overdo it. I'm a Marine just like every other Marine. I did not come here to hide and play it safe. I'm here to win the war."

"Jesus. Don't ever let your men hear you say that. You'll scare them to death."

"You're really something, Gunnery Sergeant Slate, do

you know that? Not counting ROTC, I have been in this man's Marine Corps for all of five months, though it feels more like fifty. In those five months I have yet to meet an old Marine who could not come up with some crazy gung-ho story about my dad. You've been a maniac through three wars, and here you are telling me to act like I'm made of glass. I'm a Marine too. And I'm going to fight and, if necessary, die like a Marine."

Emotion welled up in Jessie like a tidal wave smashing against his heart. A lump that felt like a rock formed in his throat, and he knew that he was near tears. He swallowed hard.

"I can't help it, Charlie. I'm scared, son. I'm scared to death."

Charlie looked like someone had slapped him with an ice pack. He stared at his father as if seeing him for the first time in his life. He leaned forward, obviously unsure of what to say. He placed his right hand on his father's shoulder and forced a smile.

"I'll be careful, Dad."

Jessie swallowed back the need to hug his son and cleared his throat. "Get that radioman over here."

Charlie Rose Slate nodded and turned. "M.G. Come over here."

"And bring your Prick-25," Jessie called.

"Yes, sir." The short, husky Marine grabbed up his radio. He walked over with a white C-ration spoon stuck in his mouth.

"Set it down here, Marine," Jessie said. "Go finish chow."

"Yes, sir, here you go, Gunny." M.G. set the radio down and ambled back to his open can of C-rats.

Jessie pointed at a small hill south of their position. "See that hill?"

"Yes."

"What do you think the distance is?"

"About five hundred meters."

"I saw NVA on that hill. I think you better lob in an arty strike on that hill."

"What?" Charlie Rose stiffened as he stood up to get a better look at the suspected enemy position.

"Go on. Call it in, Lieutenant."

"I don't see anything over there."

"Never doubt an old salt, Lieutenant!"

"But shouldn't we send a patrol over to make sure or something?"

"Already did."

Charlie Rose squatted back down on one knee beside his dad and the radio. The concern in his eyes faded, and he gave his dad a tight-lipped grin.

"I can't do that."

"Do what?"

"Waste thousand-dollar artillery rounds for the fun of it."

"Son. Trust me."

"You just want to make sure that I can call in a strike, well, take my word for it, Dad. I can call in artillery. What do you think I've been in school for all of this time?"

"Call in that strike, Lieutenant."

Charlie Rose Slate looked hard at his father. "Now don't push it, Gunnery Sergeant."

"Do as I said, Second Lieutenant Slate. I can make one call and have you relieved of duty for incompetence and failure to engage the enemy."

"You're starting to make me mad, Dad."

"Can you call in artillery or not, Lieutenant?"

Charlie clenched his teeth and his square jaw locked. He picked up the field phone. He pulled his code book out of a pocket and unwrapped the protective plastic.

"Iron Hand Two-four . . . Iron Hand Two-four . . . this is Delta Two . . . over."

Jessie watched intently as Charlie worked his compass and studied his grid map. The kid looked pretty good. Sounded almost confident for a boot as he read off the co-ordinates.

"You sure about those coordinates, Lieutenant?" Jessie asked doubtfully.

Charlie Rose pulled the phone away, "Yes, Gunnery Sergeant. I'm sure." His voice rang with irritation. He spoke into the phone again.

"Affirmative ... Iron Hand ... fire one."

Jessie grabbed the phone from Charlie. "Belay that order! Iron Hand ... switch Willie Peter to CS ... Repeat, switch Willie Peter to CS."

"What the crap are you doing, Dad?"

"Affirmative ... Iron Hand ..."

"What are you doing?"

Jessie hung the phone up and calmly took his pack off. "Dad!"

"The white phosphorous round would send up too much smoke."

"Why not just fire some H.E.?"

Jessie grinned. "Well, we don't want to waste all of that high explosive now, do we?" He calmly searched through his pack. "CS gas is cheaper."

Charlie Rose stood up. "M.G."

"Yes, sir."

"Pass the word we got an arty strike coming in five hundred meters east of us. The target is that hill over there."

"Aye aye, Skipper." M.G. shouted and stood up. He headed for the next position in the perimeter around the hilltop. "Pass the word! We got an arty strike! Outgoing."

The word echoed around the perimeter. A faraway whistle grew stronger, then became shrill. Charlie Rose turned to squat beside his father.

"What are you doing?" he asked.

Gunnery Sergeant Jessie Slate scratched at the stubble on his strong chin, then pulled down his ancient gas mask. He leaned back against his pack, staring at his son through the scratched and yellowed plastic lens.

"Real funny, Gunnery Sergeant Slate. Got that much confidence in me, huh?"

Jessie pulled the mask up enough to show a grin, then lowered it. The first CS round went silent as it passed overhead with a whoosh followed by a smallish tinny-sounding explosion. A white mushroom cloud puffed out of the ground fifty yards short of the target hill.

"Check it out, Gunnery Sergeant!" Charlie Rose shouted gleefully.

"Finish the job. Fire for effect!"

Charlie grabbed the phone. "That is correct, Iron Hand . . . up fifty meters . . . fire for effect . . . over."

A few moments later the shrill whistle of incoming rounds grew louder, pushing air out of their way as they ripped by low overhead, going silent just before impact. Two more CS explosions hit one after the other, striking one hundred meters east and west of the target hill. Boot Lieutenant Charlie Rose Slate's laugh was cut short with the fourth incoming round as the faraway whistle grew closer, then finally went silent right above them. The Marines on the hill cringed and dove for cover that was not there, since no one had been ordered to dig in. Somebody on the far side of the perimeter gave an angry shout just as the round hit. A white mushroom cloud rose from the ground on the back side of the platoon's hill. In seconds a fifth round of CS gas exploded at the foot of their hill within sight of Jessie. He tried not to laugh, for fear of breathing in the horrible stuff, but he could not help it. Men ran from the gas coughing and cussing and trying to cover their eyes and mouths with anything they could. Some ripped through their packs in a vain search for gas masks that had been tossed away long ago or left back at An Hoa to lighten the burden. Gunnery Sergeant Slate's laugh was muffled inside his mask, but even through burning, tear-filled, blue eyes he knew that the young lieutenant was very aware of the laughter.

Charlie Rose hacked violently as he tried to ask a question that Jessie could not hear. Mucus poured from his nose like an open faucet and his face turned bright red. Jessie pressed his mask tighter to his face as the CS swirled around the perimeter like a moving fog. A couple of men ran down the hill to escape, but the last round struck close by and there was no safety below.

Fifteen minutes later a gentle breeze dispersed the tear gas, leaving only the foul temperament of the platoon in the stifling tropical air. Charlie Rose finished his second canteen of halazone water, dousing himself with as much as he drank. His face was still beet-red, and his swollen blue eyes were draining almost as much as his nose. His teeth clenched when he looked at his father, but he held his words until he was calm. Finally he seemed ready to speak. He shoved his empty canteen into the pouch on his cartridge belt and faced his father.

"That was real cute. You proud of yourself? You want the men to think their lieutenant is a complete fool, well congratulations, Gunny."

"I hope that you learned something."

"Stow the lecture, Gunny."

A flash of anger shot through Jessie Slate. He straightened up in a hurry. "You listen to me and you listen good, boot! I've broken in more butter-bar second lieutenants than you've broken in shoes, and I stopped being cute when I first put a Marine in a body bag!"

Charlie Rose Slate said nothing, but he was steaming mad.

"Now hear this, boot! When you call in arty, you better know what you're doing. You better know what kind of incoming mail they're sending you, mister. You were ready to fire for effect with a battery of 105s. There is a one thousand meter range dispersion on a 105 howitzer. Any wind or rain and that useless peashooter will drop H.E. rounds right down your throat. You could have killed half of your own platoon, Lieutenant!"

Charlie Rose blinked and started to speak, but seemed to rethink. He took a deep breath. "Go on. I'm listening."

Jessie looked at the ground for a moment, then stood up

beside his son. He laid a hand on Charlie's shoulder, then slapped him on the back. "I'm sorry, son. Embarrassing you was not the intention. I could have talked all day about the dangers of calling in 105s when you're firing for effect, and no amount of words would make the impression that this will make."

Charlie forced a chuckle. "Brother, you can say that again."

"When you're in triple canopy jungle, don't even think of using 105s anywhere near your own men. The canopy will cause air burst, and like I said, those rounds can be up to one thousand meters off, even on a good day. If you use 105s in the heavy bush, it's got the killing radius of a frag because the jungle catches all of the shrapnel." Jessie paused to make sure Charlie was paying attention. He was. He looked worried. "If you're using an ARVN artillery battery, you could have rounds landing almost anywhere."

"Are the ARVNs that bad?"

Jessie laughed. "Charlie, sit down with me. I'm going to tell you a true story.

They sat down cross-legged on the hard ground, using their packs to lean against.

"I was in a spotter plane last year up around the DMZ. Me and the pilot saw about a company of NVA Regulars out in the open in broad daylight. I tried to get a Marine battery, but it was no go. I ended up having to go with this ARVN battery. I called in a spotter round and they radioed that it was on the way. Me and that pilot were high enough to see anything anywhere near the area. We never saw it hit. I called them back and said, Where's the spotter round? And they said it was fired five minutes ago. The pilot finally points at a mushroom cloud coming up in North Vietnam. Not even on the same grid map!"

Charlie chuckled, then looked serious. "That's scary."

"Find out where your eight-inch guns are. Know what batteries have 175s or 155s. Don't waste your time trying to break up a bunker system with 105s because most of the time they won't make a dent."

Charlie looked around the hilltop perimeter, then down at the ground. The weight of responsibility was already showing on his young face. "Their lives are in my hands, and I don't know if I can do it."

"You couldn't just join the Corps and be an enlisted slob like your old dad." Jessie laughed, but it was fake. "Listen, Charlie, every new boot lieutenant who ever wore the uniform or dared to call himself a Marine has known the same doubts that you're feeling right now."

"Thanks, Dad."

"You have an advantage most of them never had, son. You've got the wisdom of an old grunt gunny who's going to baby-sit you and teach you for fourteen days and fourteen nights. You be a sponge. You pick my brain, and any question, no matter how dumb you think it is, no matter how simple you're afraid it might sound—you ask it and demand an answer."

"Yes, sir."

"Now look at this terrain in front of you."

Charlie stared down at the rugged terrain and shrugged his shoulders. "Yeah."

"See that field of elephant grass?"

"Yes."

"That grass will cut your skin like a razor. Pull your shirtsleeves down when you go through it and tuck your hands inside if you can, but not your trigger finger."

"Okay."

"Let's say you step in it right in the middle of that field of elephant grass."

"Ambush?"

"Affirmative."

"I form a perimeter and call 'Guns up' to get our M-60s into position for laying down fire, preferably neutralizing the enemy machine guns."

"Right. Now let's say this firefight has gone on for over an hour, maybe two."

"Then I must be up against a numerically superior force."

"Correct. Otherwise the gooks will break off contact and run because they'll get their butt kicked."

"I would form up possible flanking actions."

"Yes. They don't work. You are now surrounded."

"I would attack the weakest point with fire-team maneuvers."

"The enemy fire is too heavy."

"Artillery strikes at one zone to break out."

"Does not always work if enemy fire from the flanks can take over. You still cannot get out."

"Air strikes."

"Or naval, if you got it. Naval is the most accurate and most punishing fire you can use."

"Right."

"Now let's say you got no naval fire."

"Air strikes."

"What kind?"

"What do you mean?"

"Choppers or fixed wing?"

"Fixed wing."

"Now what kind of munitions? Let's say you got hold of FAC, Forward Air Control. You got a Piper Cub spotter plane or an OV-10 overhead right now."

"Yes. I have the blooper man fire smoke on the target." Jessie laughed.

"What's so funny?" Charlie snapped.

"You better visit an Army outfit first, Marine."

"What is that supposed to mean?"

"Have you talked to your blooper man, Lieutenant?"

"No."

"Marines don't have spotter rounds for the M-79 40mm grenade launcher unless they've stolen it from the Army.

Which by the way many good Marines have done, but you better not rely on it until you know you got it."

Charlie shook his head and looked frustrated.

"Find out right now," Jessie said calmly.

Charlie looked up and nodded. "Right." He turned and shouted toward the closest position. "Blooper man up!"

The call echoed around the perimeter. A few seconds later a hard-faced Marine strolled over the crest of the hill and came toward them with an M-79 in hand. He stopped beside them.

"Yes, sir," he said with a slow southern drawl.

"What's your name, Marine?" Lieutenant Slate asked.

"Bill."

Jessie stood up. Anger shot through him like a lightning bolt.

"Bill, is it?" Jessie repeated with raised eyebrows and an effort to conceal his rage.

"Yeah."

"I'm Gunnery Sergeant Slate, Bill."

Jessie extended his hand, and the Marine looked at it for a moment before slowly shaking. Jessie snatched the Marine's hand and pushed toward him while he twisted the wrist back, grabbing the man's forearm with his left hand. The Marine named Bill went to his knees grimacing and let out a yell.

"Now, Bill, if you show the LT disrespect again, I'll rip off both your arms, send you home lame, and you can tell war stories about how the gooks did it to you."

Jessie twisted the wrist a little more for good measure, until Bill's face was contorted.

"Now give an officer in my Marine Corps a proper response, Marine! Minus a salute . . . Bill . . . because we are in the bush."

Jessie released the Marine's hand as he positioned himself to fight if necessary. Charlie watched the entire episode with no expression.

"Now, what is your name, Marine?" Charlie asked sternly.

"Lance Corporal Cunningham, sir."

"You are the blooper man."

"Yes, sir."

"Do you carry spotter rounds for the blooper gun?"

"No, sir. We were never issued spotter rounds, sir."

"How long you been in-country, Marine?" Gunny Slate asked.

"Six months, Gunny."

"A good Marine would have stolen spotter rounds from the Army by now."

"Ain't ever even seen the Army over here, Gunny, or I would have for sure."

Jessie tried to keep from grinning but couldn't. "Well said, Marine. But I expect you to steal or trade for some decent munitions the first chance you get, is that clear?"

"Yes, sir, Gunny."

"That will be all, Cunningham," Charlie said.

"Yes, sir. And sir, I didn't mean to act disrespectful."

"It's forgotten, Cunningham, as long as you understand that without proper discipline we might never make it home."

"Yes, sir."

Charlie nodded, and Cunningham stood up and walked back to his position. Charlie and Jessie looked at each other, waiting for the other to speak. The silence was obvious. Jessie decided to continue.

"Now you're surrounded and you got no spotter round for the blooper gun."

"I radio to the OV-10 that I will spot the enemy with my M-60s. He will fire smoke on the enemy after the M-60 tracer rounds pinpoint them. Then he will direct the fixed-wing attack."

"What are you calling for?"

"Napalm."

"Where?"

"One hundred meters due east of my front."

Jessie licked his finger and held it up. He looked accusingly at Charlie.

"You did not check the wind, Lieutenant. You now have a field of elephant grass on fire with the flames and smoke moving toward your platoon. Your men will have to rise up and move to new positions, exposing themselves to enemy fire. You will suffer casualties that are unnecessary."

Charlie looked perplexed for a moment, then he seemed to relax.

"All right. Thanks. I should have called for H.E."

"Yes. Or maybe some Snake-Eye if you judge it so. Or possibly Puff the Magic Dragon, depending on what is available, but it's up to you to radio every bit of info to that OV-10 because he just might call in that nape, not giving any thought to wind conditions or terrain."

"Yes, sir. Got it."

"Now something else boot lieutenants can forget under the stress of command."

"Let's hear it."

"You don't want your fixed-wing attack coming in with napalm from the wrong direction. You must make sure that the air strike comes in parallel to your position, over the enemy. I've seen a boot LT call in strikes in the heat of action without thinking about which direction the F-4s might approach from to drop their mail."

"I can see how that might happen."

"And if he's the least bit short, he ends up frying his own men. You have to be thinking ahead so that whatever develops on the battlefield never catches you by surprise. You'll have to make quick decisions out here, but each decision has to be thought out. The only way you can do both is to constantly plan ahead. View each new terrain situation as a probable battleground. Have a plan ready before it happens."

Charlie nodded but did not speak. He looked up and into his father's eyes, then glanced around the hilltop.

"Guess we better saddle up, Dad. We have to be eight klicks from here by tonight."

"Is that right?"

"Yes. The northwest corner of our A.O. Near this river." He pointed at the grid map, then began folding it up.

"Aye aye, Lieutenant!" Jessie said loud enough for other Marines to hear. He stood up and barked toward the next position, "Pass the word! Saddle up!"

Jessie pulled his pack straps over his tattered flak jacket. Charlie stared at the pack.

"NVA pack," Jessie said. "Twice as much room as ours and twice as comfortable. Soft canvas and the straps are easier on the shoulders."

"Where do I get one?"

"You kill an NVA."

Charlie closed his eyes and shook his head. "Duh, real bright question from a lieutenant."

"Just get all of those boot questions out while I'm here, will ya, son? It'll save you some grief."

"I'll try," Charlie said with a chuckle.

"And if one of the men asks you to radio in for a can of slack or something like that, don't do it."

"A can of slack?"

"We always do things like that to the new guys."

"A can of slack?"

Jessie laughed. "You'll figure it out. We better try humping toward the Thu Bon River or a tributary along the way. Wash off some of the CS so the men don't go nuts scratching."

Charlie rubbed at his neck and frowned. "Yeah, good idea."

CHAPTER TWENTY-FOUR

Four hours later the platoon waded into a narrow waist-deep stream that fed into the Thu Bon River about a mile away. The water was cold and soothing. They crossed the stream and humped up a steep brush-covered hill and then down into a rocky gully. Night was thirty minutes away at most, Jessie guessed. He looked at the position of the sun and slowed to let the lieutenant come alongside as they columned past a thick jungle area on their right.

"Set your ambush up before dusk," Jessie said. "Don't do anything different than you would if you were planning on staying there for the entire night."

"Affirmative."

"The gooks like to hit right at dusk with no more than a few minutes of daylight left. If they strike too early, we'll tear 'em a new hole in open combat, and they know it. They'll open fire with enough light to see us and then hope that darkness will hide them before we counterattack."

"Got it. So that if we're being watched and stalked for a strike, we want to make sure we're already down and ready for it," Lieutenant Slate guessed.

"Not quite. When you set up the perimeter, tell the men to dig in, and don't let them know that we're going to be moving out again in about fifteen minutes to an hour."

"Why?"

"If the men know you're going to make them move out again, they won't dig in. They won't drop packs. If we're being watched, the enemy will know that we're going to move again and try to ambush our move. We want to position ourselves to hit them as they move in to hit us."

"Makes sense."

"Now, after we're set in for the second time, maybe an L-shaped ambush, give it an hour then move again. Maybe fifty meters at the most. Set up a perimeter. If you can't do that because of the terrain, just make sure you got interlocking fields of fire."

"Right."

"Always set the guns up yourself to make sure they're in proper position."

"Right."

"And always make it clear to the gunners that they are not to open fire first if possible, unless they have confirmed targets. The gooks will try to draw their fire to locate the position of the machine guns. Sometimes they might even sacrifice one of their men to find out where the guns are."

"Really?"

"I've seen it more than once. They drag up one of their men and send the poor slob off to meet Buddha for the good of Uncle Ho."

Lieutenant Charlie Rose Slate inhaled as much air as he could, then exhaled like a man getting ready for the starter's gun in a marathon.

"I'm sort of nervous," he said. "My stomach is doing flip-flops. I mean, I'm excited, but . . ."

"We all are a bit. You more than the rest of us for now. The newness rubs off fast, but the stomach will be doing flip-flops ten years from today whenever you remember."

Charlie glanced at his father. There was nothing more to say.

Twenty minutes later Lieutenant Slate passed the word to halt the column. The terrain was hilly and brush-covered. Soon the shadows would make each bush begin to look like a crouching NVA soldier with an AK. The men dropped down, facing out. Charlie Rose turned and whispered back to a thin-faced Marine behind them.

"Corporal Ferguson, up."

Helmets turned as word traveled back down the column. A few seconds later a stocky black Marine with an M-14 came hustling forward. He knelt beside Gunny Slate and Lieutenant Slate.

"Yes, sir."

"Let's get the men into a perimeter. Tell them to dig in quickly."

"Yes, sir. But sir, if I might speak."

"Speak, Corporal."

"We don't always dig in for these night ambushes, Lieutenant. Makes too much noise."

"I want you to feel free to speak up when you think I'm making a mistake of any kind, Corporal. I will listen and evaluate the information. I will then make the decision."

"Yes, sir."

"Tell the men to dig in."

"Yes, sir."

Corporal Ferguson jumped up and moved through the column of kneeling Marines, touching each squad leader on the helmet as he passed along the orders.

The massive skyline turned hazy purple, streaked with red and pale blue. Jessie, Charlie Rose, M.G. Kelly, and Doc Sickle formed the C.P. group in the center of the perimeter. Jessie watched Charlie carefully plotting the coordinates for artillery support. Charlie huddled beside the radioman.

"M.G., crank it up and report our position and get a reading on the other platoons in the area."

"Yes, sir."

Jessie moved close to Charlie and whispered into his ear so no one else could hear. "Map out some preprogrammed coordinates and have M.G. radio them in. Always smart to put in some on-calls."

"On-calls?"

"Same thing as preprogrammed coordinates. If things get too hot and too heavy to give a map reference, you can just scream for the on-calls and pray the gooks have walked under them."

"Affirmative," Charlie whispered, and began to study his map again.

Jessie pointed at it. "We'll be moving over to this position."

"Right," he said. He turned to M.G. and read off a list of coordinates for on-call arty strikes. Jessie watched and listened carefully. He felt good about the boy so far. Charlie did seem to have his act together, but having your crap together before a firefight and having it together during a shootout were two entirely different animals.

The first thirty minutes went by quietly. Charlie Rose huddled down in a shallow fighting hole beside Jessie. Both stared out at the horizon. Jessie leaned toward his son, cupping a hand to whisper.

"Most beautiful sunsets on the planet earth."

Charlie nodded. "I believe it."

"The NVA will likely hit us from the opposite direction. A lot of Marines have died because they were staring at those incredible colors instead of searching for movement."

Charlie Rose looked at his father silently. Jessie got the feeling that his words had made an impression, and he was glad.

"Give me the magazine in your rifle and one from your bandoleer."

Charlie looked at him but did not give voice to his questions. He pulled one magazine out of a bandoleer and one from his M-16 and handed them to his father. Jessie searched through his pack until he found a roll of black electrical tape. He proceeded to tape the two magazines together end to end. He gave it a tug to make sure the tape was secure and handed the magazines back to Charlie.

"What in the world are you doing?" Charlie asked slowly, examining the two magazines.

"When things are hot, you won't have to fumble around for reloading your weapon. Empty one magazine, pull it out, stick in the other end. But you can't leave it that way all the time because you get dirt in the bottom magazine. Rifle jams and you die. Have it ready for every ambush."

Charlie shook his head in wonder. "So simple yet so smart."

Five minutes later it was dusk. Vision was fading fast. This was the time to move. Jessie gave Charlie a pat and stood to a crouch.

"I'll pass the word. You go get that corporal and tell him to take the point. Fifty meters due west."

Jessie moved around the perimeter, passing the word. The perimeter of Marines gathered up their gear as quickly as possible and headed out in column to the west. Each step sounded like a herd of elephants. Jessie moved through the column, whispering, "Keep together. Keep quiet."

He grabbed Charlie Rose by the arm as he passed by and pulled him aside.

"Now quickly form an L-shaped ambush facing the most logical direction of attack, if you're not breaking up into squad-sized ambushes."

"What do you think?"

"I think it's your decision, Lieutenant."

Charlie Rose froze for a moment. "Platoon size. L-shaped ambush facing east."

"Right."

"No digging in, too much noise," Charlie said.

"Affirmative, Lieutenant."

Ten minutes later the platoon was set in, facing east. Each position was no more than five to seven meters apart, two men to a position. Jessie sat in with Charlie Rose, and the nightly vigil that marked this war as different from all of his others began again, but somehow things had changed dramatically. This night was different. He glanced at his son and knew that something would never be quite the same. A fear unlike any other fear he'd ever faced was beginning to take root, churning in his gut like a piece of food that would not digest. Risking his own life was no problem. Death was always close at hand. He knew it. He accepted it. But even the notion that Charlie Rose could die out here sent shock waves of fear and doubt through him. He'd seen it happen a thousand times as young Marines, alive and full of piss and vinegar, were gone in an instant, and nothing remained but memories and a body bag. Young combat lieutenants were dying fast. Jessie shook with a cold chill and gripped his twelve-gauge shotgun a little tighter. He swiped at the whine of hungry mosquitoes circling his ears.

Charlie Rose leaned closer and whispered, "Mosquitoes always this bad?"

"We call 'em the North Vietnamese Air Force."

Charlie's teeth showed white in the three-quarter moon. "Bug juice work?"

Jessie licked his finger and held it up. He shook his head no. "Wait for the breeze to die down. Gooks can smell the bug juice. They know we use it."

Charlie nodded.

Jessie leaned close again. "It works both ways. They eat a lot of fish and rice. Sometimes you get a whiff of them and know they're close. Their body odor is unique. Learn it. Become familiar with it when you go through a ville."

"Right."

"You want the first watch, son?" Jessie asked, knowing that there was a better chance of seeing snow tonight than there was of the kid being able to sleep during his first night in the bush.

"Yes."

"Now listen. The stress and anxiety makes some Marines shut down. You become so tired that you cannot stay awake. Your body puts out so much adrenaline that the adrenaline attacks your system and you just shut down. Be aware of that."

"Okay, Dad."

"Two-hour shifts unless the men are so tired they won't make it two hours. Remember that. Know how tired your men are. If they've been in a day-long firefight, the stress can be overwhelming and can hit you that night or the next day like a hammer. Even the best Marines might just fall asleep."

"Got it. I understand."

Jessie pulled up his sleeve as he turned his palm up to check his watch. "Wake me at 2200 hours."

Charlie Rose checked his watch.

Jessie reached out and slapped his hand over Charlie's wristwatch. "Turn that watch under! Trying to get yourself killed!"

"Sorry!"

"Gooks can see that fluorescent face for ten miles."

"Yes, sir."

"Your eyes will play tricks on you, son. Bushes begin to move and look like people. Best to mark every piece of terrain mentally or in the dirt in front of you so you know that each bush or tree was there from the start."

"Right."

"Do not be trigger happy. Sometimes during the night you need to send your corporal around to check positions."

"Okay."

"If there's a bright flash, like a frag going off or a flare going up, do not look at it. You'll lose your night vision and you won't see diddly for five minutes."

"Got it."

Jessie curled up around his shotgun, pulling his collar up to his ears to stop the whining. He already knew he would sleep very little for the next two weeks.

Two hours passed with visions of Kate weaving in and out of his mind. Suddenly a loud bang ripped the dark silence. A giant sparkler spiraled out of the black landscape, sizzling into their old position. The explosion was crisp, sending fiery hot metal in all directions.

"God! There they are, Dad! Gooks!"

Charlie Rose got up to open fire and Jessie slapped him hard enough to knock his helmet over his eyes.

"They're trying to draw fire so they know where you are, especially the gun position." Jessie turned toward the nearest Marine position and whispered, "Hold your fire. Don't anyone fire until I do."

The word was whispered through the L-shaped ambush. A few moments later another B-40 rocket sizzled into the platoon's old position. The bright flash of the explosion stole Jessie's night vision and he blinked hard to get it back. Four quick AK-47 rounds cracked off, followed by the shouts of Vietnamese, then silence.

Charlie Rose nudged him. "When should we return fire?"

Jessie cupped his hand to shield his voice and whispered.

"When we know where they are. They're trying to draw fire with a few troops, but chances are the rest of their men are moving in from a different direction. If we sit tight, they might stumble around until they walk right into our ambush, but your men must maintain fire discipline."

"Looks like they already did."

"You're right. Sign of a good platoon of Marines."

"Yeah."

"Where are your claymores?"

Charlie said nothing.

"Charlie."

"Yeah?"

"Where did your men set up the claymores?"

"I forgot to get 'em out."

"What?"

"I . . . I just . . . I forgot."

"Then we don't have much covering our back do we, Lieutenant?"

"I'll do it now," Charlie growled angrily.

"We'll do it now. Together. Give me your Go to Hell Box."

"What?"

"The detonator. Always take it out with you when you set up a claymore mine. Got that? Never leave it while you're carrying the mine. That way there's no chance of someone setting it off while your face is in front of it."

"Yes, sir." Charlie reached around behind him, searching blindly until he found the claymore. It came in a bandoleer-type case with the mine in one section and the electrical firing mechanism and electric blasting cap in the other. It was a directional-fixed fragmentation mine, used primarily against massed, human wave, infantry attacks. It could be used against thin-skinned vehicles, too, perforating the outer body and killing the occupants. When detonated, the mine delivered a large number of steel ball bearings simultaneously in a fan-shaped zone approximately two meters high and thirty meters wide at a range of thirty meters. It looked like a little TV set on four tiny legs, weighed only 2½ pounds and was packed with .8 pounds of C-4 plastic explosive. Jessie had seen it mutilate an entire squad of NVA even though they were spread out.

"Looks like enough moonlight to see the wires. Think you can hook it up in the dark?"

"Yes."

"You go down the line and find another claymore. Pass the word to each position that you're going out with a claymore so your own men don't blow you away. Got that?" Jessie gripped Charlie by the front of his flak jacket and pulled him so close that their helmets hit. "They will, Charlie. Your men will hear you out there and kill you. They're scared and ain't going to wait for an introduction."

"Yes, sir." Charlie's voice sounded nervous. His eyes were open wide with adrenaline. Jessie wanted to change his mind. Just leave the claymores and gamble that the gooks would not come from that direction.

"Meet you back here, Dad," Charlie said as he rose and moved toward the next position.

Jessie watched him go. His heart began to pound blood

to his ears, and he knew the fear was not for himself. He wanted to stop Charlie, wanted to send one of the other men out, but it was the lieutenant's mistake and the lieutenant had to fix it. Jessie moved in the opposite direction down the Marine line, warning each man that two Marines would be out setting up claymores. At the end of the small part of the L-shaped ambush, he left his shotgun with two Marines flattened out on their stomachs, aiming into the darkness. He tapped them both on the back and whispered one last reminder. "I'm going out now."

They signaled with a thumbs-up. Jessie stood to a crouch and began slowly walking away from the Marine line. Each step sounded too loud. Ten feet out he knelt down on one knee, watching and listening. A bright flash followed a cracking explosion in the area of their first position, maybe forty or fifty meters away. Jessie hit the ground with his eyes shut and lay still for a moment until his night vision returned. The enemy troops were still probing the old position. Soon they would realize that the Marines had moved. They would give up or continue to search for contact. Jessie blinked. His eyes began to focus again. He stood to a crouch and moved another ten meters out. He dropped to his stomach and quickly set up the claymores. He checked and rechecked the wires, then started back. "Gunny comin' in," he whispered as he neared the Marine position.

"Come on in."

Jessie low-crawled the rest of the way. He sat between the two Marine riflemen and attached the wires to the detonator. He tapped one of the men on the back. "Turn around, Marine. You'll face the other way and man the detonator. You got a claymore twenty meters out. If you hear anything, set it off and get down or the back-blast will blow your head off."

"Right."

Jessie moved back down the line of Marines until he reached his position. Charlie wasn't there. He sat stiff with worry for ten more agonizing minutes. Finally, he could wait no longer. He stood to a crouch and started down the line of Marines in search of Charlie. He'd taken a couple of steps when Charlie appeared a few feet away. Jessie knelt down and waited.

"Took ya long enough, boot," he whispered.

"I haven't been doing this for three wars."

Jessie grinned, and though it was forced, it felt good. They moved back to their position and stared into the darkness until eyes ached for rest. Suddenly, a noise from behind them snatched Jessie's head around. A blinding flash and ripping explosion shoved his face into the dirt. His right arm hurt. He looked to his right. Charlie had a tourniquet grip on his bicep.

"What was it, Dad?"

"My claymore."

No one spoke and no one fired. Jessie glanced at Charlie and wanted to warn him that the sound of his heartbeat would pound in his ears so loud that it interfered with his hearing. He wanted to tell him a million things. Mostly he wanted to tell him how much he loved him. But there was no time. And this was not the place. One person in each of the two-man positions turned toward the blast and waited. Jessie nudged his son and whispered into his ear, "You inherited a good platoon of Marines, Lieutenant. Fire discipline is excellent."

That was the last word whispered. The night drifted by without incident. No one slept. The clanking of canteens greeted the first gray shafts of morning. Every Marine breathed easier with daylight. As the sun allowed better vision, the men began to stand and search the terrain. Jessie elbowed Charlie Rose and stood up with his shotgun at the ready.

"Let's go see if we bagged any, Lieutenant."

"Okay, Gunny."

They moved toward the end of the ambush to the two Marines Jessie had left the detonator with. They were standing up. Neither appeared older than eighteen, but both had that look in their eyes that said they were salts. One had written *Ed* on his helmet with a black marker, and the other had printed *Steve* on his. Ed looked like he should have been wearing one of those Canadian mounties uniforms and rescuing girls from train tracks. When Steve took his helmet off, he revealed a shaved head. Good Marine haircut, but Jessie wondered how he kept it like that out in the bush.

"What happened last night, Marine?" Jessie asked as they neared the two men.

"Heard something out there, Gunny. Didn't want to wait to meet it eye-to-eye."

"All right. Let's go see what it was."

They followed the wire out to a charred spot in the weeds that marked the explosion. Jessie looked beyond the charred grass. Ten meters out was a body.

"You got one, Marine."

"Hey, Ed got a confirmed last night with that claymore!"

"He did not!" Steve shouted. "I did it."

"Yeah, right," Ed scoffed. "Just like you got more in Australia."

"Yeah, exactly."

"What about Liz?"

"Oh man! Was she hot or what?"

The two Marines got a faraway look in their eyes, as if they both had mentally wandered off, away from the ugly scene before them.

"You know, Steve . . ."

"What, Ed?"

"I'd sell you into slavery for a girl like Liz."

"Yeah. I know. It would almost be worth the sacrifice just to know one of us got her."

Word of the kill echoed through the platoon of Marines like the score of a tight ball game.

"Come here, Lieutenant." Jessie gave his son a tug toward the bloody mess that was once a man.

They stood over the dead NVA soldier for a few moments before Charlie spoke.

"He looks like he was put through one of those grinders that you put hamburger in."

"You would too if you just had about twenty thousand ball bearings put through you."

"Hey, Lieutenant! Got another one over here." The Marine with *Ed* on his helmet was pointing down at another bloody mess ten meters to the right. Jessie leaned close to his son.

"Tell 'em to check the bodies for papers. The Marine named Ed can keep any single-shot weapons they find. He can tag 'em and have them sent to the rear so that when he goes home they're his to keep."

"Okay," Charlie muttered, staring down at the riddled body. "Check the bodies!" he shouted.

"Listen up, Lieutenant." Jessie nudged his son, to take his eyes off the dead man in front of them.

"Okay."

"Now you want to leave the bodies here and come back tonight or tomorrow and set up another ambush."

"Why?"

"The gooks will probably try to come back for these two. You can bag some more if you set it up right."

"Okay." Charlie's eyes were still glued to the mutilated body. He leaned over and picked up a shattered AK-47 Russian assault rifle. The wooden stock was splintered into sharp pieces.

"Charlie."

"Yeah."

"Is this the first dead man you've seen?"

"No. A kid in ROTC died in a car wreck back in Gainesville. I went to the funeral."

"Not the same."

"No."

"You ain't in the world no more, son. It's like being on another planet. The quicker your emotions become hard, the better." Jessie motioned at the dead man. "This is nothing. When you see a dead Marine, you'll know what I mean. The gooks won't seem like real people. They begin to look like the old black and white photos of soldiers who died a hundred years ago. But Marines die in color and their blood gets all over you and soaks into your skin and never washes out."

Charlie pulled his eyes off the dead man and stared at his father for what felt to Jessie like a long time. He wore an expression that Jessie had never seen on his son's face before.

For the next fourteen days Jessie trained his lieutenant in every imaginable way. They made no more contact with the enemy. The two weeks passed like two years, but that was the way it was in 'Nam. You lived each minute separately. It was like stepping into some strange time machine that caused seconds to last for hours.

The popping sound of the old Korean era chopper that would take Jessie away circled their small perimeter in a dried-up rice paddy. Green smoke swirled around like fog. Jessie grabbed his son by both shoulders of his flak jacket and stared into his bright blue eyes. For the first time in his life he felt truly close to his son. Love and dedication were never a question, but being this close to anyone could only happen when you put your lives on the line together, and they both knew it.

"Don't ever relax your mind out here."

"Yes, sir."

"Go over and over everything I've taught you."

"Yes, sir."

"If you get a kid who's color blind or slightly colorblind, use him. Put him on the point when things look hairy. Especially in heavy jungle foilage. A color-blind Marine can see shades, and gook camouflage won't fool him."

"Yes, sir. I remember, Dad."

Jessie forced a nervous smile. His mind raced to search

for anything he might have forgotten, but he could think of no more. "Sorry, Lieutenant. I'm repeating myself."

"It's okay, Dad."

"Well, guess this is my taxi." Jessie looked up as the chopper descended.

"Dad."

"Yes, son."

"I love you."

Tears welled up in Jessie's battle-aged eyes and a lump the size of a golf ball seemed to stick in his throat. He swiped at a tear beginning to trickle down his cheek and tried to clear his throat. He sniffed and felt embarrassed.

"I love you too, son." His voice cracked and he felt stupid.

"Let's do R and R together, Dad."

"There it is, son. Australia?"

"Yeah. Round-eyed girls! Write me and set the dates."

"Well, you're going nowhere for about six months, Lieutenant."

"I know. Feels like I've been here longer than that already."

Jessie smiled. He knew exactly what Charlie meant. This would be the longest six months in either of their lives.

The front wheels of the old grasshopper bounced as the chopper settled to the sunbaked earth. Jessie Slate bearhugged his son one last time, then turned and ran for the open hatch of the chopper. The old bird lifted off with a struggle and drifted sideways. The second platoon perimeter of Delta Company Marines grew smaller, like a fading picture.

CHAPTER TWENTY-FIVE

The boatswain's whistle sounded over the intercom just above Jessie's bunk with three distinct notes followed by the command that never failed to send a flight of butterflies through every Marine's stomach.

"Now hear this! All Marines report to the hangar deck with 782 gear!"

Jessie sprang out of his bunk and rushed to Captain Volke's quarters. The captain's berth was just down a narrow passageway, and Wing was pounding on the door as Jessie reached it. "Enter and be recognized!"

They went in. Lieutenant Kutler was already there, along with the other two platoon leaders and a staff sergeant Jessie didn't recognize.

"Gentlemen, listen up!" Captain Volke blurted. He seemed hyper. His face was flushed. He pointed to a map on his desk. "We're going into Elephant Valley." He looked up at the faces of the others; his blue eyes were twitching slightly. "Any of you familiar with it?"

"Yes, sir," Jessie said.

"Yes, sir," Wing said.

"I've been there once, Captain," a broad-shouldered first lieutenant said.

"And you two?" Captain Volke looked at Wing and Jessie.

Jessie pointed to himself. "Three, maybe four times."

" 'Bout the same," Wing said.

"You can't go out with us, Gunny Wing," the captain said. "You're ordered back to your Koreans. You leave 0700 in the morning." He looked at Jessie. "You know Elephant Valley, Slate?"

"Yes, sir."

"Outstanding! All right. We'll be landing in this area here. M.I. says it's a cold LZ? What do you think, Gunny Slate?"

"The LZ, who knows? But we'll run into some pretty well-organized V.C. with plenty of local support."

"Yes," Broken Wing said.

"We will land here ..." The captain went through a quick rundown of all information available and dismissed them to their platoons.

They hustled to their lockers, grabbed up their 782 gear, packs, suspenders, cartridge belts, canteens, helmets, and flak jackets. The platoon was already on the hangar deck when the lieutenant and gunnies arrived. Wing came along to say good-bye to Swift Eagle. CH-46 Chinooks were being readied for flight at the far end of the huge hangar deck as the squad leaders drew boxes of ammo, grenades, and C-rations. Navy men were rolling the Chinooks onto giant elevators on the starboard side of the deck to be lifted topside and rolled onto the flight deck. The rotors were joined together and tied down at the ends of each helicopter.

"First platoon! Over here on the double!" Kutler shouted, and waved the first, second, and third squads of the first platoon over to him. The men gathered around with mostly anxious faces.

"Squad leaders start passing out the ammo! Five bandoleers to each Marine. Break open the C-ration cartons and get 'em passed out. I want each man packing four frags. We'll have 60mm mortar support, so some of you will be packing 60mm rounds! No griping. Each platoon will have a gun, so squad leaders make sure every man is carrying at least one belt of M-60 ammo! Did those new boots get to the ship's armorer?"

"Yes, sir," Swift Eagle said.

"All right, let's get saddled up. Our taxi's waitin'."

Gonzales and Justice looked like lost, frightened children. Jessie carried his gear over beside them and started strapping his bandoleers of shotgun ammo around his neck and shoulders Mexican style.

"Gunny!" Justice sounded as nervous as he looked. "A full-grown pack mule couldn't carry all this! How's a man supposed to be able to run?"

Jessie forced a laugh. It was as fake as his calm demeanor, but part of his job. Inside the nonchalance, his stomach was doing flip-flops, as it always did before an operation that looked potentially hot.

"How can you be laughin', Gunny? I'm nervous as a long-tailed cat in a room full of rockin' chairs."

"Shoot, kid, this ain't nothing. You boys should have been in the old Corps! This is just a little helicopter landing. You want some real fear, you should have put ashore on Bougainville or Iwo."

"Holy cow!" another Marine called out.

Sally's A-gunner, Pale, crisscrossed another hundred-round belt of machine-gun ammo over his chest and pointed at Jessie. "You were on Iwo, Gunny?" he asked.

"There it is, bro. Gunny Wing was there too."

"What was it like, Gunny?" Sally asked.

Jessie smiled. "I'll tell you sometime, Marine."

"Far out! I didn't know you were that old, Gunny!" Pale said with a tone of amazement.

Jessie glared at the pale-faced Marine. "I'm not too old to take care of you, boot."

"Just kiddin', Sarge."

"Go on, Pale, kick the Gunny's butt!" Sally called out, then laughed out loud.

"Gunny." Gonzales held out his bandoleers of ammo.

"Look, boots, fill all seven magazines. Eighteen rounds per clip, got it?"

"I thought they took twenty, Gunny," Gonzales said.

"No! Twenty rounds will weaken the magazine spring. Eventually you'll have a jam and get yourself killed."

"I already filled mine, Gunny," Justice said, holding out the rest of his bandoleers of unused ammo.

"Now tie the unused bandoleers around your body Mexican style. On the outside of your flak jacket, boot."

Justice looked like a man with ten thumbs. Nerves showed on everyone differently. Some guys prayed, some went stone silent, and some got rushes like cold chills. Jessie always got scared, but the fear sort of turned into excitement. Each operation was a new adventure, and it seemed like the excitement outweighed the fear. Was he just pulling a con on himself? he wondered. Whatever it was he felt, he knew that his heart was pumping overtime right now.

"Can't get all these vittles in this pack," Justice griped as he tried to stuff in one more can.

"Here." Broken Wing squatted down beside Justice. "Where are your spare socks?"

"In the pack, Sarge."

"Get 'em!"

Justice searched through his pack and pulled out his olive-green socks. Wing took them and began shoving cans of C-rations into them.

"Fill the other sock and tie them together and sling them through a pack strap."

"Thanks, Sarge. Wish I had a pack like Gunny Slate's."

Broken Wing gave the boot Marine a serious glance. "You might get one sooner than you want. Maybe today, boot."

Justice looked at Wing as if he did not understand, but he was smart enough not to ask.

"First platoon! Saddle up!"

They marched in column to the other end of the hangar deck, where the big elevators took them, along with three

Chinook troop helicopters, up to the flight deck. Navy personnel rolled the choppers off the elevator and prepared the rotors for flight.

A Navy officer ran up to the front of the platoon and shouted, "Board by squads!"

The men filed up the ramp leading into the troop chopper. White hats, watching as the Marines boarded, had a look in their eyes that said, "I'm glad it's you and not me."

Broken Wing slapped both hands on the broad shoulders of Swift Eagle. They stared into each other's eyes for a long moment, then Broken Wing stepped back and saluted his son. Swift Eagle's chest came out another two inches as his shoulders went back, snapping to attention. He returned the salute, then filed into the helicopter. Broken Wing looked at Jessie. His eyes said it all.

Jessie signaled a thumbs-up. "I'll take care of him, Wing."

"I would choose no other." Wing turned and walked away. A stream of goose bumps sent a chill down Jessie's spine.

Jessie walked up the ramp behind the last man. "Get those harnesses on!" he shouted as he found his place on the long metal bench and strapped in.

The pilots received permission to depart. The engines cranked up, big rotors beginning to whirl. From that moment on, all normal conversation ceased. Prop wash drowned out all other sound. Soon they lifted off and were over the water racing toward land. The *Ogden* grew smaller and smaller until it was a dot on the blue horizon.

The Chinooks flew over water for a while, high enough to keep clear of ground fire but still within sight of land. Jessie felt someone tugging on his sleeve as the choppers moved inland. Justice was on his right trying to ask a question, but the engine was too loud. He finally pointed at the porthole and shouted, "Why no glass?" Jessie leaned closer, cupping his hand to direct his shout.

"So glass won't explode when hit by incoming fire!"

Justice nodded that he understood, then sat still as a statue. The helicopters headed toward distant, ominous-looking mountains, but never seemed to get closer. Other choppers were alongside. It was difficult to tell how many. The sky was hot blue, with only occasional white puffy clouds, not nearly enough cover to cool the steaming valley floor below. Doc Rice must have been thinking the same thing. He was up, moving from man to man, handing out salt tablets. A good Corpsman, Jessie thought. The chopper shifted violently to one side. It was going down very rapidly, and each man's face resembled the same startled expression you would expect to see on a roller coaster.

They white-knuckled their weapons, which were standing on butt ends between clenched knees. PFC Blaine sat across from Jessie. He was shouting something that no one could hear. The chopper was jerking violently. Blaine kept shouting. He struggled to get out of his harness. The chopper was dropping quickly. The other Marines also tried to get out of their seat restraints. They were beginning to panic.

Pencil-thin shafts of sunlight suddenly caught Jessie's eye. He looked up. Jagged holes were appearing in the ceiling and side of the chopper. He felt the chopper drop, then flare out for landing. He tore out of his harness and moved toward the open rear ramp of the Chinook.

"Move it! Move it!"

Blaine was the first man to the edge of the ramp. The ground was close but still moving. Balance was difficult. "Go on! Jump!" Jessie screamed into Blaine's ear.

"We ain't down yet! We ain't down!"

"He ain't goin' any lower, Marine!" Jessie barked, and shoved Blaine over the edge. Blaine screamed as he went. The platoon filed up to the edge of the tail ramp quickly and leapt out two at a time. Jessie and Lieutenant Kutler jumped last. The drop was about eight feet, but with a seventy-pound pack, canteens, ammo, weapons, and helmet, it felt like eighty feet. Jessie hit the ground like a lead balloon, his pack going over his head and knocking his helmet against the bridge of his nose. He rolled over and saw the helmet tumbling away. As he scrambled after it, dirt kicked up in spurts just to the right of the helmet.

"Incoming!" he shouted, but his voice was lost in the chaos.

The choppers were gone, but everything was still too loud to hear. Automatic weapons fire seemed to be all around. Men were shouting and pointing. Two grenades exploded one after the other, and then it was over. An eerie silence engulfed the area. Jessie grabbed up his helmet and searched for the platoon. He lifted his head carefully and looked around. The men were spread out in every direction. He spotted Lieutenant Kutler fifteen yards away and pushed off into a hunched-over sprint.

"Comin' in!" Jessie yelled as he slid in beside the lieutenant and Mouth, the radioman. No one shot at him.

"What's the word, Lieutenant?"

"Get 'em into a perimeter, Gunny." Kutler's orders came through clenched teeth, his face contorted in pain.

"You hit, Lieutenant?"

He grabbed at his left ankle cursing under his breath. "I sprained it when we jumped out of the chopper." He slammed down his helmet. "It's hurt."

Jessie twirled around and shouted, "Corpsman up!"

Doc Rice jumped to his feet from twenty yards away and sprinted toward them.

"Get the men into a perimeter, Gunny."

"Yes, sir." Jessie stood up. "Form up in a perimeter over here. Around me! On the double! First platoon!"

A few of the men scrambled into a perimeter, but not all of them.

"Get over here! First platoon, form a perimeter!"

Pollock and a black Marine named Bacon got up and hustled back toward the newly formed perimeter. Jessie ran at them the moment they flattened into position. He knelt down on one knee beside both men and put his face in front of Pollock's.

"I'll give an order only once from this moment on." Jessie moved to Bacon until his face was close enough to kiss. "Is that clear, Marines?"

"Yes sir, Gunny," Bacon said.

"Yes, Gunny," Pollock mumbled.

Jessie moved back to the lieutenant and Mouth the radioman. Doc Rice had the lieutenant's boot off. The ankle was swollen badly. Doc looked up at Gunny Slate as he dropped down beside them.

"I made a mistake, Gunny."

"What is it, Doc?"

The young Corpsman looked angry at himself. "I shouldn't have taken the boot off! He'll never get it on again now. The ankle is too swollen, might be broken. We got to have a medevac, Gunny."

"What?" Lieutenant Kutler barked.

"He's right, Lieutenant. Unless you can get up and walk on it."

Kutler looked around for a moment, then used his rifle to push himself to his feet. The pain in his face said it all. Forty minutes later the medevac chopper lifted off with the angry lieutenant. Gunny Slate took command of the platoon. He checked his compass and map one last time.

"Mouth."

"Yes, Gunny."

"Who's the point man?"

"Bacon Butt, Gunny."

"Bacon Butt." Jessie grinned. The Marine did have a big rear end. "Bacon! Take the point! We're headin' that way." He pointed at a field of elephant grass that stood fifteen feet high. "Saddle up! Move out by squad! Don't bunch up, ladies! Corporal Swift Eagle!"

"Yes, sir!" Swift Eagle jogged over to Jessie.

"Put out flank guards."

"Aye aye, Gunny."

"Make sure it's not the new boots. We'll never see 'em again."

"Yes, sir." Swift Eagle scanned the men as they passed. "Barry and Moose! Take the flanks!"

"Ah, Chief! Why do we always get flank guard!" Barry griped.

"Yeah, Chief," Moose said. He spat and shuffled his size-thirteen boots like a kid kicking the dirt when he's mad.

"Friggin' Marine Corps. Should have joined the Navy or Air Force." Barry trudged out into the giant elephant grass on the right flank like a man wading into water. In a moment he was out of sight. The three squads of seven men each waded into the elephant grass in single column.

The V.C. were nowhere to be seen. Jessie had done it before, but being in command was not all that comfortable for him. They humped through the valley all morning, taking a five- or ten-minute break every two hours. On the breaks, the point and flank men would drop where they were with weapons pointing outboard. The rest of the men would slump into their flak vests and sleep. Sally and Tall got in a quick game of back alley. Doc Rice moved down the column, making sure each man had taken his salt tab and a malaria pill and enough water to keep from dropping from heat exhaustion. The weight of the gear was starting to take a toll. Pack straps dug deep into shoulders after the second hour of a long hump. Men carrying the mortar rounds or 3.5 rocket rounds were starting to complain. That was okay with Jessie. It was a Marine's God-given right to gripe about the Corps, and it was a grunt Marine's God-given right to gripe about nearly everything else, and they took that right seriously.

"Pass the word to the point that we're stopping for chow at the top of that next rise," Jessie called to the doc, just ahead. Doc passed the word up the line. Ten minutes later the twenty-one tired Marines straggled up a small hill that was overgrown with brush except at the top, where it was relatively clear. They formed a perimeter, Corporal Swift Eagle barked the men into proper positions, then they broke out their chow. Jessie found a can of meatballs and beans. He leaned against his pack, pulled his P-38 opener from the band around his helmet liner and worked open the can as he watched Pale and Sally set up the gun.

"Sally, I'll play you a hand for that peaches and pound cake," Pale said, tapping the butt of the M-60 with his white C-ration spoon. His long face reminded Jessie of a caricature of Frankenstein.

"You can stuff that in your bag, bro."

"How you gonna be, Sally?"

"Gonna be fine eatin' my peaches and pound cake, bro."

"And I was making you a deal, Sally."

"I hear ya, bro. Sounds like some honky deal to me."

"Two four-packs of Salem and the use of my paperback."

Sally paused to let the deal sink in. "What is it?"

"Ellery Queen."

"I don't want no book about queers."

"Not that kind of queen! It's a mystery writer named Ellery Queen."

Jessie laughed at the two young Marines. Some things never changed.

"What ya laughing at, Gunny?" Doc Rice asked.

"Sally and Pale."

"You hear that, Sally?" Pale said. "Even the gunny thinks you're stupid for not taking the deal. You heard of Ellery Queen, right, Gunny?"

"You guys believe in déjà vu?"

"Déjà who?"

"You know, like I've been here before."

"Yeah, that's happened to me," Pale said.

"Well, I saw this same scene about Ellery Queen on Bougainville."

"Bougainville!" Doc Rice exclaimed.

"You mean World War Two?" Pale asked.

"Yeah. We had a guy in the Paramarines that would do anything to get hold of an Ellery Queen book. Perry Mason was another biggie."

"Paramarines?" Sally said with pinched brow.

"You mean they had Ellery Queen books in 'forty-five?" Pale asked.

"Bougainville was 'forty-three, Marine," Jessie corrected.

"Perry Mason is that old!" Sally said in disbelief.

"Hey, it ain't that long ago, boots."

Sally turned to Pale. "All right, let's trade, but no back alley for it. If this honky's been around that long, it must be good reading."

"Hey, lighten up on the 'old' stuff, will ya?" Jessie grumbled. "It's not like we're talking about the Civil War here."

"Can we heat our food, Gunny?"

Jessie turned to find Moose standing over him with his little C-ration can that had been poked full of holes to make a stove.

"Yeah. We don't need to observe fire discipline yet. They know we're here."

"Yes, sir," Moose said with a jaw full of tobacco. He turned and sprayed some ugly brown juice at a giant ant pile and headed back to his position. A minute later someone howled and Justice came sprinting toward the C.P. with the look of death on his freckled face. He dove in beside Gunny and Doc and Mouth.

"What is it, Marine?"

Justice pointed back toward his position. "That big guy with the M-14 is trying to kill us!"

"What? Moose?"

"He's lighting a piece of C-4 right in front of us!"

The three Marines looked at Justice and shook their heads.

"You ain't back in the world, boot. You don't know anything yet." Doc Rice sounded smug.

"Get on back over there, Pimkin. C-4 has to have an

electrical charge to blow up. It's safe to burn and it's the best way to heat your C-rats." Mouth the radioman blurted his info and turned back to eating his can of ham and eggs.

Justice got to his feet and walked away like a kid who had been scolded.

"Pimkin," Jessie called.

He stopped and looked back. "Yeah, Gunny?"

"Find a salt who's been here a while and stick close to him. Somebody who can show you the ropes."

"Aye aye, Gunny. Thanks."

Jessie winked. "You'll be all right, Marine."

Twenty minutes later Jessie gave the signal to Corporal Swift Eagle and the call went around the perimeter.

"Saddle up."

"Saddle up."

"Saddle up."

The hump began, this time with a nervous Marine named Karas walking point. The valley was a maze of booby traps, and it was unfair to make one man play human minesweeper for too long at a time. Your senses would grow dull, and that's when you wouldn't see the trip wire. Your chances of seeing it were slim anyway, but especially when you were tired. The hump got tougher and the brush grew thicker as they neared mountains on the west side of the valley. The sky grew yellow with about an hour of daylight left.

"Pass the word to pick up the pace," Jessie said quietly to Doc Rice, who was seven yards ahead of him in the column. Doc passed the word up and soon the pace quickened. Jessie wanted to make it to the base of the first mountain before nightfall, or at least close enough to move again after sunset.

An hour later the terrain grew rocky and more barren just before reaching a rugged, hilly area that lay at the foot of steep, forested mountains. "Pass the word to halt."

Word filtered to the point and back to the tail-end Charlie. The men dropped to the ground on one knee as Jessie took over the point.

"Let's go," he said as he moved past Karas, the point man.

Jessie walked forward another fifty meters to some flat terrain between two small brush-covered hills. He waved the men forward, letting them pass until Corporal Swift Eagle came along.

"Chief, get the men into a perimeter and tell them to dig in right now. Make sure we got interlocking fields of fire."

"Yes, sir." Swift Eagle's mouth said yes but his normally expressionless face was filled with apprehension. He turned to leave, paused, then looked back.

"Gunny."

"What is it, Corporal, hurry up."

"Too much light left to dig in, Gunny."

Jessie stared at the young Navajo hard for a moment, not quite sure how to respond. The kid was using his God-given talent, but orders had been given, and it was a fine line between offering advice and debating an order. Swift Eagle was right, but he did not know the full plan, and there wasn't time to take a vote.

"Did you think that order had a question mark on the end of it, Marine?"

Swift Eagle looked taken aback by the sharp reply. He cleared his throat and stood straight. "No, Gunny."

He turned and rushed through the column of kneeling Marines, grabbing and pushing two at a time into their perimeter positions.

"Dig in!"

"Ah, man!"

"Shut up, Marine! Break out those E-tools and start digging!"

Ten minutes later the clanking of entrenching shovels against the rock-hard ground reverberated around the hasty perimeter. The sky went gray with a purple and red horizon unmatched in beauty anywhere in the world. Jessie gathered the C.P. group together as the last minutes of daylight evaporated. A cool breeze drifted between the hills and it felt wonderful, but it probably meant rain.

"Give 'em five minutes more, then we'll saddle up and move two hundred meters that way." He pointed toward the small hill on their left. "We should hit a river on the other side of this hill."

"Want the men to stop digging in, Gunny?" Mouth asked.

"No."

"But—"

"Explain it to him, Chief." He assumed Swift Eagle had figured it out by now.

Swift Eagle unstrapped his E-tool from the back of his pack. "We are being watched. They will hit us after dark where they last see us, and we won't be there."

No one spoke. Jessie saw the question still on their faces.

"Digging in could be the difference in making Charlie Cong believe that we won't move again after dark."

Night engulfed Elephant Valley as if someone had thrown a blanket over it. Jessie covered his mouth and nudged the Chief. "Pass the word. Saddle up and don't make a sound. Moving out in five minutes."

Jessie gathered up his gear and waited a few minutes before standing up. Swift Eagle returned from passing the word to each position around the perimeter and began to gear up.

"I'll take the point, Chief. I want you on Tail-end Charlie so we don't leave anyone."

"Yes, sir."

Jessie moved toward the hill on their left, circled it, and went on for another hundred meters. Black clouds rolled in overhead just as the moon began to give off some light. The sound of trickling water signaled they were near the river. He moved slowly until he could feel the drop-off of the riverbank with the toe of his boot. The moon broke from behind the cloud cover above and shimmered off the swiftly running river. He held his shotgun above his head and slid down the riverbank into the cold water. It took his breath away, and for a moment he wondered if this was such a good idea. It started to rain. The moon slid behind another cloud bank. The swift, chest-deep water would be the worst possible place to get ambushed, but with the moon behind the clouds and the rain covering any noise they might make while crossing, it seemed like the perfect time.

The river wasn't that wide, maybe twenty to thirty meters, but going that far with no cover and no way to run or defend yourself was terrifying. Each man walked with his eyes up, hoping that the moon would not suddenly appear from behind the black clouds. The rain got heavier as Jessie reached the muddy bank on the other side. Beyond the river lay the mountains and, somewhere up there, according to the latest map, a village. If the gooks were coming from anywhere around this zone, he thought, it would probably be from that direction. The other two platoons of Echo Company were supposedly set in on two other routes the enemy might use to leave that village. It was a good plan, if the V.C. or NVA hadn't guessed it already.

The point man found what seemed to be a trail, and they followed it away from the river far enough to escape the sound of running water. Jessie halted the column.

"Squad leaders up," he passed the word back.

Barry Morse, Blaine, and Swift Eagle came forward. They dropped to one knee beside Gunny Slate and waited for orders.

"Chief, take the first squad fifteen meters to the right and set up a squad-size ambush, two men to a position in a straight line parallel to the river, with an L-shape on your right flank. You'll have the third squad doing the same thing on the left flank, with second squad and the C.P. group here in the middle."

"Where's the gun team?"

"Here with the C.P. in the middle. First contact any of

you make, yell 'Guns up,' and the gun goes where it's needed."

"Got it, Gunny."

"Everybody understand?"

"Yes, sir."

"Aye aye, Gunny."

"All right, get your squads and line up behind me. Blaine, where you gonna put the boots?"

"Not sure, Gunny. Karas and a couple of the others are arguing over who gets them."

"Why?"

"They know they won't sleep tonight, so they figure whoever gets teamed with a boot will get to crash all night."

"All right, just make sure they aren't together."

"Yes, sir."

"Don't dig in unless the earth is soft enough to make no noise. Fifty percent alert. Chief, I want you in charge of setting up the claymores. Each squad leader will keep the Go to Hell Box. Let's move it."

Five minutes later the ambush was set. Mouth called in the coordinates to an artillery battery for fire support and the wait was on. Fatigue gripped Jessie hard, but he knew he'd better take the first watch, just in case something wasn't right. The rain came down heavier, until chances of hearing anything were impossible.

No matter how many times you did it, the beginning of an ambush was scary. Your eyes played tricks on you in the jungle night, and every bush started looking like a man sneaking up on you. The harder you stared at something, the more tense you became and the more it seemed to move or shift position. Jessie's eyes were playing tricks on him, he was almost sure, but he could not be completely certain. A bush twenty meters out was moving . . . or was it? He crouched down into his shallow hole and stuck his K-Bar knife into the ground at arms' length and directly in line with the bush, using the knife as a site. He shifted only his eyes to search his field of fire. Nothing else seemed to be moving. He returned his stare to the bush to see if it was exactly where it had been. It was. He sighed with relief and loosened his grip on the shotgun. He repeated the procedure three times to be sure. Each time, the bush was in line with the K-Bar. Two hours into his watch he nudged Mouth the radioman.

"Mouth. Reveille."

Mouth came out from his flak jacket like a turtle coming out of his shell. He sat up slowly, realizing that he was sitting in water up to his waist. He shivered. "If I live through this, I'll never let rain touch my body again."

"Better check in."

"Yes, sir. Ah crap. That's what I get for joining the crotch."

"What is it?"

"I got a blood-suckin' leech on my balls!"

"Don't pull it off. It'll leave the head in you. You gotta burn it off."

"I know, I know. I should have joined the friggin' Navy, but no, I got to be a Marine."

"Keep it quiet."

"Yes, sir."

Jessie curled up in their shallow hole full of water. The water around him felt warm, but the rain was freezing. He was so tired he hurt, and for a moment he let himself remember that he was getting close to forty-three years old. He ached from the long hump, and his spine cracked as he tried to stretch. Being wet for so long always wreaked havoc on his muscles. Thank God for tae kwon do, he thought. How old would he feel if he didn't train all the time? He thought of his son, the lieutenant. God, please take care of him, he said to himself. He thought of the new kids in the platoon. They were no more than eighteen or nineteen years old. He knew they were terrified right now, and no matter how tired they were, he was willing to bet a year's salary that they were wide-awake and staring into the jungle. He tried to shove the thought out of his mind. He couldn't do it.

"Mouth," he whispered.

"Yes, sir," Mouth whispered as he started to work the PRC-25.

"While you check in, I'm going to check on the positions."

"Yes, sir."

Jessie struggled to his knees with his shotgun and looked around to get his bearings. He stood up to a crouch and moved to the next position on his right. The two-man positions were set up about ten yards apart.

He paused on one knee. "Psst. Comin' in."

"Okay," came the whispered answer.

He moved forward. Doc Rice, wrapped in a poncho, was sitting up in a shallow hole filled with water. Jessie knelt beside him.

"You awake? Alert?"

"Yes, sir."

"Who's that?" Jessie pointed to the Marine sleeping beside him.

"Karas."

Jessie stood to a crouch and moved toward the next position and the next and the next, until he reached Swift Eagle.

"Psst. Gunny coming in," he whispered toward a prone figure a few feet ahead.

"Okay."

He moved in beside the Indian corporal. "See anything?"

"No, sir."

"Check the other positions on your right while I check the squads on the left."

"Yes, sir."

Jessie stood and made his way back to the left. As he passed, Mouth, the radioman, grabbed the gunny by the ankle. Jessie knelt down, but Mouth was listening to the field phone. He looked away with alarm in his eyes. "Gunny."

"Yeah."

"Echo Two says to hold on. Sounds like big trouble coming our way."

"Stay on air. I'll finish checking the men. Be right back."

Jessie moved down the ambush line position by position. Gonzales and Justice were both wide-awake in separate fighting holes. Both were shivering as much from cold as fear. Jessie dropped down beside Gonzales. The kid jerked so hard he seemed to hurt his neck.

"It's Gunny. Be cool, Marine."

"Oh." He breathed out hard and began to shiver.

"You okay?"

"Yes, sir. Scared out of my wits." His teeth chattered as he spoke.

"That's normal, kid. First time out, I won't be surprised if you wet your pants."

"Me either, Gunny."

"At least it's raining."

"Yeah. Is it ever."

"Stand by. We could be moving."

"Moving? At night?"

Jessie grinned and shook his head. "There it is, boot. Get used to it."

"Did you say move, Gunny?" Justice groaned in a whisper.

"Maybe."

"Call in for a can of slack, Gunny."

Jessie turned and made his way back to Mouth and the radio.

Mouth was waiting anxiously. "Gunny. That you?"

"Yeah."

"Second platoon says there's a reinforced company of NVA, maybe more, moving our way. Right down the river's edge. They said to dee-dee-mow out of here!"

"East or west side of the river?"

"East."

"Pass the word. Saddle up. Now."

Five minutes later Jessie led the platoon back across the river. Original orders had been to spend the first night on the east side of the river, but the usual change in orders was now official. Pounding rain covered their splashing noises as the men waded back across with weapons over their heads, but Jessie would have sworn that their pounding hearts were too loud to be camouflaged. There was nothing that terrified him more than being scared and in the water. The harder you struggled to hurry, the slower you seemed to move. Each man helped the Marine behind him up the muddy west bank, using rifles to pull each other. They made their way to a small barren hill and set in a perimeter around the top.

Jessie found Swift Eagle and pulled him aside as the men moved into position. "I want two L.P.'s out on this side of the hill. If the gooks cross that river somewhere between us and the other platoons and head this way, we need to know in time."

"Yes, sir."

"Come with me for a minute. We need to plot some arty around our position. I'm going to call in some H and I fire along the other side of the river. Then I'll drop it down a klick to this side of the river so they can't get organized for any sort of assault. Maybe we'll get lucky and break 'em up all over the place."

"That's a good idea, Gunny."

They moved to the crest of the small hill where Doc Rice and Mouth had already set up the C.P. in the center of the perimeter.

"Doc, move over here with your poncho."

"Yes, sir."

"Take my poncho, here. The Chief and me are going to have to check the grid map to plot some arty. Don't let any light out of this poncho. I'm using the pin light. Got it?"

"Yes sir, Gunny."

They crouched down as Jessie pulled the map out of the inside of his flak jacket. The grid map was in a plastic cover, so it stayed as dry as anything could stay in this waterlogged country. He pulled his pin light out of a cargo pocket and huddled with Swift Eagle around the map. They verified their position. Then Jessie pointed out two places on the map.

"I say here and here would be good spots."

"I'm ready, Gunny," the radioman said.

"All right, Mouth. Got arty on the horn?"

"Yes, sir." Mouth handed the field phone under the poncho with the utmost care. Jessie took the phone and began whispering coordinates for a white phosphorous round. Then he killed the pin light and came from under the poncho.

"Willie Peter on the way," he whispered.

The sucking sound of an artillery round pushing the air out of its way whipped by low overhead. A muffled explosion followed two seconds later and a large white mushroom cloud erupted from the far side of the riverbank as the white phosphorous round hit about one thousand meters beyond the river's edge.

"Arty One ... Iron Hand Alpha ... over."

"Echo One ... Echo One ... this is Iron Hand Alpha over."

"That Willie Peter needs to come down a klick. Over."

"Roger, Echo One ... on the way ... over."

Another artillery spotter round ripped by low overhead. A moment later a white mushroom cloud exploded near the river's edge on the far bank.

"Perfect, Gunny," Swift Eagle said.

"That is perfect ... Iron Hand Alpha ... Now go left one klick at a time for five klicks and give us some H and I fire every thirty minutes ... over."

"Roger, Echo One ... over."

Jessie handed the field phone back to Mouth, who quickly rewrapped the plastic around it to keep it dry.

"Did you put out the L.P.'s, Chief?"

"Yes, sir."

"Now with the harassment and interdictory fire and a couple of listening posts out there, we should be fine till daylight. Then we can see what's up."

"Aye aye, Gunny."

Five minutes later the first salvo ripped into the earth a few thousand meters away, near the river. After five rounds the fire stopped. Half an hour later the silence was broken by the faraway whistle of another barrage of H and I fire. The shrill whistle grew louder and closer. Jessie sat up straight, cocking his ear to follow the flight of the artillery round. His spine stiffened with alarm. The whistling sound stopped, leaving only that sickening silence just before impact. It was too close.

"Short round!" he screamed, but it was too late.

"Incoming!"

The short round landed no more than fifty yards away. The brilliant flash sent white-hot metal singing past his ears. Huge rocks thudded to the earth all around.

"Corpsman!"

"We got wounded over here!"

"Mouth! Get on that radio! Tell 'em they hit us!" Jessie bellowed as he jumped to his feet.

He ran through brush and rocks, stumbling toward the explosion. Pieces of orange glowing metal lay all around, and the smell of sulfur was strong. He felt choked by it.

"Is he dead, Doc? Is he?" Jessie knelt beside a hunched-over figure, "Doc?"

"Yeah, Gunny."

Doc Rice was kneeling beside a five-foot crater filled with smoke. Jessie laid his pump down, and his hand brushed against the warm, wet limb of someone on the ground. He felt around in the darkness and realized it was someone's leg, and it was not attached to a body. "Who is it, Doc?"

"It's Gonzales," a voice in the darkness whimpered.

"Justice?"

"Yes, Gunny."

"You hit?"

"No, sir. I was taking a dump over there a ways when it hit."

"You sure it's Gonzales?"

"Yes sir, Gunny."

"Doc."

"KIA, Gunny. Nothing I can do."

No one spoke for a few moments. Two more rounds of H&I fire whistled overhead, striking the earth three thousand meters beyond, as they were supposed to.

"Should we call for a medevac, Gunnery Sergeant?" someone asked.

"No, Marine. We'll call one in tomorrow."

"Guantanamera" rambled in and out of Jessie's mind for the rest of the night. At times the lone guitar was so clear that he had to shake his head. He started to ask Mouth if he could hear it too, but he knew better. The next morning, Mouth threw out a green smoke grenade. An old 34 circled down to the perimeter like a flying grasshopper. Justice and Swift Eagle loaded the green plastic body bag onto the chopper. Justice stood staring into the hatchway until Swift Eagle pulled him away. He cried like a baby as the chopper lifted off. Four days later the operation was over. The first platoon made no contact with the enemy. The third platoon did ambush a squad of NVA, killing three and capturing two.

The men were somber flying back to the ship. Justice Pimkin still looked like Opie, but he was quiet now. The change had started, Jessie thought as he studied the young Marine's expressionless face and wondered what changes his son was going through. He took off his helmet, checked the calendar, pulled his black marker out of his writing gear, and marked off another day. R & R with Charlie Rose was seventy-three days away. In 'Nam that was about a century.

"Hey, I see home, Gunny!" Moose shouted over the prop wash.

Jessie peered out of the windowless porthole. The *Ogden* looked like a toy from this altitude. Jessie leaned back and began unloading his pump.

"All right Marines! Clear your weapons!"

The men began ejecting magazines and checking chambers.

"Corporal Swift Eagle!"

"Yes sir, Gunny!"

"Check the weapons!"

"Aye aye, Gunny!"

The big Indian took off his harness and moved from Marine to Marine, checking the chambers of every weapon aboard. He finished with a thumbs-up signal to Jessie. A few moments later the chopper circled down to the deck of the USS *Ogden*.

"Disembark!"

The Marines marched down the back ramp of the CH-46 Sea Stallion in two columns.

"Form up over here!" Corporal Swift Eagle shouted the men into formation.

They stood at port arms with bolts pulled back for inspection. A Navy officer was waiting to check the weapons. As soon as he finished, the routine began.

"Put all of your Class Two ammo in the bins below-decks!"

"Stow your gear in your lockers!"

"Weapons will be cleaned and oiled by 1300 hours! Is that clear, Marines!"

"Aye aye, sir!"

"Attttennntion!" Jessie shouted.

"Dismissed!"

"Gunnery Sergeant Slate!" A tall black corporal hustled toward Jessie.

"Yes, Corporal."

"Colonel Rockey wants you on the double, Gunny."

"Thank you, Corporal. In his quarters?"

"Yes, sir."

"Aye aye."

Jessie followed the corporal to officers' country amidship. The corporal slammed on the bulkhead three times hard with the palm of his hand.

"Sir! Corporal Rollins reporting with Gunnery Sergeant Slate, sir!"

"Advance!"

The corporal opened the door for Jessie.

"That will be all, Corporal."

"Yes, sir." He closed the door.

Colonel Rockey grinned and stood up behind his desk. Jessie stood at attention and saluted. Rockey waved a salute back. "At ease, Jessie. Have a seat."

"Thank you, sir."

Rockey sat down and leaned back in his chair. "Smoking lamp is lit, Gunny."

"Thank you, sir. I don't smoke much, but I like to chew on cigars," Jessie said as he pulled half a cigar out of his filthy jungle jacket.

"Know what you're here for, Gunny?"

"No, sir. Mind if I take off this flak jacket, sir?"

Colonel Rockey motioned to take it off. "You are here to take on that volunteer work you signed up for, Gunny."

"CAG duty?"

"There it is, Marine."

Jessie nodded.

"Second thoughts?"

"No sir. A deal's a deal, sir."

"Well, don't worry. You'll be back with your outfit as soon as you square away the situation with this CAP unit. Might take a couple of months."

"We just lost a new kid. A good Marine. Short round from one of our batteries."

"I'm sorry, Gunny. That is one lousy way for a Marine to die."

"I guess I'm a little worried about them. Sometimes they just seem so young."

"They are. Did you know that these Marines in this dirty little war are on the average the youngest Marines ever sent into combat? Average age, eighteen. In W.W. Two it was twenty-three. In Korea it was about the same. The difference between eighteen and twenty-three is a lifetime in maturity and common sense. It's the difference between a high school grad and a college grad."

"Yes, sir."

"How old was this Marine?"

"Nineteen, sir. PFC Gonzales. Could have been a great classical guitarist."

"Yes. Well, maybe we could start sending the remains of these boys to the doorsteps of people like Ramsey Clark and Jane Fonda with thanks from the North Vietnamese government."

"And these flag-burning cowards. I'd give a month's pay for one minute with one, sir." A rush of anger swept through Jessie Slate until his face flushed red.

"Had a Brit on board the other day."

"Yes, sir."

"Interesting fellow. Military Intelligence. He told me there was a group of little liberal Harvard brats mixed in with some others who were living and traveling around Europe to avoid the draft. Said they were protesting at the American embassy in London."

"Typical cowards trying to justify their own lack of integrity, sir."

"I couldn't agree with you more, Gunny."

Colonel Rockey stood up and walked around his desk. He pointed at a map on the bulkhead. "Here is Chu Lai. We got villages here, here, and here. A good distance from each other. CAP 127 is here, 138 is here, and 139 is out here in the boonies. You'll be there."

"Right on the border with Laos."

"There it is, Gunny. Separated from Laos by the Song Trabong River. The village is made up of three resettlement villages. The NVA was butchering these people and they were too far out to provide them with any protection. They were moved here so we could protect them a little better."

"So it's a platoon of Marines working with the P.F.'s."

"Originally it was called the CAC, but some Einstein figured out that in Vietnamese that was an appendage on the male body."

"CAC." Slate chuckled.

"In a Combined Action Company you have Combined Action Platoons. Made up of a fourteen-man rifle squad and a Corpsman. You move into a village, join with local Vietnamese militia, the P.F.'s, about thirty-five of 'em, and you provide security for the village. Counterguerrilla operations. The Marines are primarily military advisers providing experience and knowledge of weapons, explosives, and security."

Gunnery Sergeant Slate pointed at the map. "I'd call this out on a limb, sir. Where's my fire support?"

"You'll have an Army battery of 155s and close air support from Chu Lai. Captain Roberts will be your C.O. He'll fill you in on the details. We got a problem there."

"Yes, sir."

The short stocky colonel pretended to scan some paperwork on his desk.

"Will that be all, sir?"

"Yes."

Jessie stood up and saluted. He turned and opened the door.

"Someone mentioned that your son was doing a fine job with his platoon."

Jessie turned around.

"Heard he was one of the best young butter bars in the Fifth Marines. Shame he didn't go to Annapolis. He could have, you know. With you being a CMH winner and all."

"Yes, sir. I know," Jessie said with regret.

"General Rockey did all right for himself. He didn't go to Annapolis either."

Jessie smiled. "Yes, sir."

"Clean that mess up and get back here, Gunnery Sergeant. We have some joint op's coming up with our sister regiment. You probably won't want to miss them."

"The Fifth Marines, sir?"

The colonel nodded and went back to his paperwork.

"Thank you, sir." Jessie saluted and closed the door.

CHAPTER TWENTY-SIX

Two hours later Jessie was zipping toward Chu Lai in a fast little hummingbird of a helicopter known as a Loach. The pilot constantly sang the Marines hymn, except when he paused to point out something exceptionally beautiful in the landscape below. Jessie figured he was a frustrated artist. His name was Sergeant Lomax, about five-nine, 150 pounds. He had the pug nose of a fighter, a round face, and he wore a headset over his soft-cover Marine Corps hat. He carried an old Thompson submachine gun in the cockpit. A flare gun and some smoke grenades seemed to be the only other armament on the little two-seater. The Loach suddenly dropped down low over a mountain village.

"Used to have a CAP unit here, Gunny!" he shouted with a New Jersey accent.

"What do you mean 'used to'?"

"Got overrun last April. Couldn't get to 'em in time."

"How come?"

"Gooks ambushed the relieving column."

"That's the oldest trick in 'Nam!"

"This CAP was a lot safer than the one you're getting, Gunny."

"That right?"

"Yes. The men know it too. That's why the brass has sent for you."

"You seem to know a lot about this, Sergeant Lomax."

"Yes, sir. I know who you are, Gunny. I can't believe they're going to put a Medal of Honor winner out there on the Laotian border with orders to stir things up. It's a death warrant, Gunny!"

"How do you know so much?"

"I'll be flying you or Captain Roberts. I'm your taxi. He uses the taxi to make checks on the surrounding CAP units or to go shopping."

"I'll be using you more than he will from now on."

Sergeant Lomax did a double take, then nodded with a knowing grin. Chu Lai was a big base. The airstrip was busy with fixed-wing Phantoms as well as everything else that flew in 'Nam except the big B-52s. The Loach landed on a small, corrugated-steel landing pad near some Quonset huts.

"That hut there, Gunny!" Lomax shouted, and pointed as he let the engine idle.

Jessie jumped out.

"You forgot your gear, Gunny!"

"I'm leaving it here! You're taking me out CAP 139 as soon as I report in!"

"The captain didn't say to—"

"Stay put, Sergeant!"

"Aye aye, Gunny."

Jessie grabbed his shotgun and headed for the Quonset hut. A hand-painted red sign with yellow letters said CAG HQ over the front door. He entered and gasped as cold air hit his sweaty, wet utilities.

"Air-conditioning?" he said, more to himself than anyone else.

"Yes, sir. Better believe it." An Oriental lance corporal said from behind a typewriter. "Here to see Captain Roberts?"

"Yes."

"What about?" the corporal asked, without looking up from typing at an impressive rate.

"I'm Gunnery Sergeant Jessie Slate reporting for duty with CAP 139."

The corporal stopped typing and opened his eyes a little wider. He stood up. "Honored to meet you, sir." He extended his hand. "I'm Corporal Smith."

Jessie's eyebrows lifted as he smiled and extended his hand.

"Adopted, sir," the corporal said with a friendly smile.

Jessie chuckled. "I like it, Corporal Smith."

"Thank you, sir."

A loud howl came from an adjoining office, and what sounded like children yelling.

"Captain Roberts in?"

"Yes, sir."

The corporal knocked on the door of the captain's office and opened it. "Gunnery Sergeant Slate reporting in, sir."

"Outstanding! Send him in, Corporal."

Jessie entered the office and saluted as the corporal closed the door behind him. The captain was on his hands and knees pretending to be a bronco with a tiny Vietnamese boy and an even smaller Vietnamese girl on his back. Both children were wearing cowboy hats.

Jessie came to attention and saluted sharply. "Gunnery Sergeant Slate reporting, sir."

"It's good to have you aboard, Gunny." The captain pointed at the children with his thumb. "Mind giving them a lift down?"

"My pleasure, sir." Jessie stepped closer. He picked the little girl up first, placed her down gently, and then did likewise with the boy. The captain stood up and straightened his starched utilities. He picked up his glasses from a cluttered desk and put them on. He had a Marine jarhead haircut, was tall and lean, and looked very strong. Jessie guessed the man to be about thirty-five years old and in excellent shape. His smile was quick and genuine as he held out his hand, his grip strong.

"It is an honor to meet you, Gunnery Sergeant Slate."

"Thank you, sir."

"I've been in the Corps for fourteen years, and I don't think I've ever met a CMH winner."

"Well, sir, if you've been in the Corps for fourteen years, you already know that medals can mean many things. Men who deserve them don't get them, and it's usually just a matter of wrong place at the right time."

"And many officers get them who have done nothing more valorous than calling in air strikes or giving orders over a Prick-25."

Jessie was taken aback. Though every Marine knew that all too often a Bronze Star or Silver Star on the chest of an officer meant no more than a professional pat on the back from a superior who had a quota of medals to hand out, it was unusual to hear a captain say as much. The Army had been especially bad about such things. They gave Bronze Stars for meritorious service. Many soldiers got a Bronze Star just for making Staff Sergeant. The shame of it was that most enlisted Marines who received a Bronze Star had done something heroic to earn it. The military tried to rectify matters by putting a Combat V on some medals, signifying valor, but the damage had been done.

"I'm afraid I have to agree with you, sir."

"Someday you must tell me the story behind that CMH, Gunnery Sergeant."

"I can tell you in one sentence sir. Sometimes I think it was easier to win it than it is to live with."

Captain Roberts looked at Jessie curiously, as if seeing him for the first time. He finally nodded and turned toward the children.

"Okay, you two rustlers, let's get back to the ranch."

The children stood, staring up slightly.

"Go on. Scoot."

They giggled and left the room.

"Cute kids, sir."

"Thank you, Gunny. I adopted them six months back.

Their parents were murdered by the Viet Cong for not giving supplies to enemy troops."

"Extremely admirable sir."

"Thank you. But if I might steal your view of medals, I
was just in the wrong place at the right time."

"Yes, sir."

"Sit down, Gunny."

"Yes, sir."

Captain Roberts walked over to a map on the wall.
"These are our Combined Action Platoons around Chu Lai."
He pointed at a series of marker pins stuck in the map, des-
ignating each unit, and turned to face Jessie. "Most of these
platoons are doing a fine job. I think this is one of the
smartest programs the Corps ever instituted. Popular Forces
have been recruited, trained, and organized for security, one
squad for each hamlet. Schools and parent councils have
been started up. And a number of supporting councils
have begun getting involved, like Public Health, Public
Safety, Agriculture and Fisheries, Education, and so on."

"Sounds very successful, sir."

"Yes. But without adequate security, pacification cannot
work. The Viet Cong saw to that by assassinating and kidnapping village and hamlet officials, burning schools, and
tearing down, both psychologically and physically, whatever the government of South Vietnam, with the help of the
Americans, attempted to build. The Third MAF had recognized early that the key to the kind of security that was
needed was an effective, grassroots gendarmerie."

"A what?"

"Self-defense at the hamlet and village level. The CAG
program is downright successful in most areas, but there
are some zones that give us fits for various reasons."

"What is the problem at 139, sir?"

"All of the above." He grinned and went to the map
again. "You can see that 139 is right on the Laotian border
at the Song Trabong River. The village is made up of three
resettlement villages. High density patrolling and ambush-

ing are for the villagers and for stopping infiltration in this entire area. But as you can see, if you get hit in this area, there will be no reaction force until daybreak. You would have to hold out until the next morning."

"How about the P.F.'s?"

"The P.F.'s are not the best Popular Forces we've ever had to work with. Enemy troops are coming through this area unobstructed."

"Is the CAP unit getting hit much?"

"No."

"Okay."

"You have a thought, Gunny?"

"Yes, sir."

"Speak up, Sergeant, we run an open forum here. If I knew everything, I wouldn't have sent for you in the first place."

"Yes, sir. As you know, sir, I'm sort of used as a trouble-shooter from time to time in between—"

"Weapons expert, demolitions and booby traps, an expert on company, platoon, and squad-size tactics and Vietnamese history, culture, and language." Captain Roberts gave a knowing nod.

"You make me sound like Chesty Puller, sir," Jessie said with a chuckle.

"You have my utmost respect, Gunnery Sergeant Slate."

"Thank you, sir. I'm grateful for your confidence. I've been sent into similar situations as a troubleshooter, and just off the top of my head I would guess that we got a 'See no evil' problem here."

"See no evil?"

"My way of putting it, sir. When you get too friendly with the villagers, you also get friendly with the double agents you find in every village."

"Go on."

"You may not know who they are for sure, and probably don't. But sometimes these fellas can make a good case for minding your own business."

"You mean spend your thirteen months and go home alive."

"Sometimes, sir."

"I've had the same suspicions. This is the third time I've replaced the CAP sergeant. You'll come under scrutiny right away because of your rank, Gunny. Combined Action Platoons are run by corporals or sergeants. Rarely do they see anyone of your rank."

"Yes, sir, I figured that."

"You can tell the platoon and village chief that you're the new company gunny."

"I think I'd rather just tell them the truth, sir. That I've come to square things away so that there's no mistake about their future."

"It's your call, Gunnery Sergeant. Now, you'll get your arty support from this area in the Trabong. It's an Army battery of 105s and 155s."

"Air support?"

"Da Nang. It's about a forty-five-minute C-130 flight from 139. You'll have to go through the Forward Air Controller at Chu Lai, and he'll determine where the support would be found."

"Naval fire?"

"Too far inland."

"Yes, sir . . . Call signs, sir?"

"The call signs will be Gunfighter, Cowboy, Mustang, Fireball, Bad Boy, Bird Dog, and Rainman. This month you are Gunfighter Nine for CAP 139. HQ is Gunfighter One. If I call you, I'm Gunfighter One Actual. When I want you and only you, I'll be calling for Gunfighter Nine Actual. All clear?"

"Affirmative, sir."

"You will be resupplied by the Charlie Charlie bird from Chu Lai."

"An Army slick?"

"Yes. It brings your mail, C-rats, and other supplies two or three times a week or for emergencies." Captain Roberts pushed his glasses back up on his pug nose and put his hands on his hips. "That's about it, Gunny. Anything I can do to make the job easier, you let me know."

"Thank you, sir. I'd like to start now, if I could. The Loach is waiting. I might want to use that Loach again, Captain. I'll need to get an overview of our terrain and distance from the other CAPs, and I have a couple of ideas I might try, but I'll need to get around."

"It's yours when it's not in use, Gunny. I'll tell Staff Sergeant Lomax that he's at your disposal."

"Thank you, sir." Jessie snapped to attention and saluted.

The chopper ride from Chu Lai to CAP 139 was a good twenty-five minutes. Though the captain had made it clear that this CAP unit was out on a limb, Jessie hadn't considered just how long that limb was until he watched the jungle below grow deeper and the mountains grow bigger with each mile they flew inland. Finally, the chopper began to circle above a group of grass hooches at the foot of a steep mountain. It appeared to be a pretty big village. Not far beyond it lay the Song Trabong River. From the air the wide river looked dark with decaying leaves from the surrounding jungle. Jessie knew, as soon as he saw it, that he would have to cross that stupid river. "God, I hate to cross rivers," he mumbled out loud, but the pilot was busy bringing the chopper down to a clearing inside the village. Three Marines stood nearby, one with pack and rifle waiting for the chopper. Jessie signaled a thumbs-up to Lomax and jumped out with pack in hand.

The Marine waiting with pack and rifle ran forward as Jessie walked away from the prop wash. "Gunnery Sergeant Slate?"

"Yes."

"I'm Sergeant Jennings. You are relieving me."

"Yes."

"Good luck. Corporal Fowler is over there waiting. He can fill you in on everything you need to know. If you don't rock the boat, things will be safe and secure around here."

"Are you a Marine, Sergeant Jennings?"

"Yeah. I'm a Marine," he said calmly.

"If I find out you been playing it too safe and too secure, I'll see to it that your furry little rear end gets stationed with men trying to win this war!"

"The Marines might be trying to win this war, Gunny, but those pinkos in Washington sure ain't! I'm going home, Gunnery Sergeant. And I ain't going home in a bag." Sergeant Jennings ran for the chopper. For a moment, Jessie thought about decking him, then moved on to the two Marines standing twenty meters away.

"Which one of you is Corporal Fowler?"

"I am," said a shirtless dark-haired Marine with a pock-marked face. He was about six feet tall, lean, muscular, and ugly. Perfect Marine so far, Jessie thought.

"I'm Gunnery Sergeant Slate." He held out his hand. The corporal hesitated, then shook it slowly, weakly, as if he weren't sure that he wanted to.

"This is Doc Morphine. The Corpsman." Like many Corpsmen, this one was known by a nickname.

Jessie extended his hand to the Corpsman. They shook. The Corpsman had a weak handshake too. He was a beefy fellow, about five-ten and a soft 190. Not fat, but he looked to Jessie like he ate more than anyone else in 'Nam. It was a bad sign, because no Marine who spent any time humping in the bush could manage to keep that much weight on. Of course, he was a Navy Corpsman officially, and a Marine out here. Jessie checked their boots. They did not look salty. Something wasn't right. He could feel it and see it in the sinister dark eyes of the rotund Corpsman.

"Gunny," Doc Morphine said with a New England accent. He gave a casual wave.

"Let's see the C.P."

"Okay," Corporal Fowler said with just a hint of sarcasm.

"Right this way, Gunny," Doc Morphine said.

Jessie followed the men into the village. It was like every other village in 'Nam: grass huts, some with walls, some without. Either beside or inside each hooch was a bunker. It was about noon and many of the villagers were working in the rice paddy fields that surrounded the area. The older Vietnamese stayed home to cook the meals and do any other necessary work around the hooch. Many of the older villagers had congregated in a group on the porch of the local barbershop, where a little boy, about two years old, looked to be getting his first haircut.

"Hold up, Corporal Fowler," Jessie said.

Doc Morphine and the corporal stopped with their M-16s resting on their shoulders, each holding the barrel.

"Is the village chief in that crowd?"

"Yeah. He's the barber."

"I want to meet him."

The corporal shrugged and glanced at Doc Morphine. They headed toward the group of chattering Vietnamese, who went silent as the Americans approached. They looked apprehensive. The barber was about five-seven, which was a good size for a Vietnamese. Jessie guessed him to be around sixty years old, his hair short and gray. Staying alive for sixty years in this hard land was not easy. He was thin, his cheeks sunken and hollow. Corporal Fowler pointed at Jessie and called to the chief.

"Chief. This is Trung-shi. Trung-shi."

The old man bowed and smiled and repeated, "Trung-shi. Trung-shi."

Jessie bowed then saluted. He removed his pack and searched through it quickly until he found the little yellow can of sardines that he'd been saving for over a month. He handed his pack to Corporal Fowler, slung his gun, then walked over and handed the can to the chief. He was careful to hold it with both hands to show proper respect. The old man smiled, revealing two upper teeth and three lowers that were rotten and ready to fall out but still holding on.

He seemed genuinely pleased at the show of honor for his position. Jessie smiled and walked back to the stunned looks of the two Marines.

The CAP platoon was billeted in a wooded area across the main road from the village schoolhouse. Like so many villages in 'Nam, the only building that was not made out of wood and grass and maybe an occasional piece of stolen American plywood was the schoolhouse. It was a concrete block building with a high profile and intended to be the centerpiece of the village. The schoolhouse would usually be one of the first targets of the Viet Cong or NVA. The CAP Marines had strung a giant camouflaged parachute in between four trees to shade the compound. Some of the men had hammocks strung up between trees, and Jessie counted no less than twelve Marines sleeping around the area.

He dropped his gear under the shade of the parachute and looked around. Cases of C-rations were stacked everywhere, along with boxes of all sorts of ammunition. A PRC-25 was set up at the mouth of a sandbagged bunker. The radio was wired to a big 292 antenna, which reached above the parachute.

"How many radios we got here, Corporal?"

"One that works."

Jessie pointed at the bunker. "And that's it?"

"Yeah."

"And what radio do you use when you go out on patrols, Corporal? I'm sure you don't use that two-niner-two antenna."

"Well . . ."

"We disconnect it when we go on patrol, Gunny," Doc Morphine said.

"Who is on patrol now, Corpsman?"

Doc Morphine looked surprised. He shrugged and rubbed his belly through his olive-green T-shirt. "We don't send patrols out in the heat of the day."

"Is that right?"

"Yeah, that's right. I'm the Corpsman, and I say it ain't healthy, Gunnery Sergeant." Doc Morphine's tone was like a scratch on a blackboard. This guy was due for an attitude adjustment, Jessie thought.

He forced himself to grin at the chunky Corpsman, then turned toward the rest of the CAP Marines sprawled in various positions of sleep. CAP units wore camouflaged utilities and had CAP pins on their soft-cover hats that showed U.S. and Vietnamese crossed flags. The camouflage uniforms irritated Jessie. There were a few thousand grunts out in the bush right now unable to buy or steal camouflage uniforms, and here these prima donnas were laying around in the shade taking siestas in cammys.

"Get out of the rack, ladies!"

Two or three Marines sat up rubbing sleep from their eyes and trying to focus in on the source of the noise. Jessie flipped his gun off safety, pointed it in the air and fired, blowing a large hole in the camouflaged parachute. Some of the twelve Marines sprang up grabbing for weapons, while others hit the dirt. Gradually they realized what was happening and began to stand up, staring at the new guy with rage in their eyes.

"My name is Gunnery Sergeant Slate. I am now in command of this unit. Let us get something straight right now, Marines. You were not sent here to take siestas while grunts, your brother Marines, die in battle because you're not doing your job."

"Spare us the gung-ho speech, Gunny. These men do their job," Corporal Fowler said.

Jessie turned and put his face and inch away from Fowler's. "You shut up, Corporal, until I ask you a question."

Corporal Fowler didn't blink. He was tough, Jessie thought as he made a quick decision to deck him if he opened his mouth. He turned away to face the men. Most were shirtless, and only a couple had their boots on.

"I want three Marines to fall out for a patrol. Where are your P.F.'s?"

No one answered.

"I said where are your Popular Force troops?"

A tall, lean, barefoot Marine with no shirt waved as if the answer had just come to him. "Oh, they're all over, Sarge."

"What's your name, Marine?"

"Philly. Lance Corporal Philly, Gunny."

"What do you mean, 'all over.' Don't they have a compound?"

"Yeah," a dark-skinned Marine with tattoos added. "But some are working the fields and some are in the ville."

"Where is the Trung-shi?"

No one answered; a couple of the men shrugged their shoulders.

"The P.F. Trung-shi. Where is he?"

No one answered.

"Well, where does the man usually hang out during the day, gentlemen?"

"I seen him at the gook slop chute a couple of times, Gunny," the dark-skinned Marine with tattoos said.

"What's your name, Marine?"

"Gomez. PFC Gomez."

"Gomez," Jessie said with a smile. Memories from the old Corps flooded back to him, and for just the flickering of a moment he was seventeen years old again. "You wouldn't by any chance have had a relative in the Paramarines, PFC Gomez?"

"What's a Paramarine?"

Jessie's smile evaporated. "Never mind, Marine. Go find our Vietnamese sergeant, Mr. Gomez."

"I don't know where he is."

Jessie pointed at a blond Marine with a red face and, beside him, a black Marine leaning on an M-16.

"You two go with him. Help him find the Trung-shi."

They both looked angry at the order, but sat down to put their boots on anyway. Jessie turned to Corporal Fowler.

"I count fourteen Marines and a Corpsman, Corporal."

"Yeah, even Marines can count that high, Sarge."

"Only if they're conscious, Corporal." Jessie spoke slowly so his tone would not be misunderstood. He could see this was not going to be easy. "I understand we have a hilltop outside the ville called O.P. George."

"Right."

"Who's manning it?"

"No one."

"Why?"

Corporal Fowler shrugged. "Nobody wanted to."

"And the sergeant I just replaced allowed that attitude in this unit?"

"I guess."

"Well, I don't, Marine! You!" Jessie shouted, and pointed at the startled corporal. "Get up on that hill with two men and set up that radio. I'm assuming that this two-niner-two antenna came from O.P. George."

"Yeah, I think so."

"Get it up there! Now, Marine."

Corporal Fowler clenched his teeth, then started to speak, but seemed to rethink his position. Jessie readied himself for an attack, figuring if Fowler were going to swing on him, he would do it now. The corporal turned toward the rest of the men.

"All right, Jim and Eight Ball. Help me get this antenna packed up!"

"Oh, man! Oh, man! Cut me some slack, man!" a strange-looking Marine with a flat, pale face complained, sounding more black than white.

"Shut up, Eight Ball!" Fowler snapped.

"We found him, Gunny," someone said from behind Jessie.

He turned to see Gomez standing with a stocky Vietnamese dressed in Army fatigues, sandals, and no cover. He appeared to be about thirty, but age was very hard to guess with the Vietnamese, since they aged so quickly in the harsh climate.

"Good."

"He was sleeping right over there in that hooch."

Jessie walked up to the Vietnamese sergeant and extended his hand. "Trung-shi. I am Gunnery Sergeant Slate. Marine Trung-shi."

The sergeant shook Jessie's hand with a slight bow. He had no expression that was readable.

"You speak English?"

He indicated he spoke very little, by holding his thumb and forefinger close together.

"I want to review your troops. Have them fall out in formation with combat gear at 1500 hours."

An odd-looking expression came across the man's face, but he nodded that he understood. Jessie thanked him, and the little stocky sergeant walked away with his hands in his pockets.

"About how long will it take you to get to the top of O.P. George, Corporal Fowler?"

"Hour, hour and half."

"That would give us time to hump up there and back before the P.F.'s fall out for inspection."

"Yeah, if we don't care about blisters and heat exhaustion."

Gunnery Sergeant Slate grinned. "How long has it been since we had some men up there?"

He shrugged. "I'm not sure."

"So Charlie Cong could be sitting up there just observing the countryside, couldn't he?"

"I doubt it."

Jessie smiled and turned toward the platoon of Marines. "Saddle up! We move out in five minutes. Helmets, flak jackets, and packs! Three canteens per man. Move it!"

The platoon stood staring at their new gunnery sergeant as if he'd lost his mind. No one moved at first, then slowly the realization sank in that this guy was serious. A couple of the men began to grumble, while a couple of others started gathering up their gear. Jessie watched intently, trying to spot potential troublemakers. They were all mad as hornets, but at least there was no open disobedience. A good sign. It was obvious that this platoon of Marines had been doing absolutely nothing to secure the area. They were not to be blamed. The man in charge was responsible for this attitude. Jessie had seen it before in this strange war that America was not trying to win. This thirteen-month-tour stuff and breaking up units of fighting men the way the Corps did now was bad for morale. Old salts who only had a couple of months left on their tours would try to play it safe, and that was usually when they got killed. But if you told them that, chances were they'd spit in your eye. This was the hardest kind of war the Marines had ever been asked to fight: a night war with no objective to be taken. Neither did there seem to be any serious effort to end or win it. It was difficult to blame Marines for getting fed up with the situation, but they were not paid to question orders. Marines were "the pros," as the Aussies called them, and these particular Marines, Jessie thought, would either conduct themselves as professionals or feel the toe end of one gunnery sergeant's boot.

The platoon fell out in formation, and for the first time, Jessie noticed that they had a Kit Carson scout. He pointed at the Vietnamese scout.

"You take the point twenty-five meters ahead of the column. Don't bunch up."

"Yes, sir," the Kit Carson scout answered quickly.

"Hey, Sarge."

Jessie turned around to see who was talking. A short, stocky Marine with the beginnings of a dark black beard and a long straight nose was frowning as if something was bothering him.

"What do you want, Marine? And what's your name?"

"PFC Sammy Paul. Look, Sarge, we ain't gonna have squat when we get back here if you don't leave somebody to guard our stuff. And I got some stuff I don't want stolen."

"Villagers?"

"Yeah! But it's those useless P.F.'s too! They steal everything and anything!"

"Do you men ever talk to the P.F.'s?"

The Marines shuffled around like a bunch of kids who'd just been caught playing hooky.

"Well?" Slate asked.

"They're a bunch of thieving scumbags, Gunny," a Marine with an M-60 over his shoulder griped angrily.

"What's your name, Marine?"

"Gunner. Real name is John Eckert."

"What part of Texas you from, Gunner?"

"Hale Center, sir."

"And what do you men usually do to discourage this stealing by the P.F.'s?"

"Well, it's like this, Gunny. If we do go somewhere, we always leave at least one man here to guard our stuff."

"All right, fall out, Gunner Eckert. Guard the stuff until I can rectify the situation."

"We usually just leave old Runs here, Gunny. He can't go nowhere anyhow."

"Runs?"

"Yes, sir. He's over there on the other side of that sandbag bunker." Eckert pointed at a bunker ten yards behind Jessie on the outskirts of the shaded area.

"What's the story with Runs?"

"He's had the runs since he got to 'Nam," one of the men said with a laugh.

"What have you treated him with, Corpsman?" Jessie asked.

Doc Morphine shrugged and didn't answer.

"Did you hear me, Corpsman?"

"Yeah. I heard you. I gave him something for it."

"Why is he still sick?"

"Why don't you ask him?"

Jessie glared at Doc Morphine for a moment, considering the repercussions of knocking his teeth out. He turned away and walked over to the bunker. Just on the opposite side of it a thin, pale, young Marine lay sleeping with his head on a pack. Both hands were on his stomach. His lips were almost blue and he was groaning very quietly.

"Wake up, Marine."

Runs opened his eyes. They looked glassy. He appeared weak and semiconscious.

Jessie knelt down beside him. "How do you feel, Marine?"

"Sick," he said as he sat up straight.

"What kind of sick?"

"Diarrhea. Everything I eat."

"What has Doc Morphine given you for it?"

He reached into his pocket and pulled out two big pink pills.

"Those are malaria pills, Marine! They don't help dysentery."

"What?"

"Have you had some kind of trouble with Doc Morphine?"

He shrugged. "A little. When I first got here. But that was over a month ago."

Jessie gave the kid a pat on the shoulder. "Lay back down, Marine. I'll see that you get some medicine." Jessie stood up and walked back over to Doc Morphine. He stepped so close that their noses almost touched and spoke quietly through clenched teeth so that no one else heard. "You will treat that Marine for dysentery or I'll make you very sorry, mister."

"Aye aye, Gunny," Doc Morphine said with an evil grin that nearly pushed Jessie as far as he could stand. He stared into the Corpsman's eyes for a moment longer, searching for a hint of fear, but saw none and knew that he was going to have to deal with this guy one way or another.

Jessie waved at the Kit Carson scout in his black and green Tiger camouflage. "All right, move out."

The column walked through the village of staring Vietnamese and down the dirt road. They veered off the road just outside the ville, through some jungle brush and into the rice paddies. The point man led the platoon across the paddy dikes. A few villagers were working the fields with two water buffalo, but they pretended not to notice the Marines passing. A towering, relatively barren mountain with a peak in the shape of an eagle's head rose up from the flat terrain about one hundred meters beyond the paddy fields.

The climb up O.P. George was steep and more difficult than Jessie thought it would be. He could see why the position was important. From halfway up the mountain you could observe everything within a two mile radius, maybe more. Another hundred meters beyond O.P. George was the Trabong River.

Twenty meters from the crest of the hill four quick shots rang out at the head of the column. The Marines spread out and knelt down with weapons ready. Jessie ran forward up the steep path to the top of the hill. The Kit Carson scout was kneeling on one knee with his old M-1 carbine to his shoulder and ready to shoot at targets Jessie could not yet see.

Jessie flattened out beside the scout and prepared to fire. "Where are they?"

"I see only one," he said pointing with his rifle.

A Viet Cong in black pajamas and a pith helmet lay in the dirt five yards to the left of an old sandbag bunker. He was still heaving in search of air from what looked like a chest wound. Jessie turned and shouted, "Move up by fire team! Leapfrog!"

"First squad!" Corporal Fowler shouted.

The sound of boots hustling up behind them signaled the Marines moving in. Five men ran past on Jessie's left. He opened fire to cover their advance, spraying the area with three quick shotgun blasts. A moment later the second squad raced past the prone gunnery sergeant and the Kit Carson scout.

"Fire in the hole!" Sammy Paul shouted as he pulled the

pin on a grenade, tossed it into the bunker, and dove for cover.

The explosion sent smoke and debris pouring from the bunker opening. No one moved. Each man was tense enough to open fire on a gnat if it crossed his vision.

Jessie stood to a crouch, tapping the Kit Carson scout on his soft cover and motioning him forward.

"Get in that bunker! See what we got," he shouted as he moved over to the Viet Cong, aiming at him with his twelve-gauge until he stood over the man. Air and blood were coming out of a sucking chest wound. The V.C. would die in a few moments. A Russian AK-47 assault rifle lay five feet away with a bullet through the stock.

"All clear, Gunny!" someone shouted.

"The hill's clear, Gunny!" another Marine yelled.

"Corpsman, up!" Jessie called.

Doc Morphine came up huffing. He knelt down by the V.C. as the man heaved, violently spurting blood out of the chest wound like a fountain.

"He's dead, Gunny."

"Move around the area real carefully and check for booby traps."

"Think that's what he was doing, Gunny?" the tall, thin Marine named Philly asked.

"No. I think that you Marines have left this O.P. un-guarded for so long that the enemy just took it over for their own observation post. That's what I think! And I think this poor sap got caught snoozing. And I think things are about to change around here real quick!"

An hour later the hilltop was okayed to be safe. The PRC-25 was set up in the bunker and the 292 antenna attached. Radio contact was made with the Army artillery battery in the Trabong area. It was called Iron Hand One. From the top of the hill you could see across the Song Trabong River into Laos and Cambodia. Not that it did any good, since no one was allowed to call in arty strikes across the border, even though everyone knew the enemy was over there staging for attacks into South Vietnam. Jessie stared out across the border and shook his head. Even the Korean War could not match this one for insanity when it came to rules of engagement.

He spent an hour making sure that each man could call in artillery strikes over the PRC-25. After using up about ten thousand dollars worth of the taxpayers' money, he was satisfied that the Marines he sent up on O.P. George would be able to call in artillery if they had to. He also called in to Chu Lai for another radio.

"All right, saddle up! Not you, Fowler. You and Eight Ball will be staying here tonight."

"What? No way!" Fowler bellowed, and his lean face turned red.

Jessie looked at the young Marine with a calm expression as he lowered his voice. "That was not a request, Marine."

"But what if the gooks come up after their man tonight?"

"I'll be sending up three P.F.'s to stand watch with you two. I'd suggest putting out a two-man L.P. on this path up the hill and no less than fifty percent alert for the night. That is up to you, Corporal."

Corporal Fowler's brown eyes were bulging. He looked like he was holding his breath, but he did not speak.

"Let's move out! Gomez!"

"Yes, sir."

"Take the point!"

"Aye aye, Gunny."

"Fowler and Eight Ball. You will be relieved in two days. I'll send up supplies with the P.F.'s."

"Hey, Gunny, man!" The flat-faced Marine came shuffling forward with a deep pinch to his brow.

"What do you want, Eight Ball?"

"Hey, man, I didn't bring no ammo!"

Jessie paused and looked at the Marine for a long moment. Eight Ball became uncomfortable with the murder he was reading in his gunnery sergeant's gray eyes. He'd begun to shuffle his feet and twitch. Jessie slowly pulled his homicidal gaze away from the nervous, flat-faced Marine. He found an acne-scarred young Marine standing close by.

"What's your name, Marine?"

"Jimbo."

"Jimbo what?" Jessie snapped angrily.

"No, Gunny. PFC Jim Bow. B-O-W."

Jessie tried to stay angry but couldn't keep from smiling.

"Okay, PFC Bow. Give this moron all of your M-16 ammo except for the clip you have in your weapon."

"Yes, sir."

"Move out!"

The hump back down the hill was not much easier than coming up. Jessie rushed them along a bit to make sure they got back in time to review the Popular Forces of the village. The timing was nearly perfect, as the P.F.'s were falling out into formation in front of the schoolhouse just as the Marines reached the village. They were a ragtag-looking group, as most village soldiers were. Some wore sandals, a couple of them wore boots, and some were bare-foot. They all had on Army soft covers, and most wore fatigues, though two or three only had the shirts with the black pajama-type pants. Most carried old WWII carbines. The Trung-shi carried a nice grease gun that looked well-oiled.

When the Marines reached the CAP compound, they headed for their individual bunkers, dropping packs as fast as they could.

"I didn't dismiss you, Marines! Form up! Now!" Jessie bellowed like a drill instructor. The platoon shuffled into a line facing the P.F.'s across the road, who were doing the same thing in front of the schoolhouse.

"Fall in!" The platoon lined up facing Jessie, with weapons on their right shoulders. They came to attention with weapons at their sides. Those with M-16s had rifle butts on the ground.

"Orrrrder ... arms!"

The Marines brought their rifles to port arms diagonally across the front of their bodies. The men were in a stunned state of disbelief. They moved hesitantly, each man fumbling to remember the manual of arms.

"Riiiight-shoulderrrr . . . arms!"

The Marines brought their weapons to their right shoulders.

"Porrrrt arms!"

They brought the weapons back to port arms.

"Paraaaaade rest!"

They brought their weapons to their sides with right arms behind the smalls of their backs. Men were beginning to glance around at each other, obviously not believing what was happening. Some were fuming with anger.

"Platoooooon! Dissssssmissed!"

The Marines fell out and the grumbling began immediately.

Jessie handed his weapon to Jimbo and walked across the dusty road to review the P.F. troops. The Vietnamese Trung-shi called his men to attention as the American gunnery sergeant approached. Jessie came to attention facing the Trung-shi and snapped off a salute. The Trung-shi looked surprised. He came to attention and returned the salute as sharply as he could.

"Permission to review your troops, Sergeant."

The Vietnamese sergeant seemed to be caught by surprise, then blurted out sharply, "Yes, sir. Trung-shi."

Jessie saluted again, and the Vietnamese sergeant returned the salute with more snap. Jessie moved to the head of the line of Vietnamese P.F.'s. "Porrrt arms!"

He snatched the weapon from the barefoot soldier and proceeded to inspect the rifle. He snapped back the bolt, checking for rust, then peered down the barrel checking the bore. When the inspection was finished, Jessie marched up to the Trung-shi and saluted again. The P.F. Trung-shi was sharp with his return.

"What is your name, Trung-shi?"

"Nuy."

"Sergeant Nuy, we must train your troops with the Marines."

He nodded.

"We killed a V.C. on the mountain today. I think something might be up. V.C. might attack."

"V.C.? Mountain?" He pointed toward O.P. George.

"Yes. I want three of your men to go up on O.P. George. Mountain. Meet with Marines. Now." He held up three fingers.

"Yes."

The Vietnamese turned to his men and shouted three names. Three P.F.'s stepped out of formation. He gave them the command and waved them to get moving. They looked surprised. He barked angrily and they hurried off.

Jessie looked across the road to the CAP area. "Fall in, Marines, facing the P.F.'s!"

"What?" someone shouted back.

"I said fall in, on the double!"

The Marines strolled across the road, grumbling, and slowly fell into line facing the Vietnamese militia.

"Listen up, Marines! There are approximately thirty P.F.'s in front of you. Starting with you on the end, Gomez, six of you will step forward and point out two P.F.'s each. You will take them outside of the village for the test-firing of weapons."

"When, Sarge?" someone asked.

"Now. The rest of you will saddle up with the remaining P.F.'s for a two- to four-hour patrol. You will patrol all avenues of ingress and egress to and from the village. You will patrol from five-hundred meters to one klick around the village area."

Jessie turned toward the P.F.'s. "Trung-shi Nuy."

"Yes."

"I would like you to lead this first patrol, since you are the most familiar with the area. The Marines are in your command." Jessie saluted the Vietnamese sergeant as all in attendance gawked in disbelief.

Marines were rarely put under the command of Popular Forces or ARVNs. Jessie watched the Vietnamese sergeant begin to bark orders to his P.F.'s. He hoped that this was the step needed to begin turning these militiamen into dependable allies. The patrol started immediately, with Nuy taking the point.

By the time they returned, it was nearly dark. The Marines came in, griping worse than ever. Jessie took the Trung-shi aside with a couple of the Marines.

"See anything?"

"See camp," the Trung-shi said, this time in perfectly understandable English.

Jessie turned to a stout-looking Marine with a square face and dark brown eyes that darted back and forth. He carried an M-60 machine gun over his shoulder and had three hundred rounds of ammo crisscrossing his chest.

"What's your name again, Marine?"

"PFC Eckert, Gunny."

"You're the gunner."

"Yes, sir."

"You saw a camp?"

"Yes, sir. That's what it looked like."

Jessie pulled his map out of his cargo pocket and spread it out on the ground. He pulled Eckert and the Trung-shi down with him as they knelt over it.

"Show me where it was."

The Marine pointed to a spot near the Song Trabong River. "About here."

Jessie turned to the Trung-shi. "You show me."

He nodded and pointed. "Yes. Here."

Jessie quickly wrote down the coordinates of the spot on the map, then turned to the rest of the men. "Better chow down before the first ambush, men."

The Marines looked at Jessie with stunned expressions. They were ready to kill him and he knew it, but this was the only way to get this outfit squared away before they all died of old age.

He gathered the men together in a huddle under the parachute after they had time to eat chow. "We will send out two ambushes each night."

Someone groaned out loud. Jessie glared in that man's direction.

"Now hear this, Marines. I know you think I'm some gung-ho S.O.B., but you men volunteered for CAP duty. You volunteered for the United States Marine Corps. If you wanted to be in the Army or the Navy, you should have joined the Army or the Navy."

"I did," Doc Morphine said.

The men laughed, and Jessie couldn't keep from smiling.

"I was sent here because you Marines have not done your job. Enemy troops are waltzing right by your lazy rear ends with no fear of running into interference. And why? Look at you. When was the last ambush you men sent out?"

No one spoke.

"Yeah. That's what I thought," Jessie said with as much disgust as he could muster.

"Now wait a minute, Gunny!" Philly barked. "It ain't like we never do anything! But a few of us are short-timers. Jimbo has three months and a wake-up. I got two months left in this armpit. Then I go back to the world."

"He's right, Gunny," Doc Morphine blurted. "We leave the gooks alone, they leave us alone!"

Jessie pulled out a piece of plastic and unwrapped it slowly with all eyes watching and wondering what evil could come from a piece of plastic. He unwrapped his chewed-up cigar, stuck it in the corner of his mouth, and glared at Doc Morphine.

"If that is true, Einstein, what do you think that gook was doing up on O.P. George today? Getting a tan?"

"What do you think, Gunny?"

"He was spotting for an eventual attack on this unit. Or

he was there to make sure you clowns did not suddenly start doing your job while enemy troops waltz through your A.O. You idiots have let your guard down. That's how Marines die, and every one of you knows it."

"I don't think so," Doc Morphine grumbled.

"You ain't paid to think," Jessie said. "And I'm telling you that it don't matter what you think, gentlemen. You will now conduct yourselves like U.S. Marines. Starting tonight, and every night from now on, there will be two ambushes sent out. The first one will depart at sunset and come back in at 2400 hours. The second ambush will immediately depart upon the return of the first and will come back in at 0400. There will be one four-hour patrol every day. I'll take the first ambush out. All those men who were not on the day patrol, saddle up. Doc Morphine."

"What?"

"Go to the P.F. compound and ask the Trung-shi to send me three men for an ambush."

"Why me?"

"You need the exercise, mister. Start running something besides your mouth. Now move it!"

"Half of those useless clowns won't even be in the compound. They're out in the ville getting high or staying home with mama-san."

"Move it!"

Doc Morphine got up slowly and headed down the road toward the P.F. compound. He returned with three Vietnamese armed with old Garand rifles and two extra magazines.

"Issue these P.F.'s three frags each, Gomez."

"Aye aye, Gunny."

"And see to it they turn them back in when they come in off that ambush."

"I'll be asleep, Gunny."

"No you won't. You're taking out the second ambush." Gomez groaned.

Ten minutes later Jessie led the ambush through the village. Most of the families were just going down for the night, but were not asleep as they passed. The village was not that old yet, and since it was actually three villages combined, it was larger than most. He did not know the exact number of people here, but it had to be near eight hundred. There would be plenty of spies in a village this size, and no doubt the Marines were watched every second. If possible, the V.C. would put sympathizers in hooches that could watch roads or paths leading into and out of the village. The only way to combat such activity was from within, and the only way to get the Vietnamese to cooperate was if they were sure you could protect them. V.C. would terrorize the villagers with assassinations, kidnapping, and torture, and would not hesitate to kill women and children—in the most gruesome ways possible—to strike fear in the villagers. Jessie couldn't help wondering why none of these tens of thousands of murders ever made the evening news back home.

The point man paused and held up his hand to halt the small column. The men stopped and waited alongside the road as he made contact with three P.F.'s in a bunker guarding the road. Jessie had already arranged a password, "Apple." The guards were asleep. The point man had to awaken the one on duty, who lay on top of the bunker. Rubbing his eyes, the P.F. soldier crawled down and opened a barbed-wire gate that was stretched across the road each night. The village was built with defense in mind, but all the bunkers and wire and minefields in the world would not help if the men guarding it were asleep or undisciplined.

They moved through the wire gate and off of the main road, crossed a rice paddy by walking along the dikes, and set up an ambush in a tree line about five hundred meters outside the ville. Three hours later Jessie passed the word to move out, and the men moved quietly back into the village. The second ambush was already waiting when the first entered the wire, just as Jessie had ordered. They were still Marines, he thought, they just needed a kick in the butt.

The first group made their way back to the compound and crashed out quickly. Jessie walked over to the C.P. bunker and climbed on top of the sandbag roof. He spread his poncho liner out and curled up. He felt uneasy with no radio contact with the ambush or O.P. George, but the radios wouldn't arrive until tomorrow. He nodded off with an anxious stomach.

A short while later, he was startled from sleep by M-16s firing on automatic, followed by the crisp explosions of grenades. He shot to his feet as if stuck with a pin. Most of the other Marines were already moving around the CAP compound.

"Hey, Gunny!"

"Yeah, I hear it!"

"What do we do?"

"Get moving! If the gooks are going to hit us, we ain't gonna be sleeping. The compound will be the first target."

The Marines rushed into defensive positions around the compound. The distant firing stopped. The men in the compound sat quietly waiting. Suddenly, a red flare shot up from O.P. George, and almost instantly automatic weapons opened fire. Green tracers from enemy machine guns streaked across the peak of the distant hilltop. Muzzle flashes blinked on and off in the dark silhouette of the hill. Bright flashes signaled grenades going off, the concussion sound following a couple of seconds later.

"Gunny! O.P. George is getting hit!"

"I see it!"

"They got machine guns, Gunny! See those green tracers?"

"I see 'em, Marine."

"What are we going to do?"

"Can't do much without a radio, can we, Marines!"

No one spoke. They all sat quietly watching as the firefight on O.P. George raged. It did not last long. Within a few minutes it was all over. Around 0300 the second ambush was supposed to return to the village, but they did not.

It made sense that after making contact they would stay put for the night, but not knowing what happened had Jessie's guts tied up in knots. Maybe sending out an ambush without radio contact was a mistake, he thought. No. Not sending them out might have cost the whole village their lives. One thing for sure, this was never going to happen again. These idiots would never be without radios again, and he would see to that if it meant kicking the crap out of every man here one at a time.

As the first gray shafts of daylight touched the horizon, Jessie felt ten years older. He mustered the rest of the men and walked to the main road gate to wait. Soon the helmets of the returning ambush began to appear, coming out of the surrounding jungle area about fifty yards to the left of the road, moving along a footpath. They looked okay so far, judging by their walk. No one had their head bowed, as Marines would usually do when they'd lost men the night before. Jessie felt hopeful. O.P. George was another matter, and as soon as these men entered the main gate, he was ready to lead a patrol up the mountain to find out what had happened.

Gomez led the column of four Marines and three P.F.'s up to the main gate, where two P.F.'s on guard at the bunker had already untied the concertina wire and pulled it out of the way.

"What happened last night, Gomez?" Jessie called as the column entered the ville.

Gomez started shaking his head and whistling. "We bagged three of 'em, Sarge."

"Three V.C.?"

"Yeah. The P.F.'s have their AKs."

"How far out?"

"About three hundred meters outside the ville. Got 'em moving along one of the footpaths that lead to the paddy fields over there," he said with a nod toward the northwest.

"You leave the bodies out there?"

"Yes, sir," Gomez said as the seven men paused in front of the rest of the CAP Marines huddled around the gunny.

"How'd the P.F.'s do?"

Gomez sneered and forced a sarcastic chuckle. "They managed to stay out of the way."

"They fire their weapons?"

"Are you kidding? Not a shot."

"Now listen up, Gomez. I want you to go get the Trungshi and the village chief. Tell them what happened and tell them that I want them to go look at the dead V.C. See if they know who they are."

"Where you gonna be, Gunny?"

"We're heading up to O.P. George."

"Heard anything?"

"Not likely, with you morons operating on one radio."

Gomez looked down as if embarrassed.

"Get that done, Gomez. We'll be back by noon, I hope."

"Aye aye, Gunny."

"And listen up. The Charlie Charlie bird from Chu Lai is due in today, right?"

"Yes, sir."

"Well, I radioed before we left O.P. George that we needed at least one other Prick-25 ASAP. It should be on that Army slick when it comes in. You make sure that sucker gets here, and if it don't, you make sure that they know we must have a radio today. Got that?"

"Got it, Gunny."

Jessie looked at the rest of the returning ambush and signaled a thumbs-up, "Good job, men." He turned to the Marines around him. "Let's move out. Jimbo, take the point."

The sun was blistering hot by the time they reached the top of O.P. George. Jessie, finishing off his second canteen of water, wondered if four canteens had been enough. He had thought about bringing along another one, but any more than four made your cartridge belt so heavy that by the end of a long hump the skin on your hips felt like it was ripping off. Corporal Fowler and Eight Ball were sitting together on top of the old French sandbagged bunker when the patrol reached the crest of the hill. The tired men began to fall out, resting against tree stumps or just sprawling on the ground as soon as they reached the top.

"What happened, Corporal?" Jessie asked as he moved toward the bunker. He took off his soft cover and wiped at the stinging sweat pouring into his eyes.

Corporal Fowler pointed downhill. "The V.C. came strolling up that path like they were on a picnic, just jabbering away like they were back on the block or something."

"You're kiddin'!"

"No, Gunny. Really. I heard it, but I thought our P.F.'s were talking or arguing or something, but it wasn't them."

"Who opened up first?"

"Our P.F.'s. They knew it wasn't them talking, I guess. They opened fire all over the place. Didn't hit a blasted thing!"

"Scared 'em off, though!" Eight Ball shouted. "That's just fine with me, bro!"

"You knew the gooks would come up here, Slate!" Corporal Fowler's tone suddenly turned angry.

"Yeah, I figured they would."

"You're gonna get us all killed, Slate. You gung-ho jackass!"

"We'll talk about this when we get back to the ville, Corporal. You decide you want to discuss this man-to-man, I'm gonna take off my rank for a few minutes and me and you are gonna have a meeting of the minds."

"I'd like nothing better, Slate!"

"And you will call me Gunnery Sergeant Slate, mister. Is that clear?" Jessie showed his teeth and for a moment considered fighting the young, strong man right there and then. It would be stupid, but his anger was starting to get the better of him. He took a deep breath and looked around the hilltop. "None of your men were hit?"

"No."

"Crank up the radio, Corporal."

"What for?"

Jessie felt his face flush with rage. He took a step toward Fowler, who tensed to fight. "I said crank up that radio now." Jessie spoke slowly and quietly, forcing his words through clenched teeth.

Corporal Fowler jumped off the top of the bunker and walked down the two steps leading into it. He came back out with the radio and sat down at the bunker entrance. Jessie pulled out his map and spread it out on the ground. He pulled his K-Bar out and started writing coordinates in the dirt. He turned to Jimbo.

"You got any writing gear?"

Jimbo took off his helmet and removed the helmet liner. He produced a small plastic bag with writing paper and tiny pencil.

"Good," Jessie said. "Write down these numbers." Jessie studied the grid map for a few minutes, then began reading off coordinates, writing them out in the hard earth with his knife as Jimbo wrote them out with pencil and paper. He finished and turned to Fowler.

"Ring up that Army battery."

"Iron Hand One . . . Iron Hand One . . . this is Gunfighter Nine . . . over."

Jessie waited for Iron Hand to reply, then took the field phone from Fowler.

"Iron Hand One . . . Gunfighter Nine . . . request preprogrammed coordinates . . ."

Jessie proceeded to read off a list of coordinates marking artillery targets all around the village and O.P. George. He signed off and turned to Jimbo. "You check those numbers I read off?"

"Yes, sir."

"They match what I gave you?"

"Yes sir, Gunny."

"Good."

"What was that for, Gunny?"

"How long you been in 'Nam, Jimbo?"

"Ten months."

"And you volunteered for CAP duty? Do you know the language?"

"Yes, sir, a little."

Jessie nodded. "I just set up some on-calls. Preprogrammed coordinates. Let's say we get hit. We get hit so bad that we get overwhelmed and I can't take the time to study a map and make a call for help. I just scream for the on-calls."

"Oh. And the arty battery fires at all the spots you just called in automatically."

"Affirmative."

"My Gawd almighty, Gunny! You think we done gonna get hit that bad?"

Jessie turned to see a long-faced Marine named Hillbilly staring at him with a homemade toothpick sticking out of one corner of his mouth. The kid had the beginnings of a moustache, and blotchy-looking skin that gave him a camouflaged look.

"Where you from, Hillbilly?"

The kid's pale blue eyes looked away as his brow pinched even more with the new dilemma of answering a question. "Arkansas."

Jessie tried to keep from grinning, but this poor kid spoke as slow as he thought. That would be okay as long he obeyed orders, but Gomez had already said the kid didn't listen if he didn't want to.

"I think we might get hit, Hillbilly," Jessie said with one last look into the Marine's dull-witted face. He turned to Gomez. "Gomez."

"Yes, sir?"

"Take Hillbilly—"

Gomez grabbed Jessie's arm and leaned close to whisper, "Not Hillbilly, Gunny. Please."

"Why?"

"Last time we were in a firefight, he stuck mud in his M-79 barrel to see if it would still shoot."

Jessie leaned back and looked at Gomez questioningly.

Gomez pretended to cross his heart. "Serious as a heart attack, Gunny. No B.S."

"All right. You and Philly and that Marine over there." Jessie pointed at a black Marine standing a few feet away. "What's your name, Marine?"

"A.C."

"A.C.?"

"Yeah, Gunny."

Gomez chuckled. "That's how he got in the Corps, Gunny."

"What do you mean?"

"I stole air conditioners for a living," A.C. said.

"Stole them?"

"Yeah, Gunny," Gomez said with another chuckle. "Until he got popped and the judge gave him the choice of going to prison or joining the Corps."

"Shoulda gone to prison, A.C.," Corporal Fowler yelled.

"All right, A.C. You and Gomez and Philly stay here tonight. I'll send up four P.F.'s to stand watch with you." He turned to Gomez. "I'll be calling you up as soon as the new Prick-25 comes in on the Charlie Charlie bird. Now listen up. I'll be calling in some H and I fire tonight."

"What's that, Gunny?" Hillbilly asked.

"Harassment and interdiction. The day patrol found an area where it looked like the gooks have been camping out. If they're trying to form up for a hit on the ville, we want to keep them off balance. Might just catch them with a few rounds and ruin their whole day."

"How long we be up here, Gunny?" A.C. asked.

"Two days. Three at tops. Now start communicating with your P.F.'s. Train them on setting out the claymore mines and show them how to set up trip flares and how to break 'em down."

"Okay, Gunny," Gomez said.

Jessie was beginning to like Gomez. He had enough tattoos to be a Hell's Angel biker, but he was a good Marine.

Most of these men were probably good Marines, he figured, but they had to be led by a decent NCO. He glanced at Fowler's hard face. He dreaded the confrontation, but knew that something had to be done to straighten this clown out.

"All right, let's saddle up!"

The hump back to the village was tiring, but Jessie felt his adrenaline building for a showdown with Fowler. He knew he was giving away twenty years, but he also knew he'd been training in hand-to-hand combat since the kid was literally in diapers. He wondered how far he should go with this. If he injured the guy badly, he could be looking at another bust. He could be getting out of the Corps a lousy staff sergeant if he wasn't careful. My retirement pay is gonna be a joke already, he thought. Better just bloody him up a little. If he didn't hurt him bad enough, the guy might want to try again, but if he hurt him too bad, the guy might toss a frag into his rack one night. I'll just beat him up a little, Jessie decided.

An hour later the village was in sight. They made their way to the main road so the walk would be easier. Up ahead near the main road bunker, where the concertina wire gate had been pulled back, a group of villagers crowded around something on the ground. The wailing of women became clear as they got closer. One old woman was on her knees screaming and sobbing and beating at her own face with her fists.

The blood-splattered bodies of what were obviously her family lay across the road just beyond the main gate bunker. Some of the crowd came running toward the Marine patrol as they neared the village. The people were sobbing and wailing and speaking all at the same time. V.C. had come into a small offshoot of the main village during the night. They had tortured and murdered this woman's entire family, leaving her to tell the grim story as a warning to the others. Jessie halted the patrol to look at the dead. Three were little children. The village chief was among the crowd. He grabbed Jessie's arm and pulled him aside. The old man's face was racked with concern and anger. He spat some reddish betel-nut juice in between each sentence.

"The V.C. kill others."

"You mean they killed others besides these last night?" He nodded and spat. "Yes, yes, yes. Others."

"How many?"

"Maybe ten people. All children. Two women."

"My God. I'm sorry, chief. We will make them pay."

"Yes. We kill."

"I'll send our Corpsman back to check on the old lady. Maybe he can give her something, I don't know."

"No. No, no."

"You don't want to see the Corpsman?"

"No. No, no." The little gray-haired man shook his head as he spoke.

Something showed in his dark eyes that Jessie could not get a handle on, but it did not bode well. Doc Morphine was a jerk, but one of the most important aspects of the CAP was to gain the confidence of the people by helping them in everyday life, especially with health care when possible. The Corpsman was a vital part of the mission and most Corpsmen were proud of that important position. But Doc Morphine was not your average Corpsman. Jessie knew he had to find out why the doc was not welcome by the village chief.

He looked at the lifeless faces of the little children. It was more than he could stand. He turned away feeling sick inside. Killing the enemy was just a dirty job that had to be done most of the time, but when you saw what this enemy really stood for, it made killing them almost a pleasure.

"Where's the nightly news when the gooks murder kids?" one of the men grumbled.

"Yeah, good question, bro!"

"You boys are just fools. This don't sell papers."

Jessie looked at the dead kids one more time. This was

the plain and simple murder of defenseless children for no military purpose other than terror.

"Move out!" Jessie barked, and led the Marines past the gruesome scene. He paused until Eight Ball came along, and he pulled him out of line. "Eight Ball."

"Yeah, Gunny."

"I want to ask you something, and I want a straight answer."

Eight Ball wiped sweat from his flat face and shrugged. "Shoot."

"Why would the village chief not want our Corpsman to look at his people?"

Eight Ball looked away, then down at the ground. He began to fidget and shrugged his shoulders. "Don't ask me, Gunny." He sounded worried.

"You know something, Marine. Spit it out."

Eight Ball became more fidgety. He watched the rest of the patrol as they walked toward the CAP compound.

"It won't go any further. You got my word. No one will know that you said a thing."

Eight Ball stared into Jessie's eyes for a moment, looked down again, lifted his gaze. "You swear, Gunny?"

"You got my word, Marine."

He looked around again, then began nervously picking dirt out of the sight of his M-16. "Now look, Gunny, I don't know for sure. I don't know nothing for sure."

"Go on."

"Well, it could just be scuttlebutt. I mean, you know how guys talk."

"I'll take that into consideration. Like I promised, Eight Ball, this is for my own knowledge. It will go no further."

"Okay. Your word."

"My word."

"Well, scuttlebutt was that this old farmer in the ville was croaking. He was real sick. They said he wasn't gonna last long."

"Yeah. And Doc Morphine checked him out? Go on."

"Yeah. But the word was that the doc had heard that giving somebody a shot of water and air would kill 'em."

Jessie tried to hide his shock. "So, scuttlebutt says that Doc Morphine gave the old man a shot of air and water?"

Eight Ball looked at the ground and kicked at the dirt a little. "Yeah."

"And the old man died?"

"Yeah. But nobody knows if that's why he died. He was croaking anyway."

"Thanks, Eight Ball."

"You gave me your word now, Gunny."

"And I'll keep it."

Eight Ball gave a nod and moved on toward the compound. Jessie stood still for a few moments, not quite sure what to do. There were over 500,000 men in 'Nam right now, and ninety-eight percent of them were good men doing a tough job. It was common sense that in a group of men that big you might have a certain percentage of rapists, murderers, and just about any other possible category, including wackos. There was no proof that the story was true, and Marines were great ones for sea tales, especially if they were talking to boots or civilians. No. There was no way to be certain about the truth, but he was certain about one thing: Doc Morphine was on very thin ice.

Jessie walked toward the compound, still unsure of how to handle Corporal Fowler or Doc Morphine.

Eckert, looking worried, came up to him as he started to drop his gear next to the C.P. bunker. "Gunny! We got to call a medevac!"

"What?"

"Runs is out cold! He looks real bad!"

Jessie propped his shotgun against the bunker and ran over to where Runs was lying. The young Marine's face was ashen and his lips were pale blue. He looked dead. Jessie fell on his knees and put his ear to Runs's chest. The boy's heartbeat was barely audible but sounded rhythmic. Jessie lifted his head and searched the faces around him.

"Where's Doc Morphine?"

A couple of the men shrugged.

"He's over in the slop chute, Gunny." John Eckert, the short, stocky Texan from Hale Center pointed with his thumb at a hooch twenty yards down the road from the schoolhouse. The hooch had a couple of crude tables with chairs on a front porch. Jessie could see a Marine leaning back in a chair with his feet up on one of the tables and a beer in his hand.

Jessie turned to Corporal Fowler, who was standing nearby. He had a disinterested look on his face, which sent a wave of anger through Jessie.

"Get on the horn, Fowler! Get a medevac in here *ASAP!*"

"What do I tell 'em?"

"Tell them we got two men that have to be medevaced immediately."

Fowler looked around and so did the rest of the platoon. "Two?"

"Shut up, Marine, and follow orders, or it's gonna be three!"

Jessie stood up, shaking with rage. Corporal Fowler stepped back to get out of the way. Jessie pushed a couple of the men aside and headed toward the slop chute. He tried to calm himself as he crossed the dusty road, but there was no calm left in him and he knew it. He walked faster toward the hooch. Doc Morphine took a swig from a brown bottle of Vietnamese Tiger-piss beer and leaned back a little farther on the back legs of his hand-hewn chair. He pulled a C-ration four-pack of Salems out of his pocket and lit up as Jessie reached the porch.

"Why aren't you tending to that sick Marine, Corpsman?"

"Sick Marine?" Doc Morphine raised one eyebrow as if surprised.

"I'm talking about Runs. The radios are in. Have you

called for a medevac?" Jessie shouted through clenched teeth as he reached for his K-Bar knife.

"No. I haven't had time yet."

Jessie went blank with rage, and before he could control himself, he pulled his K-Bar out of its sheath and lunged forward, stabbing it deep into the Corpsman's thigh. He could feel and hear the crunch as he drove the knife at least four inches deep through muscle and tendon. The Corpsman's scream brought villagers out of nearby hooches, and every Marine in the compound ran into the road. The old toothless mama-san who ran the slop chute came out screaming, then went silent with her eyes bulging and her hand over her mouth. Jessie pulled the knife out of Doc Morphine's thigh as the stunned Corpsman clutched both hands over the gushing wound. He looked up with a pale expression of disbelief. Tears swelled up in his eyes. He was in a state of shock.

"You have just had a noncombatant accident. One single word out of you stating otherwise and we go to the captain and the CID to talk about shots of air and water. Do you understand me?" Jessie spoke clearly and calmly, but the words were forced and he was not sure that he would not stab this scumbag again.

Sweat poured from the panicked face of the fat Corpsman clutching at his bleeding leg. His frightened eyes darted back and forth from his leg to Jessie. His breathing was hard and labored, as if he had just run many miles.

"Okay! Okay! I promise! I had an accident! Now get me my medical bag!"

"A medevac is on the way. Be on it and don't come back here."

"All right. All right. Get my medical bag!"

"Get it yourself."

Jessie wiped the blood from his K-Bar on the Corpsman's sleeve and put it back in his sheath. He stepped forward and snatched the Corpsman's .45 caliber pistol from his holster, then turned and walked back across the road.

The entire CAP platoon, along with several P.F.'s, were staring silently from the edge of the road. No one spoke. They cleared a path as Jessie started to walk through them. He stopped and looked around until he saw Corporal Fowler.

"You call that medevac, Corporal?" he barked.

Corporal Fowler's eyes widened. He nodded nervously. "Yes, sir. They're on the way."

"Outstanding. Now get some men, Corporal, and gently carry that sick Marine to the LZ and prepare to throw out green smoke."

"Yes, sir."

"And Corporal!"

"Yes, sir."

"Get somebody on the horn and have replacements sent out right away. Tell them we need a new Corpsman."

"Yes sir, Gunny," Corporal Fowler said, then turned and hustled back toward the radio.

Jessie paused and looked around at the stunned faces of the Marines.

"Show's over. Get some chow and some rest. Whoever's on the day patrol better be ready at 0100 hours." He nodded back across the road toward Doc Morphine, who was limping their way. "One of you go help that man to the LZ. He's had an accident. Fell on a knife."

Somebody chuckled, then went silent. Jessie did not see who it was.

CHAPTER TWENTY-SEVEN

By the end of the day, the Charlie Charlie bird had brought out two new men, a black Marine named James and a Corpsman, Doc Whistle. James had a strong vocabulary; he'd been educated at Howard University. He had a quick smile and seemed like the kind of Marine you wanted to serve with. Doc Whistle looked more like a bookworm, with glasses, a small face, a long, thin body. He whistled all the time. He was a good guy too. Two weeks passed with no internal problems.

Jessie had hopes that things might start shaping up now. Corporal Fowler appeared to have gone through an attitude adjustment and was beginning to act like a corporal in the United States Marine Corps. So far there had been no repercussions about the stabbing incident, although Captain Roberts had visited once in the Loach and made a curious comment about "how sharp" old Corps discipline could be. Runs recovered but was sent out to another CAP unit nearer to Chu Lai.

Patrols and nightly ambushes continued on schedule. Three of the day patrols had come across evidence that the H&I fire was becoming effective. Torn and bloody NVA packs were strewn all over one area where the artillery fire had been called in at random during the night. In two other spots near the Son Trabong, the P.F.'s had found a shallow grave with four dead V.C. and the limbs of at least two others. O.P. George was constantly manned with Marines and P.F.'s doing three-day shifts. The two new men had to spend some extra time up there learning to call in arty from the "doggy battery" at Tra Bong. The Army battery was good. They could drop a 155 on a dime. Jessie sent them some NVA belt buckles as gifts, just to make sure they would keep up the good work. Artillery troops rarely got any souveniers, since they were never around to pick up the pieces, so they appreciated the gesture. Each day patrol called in new coordinates for the H&I fire, and each night it came whistling in right on target and right on time.

The Marines were still having trouble with the P.F.'s stealing everything that wasn't nailed down, and even though the Trung-shi was turning out to be a pretty good soldier, he was slow to discipline his men.

By the middle of July the heat was unbearable and tempers were getting short. Jessie called for the day patrol to fall out. Gomez came storming out of one of the sandbag bunkers, cursing up a storm.

"Shut up, Marine!" Jessie barked, and Gomez quieted, but was angry.

"You gotta do something, Gunny!"

"What is it this time, Gomez?"

"I'm telling you right now, if you don't do something about those thieving P.F.'s, I will!"

"Me too, Gunny," Philly echoed.

"I'm gonna booby-trap something with some C-4, and I mean it!" Gomez shouted.

"What'd they steal this time?"

"My boots! My friggin' boots! How am I going on patrol without boots? I'm gonna kill the gook I find with those boots, Gunny! I mean it! I'm blowin' him away on the spot!"

There was a ninety percent chance that the young Marine was just blowing off steam. Gomez was the kind of Marine who fed his C-rations to water buffalo. But what would have been an empty threat back in the world had to be taken seriously here, and Jessie knew it. Combat Marines were perfectly capable of losing their temper and doing something they would regret forever.

"Chill out. That's the last time we're putting up with crap," Jessie said as he turned and headed down the road. He walked past the schoolhouse and the slop-chute hooch. The bartender mama-san waved and smiled her toothless smile. He waved back as he thought about the best way to handle this. Being diplomatic was not always his strong suit. This was the third time he'd approached the Vietnamese about putting an end to the stealing, twice with the Trung-shi. He knew where the village chief lived, but the old man was rarely there. Probably at the barbershop, he thought. Jessie moved off the main road and down a wide path that was also a road, past a row of hooches with children playing some kind of game that looked like a version of hide and seek. He could see a group of Vietnamese huddled around the porch of the barbershop. The old chief waved at Jessie as he approached. Jessie waved back and nodded.

"Can I speak to you alone, Chief?" He pointed to a spot a few feet away as he spoke. The chief said something to the others and followed him. When they were alone, the old man looked up intently at Jessie, chewing on his betel nut more with his gums than his three rotten teeth.

"Chief, something has to be done about the stealing."

"Steal?"

"Stealing. Your Popular Force is stealing our gear almost every night and day. If we leave our gear to even go to the head, someone steals something."

"P.F.'s?"

"Yes. I think so."

"You tell Trung-shi."

"I have told the Trung-shi two times." Jessie held up two fingers to make sure the old man understood.

The chief grunted and nodded and looked down as if in

thought about the problem. He looked up into the face of the tall American. "I fix."

Something in the old man's eyes made Jessie think that he meant business. "Thank you, Chief."

Four hours later the day patrol came back into the village. Corporal Fowler had led the patrol, and came straight over to the C.P. bunker to report in. Jessie was on the horn to Chu Lai, giving a list of supplies needed, when the corporal approached. He signed off and turned to Fowler.

"What's the word, Corporal?"

"Hot, Gunny. Real hot. I brought four canteens and emptied every drop and still feel like I've got heat exhaustion."

"Did Doc hand out the salt tabs?"

"Yes, sir."

"Good. See anything?"

The corporal handed Jessie a piece of paper. "We saw evidence of enemy activity around these coordinates, just on the other side of the Song Trabong River."

"I figured we would see something on the other side of the river. They're trying to skirt around the ville and avoid our patrols, to infiltrate down the road a bit."

"We found another campsite."

"How close to the last one?" Jessie asked.

"A klick, maybe klick and half."

"Yeah, something's cooking."

"I think so too, Sarge. We found a trail with the branches of the trees tied together overhead. No way recon flights will spot anything."

"Hey, Gunny!"

Jessie looked around Fowler to see who was calling. Hillbilly was pointing toward the road in front of the CAP compound. Jessie stood up to see what was going on. The P.F.'s were lined up in formation on the road facing the compound. Jessie put on his soft cover, wiped the sweat from his face and walked out from under the shade of the parachute to stand in front of the P.F. formation. The Trung-shi saluted him and came to attention. He returned the salute.

"What's this all about, Trung-shi?"

The Trung-shi faced his troops and barked, "Nyugien! Front and center!"

Two P.F.'s with rifles slung and holding bamboo sticks stepped out of the formation with a frightened-looking, shirtless Vietnamese P.F. between them. The frightened man held a pair of Marine jungle boots.

"Hey, Gunny! Them's my boots!" Gomez shouted, and pointed.

"As you were, Gomez!" Jessie snapped.

The Trung-shi turned to Jessie. "This man steal Marine boots."

One of the P.F.'s holding the bamboo stick snatched the boots from the frightened-looking man and brought them forward. He handed them to Jessie and saluted.

"Thank you," Jessie said as he returned the salute. "Gomez! Front and center."

Gomez hustled out to Gunny Slate and came to attention. He was wearing a pair of Ho Chi Minh sandals taken from a dead NVA. Jessie glanced down at the sandals made of old American tire tread and grunted, "Get those things off your feet, Marine."

"Yes sir, Gunny."

Gomez took the boots and walked back into the shade of the compound area. Jessie turned to the Vietnamese sergeant.

"Thank you, Trung-shi."

"Man will now be punished," he said.

He turned and nodded toward the two men with the bamboo sticks. The two men began to immediately beat the frightened P.F. with the bamboo sticks as hard as they could swing. The sticks were about the size of broom handles and made a clear whooshing sound as they went through the air followed by a loud slap when they struck the man's sweaty back. After the first four or five blows, he fell to the ground. They continued to beat him until Jessie couldn't stand it anymore. He leaned close to the Vietnamese sergeant and said, "That is enough, Trung-shi. He's learned his lesson."

"No," he said, without taking his eyes off of the beating.

Sweat flew from the man's body with each blow and terrible red welts began appearing all over his bare back. One or two blows caught him in the head and blood ran down his face. He sat on his knees. He looked dazed and almost unaware of what was happening to him. Finally the Trung-shi held up his hand and they stopped the beating. They picked the man up by his limp arms and carried him back into formation, then marched away quietly. Jessie and the Marines watched them leave without a word. That was the last serious problem the CAP Marines had with the Vietnamese stealing gear.

By mid-August the Marines and P.F.'s were working well together. A mutual respect and bond was starting to build. Jessie was beginning to think that his job might be done. He wanted to stay until his R&R came up. Exchanging letters with his boy and planning for their big time on R&R was fun. Through the letters back and forth, he felt closer to his son than at any other time in his life. Charlie was even ending his letters with things like, "I love you, Dad," or, "I'm praying for you, Dad." Jessie had never looked forward to an R&R this much in his entire career.

One afternoon the village chief payed a visit to the CAP compound and invited the Marines to his daughter's wedding. This was a very big step in cementing relations between Marines and the villagers. It was a great honor for Marines to be invited, but would be seen as a death warrant on the chief's head by the Viet Cong infiltrators in the village. It was important that the Marines do something special for the wedding. The men weren't much for suggestions. Finally, Hillbilly, who was the least likely to come up with an idea, came up with two ideas.

"Gee whiz, Sarge, what's the big deal?" he said in his

normally stupid manner. "Cake and music, man. That's all a wedding is anyway, right?"

Jessie blinked and gave the stupid Marine a double take. He was right. That in itself was scary. Cake and music. He got on the horn to Captain Roberts. It would take some doing, but he had an idea that might really please the Vietnamese and make the event memorable. Three days later the little Loach helicopter flew in from Chu Lai with a seabag full of goodies that Jessie told no one about.

The wedding was a major celebration. Most of the village turned out for it. There looked to be around eight or nine hundred people celebrating the event. The villagers had concocted some potent wine, and two hours into the party everyone was feeling no pain. Jessie grabbed Philly and headed back to the compound as the Buddhist wedding ceremony began. He carefully carried the seabag out of the command bunker and gently laid it on the ground in front of Philly.

"What you got there, Gunny?" Philly asked.

Jessie pulled out a large cardboard box and set it on a cot beside Philly. "Wedding cake."

"Cake! You're jivin' me."

"Open it up."

Philly opened the box slowly. "Wow! Far out, Gunny. How in the world did you do that?"

"You're gonna carry it behind me right up to the wedding couple. Got it?"

"Yeah, sure."

"Carry it on top of that box so they can see it when we walk up to them."

"Look, Gunny, it's got two little people stuck in it."

"Yeah. I got Eckert the gunner to help make two little people out of M-60 rounds. I painted the tux on the little guy."

"You?"

"I didn't make the cake, just the little people. See the hair on the girl?"

"Yeah."

"Eight Ball cut if off Hillbilly's head."

"Now what are you doing?" Philly asked.

Jessie pulled on his dress blue trousers and swiped away lint from his dress blue jacket, which lay across a hammock. He sat down and put on his shoes.

"Still got a shine, huh?"

"I don't believe you!" Philly's eyes were bugging out. He started laughing hard and loud.

Jessie stood up and pulled on his jacket. He buttoned it up and carefully placed his white barracks cover on his head.

"Don't tell me you got the gloves?" Philly said, laughing.

"Affirmative, Marine."

Philly laughed harder as Jessie pulled on his gloves. "This is unbelievable, Gunny!"

"That ain't all, boot." Jessie leaned over and pulled his bagpipes out of the seabag. He checked the mouthpiece and smiled at Philly, who had stopped laughing and was staring openmouthed at Jessie's chest.

"Well, when was the last time you heard the regimental pipes played, son?"

Philly continued to stare at Jessie's chest.

"Philly? What's the matter with you, Marine?"

"God," he mumbled, and pointed. "That's the Medal of Honor."

Until that moment Jessie had forgotten all about the ribbons on his chest. He rarely wore the actual medals. They were stuffed in a footlocker somewhere in Da Nang or Okinawa. The CMH medal hung around your neck unlike any other medal worn in the Corps, so you always knew you had it on. If you were just wearing the ribbons, it was easy to forget. But even the ribbon was singularly striking. White stars on a sky-blue background. It was always placed alone above all other ribbons.

"My God, Gunny, nobody told me. I didn't know you were a friggin' Medal of Honor winner."

Jessie hated this moment. He had long ago given up on wondering how he was supposed to act. Do you fake humility? Do you say thanks? Do you tell 'em you were a coward a couple of times too? Or it should have gone to a couple dozen other guys?

"Yeah, Philly. I got the CMH. Now get the cake and wait for Corporal Fowler's signal."

Philly snapped to attention and saluted. "Yes, sir!"

"Do I look like an officer to you, mister?" Jessie barked.

"More. Much more, sir. You look like a sergeant to me."

Jessie started to speak but found it difficult. He looked at the young man for a moment, then saluted.

They waited there for the signal from Corporal Fowler and the Kit Carson scout. Soon a green flare shot into the blue sky, signaling the "I do's" were over. Jessie led the way down the main road, playing the Marines hymn, with Philly a couple of paces behind, carrying the cake on top of the box. The whole village slowly went silent and lined the road to watch the two-man procession go by.

There was no icing on the cake, but it went over very well. The village killed a sick water buffalo and laid out quite a spread for the feast. Tiger-piss beer flowed freely, as did some kind of berry wine that Jessie had never tasted. Word of the CMH naturally went through the CAP unit like a gunshot, and every man eventually came up to Jessie staring awkwardly but showing great respect. It was the duty of all Marines to get drunk on occasions such as this. The chief gave orders for the village to stand guard, allowing the Marines to get as drunk as they wanted. All in all, it was a wonderful celebration.

By the middle of August the platoon had made contact with V.C. several more times. Enemy activity was definitely on the increase. With each firefight came complaints about Hillbilly, the goofy Marine from Arkansas. He never ducked down. The men were taking bets on how much longer he would last, but he seemed to be living one of those charmed lives. On one patrol, he stepped on a trip wire attached to a Bouncing Betty and just stood there while everyone else, seeing sparks from some sort of a fuse, dove for cover. The Bouncing Betty was a dud. He remained standing there for a full five minutes before Gomez pulled him off the wire. Talking to him was no use. He would get a glazed-over stare and nod and then do the same stupid things.

Hillbilly was the blooper man for the platoon and carried the M-79 grenade launcher. It was a neat little weapon that broke in half like a sawed-off shotgun and fired 40mm rounds. The rounds looked like a giant .45 caliber bullet and exploded on impact. One day Hillbilly showed up with a 40mm round from a Huey Cobra gunship. The 40mm rounds the Hueys used were the same circumference, only much longer than those the blooper gun used and maybe more powerful.

Jessie saw Hillbilly in a field in back of the compound tossing the Huey 40mm into the air and catching it with his helmet.

"Hillbilly! You idiot! Get rid of that thing!"

The stupid Marine waved and nodded.

Jessie turned and put a match to a small chunk of C-4 in the bottom of his C-ration can stove. He set his can of ham and lima beans on the stove and poured in enough Tabasco sauce to kill the taste. He leaned back, closed his eyes, and waited for his food to heat. A minute later he opened one eye to check on his food. He noticed Hillbilly standing alone in an open area just beyond the shaded compound. Hillbilly had his M-79 and helmet in his left hand. He reached into his cargo pocket with his right hand and pulled out the big 40mm Huey Cobra round. He put his helmet on and then his chin strap, which no one ever used. He broke open the M-79 and loaded the long 40mm into the grenade launcher. Jessie sat up straight.

"Hey, you idiot!" he yelled.

Hillbilly did not turn to see if he was the idiot being paged. He calmly faced the surrounding jungle area and held

the M-79 at arm's length over his head. Jessie's shout was
drowned out by the explosion. Hillbilly flew sideways to the
ground. Jessie jumped to his feet along with everyone in the
compound and ran into the field. Doc Whistle got to him
first and was kneeling over him, checking out his hands.
The M-79 lay beside him with the barrel split wide open.

"How is he, Doc?" Jessie asked.

"What was it?" somebody shouted.

"Incoming!" another panicky voice called as they ran
forward.

"No! No, no, no!" Jessie yelled, and waved his hands at
the charging men. "Calm down! It was Hillbilly!" He
turned to look down at the stunned and stupefied face staring up at the crowd around him. "You moron! Are you trying to kill yourself, you idiot?"

"His hands are pretty bad, Sarge."

Jessie kneeled down beside the Corpsman to get a better
look. Hillbilly's hands were red, blue, and swollen. Jessie
slapped Hillbilly hard on the helmet and turned to look up
into the faces of the men around them.

"Call a medevac."

By the end of August enemy activity increased. The V.C.
were trying to booby-trap all avenues that the combined
Marine and P.F. patrols might use. Two P.F.'s had tripped a
booby-trapped 105 round near the end of July, killing both
men. Jessie instituted a new policy after getting the okay
and the money from CAP HQ. The Marines began offering
rewards for any weapons or booby traps the villagers
brought in from the fields. It paid off right away, as every
kind of imaginable weapon or bomb would be carried or
dragged up to the compound and exchanged for cash. The
Marines dug an ordnance pit, a huge hole about fifty meters
beyond the CAP compound on the edge of the village. Any
captured weapons or hardware that was brought in would
be thrown into the hole and blown up with C-4 explosive
every week or two.

Hillbilly had spent a few days in an Army hospital and

not done anything exceptionally stupid since his return to the unit. His hands hadn't been broken, and Jessie figured it might have been the best thing that ever happened to the fool. Most of the men would still give at least seven-to-one odds that Hillbilly would leave 'Nam in a body bag.

One day at the tail end of August a group of villagers hauled in an unexploded 500-pound bomb. No one knew where it came from, but it was an American bomb dropped by an American plane. How it got to CAP 139 was a mystery, but Jessie was happy to pay the farmers fifteen bucks MPC for the find. If the Viet Cong got hold of a bomb like that, they would booby-trap it and could end up killing an entire patrol. It took a few men with the help of a water buffalo to haul the thing in from the rice-paddy fields, and most of the platoon lent a hand in lowering it into the ordnance pit.

Two days later Jessie brought the day patrol back into the compound. Eight Ball met the patrol outside of the shaded area on the road. He looked angry.

"Gunny, you gotta do something about that fool."

"What fool is that, Eight Ball?" Jessie asked, taking off his cartridge belt. He gingerly touched his hip; the weight of the canteens were rubbing his hip raw.

"Look out there, Gunny!" Eight Ball pointed at the field behind the compound area.

Hillbilly was playing catch with something. He tossed it high in the air and caught it with his soft-cover hat.

"Yeah. What's wrong?"

"You know what he's playing catch with?"

"What?" Jessie asked as he strained to see the object.

"It's the firing mechanism of a 40mm round. Unexploded."

Jessie looked into Eight Ball's flat face to make sure he wasn't joking. He wasn't.

"Hillbilly!"

The goofy Marine looked toward the compound. "Yeah, Sarge?"

"Come here!"

The gangly kid jogged over to Jessie and Eight Ball, still flipping the unexploded war head of the 40mm round.

"Don't do that!"

"Do what, Sarge?"

"That thing can go off, you idiot!"

"I don't think so, Gunny Sergeant. It's a dud I found and I'm just sure it won't do nothin'."

"And why don't you think so, Marine?" Jessie asked with as much sarcasm as he could put in his tone.

"Don't it have to rotate so many times to go off? Ain't that what they told me?"

"Yes. When you fire the blooper gun, that's how it works, Hillbilly. But it is unwise for a person to play catch with a loaded explosive device. The jar just might make it go boom and blow your exceptionally stupid head off." Jessie spoke slowly, smiling all the time.

Hillbilly nodded as if he understood. He put the warhead in his pocket and walked away.

Jessie and Eight Ball exchanged looks of disbelief. Eight Ball whistled the tune of *Twilight Zone* as Jessie walked toward his makeshift hammock tied between two small trees. He dropped his gear and climbed into the hammock. Within seconds he fell asleep.

"Gunny."

Jessie groaned.

"Hey, Gunny. Better wake up."

"What is it?" Jessie moaned with his eyes still shut.

"It's that stupid Hillbilly. This don't look like such a good idea."

Jessie opened his eyes. Sammy Paul was standing beside him looking toward the field in back of the compound. His thick black beard was about an inch long already, but Jessie knew that the kid couldn't help it. He could grow a full beard in a week.

"What's that idiot doing now?" Jessie asked, trying to

look into the field without getting out of the comfortable makeshift hammock.

"He's dropping that firing mechanism on that 500-pounder! And he's hitting it! I hear it clang off the thing, Gunny!"

Jessie shot up out of the hammock so fast that he fell flat on his face. He got to his feet and stood still for a moment, staring in disbelief at Hillbilly, who was standing on the edge of the ordnance pit sighting in on the 500-pound bomb with the M-79 round by holding it to his nose and closing one eye. Jessie watched in horror as Hillbilly let go of the 40mm firing mechanism like a kid dropping a rock into a deep well and staring after it to see the splash. The M-79 round exploded against the big bomb with a loud metallic noise that blew Hillbilly into the air. He landed on his back and started yelling.

"Corpsman! Corpsman! Corpsman? Corpsman ... Corpsman ... Corpsman! I'm hurt!"

The Marine writhed in pain on the ground. Some of the men were already sprinting out to the ordnance pit, and Jessie followed them. Doc Whistle was hovering over the moaning Hillbilly when Jessie reached them.

"How bad, Doc?"

"The concussion broke his leg, but it's weird, Gunny, 'cause it never even broke the skin. Look."

Jessie knelt down to see Hillbilly's shinbone. The leg was at a slight angle, obviously broken, but Doc was right. There was no blood at all. It was turning blue quickly.

"Somebody call a medevac! Get him out of here before I kill him myself!" Jessie yelled into the agonized face of the stupid Marine.

"Hey, Gunny. Check this out."

Jessie looked around. Corporal Fowler was standing over the ordnance pit, looking down.

"What is it?"

"You gotta see this."

Jessie stood up and walked over to the pit along with a

couple of the men. He looked down into the hole. The big olive-green, 500-pound bomb lay in the bottom of the ten-foot pit. A large, charred spot on top of the bomb was still smoking from the explosion.

"Why didn't that thing go off?" Jimbo asked no one in particular.

"How could it not detonate that bomb, Gunny?" Corporal Fowler echoed.

Jessie turned slowly to marvel at Hillbilly, who was now sitting up. His hair was sticking straight up, like a man with his finger in a light socket. His eyebrows and lashes had been singed off by the blast and his nose was black against a pale, ashen face. His blue eyes were not just open, but more open than Jessie had believed possible for a human being. It was incomparable, the most superb expression of moronic shock that Jessie had ever witnessed. The others stared at the stupid Marine. No one spoke. The hush was almost reverent. There was a sense of awe in the eyes of the gawking young men, as if they were in the presence of such magnificent stupidity that mere words were totally insufficient. Hillbilly was a man destined for legendary status in the annals of Marine Corps history. Sea stories about this character would be passed down for decades. Yes, they were in the presence of a rare individual, and the men stared at Private Hillbilly with a new sense of admiration and respect, not unlike the respect that people would give anyone who had reached the zenith of his particular field or profession.

No one was sure how long that silent tribute lasted, but it seemed like quite a while. Eventually the men carried Private Hillbilly to the LZ in a quiet procession fit for no-bility. His expression never changed, and the door gunner asked the doc if he should be treated for shock. Doc just shrugged and shook his head as the chopper lifted off. A couple of the men saluted. It seemed a fitting gesture for a legend.

CHAPTER TWENTY-EIGHT

Jessie didn't like doing it, but by the end of summer it became obvious that for their own safety they had to extend their patrols across the river and right up to the Cambodian and Laotian border areas. The men did not gripe too much, but no one was happy going an extra five hundred meters into the bush with a ten-man patrol. Everyone had the feeling that Charlie Cong was not happy with the new CAP procedures either. The H&I fire had scored some hits.

At daybreak one morning in early September, two animated P.F.'s rushed into the CAP compound waving and chattering away about V.C. in the ville. Jessie tried to ignore the noise, but soon gave up on catching any sleep. He sat up wishing he'd slept inside the bunker, but no one could sleep inside the bunkers because of the giant spiders and rats that made their homes inside.

"What's all the commotion?"

Eight Ball was coming toward him with the frantic P.F.'s. "Gunny, the P.F.'s say there's gooks in the schoolhouse!"

"What!" Jessie grabbed up his shotgun and bandoleer. Some of the Marines were already pulling on boots and flak jackets. "Never take your boots off at night, Marines," he said with quiet anger in the direction of Jimbo, who was lacing up as fast as he could. "Move out."

Four of the men were out on a night ambush. They had

never gotten a replacement for Hillbilly, so the CAP unit was down to twelve Marines and the Corpsman. They moved across the dirt road and toward the schoolhouse. A red and blue flag with a yellow star in the center flew over the building. Jessie turned to one of the P.F.'s tagging along.

"How'd they get inside the ville?"

He shrugged, and Jessie wanted to slap him and every P.F. on perimeter duty. He knew that most of them slept on the lines, but there was only so much you could do with these guys. It usually took some terrible tragedy to wake them up. The men approached the schoolhouse carefully, spreading out to assault by fire team. A group of villagers appeared from across the road. An old man came toward Jessie, pointing.

"V.C. V.C. V.C."

"Where?"

He pointed toward the north gate. "Gate. Gate."

"Are they still there?"

He started shaking his head yes. "V.C. Yes, yes, yes. Gate."

"Thank you."

Jessie waved the men to follow him toward the north gate. As they neared the barbed-wire gate across the road, someone shouted.

"Gook!"

A pajama-clad Viet Cong guerrilla carrying an AK-47 opened fire from the brush near the gate. The P.F.'s who were supposed to be on guard were nowhere to be seen. The man jumped up and took off as the Marines returned fire. Jessie pumped out two quick shots, but the V.C. dove over an embankment and ran limping toward some jungle foliage nearby. Eckert cut him down with a stream of tracers from the M-60.

Ten minutes later the villagers started gathering to see what had happened. If there were any more V.C., they had made their escape into the surrounding jungle. Jessie, Jimbo, Eckert, and Doc Whistle checked out the dead V.C.

Eckert had gotten. He was a mess; only a few tendons held the body in one piece.

The lesson was not lost on the P.F.'s on guard duty. After that, they responded well to Marine training and even began to get respect from the Americans. That went a long way toward cementing cohesiveness. Five days after the schoolhouse incident, Jessie led the second ambush out with five Marines and four P.F.'s. The day patrol had come across a small footpath that looked fairly new, leading from the river toward O.P. George. The path went by an area where one of the farmers kept his cattle. The cattle were tied up and fenced in by a makeshift bamboo fence. Jessie set the ambush up on the Vietnam side of the river along the path. Since it was a three-hour ambush and they had no need for sleep, they set up in one-man positions about five to eight yards apart.

From their positions, they could cover the river from ten to fifteen yards away. Noises off the river at night were enough to make a tough man pee his pants. After being in Vietnam for a while, most men would forget that the enemy wasn't the only thing in the jungle that could kill you. One night beside a river would quickly remind you of that fact. Jessie glanced toward the sky. A quarter moon and clear. Visibility good. That was what the men wanted when they were set up and waiting. Thank God we're not humping through the bush, he thought, and pictured his son leading a platoon through the jungle night. A cold chill went through him. He tried to clear his mind. He looked to his left at the next position. Philly sat high in his fighting hole. Too late to dig deeper, he thought. They had the trail pretty well covered. No good guys to his right, but the trail curved so that part of the ambush would be able to lend fire support without hitting him. At least he hoped so.

Jessie pulled the PRC-25 close to him to make the check-in call. Each ambush would check in with O.P. George, then check in with the C.P. back in the ville. Sometimes you would check in with Iron Hand, the Army artillery battery in Trabong. Jessie checked in with all three as quietly as possible, then leaned back in his shallow hole and gazed at the reflection of the moon on the softly flowing river fifteen yards before them. He checked his watch, being careful to hide the luminous hands. It was three A.M. A light splashing sound came from the river. He stiffened and sat up straighter in the fighting hole to get a look. His heartbeat quickened. A group of figures were crossing the river downstream and coming toward them at an angle.

Jessie leaned out of his hole to whisper to Philly. "Gooks. Gooks. See 'em?"

The tall, thin Marine gave a silent wave and whispered to the position on his left. PFC Eckert was hunched over the M-60. The Texan gave no response, but his A-gunner, Sammy Paul, signaled a thumbs-up. The next two positions were P.F.'s; they were not visible from Jessie's position on the end. Now it was a matter of praying that everyone was awake and ready. One of the water buffalo made a move that stirred the small tree he was tied to, and Jessie felt himself jump. He strained to see how many V.C. were crossing the river, but branches obstructed his view. Looked to be at least five or six men, but it could be more, and he knew that if they were well-trained, they might not all cross at the same time or even at the same place. One thing was sure, enemy activity was so much on the increase around the village that something big had to be up. Guessing when it might come was nearly impossible. A prisoner might be convinced to talk, he thought.

One of the water buffalo moved again, and the sound of something slithering through the weeds brought Jessie's aim in the direction of the cows. Suddenly the sound was close, but it was moving too fast to be a human. A large snake sped past him, weaving quickly right under the barrel of his twelve-gauge shotgun and sending goose bumps up and down his spine. He regained control and aimed back to his left, away from the cattle. The sounds of a man coming out of the river brought on another shiver. A branch cracked about ten feet down the path. The rustle of wet leaves and the sucking sound of Ho Chi Minh sandals pulling out of the muddy riverbank. They were close. He chewed on the inside of his mouth and fought the temptation to open fire. His heartbeat pounded blood to his ears so violently that it interfered with his hearing.

Then he saw movement on the path. The V.C. point man came forward slowly, hunching over and carrying an AK-47 at the ready on his hip. Because of the way the trail veered around, most of the positions in the ambush had a clear shot at the V.C. coming up the trail. Jessie was nearest the advancing enemy troops. A few seconds later five V.C. wearing pointed straw farmer hats were clearly visible ten meters away.

Come on, Eckert. Come on, Eckert, Jessie said over and over in his mind. The gun should open up first, he thought as he fingered the trigger, knowing he could wait no longer without risking hand-to-hand combat. He pointed at the gook walking point, trying to make sure that the blast would catch the second man too and silently cursing himself for not putting out a claymore. He began squeezing the trigger. At that instant the 60 opened fire and the shotgun blast hit the lead V.C. almost point-blank. Orange tracers from the M-60 appeared to go through the man as if he were transparent, and he flew backward from the shotgun blast.

Jessie pumped and fired, pumped and fired, pumped and fired, never really aiming but just pointing down the path and trying to blow away everything and anything that was there. He jerked back on the pump handle the fifth time and caught movement out of the corner of his left eye from almost straight ahead. Two V.C. stood upright at the river's edge and threw something. He ducked, and the Chicom grenade went over his head. He raised up to fire on the two V.C. and something struck his ankle hard. He groaned and looked down into his shallow hole. In the moonlight he could see a Chinese grenade in the shape of a potato masher lying against his boot. It made a strange sizzling sound. Jessie's heart and breath stopped. He snatched at the grenade and flipped it out of his fighting hole, covering his helmet with both hands and driving his face into the damp earth. The grenade exploded. Then one of the water buffalo let out an agonizing bellow as Jessie rose up and opened fire with three quick shots.

The other Marines turned a withering barrage of fire on the V.C. grenadiers until the automatic gunfire became one loud grinding sound that continued for five seconds. Jessie slapped against his side, found a frag on his cartridge belt, and pulled the pin. He let the spoon loose and flipped the grenade toward the two V.C., then ducked down and began fumbling for another one. He found it as the first explosion ripped earth, rocks, and branches into the air. He pulled the pin, let loose of the spoon, counted out loud, "One thousand one, one thousand two . . ." The cow again bellowed out in agonizing pain. He tossed the grenade down the trail and ducked down again. The explosion sent out a bright white flash followed by a human scream that continued for ten seconds, then went silent.

The sound of the cow's caterwauling continued as the Marine positions opened fire with a new hail of lead. The American and P.F. fusillade was answered by a single four-shot burst from an AK-47. The muzzle flash from the enemy AK was immediately fired upon by every weapon in the ambush. Jessie pumped out five shotgun bursts himself, then ducked down and waited. His ears rang from the concussions, but even through the ringing, the pitiful wailing of the water buffalo could be heard. At last the firing ceased.

No one moved for ten minutes. Each man barely breathed until it was certain that all of the enemy were either dead or gone. Jessie wiped at sticky grime all around his neck. He ached all over. He often wondered what his body must go through during a firefight. The sweat that covered a man afterward was not like the sweat from a hot afternoon. It was as if your body oozed some sticky chemical that acted like a magnet for sand and grit and insects. His heart was still pounding as though he'd just run a marathon. Maybe the sticky crap was sheer adrenaline that came through a man's pores when he thought he was going to die.

The water buffalo's wailing was getting worse. Finally one of the P.F.'s called out in Vietnamese, then in English, "Don't shoot. Don't shoot! I'm P.F. Must help cow!"

"Go on," Jessie called to his left.

One of the P.F.'s got to his feet, walked cautiously past Jessie, and toward the area where the cows were tied up. A few seconds later the crying animal went silent with two rapid shots from the P.F.'s old carbine. He returned to his position and no one moved until morning.

They found five bodies. None of them had any papers on them. Their faces were blackened and two of them carried satchel charges. They were probably a sapper team, and the guess was that they were heading for O.P. George. The P.F.'s sent some villagers out to bury the bodies. The men chipped in some MPC to help the farmer out who had lost the cow. Water buffalos were vital to the farmers. Losing a cow could just about destroy a family economically. The Americans and the South Vietnamese government tried to pay farmers who lost cows due to the fighting. Some families had actually been paid more for the accidental killing of a water buffalo than for the accidental killing of family members.

The writing was on the wall. Two serious contacts within ten days. Each patrol and each ambush started plotting out escape routes back to the village in case they ran into more than they could handle. The P.F.'s tightened security around the village. Jessie called in more H&I fire than ever before. The Marines continued to train the P.F.'s, and they were becoming good soldiers. Downright trustworthy. Each night, Jessie, a radioman, the Corpsman, and one P.F. would make up the C.P. group. The nightly procedure was to set the command post up in a different hooch inside the village or just outside the main village area. From the C.P., the Marines and P.F.'s forming the night ambush would take off, making it impossible for V.C. spies to know where the ambush or the C.P. was located. Villagers said nothing when the Marines and P.F.'s showed up after dark to take over their hooch, but they were not real happy about it.

Daylight hours were spent helping the villagers. September marked the beginning of a new project. The CAP Marines started building a village hospital over a year earlier but had never finished the job, because the last sergeant in command had decided he didn't like work. Since then, all of the materials had been stolen by the Vietnamese, and Jessie had to requisition everything that would be needed. The plywood came overland with Army trucks escorted by Dusters. Dusters were vicious little vehicles, resembling half-tracks with twin 40mm guns on top. Jessie tried to convince more than one Army lieutenant that they should park one of the Dusters in the ville permanently, but the answer was no.

While the Marines worked on the medical building each day, Doc Whistle trained three Vietnamese women and two men in basic first aid. Slowly but surely they began to build up stocks of medical supplies, and it was not long before the village had a pretty good little hospital. By American standards it would barely pass as a first aid center, but the people were very proud of it when it was finished. The village chief performed a tribal ceremony in front of the place on the first day it opened for business, and many of the women brought food and tea for the Marines, who were the guests of honor.

When the celebration was over, the Marines could not help but feel satisfied, maybe even a little proud. They were not usually much for sentiment, but they were touched by the gratitude of the villagers. The new medical facility even got to treat its first patients during the celebration. Sammy Paul and Jimbo brought two kids to the opening who needed treatment for minor infections. They were orphans, a boy and a girl who looked about ten years old. Their parents had been killed by the V.C. a few weeks earlier on the outskirts of the village. Sammy Paul and Jimbo had made a habit of looking after the kids ever since.

The festivities ended around dusk. The Marines headed back to the CAP compound and started getting ready for the first night ambush. Jessie finished cleaning his shotgun and was giving the PRC-25 a final check before calling the men into formation.

"Gunny."

He turned to see Sammy Paul and Jimbo standing side by side. Jimbo rubbed at his acne-scarred face as if he were trying to say something but didn't know how.

"Speak up, Marine."

Sammy Paul scratched at his two-day beard. "Look, Gunny . . ."

Jimbo cleared his throat. "We was wonderin', Gunny . . ."

"What is it?" Jessie barked impatiently.

"Well," Sammy Paul began again, "how would a person—"

"A Marine person," Jimbo added.

"Yeah," Sammy said. "A Marine person. How would a Marine person go about—"

"That is, if such a Marine person wanted to do this," Jimbo added.

Jessie groaned and shook his head. "What do you men—you Marine persons—want to know?"

They looked at each other and began to fidget, then tried hopelessly to act nonchalant.

Sammy Paul shrugged. "We was just curious about how people went about adopting kids."

"Yeah. If somebody ever wanted to," Jimbo said matter-of-factly.

"Yeah, Gunny."

Jessie was stunned. He started to laugh but caught himself and cleared his throat. He put on a serious expression.

This should be treated with proper respect. He smiled at the two goofy-looking young men.

"I'm not completely sure of all the red tape, gentlemen. But if you're serious, I would be happy to inquire."

"Hey, thanks, Gunny!" Sammy blurted out excitedly, then tried to act calm. "You know, if you got time."

Jimbo leaned closer to Gunnery Sergeant Slate. "And, Gunny . . ." he said quietly.

"Yes, Jimbo?"

Jimbo nodded at the Marines who were preparing for the ambush. "Maybe you shouldn't say . . ."

"This is no one's business but yours, mister."

They both looked surprised.

"Thanks. Thanks a lot, Gunny," Sammy Paul said.

"Yeah. Thanks, Gunny."

"No sweat. Let's get saddled up."

"Aye aye," Jimbo said.

They walked away with silly grins on their faces. A warm feeling went through Jessie. He was proud of these guys. They were not really all that different from the boys who used to sing "Don't Sit Under the Apple Tree with Anyone Else But Me." Different slang. Home life not as good on the whole. But Marines all the way. He'd stand beside them any time, anywhere, and there was still no better way to die than to die a Marine.

They waited until after dark, then moved into a hooch on the far side of the village to set up the C.P. The hooch sat at the base of the O.P. George mountain and right at the edge of the village limits in that direction. It was on slightly higher ground than the rest of the ville, so observation was better than usual for the C.P. The family that lived there did not seem too shocked at seeing the CAP Marines moving in with radios and weapons. Jessie pulled the Kit Carson scout aside and told him to relay to the papa-san that it was normal procedure and would only be for one night. They should sleep in their bunker tonight. Every hooch had a bunker dug below it or beside it for family protection. They were dark and damp and miserable, but the Vietnamese people had long ago adjusted to such horrible living conditions. They had no choice.

Jessie awoke to the crackle of static on the PRC-25.

"Gunslinger One, this is Gunslinger Two . . ."

Jessie blinked the sleep out of his eyes and grabbed the field phone. He checked his watch. "Gunslinger Two, this is Gunslinger One . . . over."

"We're getting ready to come back in."

Jessie checked his watch again. "You're late. It's 0430 hours."

"We thought we saw something. Did not pan out."

"Roger."

Twenty minutes later a green flare shot out of the black jungle and into the moonlit sky, signaling the return of the second ambush. Most of the men were asleep. Jessie was awake enough to see the flare but quickly drifted back to that surrealistic zone between sleep and consciousness. Was something tapping his shoulder or was he dreaming? He opened his eyes. The Kit Carson scout stood over him, holding a carbine.

"What do you want, Vhan?"

"Dee-dee-mow!" he said, and held his crotch.

"Head call?"

"Yes."

"Go on." Jessie looked around to see who was on watch. Eight Ball was sitting upright a few feet away with his M-16 across his lap. "Make sure you tell Eight Ball so he won't blow you away," he whispered.

Vhan nodded and walked over to Eight Ball, whispered something and headed out away from the hooch. Jessie laid his head back and closed his eyes again. A few minutes passed, and he heard voices in the direction Vhan had gone. Returning ambush, he thought. He sprang up. The voices were Vietnamese. Suddenly, the familiar fire of the old M-1 carbine opened up. It was instantly answered by the cracking of Russian AK-47s. Every Marine jumped up, grabbing for weapons. The village began exploding.

A solitary figure came huffing toward them out of the darkness.

"Don't shoot!" Jessie shouted. "It's Vhan!"

The Kit Carson scout slid in beside him, breathing as hard as a man could. "V.C.! NVA! NVA!"

"Calm down, Vhan!" Jessie shook him hard.

"NVA!"

"How many?"

"Many many! They think I villager! Ask where Marines are!"

Suddenly, a voice began shouting from the radio, "Gunslinger One! Gunslinger One! This is O.P. George! We're getting hit! Getting hit big-time!"

Jessie snatched up the field phone as he turned his gaze up the mountain behind them. Green tracer fire from enemy machine guns shot across the mountain from three directions. Red flares signaling an enemy attack shot into the night sky, lighting up the mountain.

Jessie turned and shouted at Eight Ball. "Who we got up there?"

"Philly and Gomez and five P.F's!"

Jessie brought the phone to his mouth. "O.P. George! Get off the line. I'm calling in preprogrammed strikes!"

"Roger! Out!"

The sound of automatic fire came through clearly over the phone. Jessie screamed into the mouthpiece, "O.P. George, this is Gunslinger One! O.P. George! Are you there?"

The static got worse and Jessie could barely stand listening. Then Philly began shouting over the phone again.

"I'm hit, Gunny. They shot the antenna in half. Everyone is hit! Got two dead gooks laying here in the bunker!"

"I'm calling in arty! Hang on! We're getting hit here too!"

Jessie worked the radio as fast as possible, but his hands

were shaking so badly that he felt more clumsy than usual. Bullets began flying all around.

"Hold your fire, Marines! Make sure you know what you're shootin'! The gooks don't know where we are yet!"

He fumbled with his map case as the static over the field phone was interrupted by the calm voice of an Army artillery officer.

"This is Iron Hand One ... go ahead Gunslinger ... over."

"This is Gunslinger Nine! Fire the on-calls! Preprogrammed coordinates! Fire for effect! We're being overrun!"

"Affirmative, Gunslinger Nine. Adjust fire as needed. I'm listening."

Jessie turned and shouted at Doc Whistle, "Get over here! Hold this flashlight over the map! I can't see."

Doc Whistle rushed over beside Jessie as a cacophony of explosions and automatic gunfire erupted from all around the village. A flare went up, bursting an eerie flickering light over the ville. From their position on slightly higher ground, Jessie and the Corpsman could see North Vietnamese Regulars wearing pith helmets and packs running through the village shooting everything. Hooches began exploding all over as the NVA soldiers tossed grenades into each home. They were slaughtering the villagers. Agonizing screams filled the air. They still hadn't pinpointed the Marine positions. The men were in a semicircle a few yards in front of the hooch. Suddenly, they opened up with withering automatic M-16 fire on a squad of NVA that ran out of the darkness and came straight ahead. Every NVA fell dead. The Marine fire went silent.

"Gunny! Gunny!"

Jessie looked to his left. Sammy Paul and Jimbo jumped to the ground beside him, with Jimbo's flat face only inches from his own. His eyes were filled with terror, and he seemed unable to catch his breath.

"Gunny!"

"What is it?"

"We . . . we put the kids in the CAP compound! We put 'em in the C.P. bunker!"

Jessie's heart sank into his stomach, but he shook off the feeling and mustered an order. "Get back to your position, Marine!"

"But Gunny! The gooks are hitting the CAP compound!" Jimbo screamed into Jessie's face and huge tears began falling from his eyes.

Sammy Paul crawled on top of Jimbo to look Jessie in the eyes. His face was a mask of pain.

"Gunny! It's the kids! They're getting killed!"

"Shut up and get back to your position! Let me call in arty. Maybe we can save them! Move it!" Jessie yelled with as much furor as he could fake at the moment.

Both men looked stunned, then reluctantly low-crawled back to their positions. Jessie felt his heart pounding with fear, but the only emotion he recognized was sorrow. He slapped himself hard in the face as the firing in the village raged.

He turned to Doc. "Stay with me and keep that flashlight handy." He turned and shouted, "Marines! Get back to the hooch!"

The men moved back cautiously to the hooch and crouched down around Jessie.

"Follow me. They might have heard that M-16 fire. Let's get our backs up against those rocks! That'll cover our rear, and maybe we can make a stand there!" Jessie finished shouting the order as he began to move in a crouch toward the base of O.P. George where the hill met the outskirts of the village. The platoon set up quickly, and the M-60 began working right away as another group of six NVA soldiers walked right into Marine fire. They were cut down before they could fire back. The NVA continued running around the village, killing everything they saw. More flares shot into the sky, but the enemy still had not located the Marine position in all of the confusion. Jessie directed the arty fire toward a large concentration of enemy troops near the main road, probably a klick and half away from them. They appeared to be setting up mortar positions.

"Fire for effect!" he shouted into the field phone as he studied the map, his shaking finger guiding his eyes. The Army officer remained cool.

"Hold on, Gunslinger Nine . . . firing . . . Outgoing mail coming your way . . . stand by."

The whistles of incoming 155 artillery rounds had never sounded better to Jessie in his whole life. The ripping explosions sent blue and white sparks into the air with each terrific blast. The enemy mortar positions completely disappeared. Jessie snapped his eyes back to the map and began reading new coordinates off to the Army officer.

Suddenly, a hail of AK-47 fire began singing off of the rocks and thudding into the ground all around the Marine positions at the base of O.P. George. Eckert returned fire with the M-60. His fire looked effective and the incoming fire stopped momentarily. Jessie leaned closer to the map. Another blast of incoming bullets ripped into the ground and ricocheted off the rocks all around them. Doc Whistle fell back dead with a head shot. The flashlight landed beside him, its beam pointing directly at the big bloody hole in his forehead, oozing dark-looking blood.

"They're moving up on us, Gunny!" someone yelled in a panic-stricken voice.

"Over here!"

"Get some fire over here!"

Jessie looked to their right. Pith-helmeted NVA were moving in on them in squad-size groups, leapfrogging one squad at a time while the other two squads laid down cover fire. These were not cadre V.C. troops. These were NVA Regulars. Jessie snatched up the radio and started shouting new coordinates to bring fire in on the advancing enemy.

"That is your position, is it not, Gunslinger Nine? Repeat. Are you bringing fire in on your own position?"

Jessie lay flat on his stomach, listening as if in a trance

as the gunfire raged all around. The Army officer's voice was too calm to believe.

"Yes, Iron Hand . . . they are that close! Fire! Fire! Fire!"

The radio went silent for a few seconds. Jessie lifted his head to see the situation. The P.F.'s were fighting back all around the village; he could tell by the sound of their carbines. Groups of NVA fired into every hooch they came across, and he knew many civilians were dying in the village.

"Shooting. Outgoing mail now, Gunslinger Nine . . . Get your heads down," the voice crackled over the phone.

Jessie turned and shouted to the Marines on his right. "Incoming! Incoming! Incoming!"

A couple of seconds later the first whistles began to grow louder, more shrill as they neared, going silent with a loud rush of air just before impact. Jessie buried his face and waited for the blast. The ground shook from the horrific explosion that brought with it screams from enemy troops no more than forty meters to the right of the Marine positions.

"That's it, Iron Hand! That's it! Fire for effect!" Jessie screamed into the phone as explosions began tearing up the earth, spraying rocks and debris everywhere. He peeked up high enough to see the action. Two sets of green tracers were pouring into the village from a small knoll just east of the main road about fifty meters from the main gate. He flipped on the flashlight and fingered the map until he pinpointed the coordinates.

"Iron Hand! Iron Hand! Put a Willie Peter on these coordinates! . . ."

Three more rounds landed close. Jessie tightened his stomach muscles to keep from wetting his trousers. Rocks thudded to the ground all around them with back-breaking vibrations. The whistles stopped for a few moments.

"Firing now . . . Gunslinger Nine. Shoot!"

Jessie lifted his head to look for the white phosphorous spotter round. Two red flares shot up, one right after the other, on different sides of the ville. All at once the chaotic battle went silent, as if every man on both sides was reloading at the same time. The sounds of another firefight broke out on the top of O.P. George. Jessie looked up. Tracers and grenade explosions flashed all around the Marine outpost. God, I hope they can hold on, he mumbled as the whistle of an incoming artillery round drew his attention back to the village. A popping explosion was followed by the white mushroom cloud of a Willie Peter round. "Iron Hand . . . Iron Hand . . . this is Gunslinger Nine!"

"Affirmative, Gunslinger Nine . . . How was that?"

"Drop one klick!"

"Affirmative . . . drop one klick . . . Shooting . . ."

A few seconds later another mushroom cloud rose above the knoll where the enemy machine guns were beginning to open fire again.

"Outstanding! Right on target! Fire for effect! H.E!"

Within thirty seconds the knoll erupted as if ten small volcanoes came up out of the earth at the same time. The enemy machine guns went silent.

"Gunny!"

Jessie turned to see Corporal Fowler sliding in beside him. Flares glistened off of his sweaty face, and his eyes were huge with excitement and fear.

"What is it?"

"The second ambush is missing! You could be calling arty in on them!"

"It can't be helped! You know that! What's your situation? How many wounded?"

Corporal Fowler was staring hypnotically at the dead Corpsman lying behind them.

Jessie punched him hard on the arm. "Snap out of it, Marine! I said how many men are wounded?"

"I think just Eckert."

"Bad?"

"No!"

Jessie snatched up the field phone again and switched the channel to the Forward Air Controller at Chu Lai.

"Rainman One ... Rainman One ... this is Gunslinger Nine ... Do you copy?"

"Gunslinger Nine ... this is Rainman One ... We copy ... over."

"Rainman One ... we are being overrun by a company-size element of NVA Regulars! Send anything you can get!"

"I copy, Gunslinger Nine ... You must hold out until daybreak ... Do you copy?"

"Affirmative, Rainman One ... I copy ... but I don't know if the gooks will oblige that!"

"Gunslinger Nine ... Gunslinger Nine ... this is Rainman ... Will have gunships on line at daybreak ... You must hold on ... Do you copy?"

"Affirmative, Rainman! The sun should be up in ..." Jessie checked his wristwatch, then looked at the graying horizon. "... twenty to thirty minutes ... Do you copy?"

"Affirmative, Gunslinger Nine ... You will have Hummingbirds overhead in twenty minutes ... Rainman out!"

Jessie checked the skyline again.

"What is it, Gunny?" Fowler asked.

Jessie turned to face the corporal lying on his stomach beside him. "If we can hold out till daybreak, we got air support coming!"

"Fixed wing?"

"Don't know, don't care!"

"Where's Puff at?"

"Don't know! Go tell the men we got air support coming at the first crack of daylight."

"Aye aye, Gunny!"

Corporal Fowler started to rise up just as a barrage of enemy fire sprayed the hillside above their heads. He ducked back down. Enemy AK fire shot into their positions from the left flank. Suddenly, more fire came on them from straight ahead. The Marines returned fire with every weapon they had, and the enemy fire subsided for a moment. Jessie lifted up just as a shadowy figure rose from the weeds fifteen meters forward of his position and reared back to throw a grenade. He pumped out two quick blasts from the twelve-gauge and the shadow disappeared. A moment later the bright flash of a Chicom grenade exploded near where the shadow had been. Jessie rose up and fired four more shots straight ahead, then ducked back down. He fumbled for more shells, but his fingers were stiff with fear, and getting the shells out of the bandoleer seemed to take forever.

Fowler opened fire at muzzle flashes on their left flank. Bullets ricocheted off the rocks all around them, and for an instant Jessie wondered if he should have led the men to this spot. They could be killed by ricochets with so many rocks. He shoved shells into the shotgun as fast as his fingers could work, dropping at least one shell for each one he managed get loaded. The radio crackled with an urgency. "Gunslinger Nine . . . this is O.P. George . . . Do you copy?"

Jessie grabbed the field phone. "Go ahead, O.P. George. What's your situation?"

"Three P.F.'s dead . . . me and A.C. wounded . . . Repeat, three KIA and two WIA . . ." The static got too bad to hear, then cleared again for a moment. "They got inside the bunker, but we killed 'em!" The static got worse.

"You are breaking up, O.P. George . . . cannot copy . . . Hold on! We have air support coming! . . . Hold on! . . . Air support coming at daybreak! . . . Do you copy, O.P. George?"

The static crackled over the phone. Jessie turned to Fowler. "Three of the P.F.'s are dead and both Marines wounded. That leaves them with two able-bodied men."

"Want me to lead a squad up the hill?"

Jessie shook his head. "No. It's too late. They're holding for now. We got support coming." He looked toward the skyline again. Faint silhouettes of mountains were visible.

He checked his watch, his hand shook so bad it was hard to read. "It's 0600. Little after."

"Ten minutes we'll have light!"

"Ten or fifteen."

"Where are those gunships?"

A spray of machine-gun fire ripped overhead, whining off the rocks in all directions. Jessie buried his face in the dirt. Then he looked to his left and came almost nose-to-nose with Corporal Fowler.

"Got any frags?"

The corporal felt his cartridge belt and cargo pockets. He slapped his flak jacket. "I count four."

"I got three."

"Get down!" Fowler screamed, and shoved down on Jessie's helmet so hard that it felt like it busted his nose. The sizzling sound of an incoming rocket ripped by overhead and exploded on the side of the mountain. Debris stung the backs of Jessie's legs. He lifted his face and blinked to regain his vision from the bright flash. He was not sure if he saw movement or if his eyes had not yet readjusted, but he brought the shotgun to his shoulder and aimed at a shadowy blob that seemed to be moving twenty meters out. He fired and the recoil hurt. He growled angrily at himself, knowing that he should have held the butt tighter against his shoulder. The other Marines opened up. Then the M-60 began to talk its talk, and somewhere out there an enemy soldier screamed and kept screaming.

"We got to hold on for ten more minutes!" Jessie shouted into the startled corporal's face.

"Ready?" Corporal Fowler held a grenade in his right hand and put his left forefinger in the ring.

Jessie felt for a grenade on his cartridge belt. He found it and pulled it off. He brought it up in front of his face. The light of another red flare floated down under its tiny parachute somewhere over the village. Now he could see Fowler's face clearly. Chunks of dirt stuck to the sweat beading on it, and the eyes were still wild with stress. Jessie knew that he must look the same way to Fowler. He forced himself to grin.

"Now isn't this better than being bored to death?"

Fowler blinked as if unable to understand, then a hint of recognition came from his eyes. He gave a nervous smile and a quick nod but seemed unable to comment.

"All right," Jessie said, trying to sound calm. "Pull the pin."

They pulled the pins, staring into each other's eyes from no more than a foot apart.

"Ready? Now."

They let the spoons fly.

"One thousand one, one thousand two!" They both lifted up and threw, then flattened out again. The explosions were nearly simultaneous. The gunfire all around the battlefield went silent for a few seconds. Groans from dying men could be heard clearly through the night air. Suddenly, the distant popping of chopper rotors came from the direction of Chu Lai. Jessie strained to see the first chopper. The skyline was gray with dim streaks of yellow, and his heartbeat quickened with the hope of daybreak. Another round of artillery whistled overhead, then lit the village with brilliant explosions. The phone crackled with an Army officer's calm voice.

"Gunslinger Nine ... Gunslinger Nine ... this is Iron Hand ... over."

Jessie grabbed for the phone, took a quick look ahead then to the left and right, to make sure the enemy was not moving forward on their position.

"This is Gunslinger Nine ... go ahead, Iron Hand."

"Fire mission complete ... air strikes coming in on your targets ... Do you copy?"

"We copy, Iron Hand ... Good job ... Thanks, Mac ... you saved our lives, I think ... over."

"Semper Fi, jarhead ... over and out."

Jessie grinned and changed the frequency to find the chopper pilots now circling above.

"I see 'em!" someone shouted from his right.

"We got gunships above us!"

"Keep firing on the enemy!" Jessie yelled, then turned his attention back to the radio.

"Gunslinger Nine, this is Bird Dog ... Do you copy?"

"We copy, Bird Dog ... We got Charlie all over the ville, been going on for a while ... over."

"We copy, Gunslinger Nine ... What will be his probable route of egress ... over."

"Probably back across the Trabong River, Bird Dog ... Charlie must cross some open paddies to get there if he's in a hurry ... Do you copy?"

"I copy, Gunslinger ... and we got 'em crossing right now ... in the open and in a hurry ... over and out for now."

Visibility was good. Three Army Huey gunships and one of the new Cobras dove, firing rockets and machine guns at targets Jessie could not see because of trees and bush between the Marine positions and the paddies. The platoon sat up, taking shots at anything that moved as the NVA ran from the village like a bunch of roaches caught in the daylight. The gunships dove and circled and dove again, then two of them hovered over the paddies, firing at will, while the other two swept the area all the way to the river. The two choppers over the river flew up and down, occasionally opening fire. Jessie tuned in to listen as they called out commands to one another.

Fowler lifted up and called to the rest of the platoon a few feet away, "You guys should hear this! Those choppers caught 'em in the open and they got 'em crossing the river. They're blowin' ol' Charlie a new hole."

No one said anything.

"All right, let's saddle up!" Jessie called out. "We got four Marines unaccounted for. Let's find 'em."

"God, I forgot all about that last ambush," Fowler said. "Let's just hope they're alive."

"Better see if O.P. George is alive, Gunny."

The radio crackled with an incoming message, "This is O.P. George . . . Do you copy?"

Jessie looked at Fowler. "Alive."

The tired, dirty young Marine nodded.

Medevac choppers began arriving. The CAP Marines guided them to the largest concentration of casualties, but it was nearly hopeless. The slaughter was terrible. The NVA troops had fired on every living thing in the village. An hour after daybreak, an Army column of Dusters and trucks began arriving with more medical personnel, but even that did not help. The last ambush survived the massacre, thanks to the artillery. They were about to be wiped out when a barrage of 155s took out what appeared to be the better part of a platoon of NVA. Their bodies were in pieces and had been stacked into a pile not far from the schoolhouse. Marine casualties were remarkable. Doc Whistle was the only KIA. The two Marines on O.P. George were both wounded badly but lived. The P.F.'s lost twenty-four men, nineteen killed, and five wounded. The real horror was what had happened to the villagers, the innocent farmers. Over three hundred men, women, and children murdered. The enemy confirmed were 117 dead NVA and one prisoner.

The prisoner was a talkative little guy. He knew it was his only hope. The villagers still alive were going to kill him in a very special way if the Marines handed him over. Maybe that's why he was so full of information. He told the Kit Carson scout the whole plan. He said they were supposed to hit the O.P. and the returning ambush at the same time they hit the village. But they waited too long and lost coordination because the Marine's second ambush did not return on time. This caused the sappers hitting O.P. George to strike too soon, warning the returning ambush and the Marines in the village. He said they could not find the Marines during the entire battle and could not stop the artillery, as planned, by knocking out the radios. Then their officers became entangled in firefights and were unable to organize the retreat before daybreak. This allowed American helicopters to arrive.

CAP headquarters considered the episode a remarkable victory for fourteen Marines and thirty P.F.'s, but Jessie Slate found it hard to feel victorious, especially after Sammy and Jimbo pulled the bodies of the two little children out of the remains of the C.P. bunker. Huge tears rolled down both of their dirty faces as they carried the limp little bodies to a graveyard outside the ville.

Jessie led the platoon out to the graveyard, following the mourning Marines in a silent procession. They all took turns digging the grave while Sammy and Jimbo cleaned dried blood off the faces of the children. Jimbo insisted on putting them both into one body bag so they could be together. They finished building the little round mound on top of the grave, which is common to the Vietnamese, signifying return to the womb. John Eckert pulled out his Bible, and battle-weary men gathered around the grave as he read:

> "Thine eyes have seen my unformed substance;
> And in thy book they were all written,
> The days that were ordained for me,
> When as yet there was not one of them."

The 117 NVA bodies were thrown into a mass grave that the CAP unit dug by blowing up some captured munitions, satchel charges, and C-4s. About a week after the battle, the village animals started dying. No one was quite sure why. Jessie requested medicine for them. The Army flew it in, and the Marines had to give it to the animals with huge syringes. The villagers were grateful, but the animals continued to die. Jessie figured that the NVA had poisoned them somehow.

The Army brought in some Dusters with the big twin-fortys mounted, enough firepower to stop a regiment. A week after that, a reaction force from Chu Lai replaced the

CAP unit and the men said their good-byes, as each was heading in a different direction. Some of the short-timers were put in supply until their tours were up. Others were shipped off to another CAP unit.

Captain Roberts wrote Jessie up for a Navy Commendation Medal, and the South Vietnamese awarded him with the Vietnamese Cross of Gallantry. He asked the captain to make sure that the men who held on at O.P. George got the same thing. For a month afterward, Captain Roberts kept Jessie in Chu Lai to train new CAP volunteers and check out all the other CAP units, making sure that each was running aggressive patrols and ambushes.

By the time his hitch with the Combined Action Group was up, it was early October and time for R&R with Charlie. Keeping the boy off his mind had been impossible, and not a day went by that some anxious thought went through his mind, bringing on a sick, empty feeling in the pit of his stomach. It would be wonderful seeing his boy. When Captain Roberts handed him a muddy-looking envelope, he figured Charlie was confirming their date.

"Lieutenant Slate?" Captain Roberts said with a raised eyebrow.

"My boy." Jessie couldn't hide his pride.

"I didn't know you had a boy over here!"

"Yes, sir. Fifth Marines."

"No kiddin'! Outstanding. Must make a man pretty darn proud, Gunny."

"Yes, sir. It does."

"Think it would be a little frightening sometimes."

"All the time."

"Is he a grunt lieutenant?"

Jessie nodded yes.

Captain Roberts sighed. "Yeah. See what you mean."

"Do you mind, sir?"

"Of course not, Gunny. I'd be anxious too."

Jessie tore open the letter.

Dear Dad,

Been looking forward to this for what feels like forever! Telling you I can't do it is really hard, but I know that you will understand. Old Timmy is here beside me as I write this letter. He's gonna owe me big-time for the rest of his life for what the sucker has talked me into. It's a long story, but the gist of it is this: old Timmy's knocked his girlfriend up, and she's pretty upset. They're in love and were going to get married anyway, but Tim can't keep his mind on his job. He's gonna get himself killed out here if he doesn't square away.

So to make a long story short, I've given him my R&R slot, so he can go to Hawaii and marry her. She's already arranged to meet him there, and I think it's the right thing to do. I know this is a bummer for you, Dad. I'm really sorry, but I also knew you would understand. I love you, Dad. I've changed a lot in the last few months. You were right, each day feels like a week, and each month feels like a year. I feel so old sometimes that I think I'm catching up to you! Ha ha. No offense, old man.

I don't have a new date yet. Will let you know when I get one, but you should probably keep yours. I don't know when I'll finally get out of here. We have taken some casualties lately, and with all of the new boots, I feel bad leaving them. Guess this is it for now. Sorry, Dad.

Semper Fi,
Charlie

"That doesn't look like good news, Gunny," Captain Roberts said. The captain's voice sounded like it was coming out of a drum. Memories of Vella Lavella swarmed over Jessie. He tried to say something to the captain, but his mouth felt too dry to form a word. He cleared his throat.

"He can't make it."

"Oh, no! I'm sorry to hear that, Gunny. What's the problem?"

Jessie stared straight ahead. "His buddy knocked up some girl and has to get married. He gave him his R and R slot."

"Sounds like you raised a pretty good boy, Gunnery Sergeant Slate."

Fear gripped at Jessie's stomach like a vise. He managed a nod and mumbled, "Thank you, sir."

"I know how disappointed you must be. If there's anything I can do to help, let me know."

Jessie blinked himself out of his trance and looked at the tall man with the kind face. "There is, sir."

"Name it, Gunny. After the job you've done here, I'd like to do something for you."

"I'm supposed to be reassigned to the Seventh Marine Battalion Landing Team after my R and R."

"Yes."

"I'd like to get back to the BLT right away. I want to move my R and R to another date."

"Go get saddled up, Gunnery Sergeant Slate. I'll have your orders ready and a taxi when you get back."

■■■

CHAPTER TWENTY-NINE

Being back aboard ship was not quite the same as an R&R, but at least it was a clean bunk at night and hot food. Jessie made his way from the flight deck straight to the old man's quarters. Lieutenant Colonel Rockey seemed glad that he was back.

"Couldn't have come at a better time, Gunny!"

"Thank you, sir. But I'm here to ask permission to visit my son with the Fifth Marines."

"Can't do it, Gunny."

"Yes, sir," Jessie said grimly.

"We got a big op taking off tomorrow. You might just meet up with your boy on it."

"Sir?"

"Operation Mameluke Thrust and Allen Brook. I'm filling you in personally because it looks like you might be taking out your old platoon, the first."

"What happened to Lieutenant Kutler?"

"Emergency leave."

Lieutenant Colonel Rockey pointed at a map on the wall. "We're going back into the Arizona Territory."

Jessie gave a knowing groan. "What part, sir?"

"Dodge City."

Jessie whistled.

"I know, I know. Injun country. This op is directly related to the objectives of the Le Loi Campaign. Dodge City is about ten miles south of Da Nang. It's a quadrilateral bounded on the south by the Ky Lam River, on the north by the smaller La Tho River, and on the east by Highway One. The western boundary of the operation is the old railroad line. Hill 55 is here in the northeast corner; the ARVN fort and district headquarters at Dien Ban is at the southeast corner. Route 4 bisects the area from east to west. In all it's about five miles wide and three miles deep."

"Yes, sir."

"You are familiar with the area, Gunny?"

"Yes, sir. It's low ground, crisscrossed with rivers and streams."

"Yes. And honeycombed with caves and tunnels."

"Each ville is a potential fort. They have bamboo and thorn hedges and big drainage ditches around each one."

"The 27th Marines, with their command post at Liberty Bridge, have been moving two battalions around like a checkerboard in the Go Noi Island territory. They met an NVA battalion at My Loc, three miles northeast of An Hoa. Then they moved north of the Thu Bon into Dodge City to cover Hill 55 and the Seventh Marines. They had a sharp fight two miles south of the hill. On August sixteenth the Fifth Marines launched a sweep eastward from An Hoa in part of Operation Mameluke Thrust. They pushed the NVA into BLT Two/Seven, who had a blocking position set up. It was a turkey shoot. Now here, east of the Mameluke Thrust area near Hoi An, your old sidekick hit a nest of 'em with the Korean Marines."

"Broken Wing?"

"Yep."

Jessie looked at the map as if seeing it all for the first time. It was uncanny. Fate had put Broken Wing, Swift Eagle, Charlie, and himself into the same battleground. That, combined with the circumstances that caused Charlie to give up his R&R, left Jessie with a peculiar feeling. It was almost like he was watching a movie unfold before him. In this story he knew all the main characters but had no clue as to what was happening. The first tinge of worry was already scratching at his insides.

"*A-chi yeh-hes,*" he mumbled aloud.

"What was that, Sergeant?"

"Intestines itch."

"What?"

"Oh. Sorry, sir. Just thinking out loud."

Things felt like they were moving too fast and out of his control. A message from higher up cut the meeting with Lieutenant Colonel Rockey short. Jessie made his way belowdecks to reunite with the platoon. The walk through the ship felt like a dream. In fact, the whole situation felt like a dream. A very uncomfortable dream.

When he reached the squad bay, he was happy to see that most of the men were still with the outfit. They seemed glad to have an old salt in charge. Even Swift Eagle smiled. Jessie gathered the platoon together.

"All right, lads, let's get you squared away."

"Big op, Gunny?" Barry Morse, the M-79 blooper man, asked as he moved closer to hear.

"The operation sounds big, but there's going to be plenty of air support. Artillery from Hill 55, which means the big 175mm self-propelled guns, in addition to the normal 105s and 155s."

"Where we going, Gunny?" Pollock, the big farm boy from Wisconsin, shouted from the back of the compartment.

"Yeah, you didn't say where, Gunny," Sally said.

"Arizona Territory."

A nervous tremor went through the room. Jessie could feel the tension level rise.

"How soon?" Tall asked, rubbing his hand down his long face.

"Yeah, Gunny. What's the word?" Fat echoed beside Tall.

"Maybe forty-eight hours."

For the next two days Jessie watched the tension grow. Everyone tried to get a last letter out. Men's hands shook when they played cards, and some of the guys were making out wills and searching out the chaplain. At 0400 hours on the second morning, the ship's intercom crackled with the order for the Marines to assemble with 782 gear below the flight deck. That meant everything from packs and helmets to web gear and canteens. They issued the 3.5 rocket launcher, better known as the bazooka. No one liked seeing that thing. There had been some scuttlebutt about Russian tanks, but the chances of running into them seemed remote. Carrying ammo for a 3.5 was a total pain in the butt. You had to tie shoestrings to two big rounds and hang them around your neck, cushioned by one of the green towels that each man carried. By the end of a week in the bush, you'd be lucky to have any skin left on the back of your neck.

"Prepare to board!" Those words dismissed all other thoughts and took every man's mind off of his heavy load. Jessie noticed that Colonel Rockey was on deck as the men boarded the choppers. He gave him one last salute, which the colonel answered sharply, then followed it with a thumbs-up.

"Think it'll be a hot LZ, Gunny?" PFC Justice Pimpkin shouted over the prop wash as they lifted off the deck of the *Ogden*.

Jessie looked at the kid with the Opie face, and for an ugly moment knew that the kid would die today. He looked away. The sun came up over the LZ as the choppers began to flare out and dip by the stern. Marines ran down the ramp. There was no incoming fire. The men moved into a quick perimeter to await orders. The loneliest feeling in the world was the quiet that remained after the choppers dropped you off and flew away.

The hump started immediately. The plan called for E Company to work the enemy into the hands of Gulf and Fox companies, which was supposed to push the NVA into elements of the Fifth Marines' blocking action. Mouth the radioman stayed close to Jessie as they moved out. Mouth was all right, Jessie thought. Perfect for a radioman because he spoke so fast. Said he had to because he came from a family of eleven.

Barry and Moose were still alive and arguing. Justice Pimkin hung around Barry and Moose a lot, since his buddy Gonzales had been killed. He looked more like a Marine now. Tall and Fat were still together, but Sally's A-gunner, Pale, had stepped on a booby trap. Sally said the explosion was real quiet and sort of small, but it killed him. Doc Rice was still around, and it was good to have him.

After three days into the op, no contact had been made. Jessie, monitoring the radio every now and then, could hear the voice of Delta Two Actual calling in coordinates. Just hearing his son's voice filled him with hope and dread. On the third day, the second squad came across a bunch of abandoned bunkers. The gooks had left in a hurry, leaving behind some equipment, including an RDP machine gun with about a thousand rounds of ammo. This was amusing to the men. They named the poor slob who left the machine gun after carrying it all the way from North Vietnam Ralph. Everyone had a guess as to what old Ralph was doing about now. One thing for certain: old Ralph was in a world of crap with his C.O.

At the end of the third day, the platoon was told to stop and set up a perimeter near a fairly wide river. That night a heavy firefight erupted from someplace in the distance, maybe two thousand meters on the other side of the river. The call for a hundred percent alert came down from above, and Jessie passed the word to each man personally as he checked positions. It took forever to see daylight, but when it came, it felt great.

Before the men could down some C-ration breakfast, word came over the PRC-25 to saddle up and cross the river to the company's front. Jessie's first platoon was ordered across first. The second and third squads deployed on the flanks to give cover as the first and fourth squads crossed the river. It was about chest deep at the crossing point. The bank on the other side was baked gray-brown and looked steep.

"Spread out. Pass the word," Jessie growled at the Marine in back of him. The water felt cool, almost pleasant, but crossing a river was the most vulnerable feeling you could get in a war. Nowhere to run and nowhere to hide. You couldn't even duck down. It looked to be about thirty yards wide here. Jungle foliage was not bad but was still thick enough to hide the better part of a regiment on the other side.

Swift Eagle got across first and scampered up the embankment. He held his M-16 out to the man behind him and pulled him up. It took about ten minutes for the first two squads to set up covering positions for the next two squads to cross. Jessie waved, and the second squad started across the river. At the halfway mark, all hell broke loose. The water was white with the froth of bullets hitting. Marines dropped. Men went limp in the water. Others screamed for Corpsmen.

"Return fire!"

"Fire!"

The incoming fire was so heavy that the Marines could not peek above the dirt embankment. Men held their weapons above their heads and fired full automatic. Jessie pumped off six quick shotgun blasts, then turned and shouted, "Mouth up!"

Mouth came crawling over to him. Jessie pulled out his map and tried to get a fix on their position. An odd slapping sound pulled his eyes off of the map for a moment. Mouth fell back dead with a head shot. Jessie grabbed the young radioman and pulled him close, but he knew it was over for the Marine. A clean, round hole was in his forehead just above his right eye, which was still open. Jessie laid the Marine down gently and tried to regroup his thoughts. The firing was as heavy as any he had heard. It

sounded like training camp when the boots were told to fire
Final Protective Fire. That was when all was hopeless and
you shot everything you had to stop the enemy. The Marines in the second squad who were not killed had made it
back to the other side of the river, but the incoming fire
seemed to be getting heavier. Jessie pulled the blood-
covered radio off Mouth's limp body and got the skipper on
the net.

"Repeat! The firing is too heavy to hear you!"

"Stay put!" came the reply. Jessie slammed the phone
into the dirt. He snatched it back up and called in artillery
as fast as he could. A few minutes later the first whistles of
incoming rounds broke through the chaotic noise of automatic weapons fire. The first spotter round was too far
north. Jessie dropped the fire by a klick.

"Fire again."

The spotter was on target.

Just then, Sally screamed. He fell back with a bullet in
the eye. Doc Rice ran to help and was cut down. He wasn't
moving and looked dead.

"Gunny, we got a .51 cal rifle picking us off!"

Jessie held the field phone to his mouth and screamed,
"Fire for effect!"

Soon the earth trembled with falling artillery shells. Jessie peeked over the embankment. He could see NVA soldiers with pith helmets and packs scurrying around trying
to find cover from the incoming artillery. The blasts were
horrific and the screams of enemy soldiers became louder.
Jessie peeked over the embankment again. An NVA soldier
ran into the open about fifty meters away carrying an
AK-47 in one hand, but the other arm was a bloody stump.
He would never live through the day, Jessie thought. Two
more Marines took wounds on the left flank.

"Gunny! We got fire coming in on the left flank!"

Marines across the river opened up on the enemy, slow-
ing the incoming fire from the left flank. Suddenly, four
Ontos vehicles appeared on the ridge above the opposite

bank and opened fire on the NVA. Their fire was brutal. Each vehicle had six 106 recoilless rifles attached to an armored carrier. Within seconds the Ontos vehicles received hits from an onslaught of enemy fire. Two of the vehicles looked damaged as they pulled back out of sight. The enemy fire was tremendous.

Toward the afternoon, the artillery let up and close air support came in from left to right with strafing runs and napalm. Air Force F-4C jets ripped by so close that Jessie could hear the sound of the mechanism opening that slowed the bomb down and gave the jet time to clear the blast. Three more F-4Cs swept in behind the first, dropping snake-eye bombs. It looked like a thousand little bombs going off one after the other, until no one could possibly survive. He peeked over the ridge of dirt that was keeping him alive. Another jet ripped by in front of the Marine line. Something exploded in its tail, and it started trailing black smoke. It climbed, but lost power and headed back toward the earth. Jessie could see a parachute floating down as the plane crashed a couple of klicks away.

The radio crackled, "Echo One . . . Echo One . . . This is Echo Two . . . over."

"Go ahead, Echo Two . . . over."

"Move your men back on my command . . ."

"Affirmative, Echo Two."

". . . Wait for the green star cluster and make your bird, Gunny!"

Jessie took a deep breath. "Affirmative, Echo Actual . . . over." He looked around at what was left of the first squad.

"What do you think we ran into, Gunny?"

Jessie turned to see who was speaking. Justice Pimkin stared up at him with tears in his eyes. Somebody had dragged the country boy up next to him. Justice Pimkin's face was ashen with that hollow expression of death that was so familiar to Jessie.

"How bad you hit, Pimkin?"

"Don't know, Gunny. But I'm colder'n a ol' maid in January."

"Hang on. We'll be all right. We got air strikes coming in."

"Am I gonna die, Gunny?"

"Naw. You're just gonna get a Purple Heart to show your girl back in the world. What was her name, Pimkin? Sally Rotten Crotch?"

Justice Pimkin smiled and closed his eyes. Heavy enemy fire continued. Jessie monitored the radio traffic and watched Justice Pimkin go to sleep and die. There was nothing he could do to help except stick the dying boy with morphine. Messages came over the PRC-25 in bunches. A familiar-sounding voice came over the net calling for Charlie Rose's platoon. "Delta Two ... Delta Two ... this is Blue Dragon ..."

Jessie turned and shouted down the line of Marines burrowed against an embankment, "Corporal Swift Eagle! Your daddy is on the net! He's close by!"

Swift Eagle signaled a thumbs-up but kept his head down and said nothing. Jessie listened closer.

"Blue Dragon ... this is Delta Two ... over."

"Roger, Delta Two ... we hear small arms fire and are approaching from your right flank at approximately two hundred meters ... do you copy, Delta Two?"

"We copy, Blue Dragon."

"Is this Delta Two Actual?"

"Negative, Blue Dragon ... Delta Two Actual is down ... We reached the downed pilot, but medevacs cannot land at this time ... Do you copy?"

Jessie clutched the field phone to his ear and tried to block out the chaos around him. His heart felt as if it had stopped, but blood rushed through his ears like a raging river. Delta Two Actual was down. That was the code name for the second platoon leader of Delta Company First Battalion, Fifth Marine Regiment. Charlie Rose Slate was down. Tears welled up in Jessie's eyes, and he began to shake as he pressed the field phone to his ear with all of his might in an effort to crush the blood and noise from the side of his head.

"I repeat ... Blue Dragon ... this is Delta Two ... Delta Two Actual is down ... over."

"Delta Two ... Delta Two ... this is Blue Dragon ... Do you copy?"

"Affirmative, Blue Dragon."

"Is that Two ... LT ... Charlie ... Romeo ... Sierra ... over?"

Jessie held his breath and gritted his teeth until they hurt. Broken Wing was asking if it was Second Lieutenant Charlie Rose Slate.

"That is affirmative."

"Repeat."

"Two ... L ... T ... Charlie ... Romeo ... Sierra ... over ... WIA."

Jessie fell back against the embankment and stared wildly at the bullets hitting the water like rain. Suddenly, a green star cluster shot into the hot blue sky over the river. He sat up reflexively. He shook his head and tried to think. He stared at the flare as it burst into a group of tiny green stars.

He pulled the field phone to him. "Blue Dragon ... Blue Dragon ... this is Echo One Actual ... over."

"Echo One Actual ... this is Blue Dragon ... Jessie?"

"Affirmative, Blue Dragon! Wing?"

"Affirmative ... over."

"Blue Dragon ... can you get to him, Wing?" Jessie shouted into the phone, unable to hide his panic.

"Affirmative! ... That is affirmative, Echo One Actual! ... I will save him at all cost! ... Over."

"We got the green star cluster, Gunny!" someone yelled from Jessie's right flank.

He shook his head to clear his mind. "Move out!"

"You're crazy!"

Rage filled Jessie's loud bellow: "I said get moving, Marines! Don't leave one single man on this side of the river! On my command!"

"That's nuts!" somebody shouted. Another hail of incoming fire thudded against the embankment that was keeping them alive.

"We're moving out on my command!"

"Every abled-bodied man grab hold of any dead or wounded Marine!" Swift Eagle shouted.

Jessie pulled the straps of the PRC-25 over one shoulder and screamed at the top of his lungs, "Now!"

He grabbed the back of Mouth's flak jacket and dragged him into the river behind him. Another Marine grabbed hold of Justice Pimkin's lifeless body and pulled it into the river.

The sounds of automatic AK fire opened up from their left flank, down the river about fifty meters. The second and third squads laid down a withering barrage, and for a few moments enemy fire was suppressed. Jessie tugged with all his might, but movement was slow. His boots stuck to the sandy bottom of the river and the weight of the dead Marine coupled with pack, rifle, and PRC-25 was just too much.

"Yeee-Hi!" someone screamed out like a drunken cowboy.

"Get some Phantoms!" another Marine shouted.

A flight of Phantoms ripped by low, and the concussion of their bombs shook the earth beneath the river. Jessie's ears hurt from the blast. Another company of Marines was on the ridge to their front and beginning to lay down cover fire for the retreating first and fourth squads. Two more M-60 machine guns sprayed streams of orange-red tracer fire just over the heads of the struggling squads of battered men. Every muscle ached from crouching for over four hours, and it felt like it would take another hour just to get back across this river.

Finally, the first couple of men reached the other side. Jessie felt the bottom rise up as he neared the bank and the body of the radioman became heavier. Two Marines ran out to meet him, and they grabbed Mouth's body and dragged it up the shallow embankment, leaving a heavy blood trail.

Jessie glanced back. To his right and ten yards behind, a Marine rose up and twirled in the water. Neck shot. Jessie caught his eye, and it seemed like the war stood still and became quiet for a moment. The agony in the piercing black eye of the Indian corporal froze Jessie for an instant. Water kicked up all around from enemy machine-gun fire. Jessie tossed the PRC-25 to the riverbank and waded back into the river to get Swift Eagle. The Indian was facedown. Jessie ran as fast as he could move in the chest-deep water, paddling and struggling with all his might until he reached the wounded Marine. He pulled Swift Eagle's head up out of the water and put a hand over the gushing blood coming from his throat.

"Swift Eagle!" he shouted into the Indian's face. Swift Eagle opened his eyes and gasped for breath. He looked alert but near shock. Each cough brought more blood from his wound.

"Corpsman!" Jessie shouted back over his shoulder.

Another row of bullets smacked into the water all around them. He felt something tear into his hip and kidney. He sank to his knees. Swift Eagle gurgled. The boy would die if he didn't get him to a Corpsman. A sudden burst of strength shot through Jessie's body with that fear. He clenched his teeth and shoved his shoulder under Swift Eagle's left armpit. He pulled and fought for each step with every ounce of strength he had left. Ten yards from the bank he felt Swift Eagle's feet begin to help push them along, weakly at first, but then taking hold of the bottom silt and walking. Pain from Jessie's left hip sent shock waves through his body, and he feared that he was about to faint. The water around them was red with their blood. A Marine ran into the water as they neared the bank.

"I got him, Gunny!" Barry Morse yelled, and lifted the heavy weight of Swift Eagle off Jessie's shoulder. They stumbled and crawled up the slippery riverbank and into the cover of brush. Jessie fell back, and Morse laid Swift Eagle beside him and started shouting.

"Corpsman! We need a Corpsman over here!"

Jessie rolled his head to see Swift Eagle. Blood oozed from between Jessie's fingers as he clutched to the Chief's neck wound. He looked down at his hip. His utilities were dark with blood and water, but he still was not sure just how badly he was hit. He shivered. Men were shouting all around.

A few minutes passed, and Jessie could hear choppers taking off from somewhere over the ridge.

"We got outgoing medevacs!"

"Get those wounded over to the LZ!"

Jessie closed his eyes. A moment later someone gripped him under his armpits.

"Can you walk, Gunny?" Moose asked.

"I don't know. Let's try."

They struggled through thick brush on what felt like a long uphill journey until they went over a ridge and into a clearing. The sound of a helicopter taking off opened Jessie's eyes. He lifted his head. A Huey lifted off the ground grudgingly under the weight of a heavy load. It swung out over the ridge and lumbered into the air as enemy gunners opened fire with a vengeance. The sound of bullets smacking through the metal could be heard clearly, and every man looked up to see if the Huey was coming back down. It slowly drifted away to safety.

"We're gonna have to wait for another chopper, Gunny!" a Marine whom Jessie didn't recognize shouted over the noise of outgoing fire. Moose laid him down on his back near four bodies covered with ponchos and packs.

"I got 'em, Marine, get back on line," a corpsman with the second platoon said as he began to work on Swift Eagle's throat.

"Take care, Gunny! You too, Chief!" Moose gave a wave and took off.

"Can't get another medevac yet! We got a bunch of choppers picking up wounded with the Fifth Marines. The gooks retreated and ran into the Fifth." The corpsman gave Swift Eagle a pat on the head. "You're okay, jarhead. Just a ticket home."

"You said the Fifth?" Jessie asked.

"Yeah. They're blocking the gook retreat! Sounds like a lot of casualties."

"My son's hit." Jessie barely recognized his own voice. His heart fell into his stomach and, for that moment, could no longer feel any physical pain. Fear and anxiety suddenly overwhelmed him. He sat up searching for help, knowing that no one could. Someone gripped his hand. He looked to his left. Swift Eagle managed a wink and a thumbs-up with his left hand as it clutched the bloody bandage on his neck.

"How you feeling, Chief?"

He nodded that he was okay, then struggled to get a word out but could not. He gave up and pointed at the old tarnished and muddy bracelet on Jessie's left wrist. Gunnery Sergeant Jessie Slate stared at the ancient piece of blackened tin, and for just an instant saw the silver P-51 Mustang fighter plane flash across his mind and thought of Bougainville and Vella Lavella and Iwo Jima and China and Bloody Ridge and the Chosin Reservoir. He had a dim vision of that night so long ago when the star over Koto-ri appeared as if in the eye of a white hurricane. For one dreadful moment he tried to remember if he had prayed since that night Broken Wing and the First Marine Division had been saved. Something tickled his cheek and he touched it. Tears were rolling down his face, but inside he felt numb and emotionless. He wondered if he was going into shock. Swift Eagle rolled onto his side and touched the bracelet. He clutched at his throat and tried to speak again but gave up with a look of frustration. He printed John 3:16 in the dirt between them and looked into Jessie's battle-aged eyes as if saying, Now was the time.

Jessie stared at the dirt and mumbled, "For God so loved

the world that he gave his only son . . ." He could feel his life pouring out of him. "Many years ago your dad told me that I would understand that kind of sacrificial love if I ever had a son. He said that I would then understand that only God could have chosen such a way."

Jessie looked back into the dark black eyes of Swift Eagle. He had never seen this side of his godson. Maybe he had never looked. He pulled the old bracelet off his wrist and looked one more time into the dark eyes that seemed to pierce his soul. Gunnery Sergeant Jessie Slate dropped the bracelet into Swift Eagle's hand. He felt lighter as if some old weight had been lifted. He closed his eyes and prayed. The penalty for sin is death. But God so loved him that he had sacrificed his only son . . . Jessie knew what it would have meant to sacrifice his own son. How much God must love even him, Jessie Slate, to make such a sacrifice. . . .

"Gunny. You okay?"

Jessie smiled. He felt forgiven. For the first time in his life, he was okay.

"Tell Wing I understand."

EPILOGUE
October 1985

Sergeant Major Swift Eagle shivered from the cold breeze that blew against the long black granite wall. He pulled the collar of his dress green winter coat up around his neck and watched as Colonel Charles Rose Slate and his mother Kate knelt down together. Colonel Slate removed the old bracelet from his wrist and looked into the still beautiful blue eyes of his aging mother. She took the bracelet and laid it in the snow at the base of the monument. The inscription was still clear. She gently ran her fingers up the wall, feeling each name slowly until she came to his.

GUNNERY SERGEANT JESSIE SLATE

Colonel Charlie Rose Slate put his arm around his mother's shoulder. Kate stayed there for a moment with head bowed. Quiet tears fell into the snow. Finally she lifted her eyes as she ran her hand up the wall a little farther and stopped, softly touching each letter of another name as if reading braille.

GUNNERY SERGEANT BROKEN WING

Sergeant Major Swift Eagle knelt down in the wet snow beside Kate and kissed her tearstained face. He slid the other ancient bracelet off his wrist and laid it in the snow beside the first.

Two young Marine corporals stepped up behind them. Sergeant Major Swift Eagle looked over his shoulder. They were ramrod straight and pride beamed from their fresh young faces. They had no nonsense in their eyes, the old sergeant thought. They would be good Marines. He nodded to the dark-skinned corporal. "Broken Slate."

"Yes, Father?"

"You and Jessie Wing Slate help Mrs. Slate back to the car. And be sure to put a blanket over her, it is cold."

They stepped forward to help Kate as she rose. She waved them off.

"I'm fine boys," she said, wiping away a tear.

Jessie Wing Slate gave his grandmother a hug and a pat on the back. "You must miss him very much. I wish that I could have known him. I wish that he hadn't died."

Kate pulled back to look her handsome grandson in the eyes. They were familiar eyes. She had looked into those same gray eyes in 1943. Her face grew serious for just an instant.

"He would have had it no other way, son. There's no better way to die than to die a Marine."

GLOSSARY

03—Springfield rifle
782 gear—Marine Corps equipment issued to every Marine
ARVN—Army of the Republic of Vietnam
BAR—Browning automatic rifle
Barracks Cover—Marine dress uniform hat with bill
BCD—Bad Conduct Discharge
betel nut—A nut, widely chewed by Vietnamese, that stains the teeth and gums a pomegranate red
boondockers—Marine field shoes
boot—Slang for a new recruit undergoing basic training
bulkhead—Protective wall; used by Marines to describe the walls of every structure from a barracks wall to the inner walls of a tank
bush—The outer field areas and jungle where infantry units operate
Charlie—Slang for the Viet Cong or North Vietnamese Army
Charlie Charlie—Slang for certain helicopters
Chi-Com—Chinese communists
Chinook—CH-46 troop helicopter
claymores—Mines packed with plastique and rigged to spray hundreds of steel pellets
click—One kilometer, sometimes spelled *klick*
concertina wire—Barbed wire that is rolled out along the ground to hinder the progress of enemy troops
CMH—Congressional Medal of Honor, America's highest medal for bravery

Corsair—American single-engine fighter plane

C.P.—Command Post

C-rats—C-rations or prepackaged military meals eaten in the field

cruise—One tour of duty

CS—A caustic riot-gas used in Vietnam

dee dee mow—To run quickly

deuce-and-a-half—A heavy transport truck used for carrying men and supplies

DI—Drill Instructor

ditty bag—Small bag for carrying personal articles

Dogface or Doggie—Any U.S. Army personnel

Do Jang—Korean for "gym" or "workout area" for Tae Kwon Do

first dan—First-degree blackbelt

frags—Slang for fragmentation grenades

Frogs—Slang for French soldiers

gung ho—Chinese saying that means "to work together"; in USMC, an overzealous person

Gyrene—Slang for Marine

hash marks—A stripe on the sleeve of dress uniform indicating four years in the Corps; two hash marks equals eight years

Ho Chi Minh Trail—The main supply route running south from North Vietnam through Laos and Cambodia

Ho Chi Minh sandals—Sandals made of American tire tread

Hueys—Helicopters used extensively in Vietnam

Humping—Slang for marching with a heavy load through the bush

I Corp Tactical Zone—The northern five provinces of South Vietnam, called "Marineland" by some

K-Bar—A Marine Corps survival knife

KIA—Killed in Action

KMAG—Korean Military Advisory Group

low quarters—Marine dress shoes

L.P.—Listening post

LZ—Landing zone

medevac—A term for medically evacuating the wounded by chopper or plane

MOS—Military Occupational Specialty

mustang—An enlisted man who wins a commission

Nambu—Japanese machine gun

NVA—North Vietnamese Army

PBY—Seaplane; a Patrol bomber

piss cutter—Marine dress uniform hat, no bill

pogue—A derogatory term for rear-area personnel

PX—Post exchange; store

ROK—Republic of Korea

sappers—Viet Cong infiltrators whose job it was to detonate explosive charges within American positions

satchel charges—Explosive packs carried by VC sappers

scuttlebutt—Drinking fountain; also rumors often started at the drinking fountain

slop chute—Any place that serves alcohol in any form

survey—Turning in used equipment for new gear; also used to describe a man being discharged, "surveyed out of the Corps"

swab jockey—Also swabby, or squid; any sailor of any rank

Tet—The Chinese New Year

tracer—A bullet with a phosphorous coating designed to burn and provide a visual indication of a bullet's trajectory

Web-gear—Canvas suspenders and belt used to carry the infantryman's gear

white side walls—Marine haircut, no hair on sides

WIA—Wounded in Action

Willie-Peter—White phosphorous round

wing wipers—All pilots and air wing personnel